"In *After Anne*, Logan Steiner ...... up .... be-hind the story—the life of the brilliant and complex woman who gave the world *Anne of Green Gables*. Steiner writes with evident love for her character, an impressive command of the history, and lush language that conjures the gentle sunshine and floral-scented breezes of Prince Edward Island. Readers will delight in entering Maud's world and learning of the heart and mind of this heroine."

—Allison Pataki, *New York Times* bestselling author of *The Magnificent Lives of Marjorie Post*

"*After Anne* is a deeply thoughtful and moving novel about Lucy Maud Montgomery, the author whose imagination and ambition created the unforgettable *Anne of Green Gables*. With extensive research, compassion, and honesty, Steiner paints a nuanced portrait of a woman who triumphed in her professional life despite deeply personal struggles and in a society that expected so much less than she longed to give. A tragic story that also manages to inspire and uplift as we root for Montgomery and celebrate her beloved place in literature."

—Melissa Payne, bestselling author of *A Light in the Forest*

"An exquisite tribute to Lucy Maud Montgomery, the revered author who gave us so much scope for imagination. *After Anne* is for fans who long to know the woman behind Anne Shirley's story. Get ready, this book will break your heart in the most splendid ways."

—Sarah McCoy, *New York Times* and internationally bestselling author of *Marilla of Green Gables*

"*After Anne* is imbued with the love of an author for her character—both on and off the page. Logan Steiner made me want to scurry right back to revisit the *Anne of Green Gables* books, as well as delve into every one of Lucy Maud Montgomery's journals."

—Sarah Miller, author of *Marmee*

"*After Anne* is the never-told story behind one of literature's most enduring characters. Logan Steiner's beautifully written tale of the triumphs and tragedies of Lucy Maud Montgomery is a captivating read for anyone who grew up wishing they could adventure around Avonlea with Anne of Green Gables."

—Sarah James, internationally bestselling author
of *The Woman with Two Shadows*

"In this outstanding debut, Logan Steiner delivers a moving, richly detailed, and nuanced portrayal of a deeply fascinating woman. Steiner, with a loving hand, lifts the veil of Lucy Maud Montgomery to give us a glimpse of Maud, her strength, her struggles, her quiet courage navigating life as both an ambitious author and a loving friend, wife, and mother. Steiner's extensive research is evident not only in the facts but in the complex emotional tapestry she weaves. *Anne of Green Gables* fans will sure to delight in this book, but so will any fans of interesting, complicated, and clever women."

—Brianna Labuskes, author of *The Librarian of Burned Books*

"This debut is unexpected in all the best ways. It is a book for everyone. The writing is deep and powerful, charming and moving. I found myself highlighting a sentence on nearly every page, knowing I would go back to reread and apply the words to my own life. Steiner understood Maud's voice and executed it beautifully. She created a world that intertwined fact and fiction in a way that I believe Lucy Maud Montgomery herself would proud of."

—Ali Dean, *USA Today* bestselling author of *Wilder Play*

AFTER

Anne

AFTER

Anne

A Novel of
LUCY MAUD MONTGOMERY'S LIFE

◆

LOGAN STEINER

WM
WILLIAM MORROW
An Imprint of HarperCollins*Publishers*

Excerpt(s) from LUCY MAUD MONTGOMERY: THE GIFT OF WINGS by Mary Henley Rubio, Copyright © 2008 Mary Henley Rubio. Reprinted by permission of Doubleday Canada, a division of Penguin Random House Canada Limited. All rights reserved.

Any third party use of this material, outside of this publication, is prohibited. Interested parties must apply directly to Penguin Random House Canada Limited for permission.

FIRST EDITION

Library of Congress Cataloging-in-Publication Data has been applied for.

ISBN 978-0-06-324645-4

23 24 25 26 27 LBC 6 5 4 3 2

For David, who never stopped believing

AFTER

Anne

Prologue

S tuart turned onto his mother's street and instinctively slowed the car. He clutched the wheel. Swallowing hard, he fought against a scream pushing up through his throat.

He kept thinking about the patient he should have been visiting that afternoon. She was young—younger than Stuart, and far too young to be in the business of having babies. Usually the young mothers healed quickly, but not this one. He still couldn't figure out why. She had a long nose, crooked in the middle, and feminine eyes he worried could see all the way through him.

Would the doctor filling in for Stuart arrive at the woman's house on time? Would he have the medicine he needed? He would be missing Stuart's careful notes.

The woman's family had filled her bedroom with flowers—there must have been five vases of them—all in shades of yellow. They reminded Stuart of childhood summers during the good years, with the house full of vases of flowers cut from his mother's garden.

When he pictured his mother hard at work in her garden, pulling out vegetables and holding them up with a smile so big her teeth showed, his scream became harder to stifle. He shook his head. The urge to scream struck him as odd, at a time like this.

The car seemed to park itself. It occurred to Stuart that he might have tried crashing it into the curb. When else in his life would he be forgiven for such a lack of discipline?

He waited after parking, looking down to where his hands gripped the wheel. "You have your mother's hands," people said. His chin fell to his chest, and then the tears came. His mother. His mother the great author. His mother the beloved orator. His mother who made a fan of the prime minister of England, who turned a no-name island into a world-famous tourist attraction. His fervent coach and forever critic.

How could such a life be gone from the world on a day so bright and ordinary, with the newly laid pavement gleaming in the sun and the wind blowing a stray piece of newspaper down the road?

But here was Dr. Lane with his knuckles rapping on the car window, his voice muted by the glass. "Dr. Macdonald. Dr.—Stuart."

Dr. Lane must have also gotten a call from his mother's maid, Anita. Before Stuart could respond, his hands had moved, one to the door handle and the other taking the keys.

Then he and Dr. Lane slipped past the front hedges, which looked no less alive than they had the week before, in what struck Stuart as frank disrespect to the matron of the house. He pictured them as they should have looked, their top branches drooping in grief. His mother would have liked the image.

Dr. Lane handled the front door, and Stuart followed him up the staircase.

Stuart felt different when he reached the top of the stairs. Relieved. The bedroom door was closed. It would have been;

his mother kept it that way. His brother, Chester, was always barging in without asking, but Chester was not there to supply his usual dose of chaos. He must not have heard the news. And their father—fully caught up in his own inner world for years now—was surely keeping to his spaces in the house. Left to his own devices, how long would it have taken his father to open the bedroom door? And if he had, how much would he have understood?

It never occurred to Stuart that Dr. Lane might open the bedroom door, until he did.

Stuart stayed with Dr. Lane's stride on entering. He made the only choice he decided that he had: to treat this as he would any difficult day on the job. Stuart was a medical professional. His mother had made sure of that.

"Why don't you take care of things on the bedside table, Dr. Macdonald," Dr. Lane said, motioning toward it. "I'll take care of your mother."

The table was small. This could be simple. His eyes went first to the bottles of pills. He wondered why they made them all the same color, so hard to tell apart.

Stuart's heartbeat had felt too high in his chest and now it hopped up even higher. When he reached the table, Stuart picked up the bottles one by one and tried to look like he was studying the labels. He contemplated taking out his notepad and copying down the drug names and dosages.

Instead, Stuart glanced at Dr. Lane. He couldn't bear to watch what Dr. Lane was doing with his mother's body, so he noticed instead the quiet. The doctor's movements made no sound, and yet he had metal utensils. Why couldn't Stuart hear anything? He turned back to the side table and picked up the bottles again, this time putting them back down deliberately and lining them up, reassured by the small clicks they made as they touched. The sound broke up the silence in his mind. Not satisfied, he reached for a sheet of paper also on the table, which had more potential. It would crunch nicely as he balled it up.

Stuart had not noticed this paper before, even though it took up more space than the bottles.

Or maybe that was not true, he realized, no longer considering balling up the page. Maybe he had seen the paper all along, but he had been trying to ignore it. He narrowed his eyes, tried to focus.

Moments later, both paper and pill bottles had been swept into Stuart's medicine bag.

"I can take it from here, Dr. Macdonald," Dr. Lane said. He came up from behind and put his hand—too cold—on Stuart's shoulder. The gesture was startling, but the squeeze that followed told Stuart that Dr. Lane hadn't noticed anything. He hadn't seen the pills or the paper. He was only trying to be comforting, in his own stiff way.

Dr. Lane kept his hand on Stuart's shoulder, guiding him out of the room, telling him to have a seat on the sofa in the living room, he would be right down.

As Stuart walked out, he took note of the ten volumes of his mother's journals lined up on her bedroom shelf. "The decision about when to publish them will be yours, darling, once your mother is on permanent vacation," she had instructed Stuart several times. When—but not whether—to publish them.

Stuart did not remember reading the paper on the bedside table, but as he walked down the stairs, he could hear its final words, as clear as if his mother was speaking them in his ear:

"May God forgive me and I hope everyone else will forgive me even if they cannot understand."

"My position is too awful to endure and nobody realizes it."

"What an end to a life in which I tried always to do my best in spite of many mistakes."

LATER, PERCHED ON the couch in the living room, Stuart watched Dr. Lane's hand as it filled out a stack of medical forms. Dr. Lane's knuckles all had the same slight bend to them, spreading out like feathers, one behind the other. Never pausing.

Stuart had positioned himself close enough to see the forms, but he tried to look straight across from him at the wall with its pictures and paintings, carefully dusted. A photo of the fabled Aunt Frede hung in the middle. Frede had been his mother's cousin and closest friend, but she had died young enough that Stuart knew her only through the countless stories that his mother had retold about their time together. In the photo, Frede peered out from a row of trees, hiding most of her body behind one of them, with a wide smile that did not match her stance.

"Her personality was larger than life," his mother said. "If only you could have seen the way she buoyed a room."

"She understood me, parts of me, like no one else," she told Stuart once, and after that he had been more determined to ask the right questions.

The photo on the wall must have been taken at Park Corner, where Frede and her siblings grew up. Now it was another spot the tourists visited, home of the "Lake of Shining Waters" from the Anne books. "The site where Lucy Maud Montgomery was married." He did not quite believe all this, knowing Park Corner only as a farm where he had spent stretched-out summer vacation days as a young boy, with more food than anyone could eat on the table and games with his second cousins from dawn until dusk.

He remembered the photograph, of course, but not here

on the wall, dead center in the living room. His mother must
have switched it out. What else had he missed on his daily
visits?

Every once in a while, Stuart looked down at the medical
paperwork. Never for long enough for Dr. Lane to notice, he
hoped. One sheet had two columns of boxes with words next
to them. Stuart had been waiting for Dr. Lane to get to this
page. At the top, it said "Possible Causes of Death." Second
from the bottom on the right column was a single word: "Suicide." Stuart could no longer avert his eyes.

Now each moment took up more space than the one before it. Stuart's heartbeat seemed so slow that he thought to
feel for his own pulse. The strange desire to scream came
over him again, stronger than it had all day.

Stuart cleared his throat loudly, his voice squeaking a little as he did. His mother would have looked at him in that
moment, pleading, an instruction in her eyes. *Don't get upset now, darling. You must put this unpleasantness out of your
mind as soon as you can. Go on and be a strong man—the good
doctor I raised you to be. The last thing I would ever want is to
upset you.*

Dr. Lane's evenly bent fingers moved down. They passed
over the box labeled "Suicide" and checked a different one.
They turned the page over.

Stuart looked back at the picture of Frede. He let out a
breath he hadn't realized he had been holding.

*Good, now that's been settled. Please don't worry any more
over these pesky details, darling. They are not worth your attention.*

Still, there was the fact of his mother's letter—her suicide
note—that Stuart had found on the bedside table. Dr. Lane
did not know about that letter. He must never know.

But Stuart's mind would not leave it alone. He'd missed

something when he had recalled the letter earlier, he was sure of it now. But he couldn't take it out to check, not while Dr. Lane was still in the room. And the mere thought of reading those words again made him ill.

The letter had been written on scrap paper; he was almost sure of that. But if it really was a stray sheet of paper, why did it have the number "176" written in careful script at the top of the page—the same sort of numbering he'd seen on the pages of his mother's journals and manuscripts?

Now was not the time for guessing games. Dr. Lane was finishing up his paperwork, and soon there would be more questions to answer. Arrangements to make.

Still transfixed by Frede's photo, Stuart thought instead of the chickens he and his second cousins used to chase at Frede's childhood home at Park Corner, egged on by Chester. The chickens' ugly wrinkled feet moved faster than their bodies, their squawks more sluggish still. The adults were always busy laughing at their own conversation, looking over from time to time only to make sure no one was hurt.

When Stuart remembered his mother's laugh, the fullness of it and its way of implying things perpetually too old for him to understand, he thought of Park Corner. He imagined his mother's laugh, played it over in his mind.

He'd last seen that laugh a few weeks ago at supper. Her body had made the usual motions, her shoulders bouncing and her cheeks lifting and leaving hollows by the corners of her mouth. But he couldn't remember any sound.

I.

Kindling

"Dear old world," she murmured,
"you are very lovely, and I am glad
to be alive in you."

—LUCY MAUD MONTGOMERY,
Anne of Green Gables, 1908

1.

She ran the razor-cut edges against her thumb. On the frozen soil at her feet sat a cardboard box filled to the brim with papers. She'd extracted the set of journal pages in her hands from the top of the box. One of many series of days, removed and rewritten.

This particular entry consisted of ten pages describing a single weekend. Reading a few lines now, her hands shook with condemnation.

She had written these words innocently enough. It was not until rereading them years after recopying that she realized. All the while it had been there, buried beneath her descriptions of a perfectly ideal weekend. She had simply never seen it before.

So these pages must go. She couldn't risk the Reader understanding what she had not. Dropping them now from her hand into the burgeoning flames below, she watched the pages brown, curl, and crackle in the old, satisfying way. The destruction of each one a worry lifted.

The date on the first page remained visible until the rest were all but ash. "December 2, 1907. Birthday Weekend."

2.

Waves lapped at the feet of the sandstone cliffs skirting the north shore of the Cavendish peninsula. Further out at sea, each wave plodded along so slowly that it seemed to Maud they had all gotten together and decided it was high time for a nap. Watching them from her favorite rock perch, Maud's gaze fixed out past the pebbled coves and scalloped orange cliffs, and her mind settled down to match the waves' rhythm. How could she possibly stay angry at them for their rough-and-tumble ways of the past summer, tame as they were right now?

Just then, the midday sun broke through and splintered on the water into a thousand tiny diamonds. Maud blinked up at the sun and down at the sea, silently giving them thanks for the gift—on this day of all days.

But Maud's mind never could stay in one spot for long, and soon enough her knees started bouncing under her skirt. The eager energy that had accompanied her most days since childhood pulled at her heels—even more so today because of the errand she planned to run later. An errand of pure extravagance. It might even be called an act of rebellion on an island of people bred of self-sufficiency—a thrilling thought, although the fact of its thrill was one of those truths that she had learned to tuck away and keep only for herself.

"Worry not, dear sleeping one," she said out loud in the direction of the sea. Her small frame rose to face its massive one. "I'll be back to shower you with praise again soon enough."

Opening up her jacket to feel more of the air on her skin and pinning back a piece of impertinent brown hair, she made her way to the start of the closest trail through the woods. She loved these woods for the protective scarf they formed between the farms of Cavendish and the shoreline of exposed cliffs.

Walking through a layer of fallen leaves that made a happy percussion out of her footsteps, she decided she would take turns without paying any mind to where she was headed. Let her thoughts go where they pleased—one of her favorite pastimes, and a rare one these days. Then she could start the game of finding her way out, which would be a joy in temperatures so mild.

This was nothing at all like past Novembers, she realized as she walked. Not outside, and not the way she felt inside either.

The distance between this birthday eve and others in her past loomed as wide as a continent.

One birthday ago, there had been no publisher. There had only been her first full-length manuscript tucked inside an old hatbox collecting dust on the top shelf of her closet, with a series of rejection letters from uninterested editors piled on top. Anytime she'd gotten a glimpse of that hatbox, her heart had hurt.

Her last birthday had been too cold to go walking, and it was on that day, stuck indoors, that the part of her most devastated by the hatbox took shape in her mind with a personality all its own, as her deepest feelings had a tendency to do. The Fox, she named this one, and a well-groomed, gray fellow he was, with piercing eyes that knew their goal and paws that went bounding after it. The Fox had such a jolly time while writing was in progress, determined as he was to write something that would make its mark on someone, somewhere. The mark didn't have to be sizable to be profound—any happy thought that a person wouldn't have had otherwise, that was all the Fox was after. But while she stared up at that hatbox, Maud felt the Fox plain well curl up in a barren corner of her inner world. She came close to never sending out the manuscript again. If it hadn't been for her cousin Frede—well, if it hadn't been for Frede, the novel would be a different thing altogether.

Maud came to a fork in the path poised directly below an archway of maples with a good number of leaves still clinging to their outstretched branches. Walking under maple branches had always made her feel as warmed around the middle as a human embrace. She stopped for a moment to study the remaining leaves, yellow at the palms and red at the fingers. So lovely in their decay that she had never been able to imagine them being sad for it. Like the most fortunate old ladies she'd known, maple leaves got to show their brightest colors just before taking a happy float to the earth.

She did have, on her last birthday, a little diamond solitaire that she wore on her left ring finger anytime she was alone. Along with this secret engagement had come a flicker of possibility.

Long before the Fox, the Old Hen had been a persistent character in Maud's mind, a noisy but not particularly influential creature who thought that having children would be just the thing; the balm to her woes. With the emergence of the diamond solitaire, the Old Hen began clucking away, thinking that her influence might grow in kind. The Hen insisted on an immediate marriage.

But marriage had not been possible then, not with Maud's fiancé a continent away, their romance carried on in letters and postcards. And not with her grandmother getting on in years. Her grandmother had depended on her more and more in each of the years since Maud had moved back into the house to care for her—loath as her grandmother would be to admit that she depended on anything but the grace of God.

Two birthdays ago had been worse still, Maud recalled as she turned onto a path that took her directly between two straggly scrub oaks.

Two birthdays ago, there had been no engagement and no publisher. Not even a completed manuscript.

But the lowest of birthdays came before that, during those years when Maud was half convinced she would never be more than a spinster storywriter for magazines and Sunday school serials. In those years, each pronouncement of her new age stung like a wasp. "A curious thing," her grandmother said once, "for it is not as though you are unattractive or lacking for attention from men. It must be your ambition that's to blame, or perhaps the quickness of your tongue." If only her grandmother knew how hard Maud worked to hold her tongue in response.

Accompanying the sting of each of those birthdays was the old sinking feeling that would start up in her chest come November. Her habitual winter blues. Not that anyone would have known it about her. To nearly everyone, she was a "very jolly girl," "always in good spirits," no matter the season.

Sometimes Maud imagined what would happen if everyone in her life knew her real thoughts. She'd feel some amount of relief at the truth coming out, no doubt. But she'd never be able to stomach everyone's faces. Their pity would double the pain.

Maud emerged now into a small clearing and turned onto a path she knew well, looking up at more clinging maple leaves, their edges alight with the sun overhead. For a moment, she imagined them bursting into flames. She would have to run, because they would come raining down on her, but she would be tempted not to, just to experience them in their final glory.

With the coming of this birthday, Maud realized, there was none of the sting, none of the sinking feeling.

Not that her life now was devoid of concerns. But they were of a different kind. With no wedding date set for over a year now, and Maud's grandmother not showing any sign of a real decline, the Old Hen fretted. Without a marriage, there would be no motherhood.

The Fox, on the other hand, was out from his corner and pacing with excitement. The manuscript was being edited and readied for printing. The publishers were pushing for a sequel. But the Fox was not satisfied. Not in the slightest. He wanted more, much more, and he eyed the Old Hen warily, skeptical of the effects of domesticated life on his livelihood.

But one fact stood out above all the rest, acting as a salve to Maud's nerves no matter what the grievances of the minor characters populating her mind: This birthday brought with it the knowledge that determined Anne and her series of foibles and heartaches and triumphs would have a life outside of that old hatbox. And that fact alone made Maud clasp her hands together in joy as she walked out of the woods path and onto the main Cavendish road.

ON THE WAY back to the house, Maud made the single stop she had planned. How different it was from one of the usual errands she was tasked with on her walks—picking up a pound of flour from the town store, gathering a dozen eggs from a neighbor's chicken coop, dropping off a letter for a neighbor too ill to pick it up from the desk where she and her grandmother sorted mail for the town.

As she approached the tall front door of the white, shingled two-story flanked by orchards where she had lived for the better part of her life, the cake that she had purchased sat on a covered plate in Maud's hands and smelled just as decadent as she had hoped. A perfect mix of savory and sweet, with dark chocolate cake and cream cheese icing. It had been a marvelous idea: buying a cake baked by a neighbor for her birthday.

It had been Anne's idea, actually, in the way that persistent little character was always whispering in Maud's ear these days. Anne had appeared to Maud fully formed from the start, real as the ink under Maud's fingernails. After spending a solid year in Anne's company as she wrote the first manuscript, Maud was now plotting out a sequel. As hard as Maud was working to grow Anne up, she kept hearing the voice of Anne's younger self. The door to Maud's imagination reopened a crack, and eleven-year-old, orphaned Anne moved herself right back in, worn-out carpetbag in tow, with enthusiasms and whims unchecked. Once Anne started up talking in Maud's mind, Maud had a hard time not hearing what Anne would have to say on a subject. Included among this chatter had been several distinct opinions about the celebration of Maud's birthday.

You must have exactly the cake you would imagine for yourself in your wildest dreams! And don't dare bake it yourself—cakes do have a terrible habit of turning out badly when you most want them to be good.

It's your thirty-third birthday, after all, the same number twice,

*which makes it doubly special. A birthday must never feel the
same as any ordinary day of the year.*

*Oh, and you must throw yourself a party too, one that feels
like an exclamation point at the end of a stirring sentence.
There's no use waiting for someone else to plan a party the way
you don't wish it to be. No—you must conjure up precisely the
party you would like and make it so!*

Anne was difficult to argue with, which had been half
the fun in writing her—and half the trouble with having her
voice chirp away in Maud's mind.

Cake still in hand, Maud walked straight to the kitchen as
she always did, quick on her feet. Only now that she had left
the outdoors did her arms register how tired they were from
holding several pounds of cake still and upright.

Down went both cake and coat onto the old kitchen table. Maud looked around at the space, neat as always, with
the dishes put away, the heirloom paintings fastened in their
places, and the town's mail sorted by surname into the cub-
bies in the old wooden post office desk that sat against one
wall (its raised cover meaning that her grandmother had not
quite finished sorting that day's allotment). The white trim
on every window was fresh and recently dusted. People often
called it a pretty house, or a proper one. But its dearness to
Maud went far beyond pretty or proper.

"I'll get to my jacket in a bit," Maud called out to the listening ears around the corner.

A year ago, the thought of her grandmother seeing Maud's
jacket on the table—let alone the purchased cake—would
have made Maud tense and in a hurry to put things away. But
a recent change in her grandmother had made for greater
ease in Maud's shoulders.

Or was it Maud who had changed? The thought came to

her as insights often did, gone with her next exhale unless she paid it mind.

Her grandmother emerged then from the hallway, shaking her head and hiding her smile. Long, thin arms jutted out from where her grandmother's hands fixed themselves to her hips, with her graying hair pulled in a tight bun and only slightly softened by a layer of bangs.

"You've become a good deal less polite lately. Perhaps you thought I didn't notice," her grandmother said, tilting one cheek up in a way that had become recent habit.

"And you've become less ornery," Maud said, rising on her tiptoes to give her grandmother's cheek a quick kiss. "It's hard to say who's to blame."

"It is a good thing we'll be apart for a few days, I say, with you seeming to forget all your manners over such an ordinary thing as a birthday."

Maud watched her grandmother's nose lead her eyes in the direction of the cake on the table.

"I cannot say I'll be cured when you return," Maud said. "But I will do my best to save you some cake."

"Where in the world has this come from?"

"I commissioned it."

"Commissioned! What a thing to say, let alone do." Her grandmother paused. "But I suppose it is your money." Her grandmother turned away from the cake then and started busying herself at the post office desk.

Maud smiled. "It is, and plenty of it besides saved up."

"I wouldn't expect anything less, chi—" Her grandmother halted.

Her tongue caught on her usual manner of addressing Maud. Age five or age thirty, it had been the same. Child this, child that. But lately her grandmother had been using the word less often. Could it be that Maud had heard the last of it?

Maud thought back to a childhood afternoon spent crying under her covers in her upstairs gable bedroom. Gulping in insufficient air between sobs, she prayed for the day when she'd be able to live with her father instead of two old curmudgeons who told her to hush and run along every time they had interesting company. That day, she made up her mind that when she grew up, she would talk to every child like an adult. At that age, there wasn't a thing worse than being treated as a child who couldn't be told real things.

All the more so, she had since learned, when she wasn't a child at all.

Her grandmother took a breath and started again. "You know that it may make things difficult in your marriage, Maud. It can be hard on a man, to have a wife with money saved up. It can give her too much independence for a man's comfort."

Her grandmother stood still and waited until Maud's eyes met hers. Her words had been addressed to Maud as an adult, at least, but they stirred a pool of hurt and anger, making it ripple. How swiftly her grandmother could turn blessing into curse.

And then, predictably, came Anne—

I don't think a wife's money would trouble in the slightest a man who was truly worthy. He would love his wife doubly for it if there was anything romantic about him. Especially money earned by her own hand.

Anne's peppery words coated the hurt and made Maud remember herself.

"You're assuming I get married anytime soon." Maud kept her tone light, knowing her words would make her grandmother squirm. Maud had broken off engagements before.

Many of her friends had done so, especially in the early years right out of school. She thought this time was different, but she knew her grandmother had her doubts.

"You most certainly will, if I have any say. Which I suppose I don't. But I've been saving that topic for suppertime tonight. I'd like to make sure there's time for it before I leave."

"You've been saving up a discussion about my marriage?"

"I have."

"Well, I am eager to be enlightened." Maud smiled.

"And I am eager to be situated for the weekend at Park Corner, where my other family members are sure to address me in a proper tone." Her grandmother turned back to the mail with only a hint of humor.

Maud shook her head, fighting back a laugh. At times like these, Maud could see the fight in her grandmother's hands and shoulders—torn between embracing her recent loosening and returning to the perpetual clench she had used to raise Maud into the outwardly proper woman she was today.

Maud put her jacket away, then returned to the kitchen to put the cake away in the pantry.

Maud had started readying the ingredients for supper when her grandmother began speaking again, her back still turned to Maud.

"Don't get me wrong," her grandmother said. "I wish I'd had money of my own in my marriage. I'll tell you what. I've wished that many a time."

SUPPER WAS ON the dining room table over an hour late that evening.

Anne was not the least bit concerned.

More than justified by the walk in fine weather and that scrumptious cake wafting its scent throughout the whole main floor! What a word that is, "wafting." Not the most beautiful of words, but don't you know precisely what it means just by the way it sounds?

No question the cake justified the time it took to pick up. But Maud could sense her grandmother's growing impatience. Both suitcase and purse were stacked neatly by the door in the entryway and ready to be delivered into Maud's uncle's hands when he came at nine a.m. sharp to pick up her grandmother and drop off Frede. Now her grandmother was occupied re-straightening the spoons and napkins while they waited for the stew Maud was making to simmer.

An impatient grandmother did not bode well for an impending conversation about Maud's marriage.

And boring old vegetable and bean stew will do nothing to help matters.

"Let us pray," her grandmother said, and Maud's head bowed and eyes closed willingly. She always liked this part of the meal. She did usually reflect on her gratitudes first, but then she let her thoughts meander where they pleased. What her grandmother must be thinking during these minutes of silent time Maud could never guess—especially considering her grandmother's lack of any discernible imagination.

Maud could always tell when her grandmother's eyes opened. Maud's skin registered the change the same way it would register a change in room temperature.

They looked at each other now and lifted their spoons. Maud waited for her grandmother to speak.

They had a few bites.

Maud continued to wait.

Her grandmother cleared her throat. Maud raised her eyebrows.

"What do you think about planting some tomatoes next spring?"

The garden? All this suspense, and her grandmother was asking about a garden that she paid no mind to on any other day.

"Well, that's a fine idea." Maud waited a moment with her spoon in the air to cool the stew before taking a bite.

"Canned tomatoes just aren't the same. The flavor changes, and the texture too. And you know it's bad luck to count on the neighbors' tomato beds."

"I will buy some tomato seeds, then. Are you worried over your trip?"

"My, wasn't that an abrupt transition, chi—Maud, dear." Her grandmother took a slow bite of stew. "Why do you ask?"

"Well, the talk of tomatoes, for one. I did not think you cared for tomatoes."

"I like them fine. I like them in stews."

"I see; so this is about my stew. I suppose it's lacking in taste?"

"This is not about your stew lacking in anything. It's not your best stew, mind you, but I like it just fine."

Maud looked up to the ceiling to keep her eyes above her temper, an old trick. "I was only thinking of the last few times Aunt and Uncle have convinced you to come to Park Corner to see the family, when your mind has changed at the last minute. It's been quite a while since you've stayed overnight anywhere. Five years?"

"Seven and a half."

"I see you've been counting."

"Maud, dear."

"I apologize, Grandmother. I imagine that going away after seven and a half years of sleeping only in one's own bed would make anyone apprehensive."

"Well, I was not apprehensive until you started talking this way. What do you suppose will be the matter with the guest bed at Park Corner?"

"Nothing. I've stayed in that bed many times. It's quite comfortable."

"I may ask to stay in the ground floor bedroom instead."

"You don't stay on the ground floor here until winter, and it's mild out."

"Staying on the ground floor at Park Corner could help me avoid all the racket. Six people are too many for one house, I say. Especially when some of them are small children."

"Your great-grandchildren."

"I suppose."

"Since when is there any supposing about great-grandchildren?" Maud laughed.

"My dear, there gets to be a point in life when all children become the same and make one tired."

Maud fought back a smile. She had thought this herself from time to time about her cousins' children.

"It's enough to make me question whether I should be going tomorrow at all," her grandmother added under her breath.

There it was. The thing Maud had been most afraid to hear. "Am I to take it, then, that you will not be traveling to Park Corner tomorrow?"

Her grandmother stiffened. "I most certainly will be traveling to Park Corner tomorrow. I will be taking my daughter up on her offer to get out and about, so you may have the house to yourself for your birthday, as requested."

"As I requested? I recall that it was your suggestion to go this weekend."

"I remember it differently. Although I suppose you will say your impeccable memory should trump my old, feeble one." Her grandmother sighed and looked down at the table as she continued eating. The frown on her grandmother's face made her pronounced cheekbones even more prominent.

Maud was reminded once again of her grandmother's subtle flair for drama, which was interesting in someone purporting to be a no-nonsense matron. It was one of several clues Maud had compiled that her grandmother might have become a different kind of woman altogether, if given the chance.

But imagining things differently never did change the way they were now. Both Maud and her grandmother sat in silence, eating their stew. Her grandmother gazed up at Maud once, then back to the table.

Don't you see that she's playing a game? I don't know quite what it is. She is so mysterious sometimes that I have a hard time knowing what it is like to be her. But she wants something from you, just a little something. I'm almost positively certain of it.

Which is as certain as I can be, you know, because I am always sure to leave a little room in my imagination for the unexpected. In my experience, people who go around positively certain about everything are either awful bores or stubborn old ogres.

But oh, what could it be that she wants? This is all quite exciting, don't you think?

Maud shook her head. She did not find this game exciting and wanted it to end, one way or another.

"Grandmother, if you do not want to go, if you do not think you will enjoy yourself, you are more than welcome to stay for my little party. We can send uncle back with the carriage. Frede's bringing plenty of food, and of course there will be cake."

Her grandmother's eyes rose and brightened. "That is kind of you, Maud. The scent of that cake is very tempting."

Maud felt the sink of disappointment in her body and

tried to keep it off her face. The party was supposed to be a celebration with the two people with whom she could be most herself—and no one else.

Her grandmother held Maud's gaze. "But you have not had a night without tending to me in a good long time. You are right that I should go. It will make me appreciate this quiet house even more when I return. It should also silence your aunt and uncle on the subject, with any luck for the rest of my lifetime."

Oh, that was delightful! It gives me a lovely throb of joy to be right. But it gives me a pang of disappointment too. I suppose it's the pang of not being able to wonder anymore if I will be right. Achieving what we hope for is a curious thing, isn't it?

Maud did her best to look unaffected. "Very well then. It is entirely up to you."

She got up and gathered both bowls and spoons, waiting to smile until she was walking to the kitchen with her face out of sight, leaving her grandmother to sip her tea.

AS MAUD WASHED up, the stew smell faded from the kitchen, and the only smell left was chocolate.

There was something different about that cake. Its smell was like another voice in the room.

"What exactly do you want?" Maud murmured, softly enough that she knew her grandmother wouldn't hear. She'd learned long ago how to turn down the volume of the characters brewing in her mind when circumstances dictated.

The cake wasn't minding its manners, though. It had an answer, and a loud one.

Maud nodded. She liked the idea.

She took out two clean plates, forks, and knives, then removed the cake from the back pantry cupboard where she'd left it, covered loosely in wax paper. She took off the wax paper before cutting two perfect slices with her grandmother's best knife, delighted to see no crumbs left on the cake plate. A testament to its moistness. She left the cake out on the pantry counter in case her grandmother wanted a second helping— Maud was perpetually worried her grandmother was getting too thin—and brought only the silverware out to the table.

"A surprise," Maud said as she laid the silverware down.

"What's this?" her grandmother said, craning her neck to look toward the kitchen and then moving her head in a nervous bob, as if expecting a stranger to enter the room.

"You'll see."

The next time Maud emerged from the kitchen she had two plates in hand, large slices of cake sitting on top of them. "An early birthday celebration."

Her grandmother's tight-lipped smile broadened to show just a bit of her teeth. "Well, now. That's very nice."

Maud sat down. "Let's both take our first bite at once."

Her grandmother's smile disappeared. "Food is never a game, Maud."

Of course. What her grandmother liked to call "decency and decorum" perpetually crowded out any fun.

"All right then, I will take my first bite on my own." Maud closed her eyes as she raised the fork to her lips. Indecently delightful. She opened her eyes to see that her grandmother had done the same.

Although the size of her grandmother's next bite was ladylike, its quickness betrayed her enjoyment.

"Can we end the suspense now?"

Her grandmother tilted her head as she put her fork down. "Suspense?"

"What is it that you have been meaning to tell me about my marriage?" Maud was still eating, but in tiny bites that would make the slice last longer.

"Ah, yes. If you have been so curious about my thoughts, why didn't you ask earlier?"

"I was not sure I wanted to know."

"That cake has turned your tongue looser than ever."

Grown-ups love to fuss over the looseness of one's tongue as if tongues were liable to come off altogether. The looser the tongue the more interesting life is, I say.

"That being the case," her grandmother continued, "I will keep my thoughts to myself."

"But I've changed my mind. I'd like to know."

"Oh?" Her grandmother raised a single eyebrow, her pursed lips yielding into a satisfied smile.

"I would." And she meant it. She could stomach whatever it was her grandmother had to say. This newfound sturdiness surprised her.

Her grandmother placed her fork on her plate. Maud did the same.

"All right then. I have a proposal to make." Her grandmother paused for several beats longer than normal. "You have been engaged now for over a year," she continued.

"Thirteen months."

"Never mind the fact that I only found out about your engagement a month ago, and never mind how I found out." Her grandmother cleared her throat and swallowed hard. "Now, you know it is my sincere desire to see you settled down. And a man does not like to be put off forever."

"Not being a man, you are surely an expert."

"My dear. Have I told you that your humor has taken a decided turn for the worse? Ever since you had that book of yours accepted for publication." Her grandmother's tone was stern, but the corners of her mouth were turned up in amusement. She continued, "I know you may dismiss what I say, but I mean it seriously. You have lived with an old lady in an old house for more than nine years of your adult life. Taking good care, mind you. But I am a woman with more granddaughters than simply you. Granddaughters who are younger, granddaughters who are not engaged to be married. One of whom is coming to this very house tomorrow to celebrate your birthday."

Maud startled. Frede?

"Frede is less patient than you, I am aware, but she could take fine enough care of me, for as long as I have left. Now don't think I'm not preferential to you. Ever since your mother gave you my name—not that you will deign to be called by Lucy—I have felt a particular sort of connection. But that's neither here nor there. Frede and I will do well enough. Why don't you propose it to her tomorrow?"

Tomorrow? Maud's thoughts couldn't keep up.

"I am quite sure she will agree. She cares for you deeply. And she knows you are an engaged woman. She supports your marriage just as I do. You will be able to have a nice wedding then, and a child or two before you are old. More delightful great-grandchildren for me." A silent chuckle before her expression turned serious again. "It is not wise for a woman to wait too long to have children," she added.

Maud could not remember the last time her grandmother had said so many words in one string. How had they gotten all the way to children? They'd never broached such a personal subject. Maud had grown up with a wide circle drawn around baby-making in all its particulars. One of many things not to be discussed aloud, in public or private.

But at these words, the Old Hen started her regular protest. Maud had known the Hen ever since she was a girl dressing her dolls and putting them to bed at night. The Hen was convinced of the virtues of motherhood. But she was frequently hushed into submission. The Hen's hopes had an undeniable pull, but they were also ordinary, womanly. And Maud dreaded nothing more than being an ordinary woman.

She realized then that her grandmother had resumed eating her cake. The speech had concluded.

"Could I have rendered you speechless?" her grandmother asked with a satisfied smile.

"This is a lot to consider," Maud replied, because she could think of nothing better to say.

Her grandmother put down her fork again. "It is what I want."

"I had never thought of Frede living here." And she could not see bringing it up tomorrow in the middle of her birthday celebration.

"That is because you are a devoted sort."

"I don't think I could possibly—"

"Do not make up your mind now," her grandmother interrupted with a firm shake of her head. "Give it a good night's rest. Talk to Frede. There is nothing more to be said tonight." With a nod, her grandmother scooped up her last bite of cake with her fork and placed it deliberately in her mouth. Once she finished chewing, she got up to clear her dish before Maud could say another word.

Maud looked down at her cake, not sure what she felt or thought, sure only of the cake's goodness. She continued to eat, one small bite at a time. Then she cleared her plate.

As she did, her mind formed a picture of herself walking down the aisle. The man at the end would tuck his chin slightly and look up at her. His eagerness would overtake him as he went to kiss her, each of them forgetting their audience and stirring with what would come later that night.

It could be a spring wedding with mayflowers woven through her hair, done up in the most recent fashion. She had good hair that distracted from the parts of her face she liked less—its dull oval shape and the rings around her eyes. The groom (turned husband with a single line of speech—what a trick!) might come up from behind and pull those flowers out one by one, his fingers brushing her neck, then tracing their way down her spine until they landed at those small indented spaces at the base of her back that no man's hands had touched before.

Oh, the thrill of thoughts like this! Her ears positively rang with it. Knowing her grandmother would call up for her in a few minutes if she did not hear footsteps on the stairs, Maud took herself up to bed, but she gave herself permission to daydream her way into sleep—or not to sleep at all if daydreams prevented it. Anne wouldn't have thought twice about such an indulgence, so why should she?

3.

Next in the stack came an old journal with a plain purple cover. On the spine in faded script, the years 1905 to 1906. She opened it and skimmed through the pages. These memories were tender. This journal contained the origin of Anne. Just a few words transported her to the simple comfort of her grandmother's kitchen, pen in hand. In those days, she lived for the hour or two each day that she had to write. And writing Anne beat all.

Now, exclamation points and adjectives screamed at her from every page of the journal. She had fallen in love with loquacious Anne, but nearly all this silly talk had had to be stripped out on recopying, lest the Reader think her a juvenile ninny.

It was not only Anne who required stripping out. It was also the man who made his appearance the day she wrote Anne's first lines. She had imagined this a fated coincidence back then. How she had swooned in her journal, pages filled with giddy speculation and surmise. She shook her head.

One last draw of the purple book to her nose—she could almost smell the beloved old home where she had written it—and it was gone. The flames leapt to devour it, and her heart leapt a little along with them. A curious feeling to have while watching the destruction of something she loved. She wondered at herself. But she knew better these days than to squander an ounce of joy. She hurried to retrieve the next item from the box at her feet.

4.

Maud set her gardening gloves in their basket in the kitchen. It had taken less time than expected to pull that week's helping of weeds and issue the garden her stamp of approval. She'd spent the rest of the morning walking through the nearby fields with gardening gloves still on her hands and her hair falling out of its pins. She had been too busy with ideas about the novel to bother with either. She caught herself several times saying lines out loud and clapping, which made her laugh once she'd made sure no one was close enough to hear.

Maud could feel her own heartbeat now in a way that she hadn't in months. A novel was indulgent, she knew. Her short stories came easily and sold reliably. The novel might be a waste of time. She was thirty and unmarried, and she would need stable rent for a boardinghouse when her grandmother died. "Every woman with a dream better have a banker for a father or a fool for a husband," her grandmother said once.

But the redheaded girl persisted. Almost real; pestering at times.

Here's one incident: *I'll want my hair dyed raven black, but it will go horribly wrong.* And another: *I will be accused of stealing a brooch, but it will turn out to be a false, prejudicial assumption—the plight of the orphan.*

Here is how my name should be spelled, the girl instructed: Anne—with an "e."

MAUD OPENED THE pantry shelves once back at the house, eager to find the meal that would get her upstairs and writing the quickest. She decided on canned vegetables, bread, and jam.

"I see you've taken quite the morning detour." Her grandmother's voice came from just over Maud's shoulder.

Maud rose up on her toes. Her grandmother's footsteps could be so quiet, even in shoes, and the natural shrillness in her grandmother's voice often caught Maud off guard.

Maud turned around with a few jars in hand. She needed to be careful with her words. She had an agenda today.

"I worked for a while in the garden, which is coming along nicely, I think. It's a beautiful day, isn't it? I thought I could feel the rain coming in the air this morning, but now I'm not so sure. Which is too bad. The garden could use it."

"The rain will come in its own time," her grandmother said, falling into place beside Maud and slicing a loaf of bread.

"I think I'll work upstairs for a few hours after we eat," Maud said. "If you don't mind."

"I don't mind—though I wish you wouldn't use the word 'work' so loosely."

There it was. One of her grandmother's signature comments crafted, it often seemed, with the sole purpose of plucking at Maud's heart.

Maud had been barely twelve when her grandmother asked to read one of Maud's poems. Maud waited for an afternoon when her grandmother seemed particularly satisfied with the state of the household, then got up the nerve. She recopied her best poem in careful script on a sheet of notebook paper and folded it up, then said nothing as she walked into the kitchen, placed the folded paper in her grandmother's hands, and walked away.

Peering through the crack between the hinges of the kitchen door, Maud watched as her grandmother checked for her, making sure she was nowhere in sight. Then her grandmother began to read, holding the unfolded sheet straight out in front of her in the same way she would hold Maud's favorite kitten by its scruff.

It wasn't long before her grandmother put the page down and chuckled to herself. "Plump, luminous berries indeed," her grandmother said, shaking her head.

Maud soaked her pillowcase with tears that night.

When she woke the next morning, she vowed to have a poem published while her grandmother was still alive. She wrote ten new poems the next day, and ten more the day after. Not that her grandmother had read any of them—even those that appeared in print. But at least she knew they had been published.

Her grandmother was still speaking, now in her telltale tone of business to be accomplished.

"We've finally started to get some mail for Reverend Macdonald. Took some time for the new boarding address to register with his folks, I imagine. All that talk about why he might have decided to move here from a perfectly good boarding spot in Stanley, all those admirable sermons he's given, and I've yet to formally introduce myself. I don't suppose you have either."

"There was a time in Stanley, visiting Frede—" Maud began. But her grandmother wasn't looking for a response.

"Both of us should be prepared to give him a proper greeting when he comes for his mail," her grandmother continued. "And I don't mean one where you say whatever thought comes into your head. Your mother used to do that too." Her grandmother swallowed, looking away as she tended to after any mention of Maud's mother. "I mean the kind of greeting your married friends might give."

Maud tried to rid her face of feeling as she gazed out the window. Years ago, when she was still a girl, Maud might have looked her grandmother in the eyes and told her exactly what she thought of some of those friends and the mindless, obedient chatter that had gotten them married. She might have told her a little of what she had imagined about Ewan Macdonald too—the well-respected reverend who was rumored to have moved from Stanley Bridge to Cavendish after some young lady in his Cavendish parish (who happened to look a lot like Maud) caught his eye. But she had learned very well the look she would have gotten in response, accompanied by some choice phrase. "Best not to count your chickens before they hatch." "A lady doesn't excite easily."

It was much better to look out the window. Better, that is, as long as she could remember to keep the "useless day-dream" smile off her face while she dove off the ledge of this world and drenched herself in the imaginative one.

Her grandmother took out the plates and served the bread and jam and canned vegetables. Then she walked the plates to the table. "Come now, child. Let's eat." Her eyes closed as she settled herself at the table, hands folded in silent grace.

As soon as her grandmother heard Maud's chair pull back and creak, she let out her best weary sigh and opened her eyes.

JUST AS MAUD finished the dishes, the Cavendish doctor stopped by for his mail. He made it a point to report on any sicknesses around town, knowing how Maud's grandmother's deep sense of duty and deeper sense of superiority meant that she would supply any sick neighbor with a good meal.

Maud soon became charged with dropping off a pot of soup with one of those neighbors who had come down with the flu. The walk out to the edge of town would have been taxing for her grandmother, and Maud liked a good walk.

But Maud was so eager to begin writing now, to keep from losing the motivation she'd felt that morning, that she found herself issuing a litany of curses as she made her way over the first of several hills she'd have to cross to get to the neighbor. She cursed the doctor for taking generosity for granted. She cursed the tightness of her shoes. And she cursed Cavendish for what today seemed like an all-too-proud sort of spaciousness, with every family surrounding their home with as much land as they could manage, marking the boundaries with a row of their finest trees. Compensating for Cavendish's small population by amassing larger-than-needed acreage.

Maud avoided the main roads whenever she could, choosing instead to cut paths she knew well through the open woods or other families' land. Walking quickly now through a familiar pasture, her body stiffened as she recognized the figure approaching.

"Maud? Maud Montgomery!"

Nate Lockhart's voice always had sounded familiar to her, even when they first met over twenty years ago. She turned toward it instinctively.

When Nate reached her, she squinted, taking in the change in him and trying to tell what parts were responsible for the difference. Had he always been so tall?

"How are you, Nate?"

"I'm well, very well in fact. I've just been married," Nate said with a practiced nonchalance that suggested he'd been using these exact words all over town, stretching the news as far as it could reach. It had already come her way from several different sources.

"I've heard," Maud said.

"The wedding was back on the mainland, where I'm living now."

"I trust it was beautiful. With loads of bacon and poppy-seed cakes, if you had your way?"

"No wedding of mine would've been complete without both." Nate smiled. "And you?" Nate's eyes traveled down. Looking for a ring on her finger?

"Not married."

"Oh, I didn't mean—" Nate looked her in the eye for the first time. "I only meant to ask how you were."

Maud's mouth opened a little and shut. "Of course. I'm well."

"Glad to hear it." Nate hesitated.

"I'm still living in the old house with grandmother."

"I'd heard that from my folks. It's good of you—giving up teaching to be with her, and for a long while now too."

"I couldn't see it any other way, not after grandfather died."

"Right—it's just, I never knew you were close to your grandmother. She always seemed like a hard sort."

"She is that," Maud said. "But she raised me when there wasn't anyone else to do it. Kept me from being placed in an orphanage or the like after my father reached his limit. We've become quite the pair, the two of us in that old house."

"Well, that can't last too much longer. You'll find someone soon to marry. Settle down in some place nice, surely."

For a moment, Maud saw the eyes of the boy who used to read her Shelley and Wordsworth under their favorite trees near the Cavendish schoolyard, sneaking his arm around her and running the tips of his fingers along her shoulder while he did. They used to talk about being the kinds of writers who were eventually anthologized and discussed in classrooms. They had exchanged long letters, delivered behind teachers' backs. Once, Nate had whispered that he loved her as they stood outside in the dark. She used to believe they would never stop writing to each other. She used to believe that an understanding like theirs lasts as long as people do.

It had been a nice thing to believe.

"I'm not sure if you've heard I've been publishing stories," Maud said. "A fair number of them now."

"My father mentioned. Still set on those big dreams of yours, I see. Trying to become an illustrious author?" Nate shrugged his chin into what Maud took to be a smirk.

"You think I'm foolish," she said, her tone sharp.

"No, of course not. It's just—did you ever expect that I would become a lawyer? After all I used to say about the law?"

"I certainly did not."

"And I am better off for it. 'When I became a man, I put away childish things.' It took me a while to learn that lesson, but I did."

"Have you read any of my stories?"

"I haven't, but I've heard from people who have. They are said to make a fine serial for Sunday school classrooms."

Maud froze and felt the air still. A few birds called—too cheerfully—in the distance.

"I suppose I haven't been as successful as you at putting away my childhood dreams," she said. "I'm considering a novel, actually. The kind we both said we wanted to write someday."

"Oh, Maud. I hope you're not still holding on to those things we said to each other back in the schoolyard. 'Uncompromising ideals' and the like." Maud watched some knowing cross over Nate's face, and he laughed. "Those ideals aren't the sort that will get you married, I can tell you that."

Maud looked up; she pretended to take note of the position

of the sun in the sky. She pushed the bulk of her hurt back down to the base of her stomach before speaking.

"Much as I hate to end this reminiscing, I'd better go, Nate. I promised Grandmother that I'd get this soup to a neighbor."

Nate lowered his hat and looked at the ground, speaking more softly now. "I understand—duty calls. Good running into you, Maud. Hope to see you again before I leave for the mainland."

"Enjoy your day." Maud forced a smile and turned away, walking as quickly as she could.

A fine serial for Sunday school classrooms.

Those ideals won't get you married.

She had thought she was beyond words like these getting under her skin. And more often than not, these days, she was. But the problem now, on this afternoon that she hadn't wanted to go walking in the first place, was this: Wasn't it true that her stories were most often read in Sunday school classrooms? And wasn't it true that she had no ring on her finger?

She shook her head. She was a determined woman. She would see what she could do.

AS SOON AS she was back home, Maud hurried to the small desk in her upstairs room and pulled out her notebooks. There was only one way to know if she had a novel in her. And that was to begin.

Sitting her notebooks on her lap, she spread her palms wide across them. She looked around at the room's objects with their familiar colors and shapes: the pale pink quilt on the bed that had been in the family for generations, gray in the spot where the cat Daffy slept after outsmarting her grandmother's attempts at exile by coming in through an open window at night; the paintings and portraits in well-worn white and brown frames; and most of all her bookshelf lined with different-colored spines. On top of the bookshelf sat a stack of library books that had arrived last month after the terrible ice blockade in the Northumberland Strait finally lifted and ferries to the mainland started back up. She'd read those books day and night when they first arrived, copying out any parts that made her feel sentimental. On the lowest bookshelf, she kept a picture of her father—alone and smiling handsomely in his best jacket—and the lockbox that held her journals.

Opening the notebooks sitting under her palms, Maud removed a photograph tucked underneath, propping it up in front of her. It had been taken a few years earlier, at the Cavendish beach not far away. She and a friend managed to get their hands on a camera, the newfangled device her grandmother had scoffed at. They designed their own bathing costumes out of leftover scraps of fabric and made off to the beach one morning in a fit of laughter, talking about the ways they might pose and the potential suitors to whom they might show the photos.

The day had continued in laughter until it had come time to take the photo sitting in Maud's hands. For the minute or so when the picture was being taken, Maud remembered feeling not at all different from the rock where she sat or the sea that stretched out in front of her. Molecules on top of molecules looking out at more molecules. She had learned as much in school and never quite believed it, but in that moment she did.

And then, in the next breath, Maud had been overcome by a feeling that was nearly the opposite: her potential to become someone important. It was a deep, private feeling, composed less of pride than of intuition. This confidence had been followed by thankfulness, a deeper thankfulness than she could remember feeling, for being different than the rock or the sea. To be alive in an interesting world, and to tell about it. That was something.

Ever since the photo was taken, she had pulled it out whenever she started a writing project. A glance could bring back those two feelings in quick succession: the ease and relief that came each time she appreciated the vastness of the natural world and the glorious insignificance of any possible thing she could do with her life, followed immediately by the glorious significance of her own conviction.

"Chapter 1," she wrote in a large scrawl on the first page of one of the notebooks.

Maud clapped her hands against her thighs. Let the experiment begin.

She skimmed the other notebook containing her spadework—the character sketches and plotlines she had developed so far. The girl would come from an orphan asylum. Not a place so hard for her liveliness to be unbelievable. But colorless. Two trees in whitewashed cages sitting on either side of the front entrance.

Anne would be sitting at the train station, waiting, thinking about climbing a wild cherry tree. Maud thought of how Anne would describe that tree, dressing it up with adjectives; how old and quiet Matthew would respond to seeing a girl with red braids instead of the orphan boy he had expected to help with his farm.

But how to begin? Not with the cherry tree. The story wasn't only the girl, after all. It was also the story of a small island town on the outskirts of a lesser-known country, deeply tied to its Scottish roots, full of judgment and unexpected humor. It was also the story of a secluded house, nondescript mostly, with one exception: the forest-green paint on its gables. Maud had a picture of this house in mind early on, drawing inspiration from a house across the road where a shy old bachelor, Maud's great-uncle, lived with his sister.

Maud looked out the window for some action, something to start her pen moving. A few swaying tree branches. A swarm of bees emerging from a rosebush. Nothing.

Now, if she had been looking out the window of a house situated close to the main road instead of tucked away in the trees surrounding her grandmother's house, she would have been able to see anyone coming and going. She would have been the first to spot any unusual event.

This felt like a beginning. A house situated at the dip in the main road, making for easy viewing of the neighbors. An afternoon early in June. Someone would sit near a window, looking out. Someone who believed she already knew every possible thing there was to know about that town.

"Mrs. Rachel Lynde lived just where the Avonlea main road dipped down into a little hollow," Maud wrote. "Since Avonlea occupied a little triangular peninsula jutting out into the Gulf of St. Lawrence with water on two sides of it, anybody who went out of it or into it had to pass over that hill road and so run the unseen gauntlet of Mrs. Rachel's all-seeing eye. She was sitting there one afternoon in early June." Maud looked out her own window. "The sun was coming in at the window warm and bright; the orchard on the slope behind the house was in a bridal flush of pinky-white bloom, hummed over by a myriad of bees." The sentences came quickly.

She continued, stopping only to notice which neighbors were coming by for their mail, comforted in her work by the sounds of their stilted talk with her grandmother downstairs. Nothing unusual. The same sounds as before, when she had written the stories.

The sun was low in the sky, tingeing the bark of the birch trees a pale pink, when she saw a man outside the house. His gait caught her eye. Although she had seen him—studied him—in church, she did not recognize him until he paused and looked up at the house.

Then she saw his black hair with its single coifed wave and his dark mournful eyes; she saw him straighten his shoulders the way he did before taking the pulpit.

Maud flexed her feet and reread a few sentences. She liked them. When she stood, she had her notebooks and pen still in hand. She ran downstairs with them, managing to curl a few strands of hair behind her ears and situate herself at the kitchen table just before the Reverend Ewan Macdonald came in for his mail.

5.

Maud had missed overhearing her grandmother's formal introduction to Ewan in the entryway, but it wasn't hard to imagine what was said. Her grandmother would have done her best to establish in a few choice words the good breeding of their Macneill family lineage, the fine manners, the Presbyterian values. Her grandmother made a special point of this with any man who had the potential to be Maud's suitor.

"Ask questions about him and about his career and interests," she'd often instructed Maud. "Let him do most of the conversing. And don't go on about your writing. Ambition is unattractive on a woman."

Now her grandmother was showing Ewan to the kitchen.

"Reverend, I'd like to introduce my granddaughter Ms. Maud Montgomery, one of the large clan of Macneill family members here in Cavendish."

It wasn't like her grandmother to forget that Maud and Ewan had met before. But it was just like her grandmother to believe they had not been properly introduced unless she was the one directing it.

"Thank you for the introduction, Mrs. Macneill," Ewan said with a shy bow of his head in Maud's grandmother's direction. He turned toward Maud and offered her a separate nod. "Ms. Montgomery," he said slowly. A smile crossed his face as he spoke, seemingly by accident. It disappeared when Ewan caught her grandmother's eye. He straightened up.

"My granddaughter will get your mail, Reverend," her grandmother said. "I have a few matters to see to outside."

Maud closed her eyes briefly in silent grace; whatever the matters were, they were no invention. Not by her grandmother.

"Good to see you, Reverend," Maud said after she heard the door close.

Ewan nodded; he looked down at the table to where her notebooks were sitting. Then he slid his hands into his pockets, keeping his gaze low.

Maud smiled, relieved. This was not a man who was overly mannered, not one who would judge her every movement or choice of phrase. He was too shy to get a word out. She didn't see how there could be harm in continuing on the way she normally would.

"There's been quite a bit of mail that's come for you," Maud said. "I'm sure you've been busy these past few weeks settling in." She paused. "I hope your boardinghouse down the road is treating you nicely; it's been quite the spot for boarders over the years. The owner's a gentleman, and has a great chicken coop and garden for meals. Some of the biggest, ripest vegetable yields in all of Cavendish." She looked at Ewan for a few seconds in silent expectation before turning toward the shelves behind her. "I'll just check on your mail."

"Might—" Ewan said. "May I ask what you are working on?" He gestured toward her notebooks. "Another of your stories?"

So he'd heard about her stories.

"Not entirely," she said, handing Ewan his mail. "Something longer this time. A novel."

"Oh—I see," said Ewan. Then he fell silent. He began sorting through his mail.

Maud looked down at her notebooks, sliding them closer

to her on the table. It was the second time she'd mentioned writing a novel to anyone. Her dreadful encounter with Nate had been the first, and that was before she had actually begun. Her initial instinct was protective, followed closely, once she was sure her notebooks were shut, by anger. Her biggest undertaking so far in life had elicited nary a reaction.

An impulse came over her to scream, scream so her grandmother could hear, maybe even scream loud enough to reach Nate walking in a nearby field.

But then what? Then she would still be here, with a well-meaning and frightfully confused minister standing in front of her, and she'd probably need to run upstairs to her room and pull the covers over her head and cry, hoping that no one would overhear. Or better yet, that someone would overhear, put their hands on her too-small shoulders, and say, "All that sensitivity you have inside? You're not the only one. I feel just as much as you. I care just as deeply as you. I understand." But this, she had learned, was the stuff of her imagination.

Even if she had a good scream and a good cry, then what? Then half the town would find out and think she'd gone mad. And she'd never again be able to face the Reverend Ewan Macdonald and feel his storybook smile burn through her veins—the worst possibility of all.

Perhaps Ewan would turn out to be one of those kind souls cut from a different cloth than her own. One for whom understanding takes a little work, a little patience. It didn't mean he couldn't be a kindred spirit in the end. A kindred spirit could reveal himself quick as a thunderbolt or slow as the light of a lamp awakened by the growing dark. Many a friend and teacher had taught her as much.

So instead, Maud said, "I've just gotten the list of organ hymns to play for the service this week. I've started to look them over."

Ewan's eyes came up from his mail with a smile. She smiled back, reveling in the exhilaration that lasted as long as his smiles did. "I'm glad. I've begun working on this week's sermon as well."

"Oh—then I'm assuming you have the subject?" Maud took a breath, steadying herself. "I've always been interested in how you choose a text. To know what is at work in the mind of a minister before he takes the pulpit, what persons might have influenced him that day or given a little tug at his imagination—" She stopped. "I don't mean that you need to tell me."

"No, it's all right. Well—ministers are rightly a private sort until Sundays come around. And even then . . ." He chuckled, then looked down. "But you wouldn't be wrong in expecting a reading from Ecclesiastes."

"Oh!" Maud studied his face. "And tell me, Reverend, 'What profit hath he that worketh in that wherein he laboureth?'"

Ewan looked at her, his face brightening. "'That every man should eat and drink, and enjoy the good of all his labour, it is the gift of God.'"

"And yet is there not 'a time to every purpose under the heaven'? 'A time to plant, and a time to pluck up that which is planted,' 'a time of war, and a time of peace,' 'a time to be born, and a time to die.' Surely not all times are quite so satisfying?" Maud smiled the smallest version of her smile, reminding herself to be careful not to let her teeth show and reveal their crookedness.

"I suppose you're right, Ms. Montgomery." Ewan thought a moment. "A time to be satisfied and a time not to be satisfied."

"And would you call both a gift?"

"Well now, I dunno," he said, his Gaelic accent sneaking through. "I believe so. All in its proper time. All is from God."

"Well," Maud said, "I always have been interested in what is difficult to believe."

Ewan tilted his head. "I'll be seeing you Sunday, then, Ms. Montgomery. I appreciate the mail."

Ewan started to walk out, and Maud thought of a puppet suspended by marionette strings—shoulders high and steps mechanical. But just before leaving the kitchen, Ewan turned back, his chin low and his black eyes looking up at her for several seconds too long.

Then his dimples broke up the shadows on his cheeks, and his hands were back in his pockets. Suddenly he seemed like a young boy, playful and less predictable than a man.

"Good evenin'," he said.

Maud raised her hand in a wave; the newness of this last impression made her less sure of her gestures.

When she heard the door close behind Ewan, Maud closed her eyes, smiling close-lipped toward the ceiling. She reached for her notebook and pen.

She thought of Matthew, the quiet bachelor living with his sister Marilla and dreading nearly all women. She thought of him encountering the chatterbox orphan Anne for the first time at the train station.

"Oh, you can talk as much as you like," he would tell the girl. "I don't mind."

6.

Frede Campbell's voice was hoarse and loud—louder than anyone else in the family ever would have dared.

The sound of it started the itch of laughter at the back of Maud's throat, and images followed the sound: a stuffed goose at the table at Park Corner; an open fire in a parlor fireplace that kept the games and stories going long into the night; Frede and her two older sisters—all three with nearly identical sturdy builds and round faces, but entirely different personalities—bringing dish after dish from the kitchen; their father carving; their mother, whom Maud always watched carefully for any further understanding she could glean of her own mother, passing slabs of butter and homemade pickles with a close-lipped smile.

Maud decided the voice must have been part of the dream she had just woken from. She'd been working late recently, her mind tinkering with choices of phrase for the novel even after the candle was blown out, and she'd started to make afternoon naps a habit.

Then she heard footsteps on the stairs, too heavy and fast to be her grandmother's. They might even be running. After a quick knock, Frede burst into her room.

"Frede!" Maud laughed, standing up from her desk where she'd nodded off. She brushed out the wrinkles in her skirt—not that Frede cared a whit about wrinkles. "Grandmother must be out."

"Lord knows I never could have run up the stairs otherwise. Can you imagine the look on her face if she'd heard me?" Frede's voice went up an octave. "'Was that the sound of running I heard? From the dignified young granddaughter your mother assures me you are?'" Frede straightened her spine, her hands folded in their grandmother's particular way. She looked at Maud until she got the laugh she'd been after.

"What is this, anyway, where did you come from?" Maud asked. She settled on the bed next to Frede, who was working to catch her breath.

"I had the weekend free and thought I'd surprise you," Frede said.

"Well, you accomplished that much."

"Didn't count on being able to manage quite so good a surprise, though, with you in your room looking half asleep and the other half flat stunned."

"I haven't been sleeping well at night, so I've taken to napping. I thought I must still be asleep when I heard the voice of Frede Campbell ringing through this house without warning."

"How's that! In the middle of your nap. Couldn't have planned it better."

"You've always been one for timing." Maud smiled.

"So what's the latest? I haven't had a letter in over a month, so I assume things must be on the up-and-up since your last. I don't see any stifled screams stowed away in your eyebrows." Frede took the sides of Maud's face in her hands with an exaggerated frown and pretended to study Maud's forehead. "You don't look much like an old maid 'unfit for any other kind of life.'"

"I can only hope I wasn't that dramatic," Maud said. "But right you are as usual. There's been a definite improvement. In the weather, for one . . ."

"And?" Frede asked. "Seems rumors proved true about a certain handsome minister changing his boarding place from Stanley to Cavendish to be your new neighbor."

"So they have. Although not 'to be my new neighbor,' I'm sure—"

"You can't be so sure! Word is all over Stanley that some lively and very pretty lady in Cavendish caught his eye. Who could that be but you?"

"I'm sure he wouldn't have told anyone that. He's a quiet one off the pulpit, half terrified of women I think. No doubt the rumors were spread by a few Cavendish ladies bored stiff of old age." Maud looked up. "But in the hopes of satisfying you—I'll say that the same minister and I went for a walk yesterday afternoon." Maud occupied herself with her bracelet as she waited for Frede's response.

"You need to give me more than that, Maud. What did you talk about? And how did you manage to be walking in the first place?"

"The past month he's come by several times a week for his mail—"

"And?"

"And we've gotten to talking. Grandmother has given me her usual dose of instructions about holding my tongue. But I think he likes to listen. And he can make conversation just fine once he warms up. It takes finding the right topics—"

"Which are?"

"Theology, mostly. Which I can handle well—as long as we keep on the relatable parts of the Bible and keep off the long, lecturing parts. The weather too, and stories about Cavendish and my upbringing. He clams up every time I ask him too many questions of a personal nature though—about his family or schooling. Even though he seems to like to hear about mine. I'll need to find a better approach."

Frede nodded. "But how did you get from all this conversation to a walk?"

"It was my suggestion." Maud raised her eyebrows. "I was just finishing a walk when he came for the mail one afternoon, and he asked where I went. I'd spent most of my time in the graveyard that day, after my constitutional pass through Lover's Lane. I couldn't bring myself to say the words 'Lover's Lane' to him, though." She looked at Frede. "He might never have spoken to me again. So I told him about the long history of the graveyard, about all the family we have buried there. I left out the part about how it calms me down being there—no use having him think I'm morbid."

Frede shook her head. "You worry too much."

"I'd say I worry just enough. I did tell him the walk through the trees was worth taking, and passes by the schoolhouse. He hadn't responded before I was offering to show him. I needed to find my way out of the subject, is what it comes down to, and there you have it."

Frede sat up taller and clapped her hands twice, moving to the edge of the bed and turning her head so her messy brown hair was all Maud could see. "Brilliant! The minister and a graveyard, in broad daylight. The height of romance." She laughed. "How did it go?"

"I enjoyed it. We managed to talk pretty well and be silent pretty well. Especially silent in the trees, where I like silence the most. He never looked around much, though, at the trees or anything else. When I talk, he has this intense way of looking at me that makes it hard for me to get my words out properly."

"I would say that's a good sign."

"He has the funniest straight-up-and-down walk, like this." Maud demonstrated with her fingers as she laughed. "I told him a few ghost stories."

"Really?"

"Good ones from when I was younger about the souls in perdition coming round at night and knocking over the headstones of the folks they most hated in life. And the one about Old Man Ames. I used to get all the class running scared with those stories."

"Well done! I'm sure the good reverend could use a little flavor like a ghost story."

"He said he enjoyed them too. But his face never changed much during the telling."

"Only to keep up the airs of a minister, I'm sure. Who could help but be entertained by a story of yours?"

"Most flattering of Fredes." Maud smiled. "You can see what you think yourself tomorrow at church. He's a difficult one to read—different than any of the others—"

"—the many others."

Maud elbowed Frede in the shoulder. "His usual silence keeps things interesting at least. Gives me all sorts of room to imagine what might be there underneath. And I do find myself drawn to him—in a way I haven't felt in a long time. When he looks at me sometimes, I—" Maud shook her head. "He has this way of making me feel like I'm the only person who ever existed in the universe, like I'm some utterly fascinating creature."

Frede laughed. "Well, he's right about that much."

"The feeling only ever comes from glances—not words—but it's comforting. Like he's seeing all the way through me, and he likes me well enough, anyway." She paused. "You'll be here for church tomorrow? You could see him preach."

"How could I miss seeing the premier organist in all of Prince Edward Island play to win a prize beau?"

Maud took a book from the bedside table and lifted her

arm as if to throw it, then smiled and shook her head. "You know how I feel about that dreaded organ."

Frede sighed and slid back further into the bed. "I'm sorry; I shouldn't tell a lie. The premier organist in a thousand-meter radius at least!" She glanced sideways at Maud and smiled. They both laughed, with Maud closing her eyes and laughing harder even than Frede, much harder than the moment called for, until a snort rose up from the back of her throat and stopped her. She opened her eyes to see Frede's eyebrows raised.

Frede cleared her throat and crossed her hands in her lap. "Ah yes, we mustn't laugh too fully. We must always act as though someone might be listening." She paused. "Honestly, this family of ours. Macneill to their core. I dare you to laugh like that in front of one of them—just once—look them right in the eye." Frede squared her shoulders and raised an eyebrow. They both laughed again, but Maud kept hers quieter. Her grandmother might be home any minute. "Anyway, were you about to throw a book at me, Maud Montgomery? I think you were. I can only imagine what Grandmother would say about that."

Only Frede continued laughing. Maud looked out the window.

"What is it?" Frede asked.

Maud turned toward Frede and lowered her voice. "Grandmother. I cannot manage the same laughs recently—at least not until you come around." She paused. "Uncle John was here two weeks ago. He says cousin Prescott's planning to marry, and he wants this house when he does. Grandmother told them she wouldn't leave—'I've lived and worked in this house for sixty years,' she said, 'and I won't have my granddaughter and myself turned out now.' She stood up to him all right, but crumpled when he left. There's been nothing I can do that's any comfort. When she looks at me sometimes now, I cannot help but see it as resentment. If I'd been a boy . . . Well, if I'd been a boy, the farm and house would have gone to me." Maud shook her head. "The terms of grandfather's will are what they are, but he would not have stood for us being made to leave our home while grandmother still had good years left. To make it worse, no one from Uncle John's family has been to see her since."

Frede hit her hands against the bed. "How could he? His own mother? Both of them, really—you know it's with cousin Prescott's egging." She looked at Maud. "Oh, Maud. It's foolishness. They won't be allowed to get away with it. Someone in the family will put a stop to it. And if not, well." She paused before adding, in a perfect mimic of Maud's grandmother, "'We'll leave it to their own conscience.' Conscience has a way of finding you in this family."

"Let's hope so." Maud sighed. "The trouble is, it's taken my secret humor out of grandmother's ways for the time being, and you know how I need that humor. That's half the pity."

"Well, that's what I'm here for," Frede said.

Maud smiled at Frede and felt the tension leave her shoulders. With Frede around, nothing ever seemed as dire as Maud's imagination once supposed. A bosom friend and a cousin wrapped into a single package. What luck.

AFTER THE LAST organ hymn was through, Maud rushed to gather her things and made her way to the church steps. She lingered at the top, smiling at the sight of the women on the lawn, flapping their fans the way a flock of flustered birds would flap their wings. Several of them had been watching for her, eager for a story or two to break up the tiresome exercise of pleasantry after pleasantry.

The men, at an unusual disadvantage today, were stepping closer than they should to the women to catch the weak breeze the fans created. All the men save one.

Ewan stood still at the corner of the church steps, one of his feet a step lower than the other. He seemed to be paying no mind to any discomfort, including the beads of sweat running down his forehead as he extended his palm, again and again, to greet his parishioners.

Parishioners kept stopping in front of him to compliment the sermon—"The best I've heard in all my years," Maud heard one woman say. She was unmarried, as were several of the others gathered in front of Ewan.

But now he was turning, his eyes searching through faces bleached with sun. And then his eyes settled on Maud, and they seemed content to remain that way as long as anyone would let them.

Maud felt her stomach turn over.

One of the women standing in front of Ewan reached for his elbow. Maud thought she saw Ewan flinch, and then it was over.

Maud decided it was best to avoid the scene in front of Ewan until it broke up a bit. She made her way to Frede's circle, falling into conversation. Every once in a while, one of the girls would reach forward and take Maud's elbow. The other girls eyed this familiarity closely, watching for any sign of preference from Maud. It was currency to be liked by her or anyone else from the Macneill clan, a fact Maud enjoyed more than she dared to admit.

By the time Ewan finally approached the group in front of Maud, it had thinned, but only because of the heat. Ewan stood away from the others at first, his chin dipping down toward the ground. After quickening the latest conversation in ways she hoped no one would notice, Maud ended with a comment designed to draw a laugh and looked toward Ewan.

"G'day, Ms. Montgomery," Ewan said, moving a few steps forward once the remaining women started to disperse. "Fine Sunday we're having."

"Good morning, Reverend," Maud said. She kept her fan going in hopes that he'd step even closer.

"Did you enjoy the sermon?"

"It was nicely put together. I could tell you'd given it careful thought."

"I've had several compliments on the organ hymns you played. Such a wonderful thing for a woman to have musical training. To show her devotion to God and the church in that way—I've always admired it."

Maud winced. As her grandmother had declared repeatedly, it had been a good idea to volunteer as organist. Never mind how much she disliked it—being stowed away in that little box, playing the same dull hymns she'd heard as a child.

"That's nice to hear." Maud shifted her weight from one foot to another. The silence that followed made the tree leaves noisy; it turned the distant bird calls shrill.

Then she felt her diaphragm relax. Here was Frede, having finished up a side conversation and taking Maud by the arm.

"Good day, Reverend," Frede said with laughing eyes. "A little too hot for my taste, but a good Lord's day nevertheless. What did you think of our girl holding court? Quite the crowd-pleaser, isn't she?"

"Well," Ewan said once he realized the question was for him. He looked down.

"Not that I suppose you noticed with all you had going on. Few people ever fully appreciate the good hard work of a minister. On top of everything you do on Sundays—preaching as well as you just did and greeting every him-and-her-and-mister after the service is over—there are the parishioner visits, the funerals, the weddings. People never look past their own noses, I figure, to know that you are ministering to more than just them."

"I suppose that's true," Ewan said, smiling now.

"Oh," Frede said, giving Maud's elbow a squeeze. "I've spotted Grandmother over there. The rest of her group has left. I'd better go check in with her."

"Where did you find that one?" Ewan gestured toward Frede as she walked away.

"My younger cousin," Maud said, smiling now too and stepping closer. She made sure to keep her fan moving quickly enough for the closeness to be defensible. "In for only a short while, I'm afraid, but she's sure to be back."

"She's a laugh."

"She is that, and my closest friend."

"Then I doubly hope I've made a good enough impression—for her to return." Ewan smiled hesitantly. The way he looked at her, coupled with his insinuation, made Maud's stomach churn with excitement.

"Why don't we stand in the shade over that way?" Maud asked, gesturing. It wasn't only the heat that made her say so. She was eager for greater privacy.

After they'd spoken more easily for a few minutes, Maud heard her grandmother's voice close behind her ear.

"Past dinnertime now, Maud," her grandmother said. "We'd better get going."

"I tried convincing her to stay longer, but you know this one. Nothing if not stuck in her ways," Frede said, drawing a smile from Ewan.

"As I told you, Frede, I have bread dough rising," her grandmother said to Frede. Then she turned in Ewan's direction. "I believe you said just last Sunday, Reverend, that idleness is a sure sign of disrespect for the Lord."

"I suppose I did," Ewan said. Maud couldn't be sure if the reluctance she heard in his voice was her own invention.

"I'm sure you two will be able to pick up where you left off next Sunday," her grandmother said with a nod.

"You two"—Maud's heart jumped at the words, not caring for the moment that they came from her grandmother.

A predictable clearing of her grandmother's throat brought Maud back to reality. After a quick goodbye to Ewan, Maud turned at the same time her grandmother did in the direction of the walk home. Frede issued an enthusiastic farewell.

The first time during their walk that her grandmother's stride was a step ahead, enough for Frede and Maud to fall momentarily out of her sight, Frede caught Maud's attention and stuck out her tongue in the direction of their grandmother. Frede raised her large grin up into the blaring sun; she took Maud's elbow and squeezed, not letting go until Maud's rib cage started to shake in silent laughter.

"SO YOU REALLY did like him?" Maud asked finally, near the end of their walk home. She and Frede had dropped back a number of steps from their grandmother, and the noise of nearby hammering on a roof was surely all their grandmother could hear.

"I thought his sermon was splendid," Frede said. "Did you see the way people nodded along? Those women in the front pew craning their chins up to get the best view of him?" She demonstrated. "I like him too. A gentle sort. A little unsure of himself, but endearingly so. You'd never have to worry any about him going after other women. In fact, I don't think you do now. He's clearly smitten. Has he given any physical sign yet? A brush of the hand? A kiss on the cheek?"

"Frede," Maud whispered. "He's a minister. And you saw how timid he is!"

"Oh please! Ministers have wives and babies just like everyone else."

Maud's eyes narrowed as she studied their grandmother's back for any sign of eavesdropping.

Frede only looked more amused. "They've trained you so well, these women in our family." Her voice lowered. "Minister or not, you may as well try kissing him soon and see how it goes. There's nothing so terrible about one kiss."

"You act as though I'm some awful prude! It's different with him. He requires a good amount of patience, which, lucky for him, I possess."

"Funny, I disagree. I think you could have your way with him anytime you want to."

"Said with the confidence of youth."

"You know I hate when you bring up my age." Frede frowned.

"Yes, such a pity to be hardly twenty-two."

"As I keep telling you, I'm an old hag at heart."

Their grandmother turned to look for them, her arms crossed.

"Speaking of . . ." Frede whispered.

Maud couldn't help but laugh, but she also sped up her steps in hopes of fending off the speech she knew would come next. With a sigh, Frede did the same.

The heat made all three of their bodies lean toward the front door as soon as they could spot it, their legs sluggish behind them. Maud's grandmother, propelled by her jutting chin, managed to reach the door several steps ahead. Frede walked less than Maud and tired more easily; Maud stepped back so Frede could go inside first.

Entering last had another purpose, one Maud never would have said out loud: It allowed her to linger in the entryway, studying the light on the floorboards.

For a few days at the beginning of summer around dinnertime, the sun came between several branches and square through the open front door. This was one of them. Maud kept her breath soft. She'd grown superstitious about this light. She liked to imagine it turning the house into a tomb, illuminated at its entrance and dark and cavernous everywhere else.

This all fit nicely with a dearly held belief she'd never told anyone, which was that homes had souls of their own. Not conspicuous souls like people. No—old homes in particular had souls like a wise old woman standing stock-still in the haste of a crowd, wrists faceup, offering a hand, a crutch, a place to rest. Her face so ordinary it seems to disappear, the crowd pays her no mind. And then one day, when the light is right, her face is all the crowd can see; it is a collage of shadow and sun. It can crack anyone looking straight open.

The sun had been this way when Maud first walked into the house to stay after her mother died. The house, with all that it had withstood, had been the saving grace of her childhood. If the house could tolerate her grandparents for so many years, so could she.

What had her father told her that day when he dropped her off to stay? She could remember the light on the floorboards, but not any of his words. "You're to live here now with your grandparents, Maudie, just for a while," he might have said. He might have said nothing at all. Her grandmother wouldn't have given him much time before coming to the door and instructing them both on what should be done next.

Maud knew she'd been wearing her good yellow sundress that day, the one her mother had made, with the collar turned brown from overuse. Her grandmother wasted no time repurposing that dress into a set of dusting rags soon after Maud's arrival, undeterred by any amount of teary protesting.

Maud had hardly taken that dress off for months after her mother died—months mostly spent following her father around the house and the general store he ran next door. Watching as he stacked canned goods on the shelves of the store, then put them back in the original box, then took them out again—for no reason she could see. Watching him forget most of the ingredients when he tried to make a meal.

Most of all her father seemed to like Maud's chatter in those days, anything she could tell him about the worlds of her dolls or her books. He liked it far less, she'd discovered, when she asked for her mother. He liked least of all when, as he'd put it once to her grandmother, Maud "threw a conniption," crying or yelling or making any real noise. When that happened, he'd often leave the room. But sometimes he'd turn to stare at her, his perfect blue eyes that she'd always admired turned blank and unsure, as if he'd been struck blind and asked to captain a ship.

It had been better during the years after she moved in with her grandparents but before her father moved away from the Island. Those years, he had visited just enough to keep her grandmother content, ruffling Maud's hair and singing her praises endlessly whenever he did. He always had been better with words than he was with following through on them. And how she'd longed for his words back in that day.

Maud forgave her father effortlessly for the long stretches between visits—even when they lasted as long as a year. Forgave him the second he called her name after opening the door. Sometimes she thought he was the best father of all between visits, when she could decide what important work he must be doing and what words of encouragement he might bring her the next time he came. Or, best of all, how he might tell her he'd finally decided it was time for the two of them to live together again.

Maud had been standing under the doorframe of the old house for some time now; she could hear sounds in the kitchen of Frede and her grandmother preparing the meal. Strange that they had not called for her.

She went to help, desperate now to stop this painful remembering and escape into her novel. Frede had already packed and would be leaving as soon as the meal was through.

Maud wasn't ready to share the fact of her writing the novel with Frede yet. Frede always said kind things about Maud's writing, but they never went much beyond platitudes. And if she told Frede and Frede couldn't understand, well, the hurt of that might just trample all the momentum that Maud had. Better to keep it to herself, at least until she had a full draft, something concrete to show for her efforts.

PERCHED OVER HER desk later that day, Maud alternated between writing dialogue and pacing the room, dissatisfied. She turned the page and started over.

"Where is the boy?" Those would be the first words out of Marilla Cuthbert's mouth when Anne and Matthew pulled up in the buggy. And naturally so. Marilla and Matthew would have wanted a boy to help with the farm, to make life easier on Matthew in his older age.

A boy would have made life easier on Maud's grandparents too. He could have worked the farm, making it far less of a burden for her grandparents to raise a young grandchild years after they had thought themselves finished with child-rearing. A boy might have been easier for them to understand as well—easier, at least, than a girl like Maud. Or a girl like Anne.

Anne, immediately injured by Marilla's question, would linger in the doorway, not meek, but observing. And then what? It was one thing to craft Anne's speech in the unassuming company of Matthew. But it was quite another to know how Anne would respond to a no-nonsense old maid like Marilla.

Maud let herself imagine the worst Anne might say, lashing out at Marilla's insensitivity.

But people must like you, Anne girl.

Maud heard the front door close behind her grandmother. She wondered what she could have been going out for on a Sunday and if she needed help; she wondered if she would be delivered an earful at supper for not having gone down to ask.

Then she remembered Frede's tongue, pointing in her grandmother's direction earlier that day after church. Not anything Maud would ever do—the opposite of ladylike— and hadn't it only made Maud like Frede more?

What would Frede have said to Marilla? A spirited response, no doubt, but maybe not all that interesting. Then again, this wasn't Frede. It was Anne, and Anne had to be good with words for Maud to have any fun with her. Something of Frede, then, but not entirely.

"'You don't want me!'" Anne would cry. "'You don't want me because I'm not a boy! I might have expected it. Nobody ever did want me. I might have known it was all too beautiful to last. I might have known nobody really did want me. Oh, what shall I do? I'm going to burst into tears!'"

Maud laughed out loud.

And when Anne cried, she would not cry silently. She would not retreat outside to the yard or to a corner. No— "Sitting down on a chair by the table, flinging her arms out upon it, and burying her face in them," Maud wrote, "she proceeded to cry stormily."

Maud smiled. So would Matthew. Marilla smiling didn't seem quite realistic. But why bother with a character that a reader won't like, or grow to like?

Maud wrote, "Something like a reluctant smile, rather rusty from long disuse, mellowed Marilla's grim expression. 'Well, don't cry any more. We're not going to turn you out-of-doors to-night.'"

The setup, Maud realized. Hinting at an evolution into something better—better, certainly, than Maud had experienced in her many years growing up with her grandparents. The story of those years wouldn't satisfy a reader at all.

7.

Maud jumped in her seat when Ewan and her grandmother entered the kitchen together. She had not heard them coming.

Maud snapped her writing notebook shut on Anne apologizing to Mrs. Rachel Lynde. With a shake of her head, Maud attempted to shed Anne's heightened emotions and return to the world at hand.

"Reverend," Maud said, standing up.

"Please," he said, looking behind him to the now empty spot where Maud's grandmother had stood a moment before. "It's Ewan. When we're not in church, anyway."

Maud smiled. "In that case, I expect you will start calling me Maud."

Ewan nodded, looking toward his usual spot on the wood floor. His face was barely visible.

"There have not been many letters for you the past week," Maud said. "But maybe you were not expecting many." She paused. "I'm sure you have been busy preparing for the sermon this Sunday. I've heard some folks are coming from a few towns away to hear you preach. There's been a lot of talk about what the subject might be." She paused again, desperate to make the conversation normal so that he would relax and look at her again in that way she liked. "I've also been meaning to tell you that my cousin Frede's coming back into town. She's intent on seeing you preach again. We thought we'd take a long walk on the Cavendish shore on Saturday beforehand. You'd be more than welcome to join us."

She waited, exhaling slowing out of her barely open mouth. She thought of Katie Maurice and Lucy Gray—reflections of her own face in the two doors of a bookcase her grandmother used as a china cabinet and, for a time when she was younger, her confidants. She'd told her life story to Katie, the young and vibrant one, many times, watching grumpy old Lucy warily for the most part, but sharing tidbits with her from time to time so as not to leave her out.

Making her own voice fill up the space of the room, playing all the parts of a conversation, had always seemed like second nature. Good practice for her conversations with Ewan.

It occurred to Maud that she might weave Katie and Lucy into Anne's story. As an orphan, Anne would have needed to find clever ways to entertain herself.

No one ever would have suspected Maud of having some of that same need. She'd grown up with friends, after all. Never gone hungry, never suffered abuse, never been truly disliked that she could recall. But for as long as she could remember, she'd been aware of a trough inside of her that never seemed to get full no matter what she put in it. Wanting friends she could tell about her strangest thoughts. Wanting to say what she meant and not occupy half her mind watching her tongue. Wanting so much more from life than every other girl in town. Presumptuous girl!

Ewan coughed. Maud's toes raised up in her shoes as she turned to face him.

"Your letters! Here they are, the full set."

Ewan paged through them. Afraid he would leave without saying a thing, Maud cleared her throat.

Without looking up, Ewan said in a low voice, "I've had an idea."

"Well, you'd better hurry up and tell me. I was beginning to think you had nothing to say to me this week." She kept her tone light.

"I got to thinking after our walk through the graveyard," Ewan said, looking up finally. "I had a letter a while back from a friend from Dalhousie seminary. Turns out he's organized what they call a garden development in a cemetery near one of his parishes. I noticed during our walk that the graveyard has weeds where there could be bushes. Better grass would be nice too. I thought it could be a good project for—this town."

Maud nodded slowly. "It's a fine idea, Reverend. Ewan. You are right that the town will appreciate it. I've heard more and more talk lately fussing over the state of the cemetery. I think you'd be able to drum up support." She paused, then took an oratorical tone. "Alas, even the most stubborn of misers stand ready and willing to donate where their dead are concerned." She held her face straight until she saw the words register. Ewan gave a short laugh that she joined.

"Well, I hope I can count on you for support? From the looks of the garden outside, you may have some practical advice too. I've no real experience when it comes to planting."

"I'd imagine there are some differences between my kind of gardening and planting for longevity's sake in a graveyard. Why don't you see what your friend has to say first?"

"He did say he would send a pamphlet. Keep an eye out for it?"

"I'd be happy to."

"I thought I might announce the plan this Sunday. The sermon will be on purification and cleanliness after death. There could be a nice intersection."

"Well—I look forward to hearing it."

"I'm happy to know your reaction. I thought the project might please you."

Maud shifted on her feet. It was kind of Ewan—flattering, even. But something about the idea made her stomach churn.

"I'll keep a look out for the pamphlet," she said.

"Thank you, Maud. G'day now," he said. He smiled broadly and looked at her in the way she liked. She wished he'd done it sooner.

MAUD BEGAN WALKING the length of the kitchen as soon as Ewan left, images circling her mind from the day her mother was buried—her father's sun-spotted arms holding Maud over the casket; the coldness of her mother's cheek when she leaned down to touch it; the lace curtains her mother had recently hemmed swaying in the breeze. Years later, when Maud asked why she had not gone to the grave-yard for the burial with the rest of the relatives, her father told her that she would not have understood, she was too young, and anyway it was a difficult day.

During church service a year or two after her mother died, Maud had asked her aunt Emily—the coldest of her mother's surviving siblings—where Maud's mother was now. With one of her slender fingers, Aunt Emily pointed up. Toward the trapdoor on the church ceiling, Maud thought. She knew there were ladders that tall. Why wouldn't someone simply take a ladder, stand it up, open the trapdoor, and bring her mother down? How she longed then for the warm hug her mother would give her when her feet were back on solid ground. But Aunt Emily had laughed in her wicked way after each of the last few questions Maud had asked, and Maud had resolved not to ask anything else that might bring on that laugh.

Maud was eight when she first saw her mother's grave, situated in the same graveyard that Ewan was set on beau-tifying. Everyone knew by then that a graveyard meant dead people underground in boxes. Some older students were in the habit of going to the graveyard nearly every day at the start of dusk—they never would say why—and it took careful listening to find a day when they would not be going.

On the day Maud went herself, there was a low fog in the air, which reassured her. She had not admitted to herself what she was looking for until she'd been walking along the rows for some time and found herself crossing her arms across her ribs and shivering. Then she knew that she had seen her mother's name. Her mother was in one of the boxes under the ground. Mostly, she felt relief. Until then, even when she stopped looking for her mother on the church roof, Maud believed that her mother was somewhere close by—restless and uncomfortable. She had dreams of her mother's face and arms and body, pale like the last time Maud had seen them, wearing her good green velvet dress and tumbling through the air right above the family's heads, too high for anyone to reach, never getting any lower. How Maud had longed to find her mother and pull her down, to soothe the ache of all that she couldn't fully remember about her mother but that she so desperately missed.

Since that day, Maud had liked the settled quality of the graveyard. She remembered a scraggly shrub that sat about two feet from her mother's tombstone. She pictured it being pulled out, a hole where its roots had been.

No, not that.

Something far worse.

She conjured up a brush fire igniting all Ewan's new plantings, leaving only scorched earth in its wake.

Maud scolded herself for indulging her fascination with fire at the expense of Ewan's plans. She forced herself to imagine grass recarpeting the earth. The scraggly shrub back in its place. She imagined a few new trees, planted at Ewan's behest. Nice, green, and proper. Would her mother appreciate them? Maud's chest throbbed with the question. She had not known her mother long enough to be sure.

Maud's father also was buried now, in Prince Albert, Saskatchewan, the place she might have lived for more than just a year if her father had remarried a different woman—a woman who had some care for Maud other than to pull her out of school to serve as a nanny for her half siblings.

Maud imagined her father's grave the way she liked to: in a field left to grow however it would, with grasses tall and protective catching any wind, trees scattered around with plenty of space in between, and wildflowers in the summer. A nice, unobtrusive stone marking the site.

Maud had stopped walking. She held on to the edge of the kitchen table.

Purification after death, Ewan had said. As if death was a mess that could be wiped clean.

Would Ewan ever be able to understand what she had lost? What she had spent most of her life missing?

Hearing footsteps and knowing that her grandmother could smell tears several rooms away, Maud's pulse quickened. It did not ease up until she was in her room with her manuscript spread open in front of her.

Picking up her pen, Maud sank eagerly into the smaller, humorous afflictions of the residents of Avonlea.

THE TEXT FOR Ewan's sermon that Sunday was Numbers 19. His voice was clear and slow, and he did not look at his notes. "Whosoever toucheth the dead body of any man that is dead, and purifieth not himself, defileth the tabernacle of the Lord."

Then Ewan looked up to where Maud sat behind her organ, which he had never done before. It was rare that any minister would look up at that angle, tucked away as she was. His eyes were sure of himself, confident in the words he was saying. She liked him this way.

"Nevertheless," he kept saying. Nevertheless, despite their salvation, the dead leave behind bodies. Nevertheless, we owe a responsibility to those bodies; the way we handle them is important. The way their burial sites are cared for is important.

Nevertheless, the dead matter a great deal to the living. Well, he understood at least that much.

Ewan introduced the graveyard development project with an energy and conviction that had the congregation turning their heads and looking at one another with smiles. Maud adjusted to a more comfortable position in her seat.

MAUD LEFT FOR her walk in a hurry that evening, taking her usual route through the graveyard. It was later than she liked to start out—her grandmother's doing, with the chores she'd insisted on after supper.

Maud had taken to walking every evening that summer, twisting the lines she had written that day around and around until she was sure they contained the right combination of humor and truth.

When the deeper dark of night came on, she paid more attention to the trees than anything low to the ground. She liked to see the branches and leaves against the star-filled sky, imagining them as dark cutouts in a decorated cloth.

But tonight it was the gardens that had her attention, and she ended her walk in her own. She loved her garden. She could not bear the thought that she might be forced to leave it by virtue of her cousin Prescott having rights that her grandmother lacked.

She felt the old feeling again when she was kneeling and staring at the spaces between a few blue violets in the garden's corner, hearing them brush against one another with the breeze. The tingling started at the crown of her head and traveled down her neck and arms. A veil fluttering open. A fraction of real universe revealing itself, beautiful and strange. It happened only at times like these, when it was just her alone and she was listening to the sounds around her. The depth of feeling was enough sometimes to make her believe it was addressed to her, this particular place and time, with her the only one around to know she was seeing it. Other times it seemed to happen when the world plain well forgot about her being there. All she could know for sure was its effect: contentedness of the real, lingering sort, which was the closest she had ever felt to faith.

"If I really wanted to pray," Anne would tell Marilla, "I'd go out into a great big field all alone or into the deep, deep, woods, and I'd look up into the sky. And then I'd just FEEL a prayer."

When Maud stood up from the garden, in front of her sat the house where she had spent most of her childhood, dark against the night sky, with no candlelight in sight. A place so crucial to her became for the moment simply another cutout in the sky's enormous cloth.

What came to pass with Ewan mattered less in this moment than it had in some time. She wished, as she always did when she came upon a good dose of perspective, that she could don it like a cloak for the rest of her days. She knew this feeling wouldn't last.

But she could capture a bit of this feeling in Anne. And Anne, she had begun to believe, was a survivor. A girl whose peculiar ideas and ways of putting them might just stand the test of time.

MAUD CREPT UP the stairs, knowing it was later than she usually returned and her grandmother would already be in bed.

She took out her journal, a thick book with a plain purple cover, and read over her entry from earlier that day. She had written very little in her journal recently, occupied as she was with the novel. But today, she decided she owed it to her Reader—the man in spectacles whom she had always imagined opening the pages of her journals with interest one day—to write about something more uplifting than that dreadful past winter, which the last few entries had set out in exhaustive detail.

She had not included anything yet about the novel, or about Ewan. But today she indulged her desire to write it all out—her hopes and dreams for Anne's future, and her future with Ewan too. Life seemed as full as her blooming garden now, standing in stark contrast to the past few entries. My, wouldn't the Reader be pleased by this turn of events.

She reread, adding sentences here and there, but stopped when she heard her grandmother's footsteps in the hall. They paused by her door, then got lighter as they retreated.

So she had been awake and was checking. She would never ask where Maud had been, but she would make her assumptions.

If Maud told her grandmother she was walking by herself every evening because she enjoyed it, because the natural world had never stopped astonishing her, her grandmother would shake her head. She would ask herself again where Maud came up with such fanciful notions.

Maud turned back to the journal. "The Bible was wise to place the creation of life in a garden," she wrote. Anne surely would have agreed.

8.

The next time Maud unlocked her journal that summer, it was to write about Ewan's regular visits, along with the inspiration she had gleaned from rereading a stack of letters from Nate.

The novel had given Maud the idea to reread Nate's letters. She wanted to put herself back in the mindset of her schoolgirl days, relearning the cadence of the speech, the sources of laughter and tears. Her budding relationship with Ewan put her childish romance with Nate into proper perspective, allowing her to look back on it with understanding and humor.

Now, with Nate's letters read and stacked at the corner of the kitchen table, Maud started to write someone new into the novel—the boy only roughly sketched out in her spadework, whose manner had been slowly solidifying in her mind.

Gilbert Blythe would only be trying to get Anne's attention. Anne would be looking out the window, distracted by the pond that her romantic soul had named the Lake of Shining Waters, and Gilbert wouldn't stand for it. No other girl in school would have paid him so little attention. And what would he do? What could he say to put something memorable between him and Anne that would follow him through the rest of the story?

Maud wrote, "Gilbert reached across the aisle, picked up the end of Anne's long red braid, held it out at arm's length and said in a piercing whisper: 'Carrots! Carrots!'"

Maud smiled.

Frede had once told Maud a story about a terrible day in grade school. A boy had been teasing her about her arms—pinching the backs of them and calling her Chub-erica (from Frederica, her full name). "Legend has it," Frede said, "that I cracked my slate in half on top of his head. Of course," she added, winking, "no daughter of your aunt actually would have done such a thing."

Maud wrote, "And then—thwack! Anne had brought her slate down on Gilbert's head and cracked it—slate not head—clear across."

Maud heard herself laugh, and immediately thought of Marilla.

Marilla would need to be told about the slate, but Maud hadn't fully sketched out how the scene would go. Maud had, however, begun to make Marilla into the kind of older woman who does not entirely forget the way she felt as a young girl—something Maud herself could never imagine forgetting. Although Maud preferred an older woman whose youthful spirits were fully intact, she had also met some rough-and-tumble older women who still had an understanding of their young selves inside of them, even if it took some digging through the rubble to get there.

Or maybe all women had some sense of their younger selves, but for some there was too much rubble. Maud had always suspected as much about her grandmother.

But as for Marilla, it was all up to Maud.

Perhaps Marilla could have carried a similar grudge against a boy. Small town that it was, it could even be Gilbert's father. He could be an old beau, which would also help explain how Marilla had ended up unmarried—something readers would be wondering. People always were in the business of speculating about old maids—

"G'day, Maud. I've come to see about the mail."

Ewan's deep voice was especially startling in contrast to the pebbly and uneven boy tones Maud had been imagining for Gilbert. It made her jump from her seat.

It really shouldn't have. Every day it was the same, whether to Maud or her grandmother. "I've come to see about the mail," usually followed up with "fine weather today." Sometimes he held on to his breath along with his words, which made her nervous.

"Ewan—you've caught me distracted," Maud said. She pushed her papers together on the table and smiled. "I'll go check on your mail."

As soon as she turned, Maud heard Ewan's breath release.

With her back to Ewan, Maud recalled her spontaneous banter with Nate. How much easier it all had seemed back then. Back when possibilities seemed strung on a line. Back when she'd decided to let other girls worry over marriage while she concerned herself with building the kind of life that happened to other people, in more important places.

"Fine fall weather today," Ewan said now through the kitchen doorway.

It got better after the first few lines were behind them, she reminded herself. Especially once she came up with a line to make Ewan smile.

But each day, the questions remained: Where were they headed? And when?

9.

The sweet peas and asters always had been the last in her garden to go. Maud watched their first petals fall and felt one of her pesky old headaches rise up from the nape of her neck. She'd been free of headaches all summer.

Later that day, she cut a few of the sweet peas that were still blooming and brought them into the kitchen, arranging them in a vase and working to memorize their scent. Looking out the window at the trees, she tried to imagine them bare and couldn't. "Winter is impossible to believe until it comes," she whispered.

"Good idea cutting them while we still can," her grandmother said to Maud's back. "It might be the last year for the garden."

Maud tried not to let her surprise show in her body like it sometimes did.

"It won't be the last year," Maud said too loudly. Then she turned around, and her voice softened. "It cannot be. I will not have us turned out of this house just because Prescott's getting married. He and Uncle John are no better than bullies, and it will not work. And as long as we are living in this house, we can manage a small plot for flowers. They cannot possibly use the whole yard for farming. It wouldn't be fair."

"I would not count on anything more than those roses and chrysanthemums you replanted to keep indoors this winter, which we could take with us somewhere else."

"Grandmother—"

"I know how you get your heart set on things is all. I'm only trying to soften the blow if it does come. There's no fairness, child, not in this life. Life brings us what it brings, and success lies in how many times we can become someone new. I learned as much when you landed on my doorstep. If I have taught you anything, I hope I have taught you that."

Maud felt the start of tears tickle painfully in her sinuses. She walked across the room, trying out places for the vase.

"The reverend came by earlier today, when you were out," her grandmother said to Maud's back. Her tone had something new in it—regret?

"Oh?" Maud turned her head.

"Seems his graveyard project's near finished. At least they have finished planting all the shrubs hearty enough to live through winter. It is a good idea he had."

"It has earned him a lot of attention," Maud said.

"I like the idea of being buried there better now."

"Grandmother!" They both laughed.

"Well, it's the truth. Your grandfather would too. He liked things presentable."

"He certainly did."

"I think he'd forgive the reverend for being a Highlander. What he lacks in culture and charm he makes up for in a good, solid career and a fine enough disposition. Serious, but I do not think morose." Her grandmother looked directly at Maud. "I hope you agree?"

"I do."

"Fine then. I want you to know you have my approval."

"Your approval?"

"In case anything should ever come of the two of you, which I'd like for it to," her grandmother said slowly. "I'd like for you to have a husband and a family." Maud thought she saw tears starting to well in the corners of her grandmother's eyes. "Your mother too. She would have wanted this for you."

"I'm happy to know it," Maud said, and stepped closer. She had half a mind to reach out for a hug. But her grandmother's eyes were already elsewhere, plainly uncomfortable with how much she'd said. After a nod, she made quick business of escaping to the parlor.

Soon after hearing her grandmother leave the room, Maud noticed her pulse speed up. She let herself realize that she had not been on another walk with Ewan since that first one through the graveyard. Never anything resembling a date. It was not as if he had expressed any intent with respect to her. He had never even paid her a compliment, not directly. And he had a good reason for coming so regularly, same as everyone else in town. What if she was wrong about his intentions? Now, with her grandmother's hopes layered on top of her own, the thought of that disappointment was hard to bear.

She went upstairs and took to her journal to wring herself out. She'd write about the last of her garden, her fears about Uncle John and Prescott and losing the old home, and her fears about Ewan. Then she would be ready to go back to the novel and write something else entirely.

10.

Despite the return of the usual headaches that fall and winter, there was a difference from the past several years. Maud felt propelled by the thought of the next day, interested in life in the old way she had felt up through her first year of teaching school, before she returned home and the bad winters started. Frede visited three times, and each time Maud came away with her tears laughed out.

Her writing went well, up until just before her second cousin's wedding on Christmas Day. There was the work of being a bridesmaid to blame, but there was also this: She did not know how Anne's story would end.

She admitted it to herself just before the wedding ceremony, when her mental defenses were occupied with fluffing the bride's dress and instructing her not to lock her knees because a reputation for fainting sticks with a girl. That's when she realized that after the wedding ended, it would be January; there would be no excuse but to finish the book.

She hated every ending she'd thought of so far. What if she never finished? What if those blank pages at the end stayed blank? She hadn't been able to bring herself to read it through yet. Worse still, what if the entire novel was terrible? Then she'd be a failed novelist. An unmarried, failed novelist. The thought made her want to curl up into a sad, sorry ball right there on the aisle.

On the heels of this awful imagining, Maud looked up

and saw Ewan holding his Bible. She knew he would be officiating the wedding, but she hadn't seen him yet that day, and he hadn't come by for his mail in quite some time. He looked the part of a wise minister, focused on his task. Maud held her chin up and forced a smile.

Later in the ceremony, as Maud sat and watched from the front row with the other bridesmaids, Ewan's eyes took hold of hers, and they were warm and reverent in a different way than she had seem them before.

He was saying, "God gave us marriage for the full expression of the love between a man and a woman. In marriage a woman and a man belong to each other, and with affection and tenderness give themselves to each other."

Ewan looked at Maud then like he had asked her a question. His mouth smiled without moving much, and she felt her stomach drop.

Then Ewan's eyes were back on his notes. Maud studied him, willing him to look toward her again so she could decide how she felt about what he had just said. But he didn't look up again. He said, "This way of life must not be entered into carelessly, or from selfish motives, but responsibly, and prayerfully." He glanced up to take note of the couple, waiting for them to nod.

As he continued, Maud watched other guests' responses to Ewan, glad to see that they looked content. She could appreciate the sincerity of this speech, the appropriateness of its message. But the delivery felt too grave for the occasion. She imagined joining Ewan at the front of the room and saying a good-natured line or two about the couple that would shake the somberness out of the crowd. Something that would make Ewan chuckle and settle down a little. It was something Anne would do.

But this was not the time or place for such gestures. No

one would laugh, most likely. They'd only shake their heads and wonder what in the world an unmarried woman was doing standing beside a minister at a wedding.

What a dreadfully predictable place the real world could be.

AT SUPPER AFTER the ceremony, Ewan chose a seat at the opposite end of the table from Maud, despite the seat open next to her. But he kept glancing at her with a nervous kind of smile, and when the meal was finished and everyone was gathered in the parlor, he walked toward her. She noticed that he'd waited until just after two companions had left her side.

"Sorry I've let it go so long since coming for the mail," he said. "It's been a busy time."

"I can imagine," Maud said. "Life gets away from us all around the holidays."

"Between travel to see my folks, the Christmas concert, and weddings too. I never would have expected winter weddings to be so common around these parts."

"It seems to be a new trend. I thought this one was beautiful, especially with all those berries and pine branches."

"It surely was."

"You did a fine job up there. And the bride of course was lovely."

"She was, though not the loveliest in the room," Ewan said, smiling.

Maud found herself searching his face. Could he have become so forward all at once that he meant her?

The way he was looking at her left little doubt. She felt her stomach drop for the second time that day. The air between them felt vacant, like there was nothing to it. She wanted to kiss him, then and there. Minister or not.

She took a half step back. A little more space and she could take a full breath.

"All the ladies certainly are dolled up tonight," Maud said, keeping her voice light. "Wearing their holiday best." She tried not to look at Ewan's face. "How was your holiday? How were your folks?"

"Oh." Ewan seemed to be deciding what to say. She'd learned to shy away from his family in their conversations, but that couldn't last forever. Not with the way he was just looking at her. "It was a wonderful treat to see mother," he said finally. "We always have been close. My half sister, Flora, too."

Maud's curiosity almost certainly showed through on her face. Ewan continued, seeming eager to explain. "My father emigrated with his parents from Scotland as a boy, on account of the famine. He married young, and his first wife passed away, leaving him with my half sister, Flora, to care for alone, until he met my mother—"

"And he managed, caring for Flora alone?"

"He did, somehow, poor as they were."

Maud felt a lurch in her chest. Her own father surely had more resources, and still he had left. "I didn't realize your father emigrated," she said, hoping to shift the subject.

Ewan coughed. "I don't tell many people."

"I'm not many people," Maud said.

"That's true. Still, I worry."

"Why?"

"My father wasn't educated. I don't know what you might make of that, coming from a family like yours."

"A family like mine?"

"You know," Ewan said, looking at the ground. "Well, everyone knows what it means to be a Macneill. Proper and the like."

"I wouldn't—" Maud swallowed. "I would never judge you based on your father emigrating, Ewan." She looked at him until he met her eyes. "Besides, my father was a Montgomery, and the Montgomerys have a livelier reputation." She smiled, trying to lighten the mood.

"Well then." Ewan looked down again and smiled. "I was saying about my half sister. She has a real kind heart. It's a strange position that she's in, being older and not quite one of us. I've been the best to her of any of my siblings, I think. The rest of them are . . . difficult. I'm not a lot like any of them, which made it hard growing up." He searched the floor again. "Guess that's the long and short of it."

"I've felt much the same about my family—not a lot like them, aside from Frede. I'm envious of you and your mother though, what that must be like." Maud's voice caught.

"It's hard to be away from her," Ewan said, not seeming to notice the change in Maud's expression. "She's encouraged my career so. Without her, I might have ended up working the fields like my father and brothers. Not that my father ever let me forget where I was from. He always warned me against getting too big for my britches. God punishes the proud, he said. He hated how my mother would console me. Coddling, he called it. But I don't see how I would have done much without her."

"I am grateful to your mother, then," Maud said. But something about the way he described his mother's encouragement—and his father's response—unsettled her. She couldn't put her finger on it.

His mother seemed like the safer territory for further inquiry. "What's your mother like? As a person, I mean?"

Ewan smiled. "I admire so much about her. No better mother or housekeeper in the entire town. Always put us kids ahead of herself. Devoted to her Bible too. 'A fine sense of duty looks better on a woman than any amount of makeup'—my father used to say that about her."

"She sounds like an excellent wife." Maud's tongue caught on the final word as she began to perceive Ewan's narrow understanding of its meaning. She batted the thought away.

"She certainly is," Ewan said. "She has her wits about her too though, make no mistake. She can defend herself all right with Father when she has to. Used to defend me too."

Ewan looked uncomfortable on his own two feet now, swaying from side to side with his hands in his pockets.

"Defend you?" Maud lowered her voice to match Ewan's volume. "How do you mean?"

Ewan shook his head, straightening up. "This is why I don't like talking about the past. Concerning you with things you shouldn't be concerned over."

"But—"

"Besides, we have a party to enjoy. It's Christmas."

Maud studied him. "It is Christmas," she said finally.

When Ewan looked away, Maud noticed for the first time that music had started up. A few couples were dancing in the corner.

"Would you dance with me?" she asked.

"You go ahead," he said. "I'm not—I mean, I don't."

After tucking in a few loose strands of hair, she looked at him. "I hope you don't mind if I do. I've always loved to dance."

"Of course, you should. Go right ahead. I'll be around." His final three words were lower than the rest.

When Maud turned, the side of Ewan's face was beside her ear, his hand touching her arm from behind.

"You look really lovely today, Maud," he said.

She thought about turning around. Instead, she smiled close-lipped and small, shifting her face toward him to make the smile visible. Then she walked away, the arm he had touched still tingling with the sensation. She kept the feeling of that touch with her as she danced. She told herself that he'd be watching.

WHEN SHE ARRIVED home the next night, Maud was tired behind the eyes and in her feet, and she could feel the start of a cold in her swallow. Still, after she had greeted her grandmother and given some much needed food to Daffy, she couldn't sleep. She could think only of the novel.

Gilbert had become the problem. Maud had taken the story up to Anne learning that Gilbert had given up his teaching post in Avonlea, all so Anne could stay at Green Gables and care for Marilla now that Matthew had passed away. Anne would start to come around then. Forgive Gilbert a little. But how much further to take it? Maud went up to her room and took out the manuscript.

The traditional way would be to go forward in time a ways, to marry Anne and Gilbert. Or to have a proposal at least.

But when she had gone to try out these endings, she hadn't found the words. Not even one good sentence.

Now she was coming to understand. Anne had only been young as far as Maud had seen her. So the book would end young—right up against the rest of Anne's life. But it could not end simply with Anne living with Marilla, teaching at the Avonlea school. That existence was good but small. Other possibilities must be implied.

A road came to mind just then—one that always caught Maud's attention about halfway to Charlottetown from Cavendish. It branched off the main road and then curved around a field of purple lupines like the copper rim of a pan. She thought of the point where the bend took the road out of the known and on to the possible. This image simplified things. She wouldn't need so many of the blank pages.

Anne would tell Marilla, "When I left Queen's my future

seemed to stretch out before me like a straight road. I thought I could see along it for many a milestone. Now there is a bend in it. I don't know what lies around the bend, but I'm going to believe that the best does. It has a fascination of its own, that bend, Marilla."

Not so much more now. Maud thought of that first walk she had taken with Ewan through the graveyard, their feet stepping just in front of the place where her mother was buried. She had watched as Ewan registered the name on the headstone. She liked to believe that Ewan had sensed the graveyard's significance to her in that moment. That his intent to beautify it had come out of that recognition, even if he never said as much. *Nevertheless, the dead matter to the living.*

Maud wrote, "Anne went to the little Avonlea graveyard the next evening to put fresh flowers on Matthew's grave and water the Scotch rosebush. She lingered there until dusk, liking the peace and calm of the little place, with its poplars whose rustle was like low, friendly speech, and its whispering grasses growing at will among the graves."

On her way down the hill from the graveyard, Anne would see Gilbert, obscured because of the dull light at sunset and taller than she remembered, a whistle dying on his lips as he recognized her. He'd offer to walk her home. "We were born to be good friends, Anne," he would say.

The Reader would believe in their friendship, the long walks they would take covering all manner of subjects. The Reader might dream up a future for them too, discovering a deeper love and building a home together.

But what if the Reader was not so optimistically minded? What if the Reader was the sort who couldn't help but fear a darker future? She owed it to that Reader to provide some assurances. "The joy of sincere work and worthy aspiration and congenial friendship were to be hers; nothing could rob her of her birthright of fancy or her ideal world of dreams," Maud wrote.

She looked down at the hand holding her pen and shook her head, fighting the desire to cross out the lines she had just written. Was it too bright a vision to be believable?

Then again, it was all up to her, wasn't it?

She added, "And there was always the bend in the road! 'God's in his heaven, all's right with the world,' whispered Anne softly."

Maud put her hands behind her head to stretch and closed her eyes. She would not be sure until she reread it. She put the manuscript aside and walked the square of the room, touching some of its small objects as she passed, each in its place. Bringing herself back to her own reality.

Then she sat down and picked up her journal.

"The wedding was lovely," she wrote. She was surprised how well she'd enjoyed it.

11.

Maud had never experienced a turn from winter to spring quite like this one, without any snow to speak of and with easy conditions for walking. New flowers bloomed in the window planters: white narcissi and yellow crocuses.

After months of steady typing, she reached the last chapter of *Anne* in mid-April. On rereading, it seemed half-decent. At times she dared to believe it was good.

She took out the large envelope beside her desk where she had written the address of the first publisher she planned to try. But before she could worry about that, she needed to make sure her grandmother was stowed away.

"Grandmother!" she called, then went downstairs, light on her feet. She repeated herself more softly.

She found her grandmother sitting in a rocking chair with a blanket wrapped up to her shoulders and her head leaning back. Seeing her this way, with her eyes closed and her mouth drooping, Maud nearly cried out. In Maud's mind, her grandmother still looked exactly the way she had when Maud was young. But looking at her now, she seemed to have aged overnight. A dull ache started up in Maud's chest.

"Grandmother?"

"What is it?" Her grandmother opened her eyes and blinked.

"Oh good, you're all right."

"And why wouldn't I be?"

"I—I'm sorry for waking you. Why don't we get you up-stairs so you can keep on with your nap? I'll take over mail duties, and I'll fix supper too."

"All right. I'll go upstairs, since it will satisfy you, it seems. But I thought you were typing for the day."

"I've finished."

"Well then. Another of your stories or a poem?"

"A—story."

Slowly, her grandmother rose from the chair and folded the blanket. She picked up a cup of tea from the small bench beside the chair. "It has occurred to me to ask . . ." She trailed off.

"Yes?" Maud felt her heart hop in her chest at the thought that her grandmother might ask more about what she was writing. She might even ask to read something, now that she had less of the buzz of energy that used to keep her endlessly occupied on household tasks. Would that be a good thing? Or an awful one?

"I trust there's none of me in these stories you write. Or your grandfather."

She didn't know what she'd expected. A person can change only so much.

Regaining her composure, Maud walked toward her grand-mother, taking her arm and the blanket to lead her to the stairs.

"Grandmother, I would never make a character out of you," Maud answered.

Her grandmother nodded, seeming to accept this. She said, "I don't suppose you've heard any more about cousin Prescott around town? How his health is faring?"

So Maud hadn't been alone in fretting over the possible ouster from their home. But she had forgotten to share the latest news.

"Last I heard, the doc's still going up there every day. Tuberculosis," Maud said.

"A true pity," said her grandmother, with a hint of a smile.

"It is," Maud said with her eyes cast down, doubly remorseful for the ounce of pleasure she felt on seeing her grandmother's expression. She waited while her grandmother settled onto the bed, then tucked the blanket in around her. "You get some good rest."

Maud closed the door.

It was time now. She would mail the manuscript while her grandmother slept.

"SEEMS JOHN'S DECIDED to leave this tired place alone once and for all." Her grandmother's words were matter-of-fact; she said them while she poured tea. Her pinkies stretched away from the other fingers, straight as arrows. "Now that Prescott's so bad off. I got word today."

"Oh!" Maud turned her head toward the kitchen window to hide the full extent of her delight.

"Your love for this drab old place is something else," her grandmother said.

"You know how I get attached."

Maud breathed in the air of the kitchen—the kitchen that would now be hers for as long as her grandmother lived. Thanks be to God. The best of smells were baked into its wooden floors and walls. She could separate out a few if she concentrated: the lemony mixture used for cleaning; good red meat stewed with tomatoes; a piecrust just crisping; and underneath everything, a spicy cologne that used to fill her grandfather's sweaters and hats, everything wool that he owned; after he died it spread out everywhere, his stubbornness no longer trapping it on his person. The kitchen air held on to sounds too: the pat-pat of hands on an apron, finishing work or just beginning; the accommodating grunts of the pickling jars as Maud and her grandmother added a new one to the rows on the shelves in fall; the *whisk whisk whisk* in a metal bowl, the noise just like the word. Her grandmother let her sit on the table one holiday when her grandfather was away to make eggnog, showing Maud first, then handing her the whisk with a look that ensured Maud's seriousness. "Stop putting your nose up to the vanilla, child," she'd said, "it takes away part of the taste when you do that."

"I hope you will not go caring quite so much after I'm gone," her grandmother said now. "It is no use is all. Clinging to things. I have wanted to help you see that. I suppose I have not done the best job of it, letting you stay so close to me for all these years."

"Caring is different than clinging, Grandmother."

"Do not go thinking me ungrateful either. But these are the facts of life, child; it goes on changing until one day it doesn't. A house cannot stay the same forever. Neither can I. And neither can you." She stopped and came closer to Maud. "Tell me you don't care quite so much as you used to about this old place. That you will not stubbornly insist on staying when life—or dare I say a man—summons you elsewhere."

Maud thought about this. "My pen at the very least keeps me aimed to the future," she said.

"Very good. Someday everything may shift at once, and you don't want to be caught unprepared. Or, heaven forbid, resist what's inevitable. The resisters, those are the sort who end up miserable."

"I'll resist only misery, then," Maud said, hoping for a laugh.

"Misery can be easier than happiness, you know," her grandmother said, this time looking Maud straight in the eyes and surprising her, as she sometimes did, with what she understood.

"I know," Maud said eventually. She put her hand on her grandmother's shoulder the way the cat sometimes did, tentative but pressing.

Maud closed her eyes briefly, and when she opened them again, her grandmother's eyes were wet and redder than usual. She took Maud's hand in hers.

"Good girl," she said softly.

12.

*W*ake up, *it's your birthday! You will have the entire house to yourself, and cake, and Frede and her delightful cooking. Oh, isn't it a scrumptious thing to wake up on this kind of morning? It makes one appreciate all the perfectly awful mornings, because they make one feel the difference on a morning such as this.*

Maud sprang up to sitting and went immediately to the bedroom window, where the morning light poured in. Pulling the muslin curtains aside, she looked for the sun's position in the sky.

And a sunny day besides. What a positively poetical thing to have the outside day match one's inside feelings.

It was sunny. It also looked to be past eight o'clock. Maud had slept in far later than usual.

She went to the porcelain washbasin in the corner of her bedroom to splash some cold water on her face. After drying her face with a towel, she pinched her cheeks, pinned up her hair in the quickest way she could in the small mirror that she loved so well because it had once been her mother's, and hurried downstairs, full of exhilaration.

Halfway down the stairs, Maud spotted her grandmother

standing at the window in the parlor where the front staircase landed, bent at the waist and peering out in earnest. Maud paused for a moment to take in the sight—the backlight had turned her grandmother's darkened body, with its pronounced nose jutting forward, into a comical figure.

Her grandmother turned as she heard Maud's pattering feet come closer to the window.

"I've overslept," Maud said. "I apologize."

"I noticed. But never mind that. Happy birthday, Maud," her grandmother said, showing her nerves in the movement of her jaw from left to right.

Maud kissed her grandmother on the cheek and smiled. "It is my birthday, isn't it?" She checked the old grandfather clock in the parlor to make sure of the time. "But uncle isn't due for another half hour. What do you say we sit down and have a quick bite of porridge?"

"I could not eat." Her grandmother had turned back to the window.

"You must eat something. It will take at least until noon to get to Park Corner, and by then you'll be starving."

"'Starving' is not a word to use lightly, my dear," her grandmother said, craning her neck to get a better view of the road beyond the long path leading to the house. "Your ancestors never would have tolerated such usage."

Maud smiled and shook her head. "If you arrive with a significant appetite, they'll think I'm not taking good enough care of you."

"All right, but there is no time for heating up porridge. Your uncle might arrive early. I will make do with a cold biscuit and butter."

"I'll prepare it now and leave you to continue inspecting the window," Maud said, not wanting her excitement to be further drained by her grandmother's nervous energy.

Maud hurried to pull small plates out of the old wooden sideboard in the dining room. The biscuits and butter were covered on top of the sideboard, making things easy. As she worked, Maud anticipated the thrill of having the house all to herself, aside from her two treasured guests. Other friends would be hurt if they learned they weren't invited. But Maud had taken Anne's advice about planning exactly the party she wanted, and she had invited only those whose company didn't feel like work—which these days meant Frede and, somewhat miraculously, the Reverend Ewan Macdonald.

Just after Maud set the plates and biscuits on the table, her grandmother came into the dining room with a few letters in hand.

"I set these aside for you yesterday. Mail that came while you were on your walk."

Maud took quick stock of the letters. One addressed from the hospital in Charlottetown, a thank-you note for the quilt-making event she'd helped organize, surely. Another addressed from a friend busy teaching on the other side of the Island, a birthday card, almost surely. And—Maud startled at the handwriting on the final card. Ewan's. He could be sending a birthday note, but why would he? He was due to arrive in less than eight hours.

Maud sat down at the table with Ewan's card and noticed her grandmother eyeing her warily.

"I gather that my company on our last morning together is not worthy of your attention," her grandmother said.

Maud looked at her. "Did you see that one of these letters is from Ewan?"

"I did not."

"You might have looked and given it to me yesterday."

"Making note of who has sent a letter to whom is as good as gossip, Maud." Maud knew this already about her grandmother, the way she treated mail from Maud's publishers the same as any ordinary advertising flier.

Maud opened the letter. At the first few lines, her stomach sank. "He says he is very sorry, but he will not be making it for my birthday," Maud said, and put down the card.

Well, this is a tragical development! A birthday cannot dream of being the romantic and memorable affair it is meant to be without one's beau in attendance.

"I should have known something like this would happen. I got my hopes up too far, which tends to mean they will be dashed." A few tears fell down her face in spite of herself. Girlish tears, but she felt them all the same.

"Maud, dear, I must say you've romanticized this birthday something silly. A birthday comes every year."

"A birthday may come every year, but that's no reason it cannot be a particularly special day," Maud said, hearing Anne's voice in her own. "And I do not see how my little gathering can possibly feel complete without Ewan." Shaking her head and putting her hands to her face, Maud felt herself sink back into the self she'd outgrown.

"Now, my dear."

"Yes," Maud said, still covering her face.

"Do try to react calmly." Her grandmother paused, but Maud's hands did not move. "I must put a stop to this stuff and nonsense." Maud bristled at the expression her grandmother had used so often when Maud was young. The combination of words and tone recalled Maud's childhood to her in an instant, and with that reminder, she regained a sense of herself.

"You're right," Maud said, straightening up. "Let's not discuss it any more. What needs to be done to get you off?" Off and out of the house so Maud could feel what she was feeling in peace.

But her grandmother wasn't finished. "You know, if Ewan is so very important to have at your party, you might consider why you have been treating his marriage proposal so trivially."

"Grandmother! I assure you I am not."

"Just something to consider. Now, what else does Ewan say in his letter?" her grandmother asked.

Maud frowned. Had there been anything else in the letter? She picked it back up. "It does go on. He says—well, he says he's been given the opportunity to deliver a speech for the members of the Presbyterian General Assembly this week, on means of improving the ministry, and he must prepare for it. He's terribly sorry, and he hopes I can understand."

"The General Assembly—that sounds mighty impressive."

"It is." Maud looked up, now more fully embarrassed at the leaking out of her childish ways. "This is quite the opportunity for Ewan. I wonder how it came about. It could earn him all sorts of goodwill on the Island."

"Well, you see, there's a lot to be said for not overreacting." And on that note, her grandmother set her fork on her plate and rose. She started to reach for her plate to carry to the kitchen, but Maud stopped her.

"I'm happy to clear the plates. You can return to your window perch."

"All right then," her grandmother said, her quick acceptance betraying her continuing nerves.

Maud took both plates to the kitchen, still trying to sort out her feelings about Ewan's letter. As soon as she walked past the pantry entrance, she felt a jolt run through her body.

The cake.

She hadn't remembered to cover it the night before.

She went closer to inspect.

She spotted an area on the top rim where the frosting had

worn away, and beside it a set of dents. A cat's pawprint. It had to be. Daffy had smelled the cake and wanted a few licks of the cream cheese frosting for himself. She could hardly blame him. Worse, she could tell by the way the frosting looked that it had dried out considerably.

Her head fell back in exasperation. When had she last been so careless? She could only imagine what her grandmother would have to say about this. Her grandmother never could be bothered with whether something was accidental.

That's hardly fair! To blame someone equally no matter her intent? I cannot tell you what horrendous blame I would have suffered with all the scrapes I've gotten into. But oh, I wouldn't trade the places my imagination has taken me for a million perfectly made recipes or unwrinkled dresses. To live with someone who cannot understand the difference between accident and sin is a tragedy beyond all comprehension.

Who would Anne be without equal parts sincerity and hyperbole? And what a treat it had been for Maud to write Matthew, with all his heart for Anne no matter what trouble she got into. He could see her earnestness, and that was good enough for him.

But that was Anne.

Maud did not make mistakes. Not anymore. She had mastered equally well the precise angles at which to hold her arms at a party and the dreaded angles of geometry.

No doubt Maud's imagination was just as adamant a thing as Anne's, but she'd learned to discipline it, to keep it in check until she had a long walk or a writing afternoon to herself. And yet here she was, on her thirty-third birthday, letting a cake dry out because she had been occupied the night before picturing a wedding to Ewan that in all likelihood wouldn't be happening anytime soon, and might never happen.

You did not mean it, and you must keep that knowledge in your heart and not suffer with it so.

There was no one in the kitchen but her. She could doctor the frosting, and then cut off the side pieces that would be the driest. Take them outside and sprinkle them for the birds, in a place no one would notice, and—

What if you were to bring the cake to the table just as it is? You could tell the whole story. A mistake is just a mistake, and a bosom friend would never blame you for it. Or else she isn't much of a bosom friend.

Only Frede would be sharing the cake, that was true. Maud couldn't imagine Frede being bothered by this. No—as the realization registered, Maud smiled in spite of herself. It was she who was bothered. It was from her own self that she wanted to hide all the evidence.

A point to remember. One she might tuck in her pocket for safekeeping. She had a feeling its applications might extend to more than simply cake.

Just then she heard the sounds of her uncle's and Frede's voices nearing the front door. The door opened, and cheerful greetings followed.

Maud smiled in the direction of the cake. It smelled as delightful as ever. She closed the pantry door and went out to the entryway to let her birthday begin.

13.

Next in the stack came the most worn of all her correspondence folders. Contents sifted through so often that she could recite some of it by heart. "Correspondence—Frede," she'd written in large, scrawling script on the cover.

The contents of this folder had been sick, palpable comfort to her through the years. She didn't think she could bring herself to burn it all. But some of it surely needed to go.

The handwriting that greeted her inside the folder still elicited a weak approximation of the joy she used to feel each time she opened a new letter from Frede, anticipating how her nerves would be calmed by the reading. The script was so utterly Frede: boxy and bold, nothing subtle about it. She didn't think she could bear to part with any of this.

But Frede's letters weren't the only ones in the folder. Her own letters to Frede were stacked in the back. Skimming, she paused at a suspect date. April 22, 1906. She thought she remembered this one. A letter reporting that Frede had been right as usual. Concerns misguided. Silly imagination. How adult she had fancied herself back then. How wise. The hubris of her younger self!

In an instant, this letter could be gone from the earth. As good as unwritten. She dropped it from her hands into the flames with a feeling close to glee.

14.

Cavendish, Prince Edward Island
April 1906

Frede at last came in from Stanley after months of promising a visit. Maud woke at dawn to sweep the spare room and have breakfast waiting for her grandmother when she woke up.

She and her grandmother were in the kitchen together, shaking off water from the plates before drying them, when Frede gave her usual single hard knock and holler of a "Hello!"

Her grandmother shook her head. "That can only be Frede."

Maud hurried Frede up to the spare room with her things and then out the door for a walk.

The news about not being ousted from their home had a lingering positive effect on her grandmother's mood, but with her increased satisfaction came inquisitiveness in equal measure. She kept asking when Maud next expected the reverend for a visit, no longer trying for subtlety. Now that her grandmother had the house business settled, her sole devotion was to have Maud settled too. Not that Maud minded that agenda too much, especially not with Ewan visiting regularly again. She found herself basking in her grandmother's shared enjoyment—rare as such a thing had ever been.

Maud took Frede through lesser-known paths, some with only patches of bent grass to reveal them. The bare branches of the trees exposed a few chipmunks, their compact bodies stopping and starting, looking up occasionally like they were seeing the sky for the first time.

"Brown all around, but doesn't the air have a new green in it?" Maud asked. "Spring is nearly ready to raise the bleak old cloak and remind us again of what we'd almost forgotten was possible."

"I'm not sure I know what any of that means, but it sounds lovely," Frede said. She shook her head. "I don't know, Maud. Jim's been very kind to me and father likes him. Stella says I should count my blessings. You know my sister—never mincing her words. But how can I tell whether it's meant to last?"

Maud was looking up at the bare-skinned tree limbs with their gnarled fingers. The buds were still scaled over, containing themselves despite the relative warmth of the thaw. She imagined budbreak when it finally came, the different shapes of leaves that could grow out of just the few trees above her. She forgot to respond.

"Come on, you're the old wise one," Frede continued. "Use those nine extra years you have on me and help a fellow out. Lord knows I can't confide in either my sisters. Much as Stella would love to tell me all about how it is, no matter that she's never experienced anything like it herself. Probably making me feel like I owe her something for the telling."

Maud laughed. "That's Stella for you."

Frede shook her head.

"I'll give you that I'm old," Maud said, "but I won't give you wise. I can tell you one thing, though"—Maud looked right at Frede—"love is not the way it is told in most books, with everything clear from the start and steady all the way through."

"If that's true, someone should have told me a long time ago," Frede said.

"I'm not sure I would have listened when I was younger. Would you?"

"You're probably right." Frede slowed her steps.

They walked quietly for a while, until Frede broke the silence. She'd always had less tolerance for quiet than Maud.

"And what do you think about children? Not what we're supposed to think, but how you really feel. Can you begin to imagine yourself with them?" Frede asked. Her words were light enough, but her tone was urgent.

"Well," Maud said slowly. "I guess I have always had a feeling that children would be my greatest life's joy. I could love them the way—" She stopped. "Well, the way I have always imagined a child should be loved. I cannot imagine I could have another quite-so-lonely night as I have had in the past with a child to tuck in bed and read a story to."

"I wish I could be like you. I have a hard time thinking of children as anything but a burden."

Maud shook her head. "I could use a healthy dose of that perspective. Grandmother would warn me against counting chickens."

"Oh, I have a feeling all this is not too far around the corner for you," Frede said. "And besides, you'll always have your stories for company. You have something real to live for, children or no children."

They walked in silence until Maud said, "You might as well know I've finished a novel."

Frede grabbed for Maud's wrist, then stopped walking. "And?"

"Just as I said."

"Well, when will it come out? When will you be a world-famous authoress?"

Maud shook her head. "It does not have a publisher yet. It is out in the ether as we speak, in search of kindred spirits. Probably no publisher will accept it, and I will end up stripping out bits and pieces for some Sunday school serial. I should not have mentioned it."

"Of course you should!" said Frede. "At the very least tell me where it stands."

"I mailed it to a publisher last week," said Maud. She turned back toward Frede, her thumb tapping against the tips of her fingers. "No one else knows. I spouted out something to both Ewan and Nate right at the beginning, last year—"

"Last year! You've been at this a whole year and this is the first I'm hearing of it?"

Maud sighed. "Not quite a year. You can be glad for being the first to know I have finished."

"I suppose I can manage a little glad."

"I owe you for it. I did want to tell you that much, regardless of what comes of it."

"Owe me?"

"For the main character. If people like her, it will have a good deal to do with you."

"Well." Frede smiled and shook her head. "I know it will be published. And if the main character has any resemblance to me, I'm sure she's a gas. But you said you told Ewan?"

"Sort of. It was the first day he came for the mail, which happened to be the day I wrote the first words of the book. The word 'novel' came out of my mouth before I could think about it. But he never asked about it again."

Frede shook her head. "I'm sure he didn't mean anything by it. Probably just didn't know what to say." She paused. "Speaking of the good reverend—has anything changed?"

Maud started walking again, taking a few steps before turning her head back toward Frede. "Not quite—"

Frede caught up to Maud's stride, grinning.

"But?"

"A little. It might. I've been seeing plenty of him."

"What's the feeling like with him?"

"The feeling?" Maud asked. "It's hard to say."

"Don't go close-lipped on me just because he's a minister, Maud Montgomery. Have you already assumed the propriety of a minister's wife-to-be?"

"No!" Maud's heart pounded. "I am sorry, it's just—'a minister's wife.' The sound of it. Hearing it, I cannot help but think of endless visits to congregation members and boring church benefits. How would I ever find time to write?" She frowned. "I know I should want it. I have been telling myself I do. But I do not need to decide now. With her persistent good health, it will almost certainly be years more that I am graced with Grandmother's ways, and I do not see that I could ever marry and move out while she is still alive. Maybe I will be a successful novelist by the time she passes, so entertained by my own books that I will have rid myself of any notion of the loneliness of spinsterhood."

Ever since she'd first had real feelings for a man, Maud had suspected that marriage could be heaven with a man she loved, and hell with one she did not. The difficulty was telling the difference between love and its imitators.

"But Maud—you do like Ewan, don't you?"

Maud sighed. "I do." Her speech slowed. "I do like Ewan. I imagine the beautiful children he would have, raised in a proper home. I picture his broad smile with those good teeth of his coming through the door at the same time each day like clockwork after visiting his congregation members. He is serious about being good—that much I am sure of." She looked at Frede and managed a smile. "I do like him," she continued. "But there's a strange feeling I get sometimes around him. When I talk, you would think I was the most interesting person around. On the one hand, it feels wonderful. Like he honestly cares only for me. It can give me some of the old thrill I used to have with Nate—that tingling down the spine—with even more certainty of devotion. But those looks also turn my stomach sometimes. I cannot explain why. When I look in his eyes, it can be like looking in a dark tunnel made up of something that wants to pour itself all over me and pull me in and never let me go."

"You make it sound so frightening." Frede was looking the other way.

"It can feel that way."

"Having a man look at you like he only has eyes for you? Never wanting to let you go?"

Maud shook her head. She felt her eyes grow wet.

"I cannot explain it. Sometimes I am not so sure his long stares are about me. It is like there is a cloth covering half his face that I cannot pull aside. And shouldn't I manage that before I think of marrying him?"

"You know, Maud." Frede hesitated. "No other girl on this Island would be telling themselves these scary stories. Any of them in your shoes would have found their way into a marriage already if they had a handsome minister courting them. Do you ever think you may be expecting too much?"

Maud stopped moving and looked over. A knot in the pit of her stomach hardened. "I know what everyone else would say if I told them my darkest fears." The knot loosened, replaced by tears. "But I've always thought I could speak to you without thinking first. That you would listen and at least try to understand."

Frede walked a few more steps, and then stopped. When she turned and saw Maud's face, her shoulders dropped.

"Of course you can, Maud. I may not always perfectly understand you," Frede said. "But I promise I'll never stop trying. I've been spending too much time around Stella and my mother is all."

Maud pulled a handkerchief out of her pocket and wiped her eyes. "It's not just Stella and your mother. I can see how you admire Ewan. I can see how you worry."

"I do worry. For myself as much as for you, about where our free-mindedness will land us. And it's true that I admire Ewan. But I'm not the one courting him." Frede pulled out her handkerchief and exchanged it for Maud's wet one. "Damn all those watchful fools and their opinions."

Nodding, Maud sighed and wiped more tears.

"Now just look where all my questions have gotten us. Not too polite to ask about much, am I?" Frede asked. They both managed a short laugh, then turned quiet again. They continued walking until they felt the start of hunger, then went back a different way.

THE NEXT DAY was Sunday, and Ewan preached well.

All through the service, he kept looking up at Maud in the organ box, less cautiously than ever. Toward the end, his eyes looked the same way they had at the wedding on Christmas Day, when he spoke about men and women and marriage. Once again, he seemed to be asking her a question. Maud felt light and tingly all over her body, and this time she did not let herself worry when his eyes went down to his notes.

The next time he looked up, Maud felt her head nod. In response, Ewan smiled and tripped over his words. Ewan's smile made its way immediately into her own, and Maud wondered if Frede was right. Maybe she had let her own imagination frighten herself silly. It would hardly be the first time.

The image of her mother stranded on the church roof came back to her then. How literally her young mind had taken her Aunt Emily's finger, pointing upward. How many nights had Maud spent worried for her mother, imagining her alone and desperate to come down from that cold roof and tuck Maud into bed?

It had been a relief to learn the truth about her mother being buried at the old cemetery. But it had been a bitter disappointment too. All because she had let her imagination get the better of her. She resolved not to succumb to the same fate now with Ewan. She would trust his kindhearted smile and admonish herself for any further foreboding thought.

15.

There she is," said Frede, bounding forward to give Maud a fast hug. Frede pulled back and studied Maud's face. "It's been so long, I almost forgot what my favorite friend in all the world looked like. Happy birthday!"

"Older, that's what I look like."

"You look younger, if anything! All fresh and rejuvenated. Doesn't she, Grandmother?" Frede turned toward their grandmother, who was buttoning her coat by the door. Frede's father had left to take the luggage out to the buggy.

"I hate to be the bearer of bad news, but age only goes in one direction, my dears," their grandmother said. "I am one to know. Now I am off. You will be happy, I am sure, to have the house to yourselves while I am subjected to the scent of horses and the reverberation of every bounce of the buggy through my spine for what I hope will be the last time in a long life."

Maud's excitement propelled her to the door in no time, and she pulled their grandmother in for an unwelcome hug. "Goodbye, Grandmother. Aunt and Uncle will take very good care of you and hopefully return you a little plumper than when you left."

Their grandmother's back stayed stiff, but at least her arms lifted the way they should. "Goodbye, Maud, dear," she said awkwardly over Maud's shoulder. When Maud released her grip, their grandmother added, "Remember what we've discussed, now." She looked pointedly in Frede's direction. "And do have a happy birthday."

Frede came over and put her arm around Maud's shoulder. "Oh, we'll have a grand old time." Frede gave their grandmother her signature smile that overpowered the rest of her features, momentarily transforming their plainness into radiance. Their grandmother nodded, issuing Frede a fraction of a smile in return. She stepped out the door.

After a few feet, their grandmother looked back at them, the sun turning her graying hair into gold silk. She seemed to be taking in their two forms in the tall doorframe, Maud's small and tight, Frede's sturdy and loose.

"Please, whatever you do, don't make a mess of the house." She paused before issuing the final word. "Ladies." With that she was off, her long, purposeful gait betraying none of her age.

"Freedom, at last," pronounced Frede as soon as the door was fully closed.

"Freedom, indeed," said Maud.

"What should we do with it?" Frede looked around the wide entryway, as if an idea would call out to her from its wood paneling, then walked through the entry into the parlor. Maud followed.

"Have a catch-up for the ages, to begin with. It has been far too many months since we have had one, what with you studying yourself to death, through the entire summer, no less."

"I know. I can't seem to get enough of my studies. Taking after someone else I know. Your cousin the future professor, at your service." Frede gave a bow, her mess of brown hair coming out of its clips. Usually, she didn't bother with clips.

"A professor indeed! You'll far surpass me in my lowly schoolteaching career, as I always knew you would. And what will you profess?"

"I don't quite know yet, but I'll be brilliant at it," Frede said. "It will just be a matter of working for a few years and saving up the money to finish my degree, and then I'll be off to the races." Frede's whole face smiled. Her eyes were bright as sun on the top of a water glass.

Maud recognized those eyes. They were the same ones she saw in the mirror after she read something over that she'd written and particularly liked.

That settled it. There would be no asking Frede to live in this house, no matter what their grandmother might say.

"You certainly will be. I will be cheering you on every step of the way. Now let's sit down and get settled in." Maud gestured to the sofa.

"Yes, only I'm taking Grandmother's spot," Frede said, springing toward their grandmother's rocker, a faded crocheted blanket folded in a perfect square over its back. As Frede sat, the blanket fell around her shoulders. Frede pulled it out and sat on it instead. "We must do absolutely nothing that we would normally do this weekend. We shall call it—" She paused. "The weekend of nothing ordinary."

"That is exactly what I had in mind. You know how I dread the ordinary." Maud looked around. She pulled a cushion that belonged on an armchair over to the sofa and pulled it onto her lap, stacking her legs beside her on the couch like she had when she was a girl and there was no one around to instruct her otherwise.

"So how long do we have?" Frede asked.

"How long?"

"Until Ewan arrives? I want the full measure of our uninterrupted time."

Maud felt the hot bath of disappointment wash over her again. "Ewan's not coming."

"He's not? Why?" Frede's eyebrows gathered in the middle so there was hardly any break between them.

Of course Frede would be sad. Frede and Ewan got along famously. But Frede's disappointment layered on top of Maud's threatened to drown out all hopes for the day.

Fiddlesticks if you'll let something like that sink your spirits. On the birthday that we have planned so brilliantly.

"He's got a good reason for it. He's been asked to give a speech about the ministry to the General Assembly this week. He needs the weekend to prepare."

"Well, that is something. How do you feel about it?" Frede studied Maud.

"I am sad for my own self, but that's the girl in me talking." Maud thought about it more, willing herself to look past this particular day to the days that would follow. "Deeper down, I am grateful that he has this opportunity, and that he is taking it seriously. I have always dreamed of being married to a man who cared as much about his work as I care about mine."

"I can understand that."

"Ewan is cut from a different cloth than me, as you know. He does not take an interest in my writing. But I do not suppose it matters so much to have particular passions in common as it does to have passion in common."

"I agree. And what a wonderful thing that you do."

"I've had my doubts. Back in those days with Ewan in Scotland . . ."

Frede frowned. "You gave me some idea of what happened there, but not all of it."

"His letters from Scotland were so strange. He came back

nearly despondent, and without his degree, as you know. I worried then that he did not care so much about his work. But maybe it was, as he said, just the weather that was the matter. And his being so far away."

Maud looked at Frede, trying to convey the picture that was becoming clearer in Maud's mind. "It would be wonderful if this speech went well for him. I can see it taking him further in his career than even he may think." After returning early from Scotland without a degree, Ewan had struggled to find a new ministry charge, eventually accepting one on the east side of the Island, far from Cavendish. Maud longed for him to regain the momentum he'd had before leaving, when he'd been invited to preach at large venues.

"Well, then we will not waste one more minute being sad about his lack of attendance," Frede said. "In fact, I know just the thing. I meant it for tonight, over supper, but in the interest of doing nothing ordinary, I say we have it now."

Frede got up and went straight to her luggage, which she'd left out in the parlor instead of placing it in the spare room— something she never would have managed had their grandmother been in the house. She rummaged around in one of her several suitcases until she found what she was looking for and then stood up, holding a large green bottle.

"Is that champagne? Frede, where in the world did you find it?"

"Here and there."

This was a lie. No one found champagne "here and there" on the Island. Maud couldn't recall ever seeing it in a store.

"You've spent a fortune," Maud said.

"Have not."

"I will pay you back."

"You will do no such thing. It's your birthday present. And we shall drink it now while you tell me the entire story of your book publication, from front to back, with toasting along the way. Your descriptions in your letters were far too modest and short. For a writer, no less. Now, you get the glasses, and I will pop the cork."

AROUSED FROM THEIR afternoon slumber by Daffy's meow, Maud and Frede looked at each other and laughed at the picture they made. With the empty champagne bottle and two crystal tumblers sitting on the floor beside her, Frede's arms were flung out over the arms of the chair where she sat. Maud had one leg over the arm of her chair and one leg on the ground, her long skirt stretched between. They had moved their grandmother's prize armchairs in front of the open front door when the sun had been strong, but now it was close to setting.

Daffy shared none of their amusement, and let out another meow piercing enough to start their legs moving.

"I don't know about you, but I'm starving," Frede said. Frede closed the front door as Maud indulged Daffy with a neck scratch. "And I've brought your favorite casserole for supper—broccoli, garlic, and cheese, with those curly noodles you love."

"You know me too well. Let's get it in the woodstove."

Maud felt a slight letdown in her body as Frede went to pull the casserole out. The aftereffect of the champagne? Or the fact that the day could not be quite what she had imagined without Ewan joining them? Seeing Frede walk back into the entryway, Maud shook these thoughts away and smiled, taking Frede by the arm.

Frede and Maud worked together in the kitchen to ready the casserole and boil red potatoes for supper, the continuing effects of the champagne making them easy in their movements.

"Now, Maud," Frede said as she placed the casserole in the woodstove, "how is it exactly that you imagine having the children you are intent on having with a grandmother underfoot and examining your every stray gesture?"

Maud turned her head from where she was occupied washing potatoes. "Having children with Grandmother around would be as impossible as running a distillery under the nose of a provincial policeman."

Frede laughed. "That sounds about right," she said as she carried the crystal champagne tumblers over to the sink for washing. "Hey, we both know I don't want children—maybe I should move in with the old lady."

Caught off guard, Maud turned fully around to face Frede.

"What is it?" Frede asked, the easy smile fading from her face.

"Oh, nothing," Maud said, shaking her head. "Only something preposterous that Grandmother said last night."

"What did Grandmother say?" Frede asked.

Maud hesitated, which only made Frede's volume increase as she abandoned the tumblers and started wagging a finger. "We do not refuse to tell things to each other, Maud Montgomery, so spill the beans now." Frede could deliver a mandate as well as anyone, with her thunderous voice and her mouth a straight line that cut her face in two. Her face looked all wrong this way, without its habitual laugh or smile.

"Fine," Maud sighed. "Grandmother had the idea that you move in here with her for a while, and I go ahead and marry Ewan now. She wanted me to discuss it with you. I have been fully committed not to."

"And why is that?"

"No." Maud shook her head vigorously, walking over to the stove to place the potatoes in a pot of hot water. Frede followed. "You will not, so stop considering it."

"Why not?"

"Your dreams, Frede," Maud said as she dropped the potatoes in one by one. "How do you think you can be a professor
of anything from the kitchen table in this old house? Consider what you would give up."

"And what about your dreams?"

Frede looked as serious as Maud had ever seen her.

"My dreams—" Maud's mind was fuzzy with leftover tip-
siness. "My writing can be accomplished right here from this
kitchen table, that's the difference," she said. "The crucial
difference."

Frede studied the floor for several moments without
speaking.

"Let the record show that I'll do it," Frede said finally,
looking Maud in the eye. "You have done your good granddaughter's duty for nine years now, and you are allowed to
have more than one dream in your life. You say the word, and
I'll be here. All right?"

"All right," Maud said eventually, because she knew nothing else would satisfy. Frede made her decisions quick and
firm, like her hugs.

Frede nodded. As she walked back to the sink, she turned
to Maud, grinning. "Besides, how much longer can the old
lady possibly live?"

WITH A GOOD twenty minutes remaining before the casserole would be ready, Frede suggested a return to the armchairs by the front door to wait and chat—on non-habitual
subjects—until the smell of bubbling cheese summoned
them back.

As they walked down the hallway, Frede suddenly clutched
at Maud's hand. "Maud, did you hear that?"

"Hear what?"

"That noise outside the house."

Maud turned around to look at the front door, half expecting it to deliver an answer. "I didn't hear a thing."

"Really? I heard a sound like leaves crunching."

"Oh, it's probably only an animal of some sort. It's nearly dusk, which is their favorite time to roam." Maud paused. "But what could we imagine it to be?" she asked, her expression bordering on delight as Anne's love of fright washed over her. "A ghost of one of our deceased relatives, perhaps, coming to see where Grandmother has gone off to for the weekend?"

Frede gave Maud's hand another squeeze, accepting the invitation. "Or maybe," Frede said, "it's that crotchety old man who used to live in this house before our grandparents, coming to reclaim it?" They both shivered and put their heads down to laugh.

Then Maud heard a noise herself. A distinct noise.

"I hear it now too," Maud whispered, her heart starting to beat wildly. "And you know what's funny? I have never once let myself get good and scared like this with Grandmother home."

"I just had a picture of Grandmother, with those rail-thin arms of hers, trying to fend off an intruder," Frede said. "That idea is enough to give anyone a good, hard laugh."

"She would never need to fend anyone off from an intruder," Maud said, her voice still a whisper. "No one would ever dare go near enough to harm her. I can only imagine what she would say to us now, letting our imaginations run wild like this." Maud shivered.

Then a noise at the front door.

Frede gasped.

A creak of metal—the door handle turning.

They hadn't locked it after their nap. They rarely ever did lock it.

"Anyone home?"

They heard the voice before they could see who waited behind the door. Maud felt the fear leave her body before her mind recognized the voice, kind and familiar.

"Maud? Frede?"

"It's Ewan!" Frede exclaimed.

Maud pounced on the door. "Ewan, you devil!" she said when she reached it. "You've nearly given us collective heart failure."

There her fiancé stood, his hat in one hand and a bundle of late-season flowers and reeds in the other—a striking assortment. His smile grew larger as he caught sight of Maud, then even larger as he took in the armchairs by the door, apprehending some of the afternoon's fun.

Maud could see Ewan's mind at work. He did not ask about the armchairs. Instead, he straightened up the way he did at the pulpit, with the authority that never failed to send a thrill down Maud's spine. She loved the contrast between this authoritative Ewan and the shy man he was most of the time. She never knew when his commanding side might appear, and although she would have been loath to admit it to Frede, it gave her such joy whenever it did.

"Surprise!" Ewan bellowed, his dark eyes on hers. "And now"—he gave a slight bow—"the party may begin."

Maud wrapped her arms around Ewan's neck, and he kissed her long and hard. Yes, this was the sort of kiss she dreamed of in the night—the kind that made all thought leave Maud's mind.

I don't recall a time when my thoughts have ever left my mind, not even for a moment. What a lovely and interesting experience that must be, for a short time at least. Like a dip in a deliciously cold pond. I cannot wait until I am kissed in a real way. I will simply drink it in.

Anne's voice had not, it seemed, left Maud's mind along with her other thoughts.

"I cannot tell you how wonderful it is to see you!" Maud said as she pulled away from Ewan. "All day I've kept some secret hope that you would come, and here you are."

"I wouldn't have missed it," Ewan said. He put down the flowers and his hat on the small entry table so he could take Maud by the waist, picking her up and then pulling her in for a kiss even longer than the first, taking advantage of her grandmother's rare absence.

"I'm still here, you know," Frede said eventually.

Maud started laughing with her lips still on Ewan's. They pulled apart and turned toward Frede.

"It shows you how comfortable we both are with you," Maud said.

"I'll take that as flattery." Frede started fanning her face with a hand. "But now I need to reduce the simmer in this room and check the casserole," she said. Frede shimmied through the armchairs in a way only she could—too unself-conscious to be awkward—and grabbed for the bouquet on the entry table. "I'll put these in a vase, and give you two a few minutes to finish up where you left off."

"Thanks, chum. I will meet you in the kitchen in a minute. But oh, Ewan, I almost missed thanking you for the bouquet!" Maud reached out a hand and touched her fingers to a plump pussywillow as Frede passed. The bouquet's assembly bordered on artistic. Could Ewan have put it together himself? It was thrilling to think that he might have. "It's beautiful, Ewan."

Ewan studied his shoes with the modesty that was part of what endeared her to him. "I picked them out myself."

"You did?"

"I bet you didn't think I had it in me."

Maud shook her head. "I have never heard you take an interest in flowers. But the composition is lovely."

"You, my dear fiancée, are worth every amount of loveliness," Ewan said, now issuing the fully dimpled smile that came over his face whenever he knew he had pleased her. "I know flowers are friends of yours, so I thought I better learn how to befriend them as well."

"Thank you, Ewan." To know that Ewan had this talent surpassed the bouquet itself.

The soft light caught on his dimples. The disheveled curl in his hair, which he hadn't bothered to fix after taking off his hat, gave him the look of a schoolyard playmate rather than a grown minister. Maud thought of accompanying him upstairs while he settled into the guest room, resuming their last kiss where it had left off. But no, there was the smell of casserole to remind her she was hungry, and Frede was working away in the kitchen. She had promised to join her in a minute.

Maud stepped closer to Ewan instead. Reducing the amount of air between them, she had learned, could make her body feel anticipation even greater than when they were pressed against each other.

"What made you think to surprise me?" Maud asked, her voice soft.

"I got to picturing the look on your face, seeing me after thinking I wasn't coming," he said, touching his thumb to the middle of her cheek. "Of course I would come. I wouldn't have missed it."

He wouldn't have missed it. She hadn't wanted to think so. But then she'd read his letter—"What about your speech, Ewan? Will you be all right for it?"

"Never mind that," Ewan said. "You are more important." His thumb, which had stayed on her cheek, made a stroke down to her chin that Maud felt in her lower spine. Then his mouth drew into a smile. "Now how on earth did a pair of armchairs make it into the entryway?" he asked.

Maud laughed and took his hand. "It's a long story," she said, as she led him around the chairs and down the hallway to the kitchen. "But the short of it is that we are doing nothing ordinary today."

"Nothing ordinary, eh?" Ewan put his arm around her waist. "I like the sound of that."

WHILE EWAN WASHED up, Frede and Maud stood together in the kitchen. The floorboards were warm from the stove, and Frede had had the idea that they should take off their shoes, an idea that would have scandalized their grandmother. The heat warmed the soles of Maud's feet. She did not want to leave that room.

"And why should we need to?" Frede asked. "Let's set the old kitchen table instead and eat right here."

Maud raised her eyebrows and clapped her hands. "An excellent idea. Ewan will agree, I'm sure. There is nothing formal about him, not at his heart. It's one of the things I like best about him."

They busied themselves setting the table, humming around each other with comfort that did not require speech. While Frede checked on the casserole, Maud set the large glass pitcher of strawberry lemonade she had originally intended for that afternoon on the table. The color of the liquid seesawing in the pitcher matched the lowest band of sunset out the kitchen window.

Maud went to the window and granted herself a few moments. Whenever she saw a sunset like this, she liked to imagine herself traveling along the ground just below it, looking up. She saw herself skipping along the tops of the birch trees and soaking in all the colors above her.

If she were to plan a wedding soon, it would be a sunset wedding, with pink, purple, red, and orange flowers all bundled together and tied with sky-blue bows. *Too much color*, everyone would say, but it would not be. *A tasteful wedding*, the guests would comment. But best of all would be the words she and Ewan would whisper to each other that night in the dark. When there would be no more limit on what was possible to do.

"Let the record show." Frede's eyes had been solemn as she said it, her unkempt eyebrows furrowed together. There was no question that Frede meant what she said.

But would she mean it a year from now, after Lord knew how many veiled criticisms and sighs had issued from their grandmother's rocking chair? Maud suspected she would not. She knew her cousin.

Then again, it wasn't exactly a life sentence. As Frede had said, their grandmother couldn't have that many years left. And there were other cousins. Stella, for one—Frede's older sister, with the same laugh as Frede and an incredible aptitude for finding Maud's last nerve and striking it with an endless string of complaints and conventional wisdom.

Stella didn't have an engagement, or even a hint of one in the making. Stella had no ambitions of professorship either. If Maud did decide to marry soon, she would have a talk with Frede about trying Stella first. Not now—not with Frede's determination still fresh. Tomorrow perhaps, or the next time they saw each other.

Just then, both Frede and Maud turned toward the sound of footsteps coming down the back stairs.

"Nothing more to be afraid of, lassies," Ewan said, his eyes catching on light from a source that Maud couldn't place. "The trifecta is together."

"SO YOU REALLY drank that entire bottle of champagne and didn't save a lick of it?" With a last bite of casserole suspended in the air on his fork, Ewan looked back and forth from Frede to Maud.

"We had nothing to save it for, lad," Frede said, smiling. "But we can get the bottle for you. There may be a lick left in the bottom."

"Is that so?" Ewan asked, looking up at Maud across the kitchen table. He had started to break from his shyness more often these days, especially when Frede came around. "Where is that bottle? I'll perform an inspection."

Maud laughed. "I've washed it out, I'm afraid. But I do have a surprise that might make us all forget about champagne. Frede, would you mind clearing the table while I go make a few arrangements?"

"Gladly," Frede said.

Maud disappeared into the pantry, careful to shut the door fully behind her. Apprehending the cake now, Maud couldn't bring herself to be concerned by either pawprints or licks. Not with her whole body simmering with gladness in the day, and especially the unexpected joy of Ewan's presence. A bouquet he'd put together himself!

She decided to bring the cake out in its current state and tell the full story, just as Anne would have her do.

Maud opened the pantry door, picked up both cake and serving knife, and presented them to the table with the casual delight of an experienced waitress.

"The most delicious cake you'll ever eat," she pronounced with a smile so big her teeth were exposed—a rare moment.

"I did not make it myself, so it is not self-flattery to say so either. Just you wait until you try it."

When Maud turned around to gather three small plates and forks from the wooden sideboard, both Frede and Ewan started laughing.

"What is it?" Maud asked when she was facing them again.

Frede straightened up from where she'd been whispering in Ewan's ear. "You should have seen yourself coming out of that pantry, like a cat parading a mouse."

"I'll say," Ewan said.

"A cat parading a mouse, eh?" Maud asked, raising her eyebrows. "You'll be happy to know that this cake's superior taste has, in fact, been confirmed by the cat himself. He's taken several licks off the top," she pointed. "And stuck his paw in for good measure." She sighed and then laughed. "I forgot to cover the cake last night."

Frede gasped in mock horror.

"It's true." Maud shook her head and smiled. "I, Maud Montgomery, made a mistake. Oh, the dishonor of it all. I got myself into such a state about it this morning I thought I couldn't possibly bring myself to tell you."

Ewan laughed, plainly delighting in this admission.

"That does it, we should trash the whole thing," Frede said.

Maud joined in with Ewan's and Frede's laughter, surprised at how genuine her humor felt.

Then Maud noticed that Frede was already at the cake, digging in with the knife. Maud put a hand out to stop her. "Oh, please Frede, don't cut one of the side pieces for yourself. Let me do away with the dry parts before we dish any of it up."

Frede cut Maud a sideways look as she handed over the

knife. "It has been a while since I've cut a cake myself, so I appreciate you taking control of this situation. Honestly Maud, you sure are funny about this cake."

Frede and Ewan laughed again, but Maud stayed focused on the task at hand. She sliced off one of the edges, then cut three large slices and dished them out onto the plates without a single crumb.

"Grandmother and I had a sample last night, as you can see," Maud said. "Oh! Let's have the first bite all together. I said the same thing to Grandmother and she refused, but I expect better of you both."

Frede already had a bite halfway to her mouth.

"Well hurry up, then, you two," Frede said.

Ewan and Maud quickly followed suit. They all laughed before placing the bites in their mouths.

"Lord almighty," Frede said while she was still chewing, then froze. "I'm sorry, Ewan. I didn't mean to speak that way so casually."

Ewan shook his head. "This cake is worth thanking the Lord for." Ewan never seemed to take anything Frede said too seriously.

"I tell you," Frede said, inching the cake plate closer to herself, "there is just about nothing more I want in this whole world than to have the rest of this cake all to myself. I'd eat it three meals a day."

Maud nodded, vindicated. "Now who is funny about this cake?"

"It's a good thing I never mind being funny about anything," Frede said. They all took another bite.

"It can't be true though, can it?" Ewan asked.

"It can't be true that I'm funny?" Frede asked.

"No, not that." Ewan shook his head. "I meant that you must want something in the world a whole lot more than having this cake to yourself." He looked at Maud. "Not to say it isn't very good cake."

Frede stopped her fork briefly on its way to her mouth. "This cake is too sinful for Reverend Macdonald. He refuses to accept my devotion to it." She finished the bite before continuing. "It's a good thing I have a repentant heart."

Maud laughed.

"What would your answer be to the same question, Ewan?" Frede asked with a flicker in her eye. "I'll answer, but only if you tell me first."

Ewan raised an eyebrow, readying himself to play along. "Why should I tell you first? I was the one to ask you."

Frede shrugged. "My rules."

"I'll humor you, but only because my answer is easy," Ewan said. He looked at Maud. "What I want most in this world is to have you as my wife, for as long as either of us should live." Maud could feel his words course through her like a happy salve. She saw in his eyes that he meant them.

"Mine's easy too, for what it's worth," Frede said, interrupting Maud's reverie.

They both turned toward Frede. "And what's that?" Ewan asked.

"To be a professor at an honest-to-goodness college."

"Oh?" Ewan asked.

"I want to master a subject completely, so well that I can inspire others to love it as I do," Frede said, her eyes uncharacteristically serious.

Ewan looked from Frede to Maud and then back again.

Frede added, "I love the word 'professor,' don't both of you? It sounds so wonderfully worldly." Frede stretched out the last word on her tongue. "I've always wanted to explore enough of this life to be thought of as worldly. And you can't be a professor without being at least somewhat worldly, don't you think?"

"I do," Maud said.

"Well, that sounds mighty nice," Ewan said with an earnest smile. "I didn't know you had those ambitions. You've never spoken about them before."

"You've never asked," Frede said, looking Ewan in the eye. "Consider whether you would have asked, had I been a man."

Ewan looked at Maud, who gave him a small shrug and an encouraging smile. "It is worth considering," Maud said.

"I suppose it is," said Ewan. "I apologize for any offense taken."

"Oh, there's no offense, I assure you," Frede said. "It's just an interesting question."

"Am I to take it, then, that you don't have any womanly ambitions?" Ewan asked.

Catching Frede's raised eyebrows, Ewan looked down.

"I don't mean 'womanly,' exactly," Ewan continued. "I only mean—do you want a husband eventually? Or children?"

"Womanly" to Ewan meant a husband. Children. Of course. Then again, he had also said that Frede's professorship ambitions were mighty nice.

"Children—Lord, no!" Frede put her hand over her mouth once she registered her words. Then she smiled. "I meant that as a prayer, Ewan. And a sincere one!"

"Does the same prayer extend to not having a husband?" Ewan seemed genuinely curious.

"Not exactly," said Frede. "A husband would be all right, but having one is certainly no great ambition of mine. I'd rather stumble upon a husband on the side of a road I'm already headed down than go looking for one." Frede paused. "And if I never do stumble on one, my path will probably be easier for it—and my skirt will be cleaner too," Frede said, her eyes lighting up with her laugh.

"An enlightened plan," Maud said.

"I'd say so," Ewan said, and Maud warmed at his words. "A mighty impressive friend we have here, don't we?"

"We do," Maud said. "Frede, tell Ewan about—"

But Ewan interrupted her. "And what about you, my dear?" Ewan asked, his eyes bright spots on an otherwise shadowed face in the darkening kitchen.

How had the spotlight turned to Maud so abruptly? The question just so happened to be the same one she'd been trying to answer herself: what she wanted most in the world. Now she was meant to answer it casually, over her last bites of cake?

She'd try some light, deflecting humor to start. "Oh, I'm afraid I've already done my stumbling," she laughed, looking pointedly at Ewan. Then she turned to Frede. "Frede, any recent times you have caught your toe on a man that you care to share?"

Ewan only looked confused. "No, I meant about what you want most in the world."

"Oh," Maud said, gathering a few crumbs with her fork and lifting them to her mouth, careful not to look Ewan's way. "I misunderstood."

Maud looked at Frede, who gave her a nod that said simply to go on.

Now both Frede and Ewan had their eyes on Maud, and her usual quickness of thought was failing her.

"I have significant ambitions too, of course," Maud said. "Always have had, rising from somewhere deep within me."

She looked at Ewan, whose expression remained jovial.

"Ambitions in marriage, do you mean?" Ewan asked.

Maud felt the sting of disappointment. Ewan might admire a deeper sort of yearning in Frede, but would he ever accept the same in Maud?

"Well, yes, I do have those." Maud paused. She must tread carefully here. "Ambitions for children too," she said, looking at Ewan. "Even if that does make me less sane than dear Frede," she added, looking at Frede.

No one spoke in reply.

As she tried to think of what else to say, Maud's gaze caught on the kitchen window. Outside it, a moonless black night greeted her like a warm blanket, calming her until she felt the faithful kick of her imagination. "As far as children go, I have always had a premonition that I would have sons instead of daughters. My fate, since I understand girls better. But I think I would do just fine with boys. I see them as interesting, imaginative lads, good readers, who love the outdoors as much as I do. They would grow up to put their minds to good use, as doctors or lawyers or the like." She looked at Ewan again, who was smiling. "And they would have a good man for a father," she added. "One who excels at things such as picking out a late-bloom bouquet."

Ewan followed Maud's glance toward the tall vase Frede had set out on the kitchen counter, with the bouquet placed inside it. Ewan's face lit up, and Maud felt her own joy rising to meet his.

Nothing she had said had been untrue. Not the facts, at least.

Ewan rose then, and came over to Maud's side of the table. Leaning down, he took Maud's face in his hands and delivered a kiss. Then he said, "I mean to make all of that possible for you—if you'll allow me, that is."

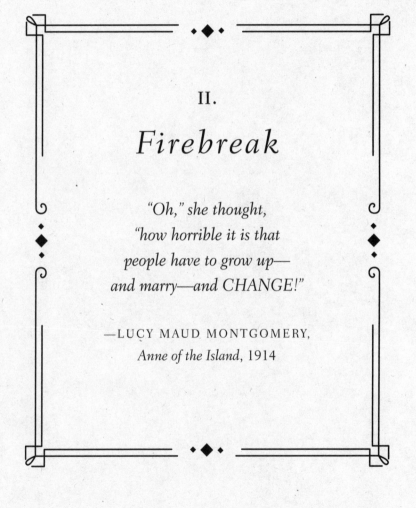

II.

Firebreak

*"Oh," she thought,
"how horrible it is that
people have to grow up—
and marry—and CHANGE!"*

—LUCY MAUD MONTGOMERY,
Anne of the Island, 1914

16.

A letter from Frede predicting the contents of their old-lady chats. Another letter rejoicing in the success of Anne. And further on in the folder, a letter outlining the book she hoped to write one day—a book telling the story of a full adult life. She could feel it in her bones, she told Frede. She only needed a few more bestsellers under her belt to provide for her boys. A little more time in her days once they were both in school.

She was aware of a dull throbbing somewhere in her body as she reread the contents of this folder. But she could not locate the source. She pictured herself looking down from one of the large cherry trees in the backyard, her body a small thing standing beside a bonfire, hurting as bodies do.

She was growing impatient with herself. It would be so much simpler to let the whole folder go. No more of this painful sorting exercise. What would the Reader care about a few old letters exchanged with a cousin?

She opened her hands, and the entire folder fell. For a moment, she willed it back so strongly she could have been sick. But it was too late. There the first lick, then the hungry brightening.

17.

Leaskdale, Ontario
January 1919

Two broomstick horses had been Christmas gifts from Frede, with sock faces different enough for each boy to pronounce his own superior. They had supplied gobs of entertainment ever since. Leave it to Frede to know just what boys of six and three would enjoy equally and together.

Maud relished the boys' banter alongside the Christmas music playing on the Victrola as she attached hooks to curtains and handed them to Ewan. He kept interrupting his work to smile down at her or to joke with the boys about training their horses. But she did not mind if this project took all day.

"Scoot, scoot," Stuart kept saying to his broom, a phrase he had picked up from the maid Lily as she ushered the boys from one room to the next. Now and then, when he thought no one was looking, Stuart would smile down at his horse's face and tenderly pat its button nose. Chester would roll his eyes at this if he noticed, fancying himself an adult lad already, but Chester paid much more attention to where he was headed than to anything Stuart was doing.

"Off to another land!" Chester exclaimed, smiling wide as he traipsed in and out of the room.

Maud and Ewan had been laughing right along with the

boys all afternoon, asking questions about the imaginary lands they visited and who populated them.

"Sharks and tyrants," Chester answered, and Maud shook her head at the difference between boys and the young girl she had been. Never would shark or tyrant populate her imaginary worlds. But how wonderful for Chester to have an audience for his dreams—something far surpassing the looking-glass companions of Maud's childhood. Maud delighted in being this kind of compatriot for her boys. They would never be so lonely as she had been.

"Mummy and Papa too," Stuart added for his part, his voice high and sweet.

"And Chester and Stuart and dozens of kittens," Chester added, smiling.

"Kittens!" Stuart exclaimed, laughing at the image his mind had formed.

"I fear these curtains would not last a minute in such a land," Maud said with a rueful smile. "Those kittens would be crawling the walls!"

The boys looked at her and laughed in unison, then started a neighing lap around the room, Stuart on Chester's heels.

Maud handed Ewan another screw, letting her hand linger on his as she did. He smiled, and gave her cheek a playful pinch.

Ewan Macdonald. Her husband.

Ewan had turned into basically the husband she'd thought he would be on the most realistic days of her youth. Gloriously dependable. Good to Maud and her relatives both. He had been especially kind to her grandmother, always.

The thought of her grandmother brought its habitual pang to Maud's heart. Incredibly, her grandmother had kept her determined wits about her until her death nearly eight years earlier. While taking the old house apart so it could be sold and its contents parsed out among family members—an awful undertaking, and one that she never could have managed without Frede's humor and practical wisdom accompanying her every move—Maud found in her grandmother's trunk several new blankets with Maud's name stitched on them in her grandmother's hand. Meant, surely, for an occasion too special ever to occur. Maud kept one of them at all times under her comforter now, running her fingers across the stitching at night and feeling a surprising amount of relief to discover how much she missed the woman to whom she had devoted many good years.

Not long after she and Ewan married, she moved to Leaskdale on the mainland, where Ewan had become a minister of two parishes a few years earlier. He made a nicer income than he had on the Island, and he'd been determined to make a life in a new spot and bring her to it. To say that Maud was unhappy to leave the Island would be an understatement—both she and the cat Daffy, who had to be shipped by train, were depressed for a solid few months. But soon enough the boys came, and the house turned into a home.

Not a home furnished the way Maud would like it to be, however, until recently. The curtains were the pièce de résistance in Maud's new decorating scheme, and they had just arrived on special delivery from England. She loved the feel of those curtains. The decadence of them. They were heavy and velvet and came with a square card printed on heavy stock promising they would last a lifetime. She ordered them with her own money. She had been diligent about putting money away for the boys' educations for years now, and with nine books published and trotting around the world quite nicely, she finally felt she had money to spare.

"They're sure beautiful, aren't they, monkey?" Ewan asked now. Maud couldn't tell whether he meant the curtains or the boys. She smiled and kissed him for both meanings, cutting the kiss short when she realized that the boys' footsteps had slowed. They would probably start groaning soon, as they did at any semblance of romance between their parents.

Maud turned to the boys and smiled.

"What a perfect gift from Aunty Fred those horses are. She knows you so well," Maud said. "We must arrange a time for her next visit, what do you say, boys? She won't believe how much you have grown in a few short months."

"I can't wait to tell Aunty Fred that I lost a tooth!" Chester said, pushing his tongue between the space in his front teeth.

On his way over to pour more coffee, Ewan nodded his agreement. "You should write to Frede about coming during her next school break."

"I just might do that tonight," Maud said.

Looking at the boys' beaming faces, their cheeks as rosy as if they'd been out in the snow, Maud had an idea.

"I know what might be the perfect afternoon treat for us all—hot cocoa. Should I go make us some?"

Chester's eyes grew wide. "Oh, Mother, do you mean we can have cocoa and music all at once?"

Maud laughed and kissed Chester's forehead on her way to the kitchen. She remembered all too well the feeling of being young and not daring to dream that two lovely things could occur at the same time.

"I'll tell you what, Chester," Maud said with a twinkle in her eye. "I'll bring out some cookies too."

LATER THAT NIGHT, after dashing off a letter to Frede about a visit—quoting Chester in his full front-toothless enthusiasm—Maud opened the first volume of her new journals. She had purchased a ten-volume set after seeing an advertisement in a magazine: "high-quality binding will last a lifetime." She hoped for longer than that. These volumes were to house her journals, recopied in the uniform hand and sound mind of middle age. Her old, haphazard set of journals, the first few full of girlish handwriting, would never be fit for publishing. They were missing a storyteller who knew what parts to keep—and what parts to excise.

Maud had been recopying for at least thirty minutes each night, having more fun than she had expected. Tonight, after the boys were sound asleep, she opened the oldest journal she'd deemed worth keeping to the place she'd left off the night before.

The next entry on deck was about Nate, whom she had nicknamed Snip, on a day she'd been confused by some remark of his and spent hours pondering it. After a few laughs, she settled into a good rhythm. Most of this was harmless; it could be recopied verbatim into the new volume.

The ring of the telephone was shriller than it had ever sounded in daytime. It made her heart and legs hop in unison.

It was too late in the day for a call to mean anything but worry.

After she picked up the receiver, it seemed to take an eternity for the operator to connect. She delivered the telegram in the usual mechanical tone: "Telegram for Ms. Maud Macdonald. Frede is ill. Come at once."

18.

Situated in their nonhabitual seats with cut crystal tumblers of champagne in hand, Frede repeated her demand to hear the full story of Anne's publication. "Leave nothing out."

"I don't know where to start." Maud raised her eyebrows as she took her first sip of champagne. The most alcohol she'd ever had was a glass or two of wine at some of the gatherings of young people that used to happen at the less strict households in Cavendish, back when more among her cohort were unmarried. She smiled, thinking of how, in her old journal, she had referred to those drinks of wine as "etc." A note for her to remember, and for the Reader to claim ignorance.

She'd only tasted champagne once, at the nicest wedding she'd been to, and that taste was a single distracted gulp after everyone in the room raised their glasses. Now, a tumbler of champagne sat in front of her. This particular tumbler had traveled all the way from Scotland and been passed down through the generations—never before used to Maud's knowledge for anything more than cherry cordial, and that only when the minister or a faraway relative came for a visit. The bubbles of this new, upgraded beverage played on Maud's tongue, the sweet notes cut with the perfect amount of sour.

"Oh, Frede, this is magnificent."

Frede, never one for patience, had already finished half her own tumbler.

"A toast to the soon-to-be-published authoress!" Frede raised her glass, and they stood up to cheers. "Now, what exactly happened during those many months when I had no report?"

"Last fall, you mean?"

Frede nodded.

"Oh, it was an awful time. The manuscript was sitting in a hatbox on the top shelf of my closet. With a stack of rejection letters all I had to show for it." Maud met Frede's eyes. Saying these words out loud for the first time to anyone, Maud felt as exposed as a field mouse spotted in the middle of a newly swept kitchen. But Frede did not look away.

"You must have felt so miserable."

"I did." Maud sat down and took another sip. "It hurt something terrible in my chest, especially at night. Each time I'd get one of those rejection letters, I'd sink a little lower."

Frede nodded. "I understand. It was a part of you they were saying no to." She came over to the couch so she was sitting next to Maud.

Maud wiped away a few tears, half made up of remembered pain and the other half made up of the understanding filling the room as palpably as a gust of warm wind.

"Yes," Maud said finally. "That's exactly it."

"And yet you dared to keep sending your book off to perfect strangers! That's brave if anything is."

"It felt more like my old heedlessness than bravery."

"Regardless, the book did find its way out from that hatbox. What prompted it?" Frede took the last of her champagne down in one final gulp.

Maud's face broke into a smile. "You did."

"I did?" Frede bounced a little on the couch but shook her head dismissively. "I'm sure I had nothing to do with it."

"Well, the both of us together." Maud gave a half smile. "I think I'd better go get the rest of that bottle," she said.

Maud came back from the kitchen, pouring both glasses a quarter full, then watching to make sure the bubbles died down before pouring them half full. Looking up at Frede a few times, Maud laughed to see that impatience had set Frede's legs hopping.

"Enough!" Frede said. "No more suspense."

"You wrote to me last December, do you remember? Asking how my publishing trek was coming along. That's what you called it, a trek. 'And no trek is ever finished until you reach home, however long it might take,' you said."

"Well," Frede said. "No use staying lost out in the woods."

"It was because of you that I dragged the hatbox down from the closet late one winter night when grandmother was fully asleep." Maud paused. "And a good thing she was so asleep too, because I bumbled the box something silly, and it fell to the ground. Thank goodness none of the pages got out of order." She smiled and shook her head, remembering.

"I hid the rejection letters away in my desk drawer upside down, to keep myself from reading any of those dreadful words again. And then I lit the lamp in my bedroom and started reading the manuscript over."

"Good girl. And?" The refilled champagne glasses sat untouched and un-coastered on a wooden side table.

"And"—Maud smiled—"I still liked it."

"No doubt you did! I am sure it is brilliant."

"I assure you it is not. But it wasn't terrible."

"And?"

"A few weeks later, I packaged it up and sent it away to L.C. Page and Company in Boston, Massachusetts."

"Excellent. But I may leap out of my skin if you keep pausing your story at the end of each breath."

Maud laughed. "I'll do my best to continue without taking in air." Maud quickened her speech. "This past April a small, inconspicuous letter arrived, with L.C. Page and Company as the return address. I ran upstairs with it—suspecting already, because rejections come with the entire returned manuscript—but not believing it could really be so. I even held the letter up to the window, trying to get a hint of what it said before opening it." Maud laughed again and shook her head. "The strangest waves of emotion flooded through me. I was laughing and crying and wringing my hands against my chest like the sort of overcome bride we like to mock." Maud demonstrated.

Laughter distracted Frede, but only for a moment. "What did it say when you opened it?"

"'We are pleased to inform you,' it started." Maud felt tears prick at the corners of her eyes, remembering. "It said they'd like to extend an offer of publication."

Frede bounced to her feet. With champagne in hand, Frede pulled Maud up to standing too.

"To you," they said at the same time as they toasted.

"Don't you go giving a bit of credit to me," Frede said. "You wrote a whole book. A book that will be published!" Then Frede started singing a happy song they knew from childhood and dancing around the room with movements that made no sense whatsoever except that they were Frede's.

"So it was the first publisher you tried after the hatbox. I knew it." Frede kept dancing while Maud laughed, and they both kept sipping.

Suddenly, Frede stopped. "Oh, Maud, can you imagine if your book made it big in the mainland?"

"Oh, the thrill of joy as would run over me!" I heard that somewhere once. Isn't it a perfectly elegant sentence?

Maud put her head back and laughed. "That seems far too much to hope for. I cannot imagine what people as far away as Vancouver would have to say about Anne and her odd little ways."

Odd little ways?

"I shouldn't have said 'odd'; I didn't mean that," Maud said.

Frede gave her a quizzical look. "I took no offense, I assure you."

"The truth is this character of mine has established something of a residence in my mind and heart. I am beginning to think her place might even be permanent." It felt vulnerable to say so, but this was Frede she was talking to. "I wonder what you will have to say about her."

"I cannot wait to see. Will you keep writing about her?"

"My publishers are insisting on it. They're contemplating several sequels. But I've never been able to imagine this girl of mine taking college courses, or facing any of the sobering realities that come after that." Maud took a long draw of champagne. "As we both know too well."

"Oh, adult life isn't so bad," said Frede. "How can you say that it is, today of all days?"

Sourpuss.

"Do we need to start calling you a sourpuss?"

"Not you too," Maud said. Then, spotting a cushion nearly falling off the couch, she set her champagne back on the table and grabbed the cushion. She mockingly took aim at Frede's bemused expression.

"I dare you to do it," Frede said.

So she did, hitting Frede in the side with the cushion, with Frede lifting her tumbler high in the air and crying out, "Save the champagne!"

They both ended up falling back on the couch in a pile of laughter.

"Most importantly, not a single drop spilled," Frede said, looking down at her glass. "Of course, that is likely because there were only a few drops left."

"You can still call yourself a savior if you'd like," Maud said, pouring the rest of the bottle.

"Look at you—I believe the champagne has made you sacrilegious," Frede said.

"It's a good thing Ewan isn't here," Maud said, although she felt confident Ewan would have only felt joy seeing her and Frede joke in this way. He loved their jolly banter, even if he rarely joined in.

"Now," Frede said. "Why couldn't you write exactly the next book you most want to write? Who says you need to write sequels at some publisher's say-so? I think you could write all different kinds of books."

Different kinds of books! Does this mean you are bored of me? Have I become a chore to listen to? People have told me before that I can be a chore to listen to.

"Oh, I'm not finished with Anne. I only wish I could keep writing her young. Or very old. The in-between years will not be quite as much fun, I'm afraid. And it mars things for me a little, receiving my publishers' notes about what they believe will sell. But I suppose it behooves me to pay attention to what they say. I do want to sell books, after all. I've also started to sketch out a few new characters—young ones—who will ensure my own continued amusement."

"Good, because it is not up to any publisher. You must have a grand adventure with the next book. Oh, Maud, what if you moved cities with each new book you wrote? You and Ewan together?"

Maud laughed. "I don't see how that would be conducive to having children, exactly. Or to a ministry."

"I suppose not. So I take it my letters still haven't convinced you to do without the children?" Frede sighed.

"I'm afraid not," Maud said lightly, but her stomach turned. The Fox and the Hen, squaring off.

Frede didn't seem to notice any shift in the mood. "Just promise me you will not come crying to me when you have suffered for sleepless nights and you want to give your children right back to the good Lord."

"I vow never to bother thee with such afflictions," Maud said in a solemn voice, the champagne making her forget her worry of a moment before.

Frede nodded. "It's a pact."

An idea came to Maud then to open the front door wide and let the bright light of day into the house.

It was the happiest light the house had ever seen, she was sure about that, and she told Frede so.

"I'd say that's indisputable," Frede said.

They moved two striped armchairs from the parlor that had never been moved in all their lives to the entryway so that they faced the open front door. Then they laid themselves over them so they could feel every ounce of the fragrant sun.

"A published novelist. You will be a published novelist," Frede said as they both closed their eyes, having finished the last of the champagne.

With the heat of the afternoon sun coaxing her eyelids shut, Maud realized that any other friend would have grown tired of such talk long ago.

It was oddly familiar, this relentless delight. From where?

She is wearing her good yellow sundress and she is twirling, over and over again, on this same old wood floor, and she doesn't need to stop because someone is clapping. Clapping and exclaiming. Someone with dark hair falling out of its pins and a contagious nonchalance. Paying no mind whatsoever to the grandmother and grandfather huddled in the dark corner of the room with their forever frowns.

Her mother.

She opened her eyes and saw Frede asleep on her chair, the light pouring over her. How many people in life ever love us with the selfless fervor of a mother?

"Thank God for you," she whispered to Frede, and Frede answered with a loud snore, which was just like her.

19.

Maud wrapped her hands around the cold metal bars on either side of her waist. The cot had given Maud no sleep and bruises on her hips and shoulders, but she could not will herself to get up from it. To get up meant going back to the Macdonald College infirmary where she'd spent her first fifty hours after arriving. It meant hearing another somber progress report, and then trying to find any possible words to say.

The doctors were calling it the Spanish flu. The pandemic had taken Frede's brother and his son at Park Corner a few months before. "The Great Aftershock of the Great War," said a newspaper headline. The war had coughed up the epidemic like contagious phlegm, bringing home the devastation that had always been contained a ways off. But that didn't mean it was allowed to take Frede.

At Park Corner that past November after Frede's brother's funeral service, Maud and Frede had walked back and forth over the pond bridge in complete darkness—and cold; in all their walks together, there had never been one so cold. They mostly did not talk except when Frede said, "My heart isn't right." She added right away that it was only stress, it had to be. "All this loss, and the finances to figure out now with only women left at Park Corner."

"You'd better take care," Maud had said. "You're essential, you know."

Essential to whom? Essential to Maud, yes.

She had not thought then, as she probably should have, of Frede's boy soldier husband back from war and ready to settle down and have a family.

Maud never had been able to fully imagine Frede as a mother, established in a home without the professorship at Macdonald College that she adored. Frede had graduated first in her class and become exactly who she had her sights set on becoming all those years back. But no woman they knew had become a mother and kept a profession. And she couldn't bear to see Frede give up her livelihood. Had all this occurred to Maud as they walked that day in the cold?

She shook her head. Foreshadowing was for novels and child's play. Not for real life.

A different memory now: Frede holding Chester as a round-faced baby on her knee, bouncing him up and down and smiling as proudly as she would if he was her own son.

She must get to Frede's bedside immediately, must see her again, must make her recover. She'd wasted too many precious seconds attempting sleep in this dreadful cot already.

THE DOCTORS INSISTED on Maud wearing a mask any time she was near Frede's bedside, which Maud hated for the barrier it created. But it also helped in a way. She never knew what might show up on her face and undermine the work she was doing to keep her gestures reassuring.

Through each movement, Maud tried to communicate the words that wouldn't come. Tried as she held Frede's hand to turn their friendship into one solid entity that must come and go together. Tried as she tucked the hair off Frede's face to move grace through the tips of her fingers. But she was finding it hard enough just to keep her habitual finger twitch at bay. Her jaw was grinding horribly under her mask. She was busy cursing herself for her own weakness when Frede began to speak.

"You know, I'd like to see Stella with the influenza," Frede said. "I'm sure the specific gravity would go all the way up to one hundred. Highest level yet."

Frede had barely enough air for two words at a time, but she managed these lines perfectly, imitating her older sister's reasoning for any ailment she'd ever had. They laughed together then, with Frede managing a few wheezes and Maud joining a few seconds late, the way she usually did. For a few generous seconds, Maud managed to forget the steamy wetness of tears on her cheeks under the mask, and even—momentarily—the reason for them.

"Take care," Frede said breathlessly. "Of you."

"No, Frede."

"Ewan, he"—she took a breath—"means well." She took another breath. "Lean on each other" was what Maud thought she heard in Frede's wheezing words.

Lean on Ewan? To lean on a man was not something either Frede or Maud had ever suggested to each other. But it was what Frede said.

"Sorry to leave the party," Frede added, in a voice so soft Maud could hardly hear. "So soon," she added.

Maud grabbed for Frede's hand suddenly, violently, but she still couldn't manage any speech. She could only close her own eyes, willing her own breath into Frede's lungs.

Some time later, after Maud's head lay by her friend's side for what could have been minutes or hours, a change registered in Maud's heart.

Frede was no longer breathing.

Maud's head rose until she saw the whole of Frede's cot, everything starch white except the brown mess of hair on the pillow. She didn't see how she could stand this feeling for another breath, or another after that. The crimson sunrise out the east-facing windows only made matters worse, bleeding its indifferent beauty into the room.

Then Maud felt a hand touching hers, with thick and sweaty fingers tightening around the side of her palm. A hand like Frede's.

It couldn't be.

A nurse, she realized when she turned her head—trying to be kind and lead Maud to a nearby chair. But Maud couldn't tear herself away, couldn't stop trying to come up with the right words. The right words, she only had to find them and speak them out loud.

Then, the terrible realization that no matter what she said, Frede would never laugh again.

With a choke, Maud found herself clinging desperately to the nurse who had only meant to offer a hand. Her hysterical sobs, close to laughter in their pitch, shook the poor woman's body, but she couldn't stop, didn't know how to stop, didn't know how to live in a world from which the most kindred spirit she had ever known was missing. She sobbed until her stomach ached and the nurse's arms gave out, and then she sank to the floor and shook until she slept.

20.

Maud pulled out a folder from a drawer in the manse's library labeled "Correspondence: Frede," sliding out the letter on the top, dated March 24, 1907.

Maud found this letter in the large drawer in Frede's writing table that Maud had been tasked with sorting a few weeks after Frede died. A heart-wrenching endeavor. With each paper that Frede had deemed worth saving, Maud felt the pain of loss cut through her again like glass. Not that Frede had the time or the type of mind to curate her papers. No, Frede's writing table was as unkempt as her hair had been, and yet the layers of students' papers thoughtfully marked and birthday cards saved and letters half begun to nearly every family member spoke volumes.

Once sorted, the largest stack of all consisted of letters from Maud. And at the top of the heap was the letter from March 1907, with "Ten Year Letter" spelled out on the top.

Back when Maud was in her teenage years, the idea of a letter to be opened in ten years had seemed like harmless frivolity. She wrote one after the other. Ten-year letters were a fad of the times; a test of what felt back then like a heroic sort of patience; a means of delivering honesty while delaying any of its consequences.

Long after the fad had passed, when Maud was in her thirties, Frede had pushed to exchange ten-year letters. Maud had hidden her reluctance at the time, but now she was glad she'd gone along with it. Glad she had gone along with anything Frede wanted while she still had her.

Reading it now, she was surprised that the letter she had written to Frede twelve years ago started somewhat morbidly. It predicted the loss of familiar places: the home she shared with her grandmother in Cavendish demolished or a residence for bats and spiders, Frede's old home at Park Corner absent the personalities that made it live. In return, Maud hoped for marriage for them both, with Maud a minister's wife and a mother. (She hadn't mentioned children for Frede, not wanting to suggest a possibility that Frede had never wanted for herself.)

But Maud also might be an old maid with books for children and a pen for a husband. She would not be unhappy if so, she'd written, because what she'd put into life mattered more than what she got out of it.

She thought herself wise to end with contingencies. If their friendship pulled away from them during the intervening years. If Maud died. Herself she had thought of, but not Frede. It was never supposed to be Frede. Not the one nine years younger who seemed to bob on top of all life's troubles.

In case of death, Maud wrote, Frede should not feel badly. Maud would still be roaming close by; she did not believe that all laughter was banished from the Beyond.

How lightly she had written these words at the time. How desperately she now hoped it to be true that Frede was still somewhere about, laughing. She squeezed her eyes shut in prayer.

"Truly and lovingly and good comradely," Maud had signed her letter.

Maud worked her fingers down the side of her nose. Her sinuses were throbbing with the residue of the tears from that morning and the past three months. Even when the tears dried up, her stomach still turned sick with each realizing: each time one of the boys would have a small success or put things in a way Frede would love, each time they sat at the dining room table looking at the seat they'd always left open for Frede, each time Maud wanted to laugh and didn't, each time she had a late-night craving for her and Frede's favorite snack. And Ewan—Ewan had loved Frede so well. "We've both lost a great comrade," he said when he heard.

Curling up in bed at night with Ewan was a real comfort. His steady breathing, his arm heavy around her shoulder. Ewan was her solid ground.

But there was only one voice Maud found herself longing for these days, one voice she wished would return to her on the most sluggish mornings and torturous nights. Not Frede's. Maud couldn't bring herself to hope for the return of that voice. No—this was a voice she should be capable of conjuring at any moment. How often had it flowed from her pen as easily as morning tea from the kettle? Yet Maud couldn't remember the last time Anne's voice had entered her mind. When had Anne last spoken solace or wisdom in the way that only Anne could?

One of the great pains of Maud's middle age was that Anne's middle age, the playing out of tired tropes in sequel after sequel, had flattened Anne from full living being into lines on a page. No longer was she the lovable truth-teller bounding about Maud's most private thoughts.

Now, when Maud needed her most, Anne was nowhere to be found.

Maud had just started to close her eyes, dizzy with the ache of it all, when she heard a noise like a cat scratch behind her.

She scanned the furniture for where Daffy might be clawing. But it wasn't Daffy.

A flash of something small and pale passed under the locked library door. A mouse? Maud was almost at the door when she heard a squeak and then saw another pale flash. Not a mouse, but a small hand, flattening to slot under the bottom of the door, then retreating.

"Stuart, is that you?"

"Yes," said a high-pitched, eager voice from behind the door. Maud heard shuffles that meant he was standing up.

Maud opened the door and laughed. It was such a relief, the simple reality of three-and-a-half-year-old Stuart standing in the doorway, smiling and happy to be caught. Such an antidote to the pain she could do nothing about. The pain that was driving her half-mad.

"I thought you might have been a mouse! What do you need, darling?" She ruffled his hair. "I'm sorry I locked the door. You know I only do that when I'm hard at work and having trouble concentrating." She hadn't locked it in a while. Maud had been avoiding her writing since Frede died.

"I blow kisses real strong for Mummy."

"Oh, Stuart," said Maud, a tear falling down her face. She wiped it away so Stuart wouldn't worry about having made her cry. "You always have been my little dear." She took Stuart's hand and squeezed it.

"I worry," Stuart added, in a pleading tone that made Maud kneel down and look in his eyes, searching for his full meaning. When she saw his eyes start to well up, hers welled up again too.

She had been busy thinking only about Frede, about her future without Frede. She had convinced herself the boys were too young to be affected. She'd been wrong.

Maud took Stuart into her arms for a hug then, squeezing tight enough that he wouldn't feel the fullness of her tears.

"Oh darling, please don't worry about me," Maud said while she was still holding him. "It's my job to worry about you. I've been very upset about your aunty Fred, but I'll be all right. You and your brother—you're what's most important to me in this world. Don't ever forget that."

Maud pulled away enough to see Stuart nod, but not to meet his eyes. She couldn't bear to let Stuart see the fear she knew her eyes would reveal—fear about how to live through pain like this and still be a mother. She rose and steadied herself, gripping his hand.

"Let's see if we can't fix you a snack," she said, leading him into the kitchen.

She needed to bring her attention back to her boys now. Ewan too. She may have lost Frede, but she still had the other element of their trifecta, sitting in the other room alive and well. Her pain had caused her to pull away, but that didn't need to continue.

"Ewan," she called out from the kitchen. "Stuart and I are making a snack. What can I fix you?"

Maud decided that she would wrap her arms around Ewan the next time they were in the same room, letting him hold her as long as he liked.

21.

The moonless night cloaked the kitchen windows, turning the room as cozy as Maud ever remembered it. The woodstove, still warm, smelled of crisped cheese—the perfect complement to the lingering smell of cake.

Ewan rose from the kitchen table and cleared his throat.

"Now that we've finished our cake," he said, his voice commanding.

"Oh, I have not finished my cake," Frede said, and cut a new slice for herself. Maud laughed.

"By all means, I shouldn't have presumed," Ewan said. "Are you finished, Maud?" he asked.

"I am," Maud said.

"My surprise can accompany Frede's cake eating without a problem," Ewan said, standing up.

Maud's eyes widened. "Another surprise?"

Ewan scrounged around in his pockets, and Maud smiled. Ewan never could keep track of his things. It was one way she thought she'd be of use to him.

"It's a poem I dug up for you," Ewan said. "I've heard you talk about how much you admire Dickinson."

Emily Dickinson? So he did listen when she went on about books and poetry.

"Read a whole volume, and it wasn't half-bad. Can't say I understood all she was getting at, but this one seemed pretty good and comprehensible."

Ewan looked down with the shy, melancholy expression he had worn so often in their early courtship.

Melancholy eyes are my absolute ideal in a man.

And then he began to read.

"Wild nights! Wild nights!"

His voice caught, and he swallowed. He looked up at Maud then, and seeing her face seemed to renew his confidence.

"Were I with thee,
Wild nights should be
Our luxury!"

His words were soft and deliberate, not at all in keeping with the tempo or exuberance of the poem. But the hopeful way Ewan kept looking at Maud told her he understood something of their meaning. She felt a stirring inside.

"Futile the winds
To a heart in port, —
Done with the compass,
Done with the chart."

Ewan's frown told Maud he didn't understand this stanza quite so well. But then he looked on down the page, and his hopeful expression returned.

"Rowing in Eden!
Ah! the sea!
Might I but moor
To-night -"

He colored as he read the final phrase.

"in thee!"

At the end, there was a long pause, until Frede jumped in.

"Bravo! Well done," Frede said, rising and clapping her hands.

Maud felt a pang of guilt, realizing she had forgotten about Frede entirely. Looking over, Maud saw that Frede's plate was clear.

"Now," Frede said, "I am stuffed full as a holiday goose." She gave an exaggerated yawn. "I'll clear everything. You two lovebirds go on upstairs," she said. "I'll stay in the little spare room down here for the night, and I'll see you in the morning for a continuation of our birthday celebration."

Maud looked at Frede closely, checking her sincerity. Frede issued a reassuring nod.

"I sleep like a log too," Frede said. "Don't hear a thing."

"Frede!" Maud said under her breath. Ewan cleared his throat.

Frede laughed and picked up all three plates and forks, taking them to the sink. "Not a thing," she added for good measure.

Maud couldn't bring herself to bother any longer with what Frede might be thinking but not saying. Ewan had found a poem. He had found a poem, by a poet she loved, and read it out loud to her.

She went to him, took him firmly by the hand, and led him up the back stairs.

AS MAUD TURNED the doorknob to her old gable bedroom—a room that Ewan had never stepped foot in before—he came up from behind her and traced a line down the side of her neck with the light touch of a finger. Then he kissed the spot where his finger had started, just as lightly, and Maud leaned back. She remembered the feeling of Ewan's breath on her neck at her cousin's wedding, back when she was still trying to discern his feelings. She loved him this way, his movements designed to tease, not leaving any room for her to guess his mind the way she often did when they were facing each other.

Then his lips were against her neck again. Slowly they moved their way from her hairline to her blouse collar, and then he pulled her blouse collar aside and kissed there too. Her hand found its way up to his hair, and she ran her fingers through it. Then he turned her to face him and pulled her in.

She searched for his intent. He slid both hands down from her waist. And he was—oh, lifting her, carrying her to the bed, where he dropped her on top of her old feather tick mattress with a gleam in his eyes and then pounced on top of her.

Innocent fun quickly gave way to urgency, and now his hands were finding her legs under her skirt, which they'd never done before, and this was making it hard to think.

"Let's get married now," he said, pulling back briefly. "I can't wait any longer. Can you?"

Desire surged through Maud as Ewan pulled her back in, not giving her time to answer.

They could do it. They could marry next week and have a baby in a year. Grandmother could be stashed in a spare bedroom. Surely whatever manse Ewan occupied would be big enough, at least while they had only one child—

"Answer me," Ewan said.

Insistent man. This bold Ewan was good. She liked him.

What if she were to take Frede up on her offer? Why did she have to be the responsible one? The desire to do just what she wanted had been drilled out of her for so long that it could only be experienced in secret pockets like this one. And the person responsible for the drilling was the same person she felt obligated to dote on for the remainder of her days?

Maud's body tensed at the thought, but Ewan didn't seem to notice.

Now his hands were everywhere, on her chest and her upper thighs, abandoning all restraint.

"Answer me," he said again, pulling away this time and looking at her. Want was sending a ringing through her body.

"Yes," she said. "Yes."

Ewan broke into a wide smile, put his hands on either side of her and pushed away so he could study her face.

"You mean it? You can't know what this means to me, Maud. I care about you more than anything. More than any reason to wait. Do you—" He cleared his throat. "Do you feel the same about me?"

More than anything?

"Tell me that you do."

Her body felt emptied of all its contents. A curious thing. One minute ago, it had been full to the brim with want.

Ewan pulled back to look at her again. What had he asked?

"Do you?" he asked, his eyes insistent.

"I do," she said, because it seemed like the right answer, and he pulled her close and kissed her again with the urgency she liked.

"I should make my way to the spare upstairs room soon," Ewan whispered finally, as he pulled up for air.

No, her body insisted.

"No," she said. "You can stay. Sleep here with me."

Ewan was silent for a minute. "All right," he said.

Then, deliberately, Ewan pulled the pins out of her hair one by one. "That part's finished," he said. He added in a coarse whisper, "Go put on your nightdress."

She pulled up to look at him. Seeing his seriousness, she gave a small, secret smile and hurried over to the dresser.

"Keep your back turned toward me," Ewan instructed as she opened her bureau. She could hear him making rustling noises. Undoing his trousers? It took everything in her not to turn around.

"Now," he said. "Undress slowly." She did, feeling light all over her body. "Wait just a moment, then put on the nightdress," he said.

Her body was now prickling with awareness. In the past, whenever she'd kissed Ewan or anyone else, her imagination had been an active participant, putting herself in the other person's head, or sometimes in a different space altogether. Often, she imagined the same kiss, but outside in an orchard, garnering the applause of the trees and flowers she liked best. Now, her imagination was quiet. Satisfied where it was, evidently.

Ewan made a noise that didn't quite sound like a word, but she took it as approval. When she picked up the nightdress, she put it on carefully, conscious of this newly discovered sense of her body as a vehicle of interest.

When she had the nightgown fully on, she was surprised to feel Ewan behind her again, kissing her neck and pulling her back toward the bed. He remained clothed, but less so than before. Without words, they reached an understanding that any more kissing would lead to no good. Then they settled down under the covers, Maud's head on Ewan's chest, until her heart slowed down enough that all she felt was a deep sort of peace. This was what it was to fall asleep with another person.

22.

*T*he next paperclipped set of journal entries was the thickest yet, each page razored out with surgical precision.

Spring to fall of 1919.

How naive she had been during these months. How she had struggled to understand. And all in Frede's tremendous, terrible wake. None of this would do for the Reader. Here were two recopying attempts clipped together—back-to-back failures.

Into the fire, all of it. This time, the burning was pure delight. Gone, gone, gone went the pages! What power there was in the flames at her feet. What freedom there was in her hands letting go.

23.

Leaskdale, Ontario
May 1919

Routine had finally begun to lay itself over Maud's days, covering the pain for longer and longer stretches. She still allowed herself ten minutes each day to cry out of the boys' earshot, and the rest of the time she thought mostly of keeping her feet moving. She hadn't yet managed to get back to her writing, but the way she felt after indulging the boys' energetic pleas for her to come play in the yard or see their latest magic trick told her that her heart was still working.

Today, she had plenty of cause for distraction. The garden needed attention, and in two days, the first of a brigade of visiting ministers would be coming to Leaskdale to preach. One after another for a full week of sermons. Ewan would pick each of them up from the train station at Uxbridge, ferry them back to the manse for supper, and attend their sermons the next day. Maud was explaining this to their maid Lily; it would mean an involved menu.

"Not a problem," Lily kept saying.

Maud said, "Of course, you have a scheduled holiday tomorrow—Toronto, is it?"

Lily nodded.

"That's fine. I can do most of the setting up myself so long as you help me with the prep work today."

This would mean no digging in her garden for the week. It was a good thing Maud had gotten an early start that spring, during those days when working with her hands was one of the few things keeping her on the right side of sanity.

"Sure," Lily responded. Her voice lowered. "You know, it's the minister coming second that everyone has been talking about. My friend got a look at him when she was visiting her cousin in the area, and she has been all talk of his shiny blond hair and glowing blue eyes. Quite the catch, it seems." Lily looked toward Maud and away from the lettuce she was washing.

"Is that so," Maud said, drying and stacking dishes.

"Her cousin says the sight of him is nothing compared to how he preaches. He has people coming to see him whose relatives thought they would never go to church again."

"I suppose you'll want to go to his sermon, then?"

"I'd like to."

"We'll need to work around it in the meal plan, but that's just fine." Maud turned back to the dishes. "I remember those days—" She stopped herself.

"Hmm?"

"Oh," said Maud. "A new minister in town. Girls wearing their newest dresses. We had some lookers in my day too. Some with sermons so fine you could feel a shiver go through everyone in the room at once."

"You mean Reverend Macdonald?"

"Ewan, yes. Others too." Maud picked up a plate to dry.

"I bet the visiting ministers will sure be excited to meet Reverend Macdonald's famous wife," Lily said.

Out of the corner of her eye, Lily seemed to be watching closely for Maud's response. Half the time they talked, Maud suspected Lily was performing some sort of test. One she could never be sure if she'd passed.

"I don't know about that," Maud responded eventually. "I only hope these visiting sermons all across the country have their intended effect. 'The Forward Movement,' they are calling it. 'Healing the wounds inflicted by war.'"

"Is that right," Lily said.

Maud nodded, keeping her eyes on her drying. "Ewan and I have been so concerned for his congregations, between the war and all that has come after it. Though I'm not sure how a troupe of traveling ministers can help, exactly. And I do worry that Ewan may be overshadowed, embarrassed in some way by these young men in town impressing his congregations. That he might worry about being replaced—"

Maud's hands stopped drying. She had gotten carried away, forgotten her audience. She had been talking as if it was Frede standing there with her in the kitchen.

"I didn't mean that," she said quickly. "I've been so tired these last few months, I don't know what I'm saying. It's a fine thing that they are coming. I'm sure Reverend Macdonald agrees."

"Of course," said Lily, her tone sobering to match Maud's. "A fine thing."

Then they both turned their heads toward the closed kitchen door. It had to be Ewan's footsteps they were hearing. They were too loud to belong to the boys. Both women's necks bowed in different directions; Maud picked up a stack of dishes and walked toward the cupboard; Lily stacked the silverware. Neither did anything to show her realization that Ewan had been standing there listening, not saying a word, and not quieting his footsteps as he shuffled away.

SUPPER HAD BEEN on the table for a full five minutes that night, and they were all waiting on Ewan. He always came down to supper before anyone else, smiling in a way that showed his dimples as Maud and the boys entered, ready with a few jokes to make them all laugh.

Maud called for him, but when he didn't come, she busied herself helping Lily take the serving dishes to the table.

"Go ahead and sit down, boys. I'll go check on your father."

Maud went to the top of the stairs. "Ewan? It's suppertime," she called down the hall. Hearing nothing, she returned to the table.

When she finally heard Ewan's footsteps start down the stairs a few minutes later, Maud felt her hands jump to life; she got to work serving the boys.

Ewan entered the dining room slowly. His chair screeched as he pulled it back.

"There you are, dear," Maud said.

"I've had a pretty bad headache," Ewan said.

The fork scraping stopped first, followed by a gradual halt of the boys' high-pitched banter. Ewan served himself without looking up.

"Oh dear, I'm sorry to hear it," Maud said eventually. Could this be his way of showing his upset over her comments in the kitchen?

"Sorry, Papa," echoed Stuart. Chester nodded and smiled; his swinging legs kicked the table a few times.

"Not your faults," Ewan said with a halfhearted smile. "Sorry to delay supper."

MAUD USUALLY LET Ewan be when he was working, but the day after the headache she made an exception. She waited until a few minutes before they needed to leave to pick up the first visiting minister, then gave a quick knock on the dining room door.

"Ewan, dear," she said as she approached the back of the

chair he used for both working and eating. "Are you feeling any better?"

"A little," he said.

"I'm glad to hear it. A headache is so unusual for you." She put her hand on his shoulder, which drew his eyes away from his work.

Ewan leaned into her a little, and her nerves began to dissipate. He may not have overheard what she'd said to Lily, after all. Or overheard it but thought nothing of it. It might have simply been a headache, there one day and gone the next.

Then her eyes focused on the paper in front of Ewan. She reached around him. "Ewan, what's this you are working on?"

"My sermon for next Sunday."

"You usually don't start on your sermons until the day before. I thought you'd be working on your introductory remarks for the visiting ministers."

"I thought I might start my sermon sooner than usual. Try to make it a memorable one."

"Your sermons are always memorable, dear." She came around to face him.

Ewan grunted, then looked up like he wasn't sure whether to believe her or not.

"We need to leave soon to pick up the reverend at Uxbridge." He rose slowly. "I'll get the car started. We don't want to be late."

WHILE THEY DROVE to Uxbridge station, Ewan's joy at being behind the wheel seemed to overcome any other feeling. From the minute they purchased the car from a dealer in Toronto, driving had been one of Ewan's deepest pleasures. He was in his element in a car, scaring Maud sometimes with his wild turns, asking rhetorically if she trusted him. She had said once that she might like to learn how to drive herself, and he had looked so disappointed that she had dropped the subject.

Ewan's talk turned cheerier than it had been in days the minute the motor started, and the effect persisted after they picked up their visitor.

The next day came the second minister—the one Lily had been looking forward to meeting. To Lily's dismay, this particular reverend was accompanied by a new bride.

Two nights of normal conversation with Ewan and their visitors made Maud realize how frequently she'd been holding her breath the few days before. The sudden swing in Ewan's mood from bad to good had her shaken. She counted on his steadiness.

As talk with the second minister and his cheerful young wife crept on toward one in the morning, the subject turned to Maud and her writing. Loosened up by good food and the long evening, the guests had started to pepper Maud with questions.

"How do you come up with characters?" "In just how many countries have your books been published?"

She tried to keep her answers short, but the questions only got bolder.

"And how do you manage all the money you must be making?" the reverend was asking now. "Ewan must have a lot of bookkeeping to do."

Maud was loath to reveal that she managed her own accounts—Ewan hated that fact—but she couldn't think of how else to respond. She turned to Ewan, hoping he would jump in, but he only yawned.

Then, with a sudden awkwardness that made Maud cringe, Ewan announced that he was off to bed, avoiding everyone's eyes as he rose from his chair.

Thankfully, neither of their guests seemed bothered by Ewan's exit. Without him there, Maud was at least able to answer their questions with less hesitation.

AS SHE CREPT upstairs later that night, Maud listened for any sound coming from the bedroom. Nothing unusual.

When Maud got up the nerve to enter the bedroom, it was dark; she assumed Ewan was asleep. Then her eyes adjusted.

The downright strangeness of what she saw startled her. Ewan sat upright in the bed. He had wrapped a red bandanna around his forehead and tied it in the back. She could not imagine where he'd found it. His eyes were open but glassy, fixed on the wall across from his head.

Maud tried a few questions: Could she get him anything? Would he like some tea?

Ewan gave a weak grunt and shook his head.

Maybe the bandanna was helping to relieve his headache. Or he might be feverish and using it as a cool compress.

Whatever it was, it startled her. Ewan was never sick. It seemed best to stay awake for a while and keep an eye on him. She moved to her small desk in their bedroom, adjusting the accordion-like screen she used for changing to block the light from the lamp. She shifted her desk chair enough that she could make sure Ewan was still breathing, but not so much that the odd bandanna was in view. She pulled out a novel. When Ewan had been breathing steadily for some time and appeared to have fallen asleep sitting up, she changed and got into bed.

In her dream that night, Maud was hurrying to dress for a presentation that she hadn't had a chance to rehearse, but there was no time for that, she was already late. When she opened the front door, it did not lead outside but to another, dimly lit room with shadowy furniture. She searched the walls until she found a door with only a hole for a handle. She opened the door and believed she was finally outside; her skin knew it by the hollow chill of a damp and moonless night. Then her eyes began to adjust, and no, this was only another room, darker than the last. She tried to feel for a door, hitting and tripping against furniture every few steps. Suddenly, a relief; she wasn't in the dark room anymore; she could feel Daffy's fur under her hand. All the surfaces she could feel were soft. With her body sweating, her limbs reached out for the cooler places in the sheets and found them. Her hands and feet spread long and ran into nothing. She opened her eyes.

The sky out the window had no blue in it, no sound of birds calling, which meant there was still time to sleep. She shifted, keeping one hand on Daffy for comfort. She turned toward Ewan's side of the bed and turned again, thinking she might still be asleep.

But no. She was awake, and Ewan was gone. She remembered his strange, sad expression the night before, the odd bandanna, and the whites of his eyes in the dark. Her stomach churned. She got up to make coffee, her hands shaking as she did.

For Ewan to be suddenly acting like a different man, on top of losing Frede—how could she be expected to withstand this?

Once again, she longed for an inkling of Anne's voice. Anne had a knack for supplying just the dose of humor needed to take the sting out of heavy subjects without diminishing them. But no words came.

The coffee sloshed out of the cup as Maud tried to pour, spilling off the counter and down the cabinets. Her grandmother's face came to mind, a single eyebrow raised, but Maud could not bring herself to reach for a dish towel.

"Mine are not problems a dish towel can solve," she whispered out loud, to no one.

SHE AND EWAN had no privacy until later that night, with a new set of visitors stowed away in bed. The red bandanna was back on Ewan's head when Maud came in the bedroom, but this time at least the light was on and he was studying a newspaper spread wide on his lap.

"Ewan—dear—how are you?" Maud asked.

Ewan mumbled something she couldn't make out and closed his eyes. She walked toward the bed.

"Ewan, you've never not answered me this way. Are you feverish?" She put a few fingers to his forehead, mindful of his bandanna. When she touched him, he opened his eyes, seeming to relax a little.

"Do you remember all the kind things you used to say to me, Maud, the way you used to look at me?" Ewan murmured.

"What do you mean, Ewan?" Maud asked.

"Never mind," he said, furrowing his brow in an exaggerated way that struck her as something one of the boys would do.

"What is this on your head?" Maud asked, gesturing toward the bandanna.

"I found it in an old box in the attic," Ewan said. "It helps my headaches to tie it tight."

She felt the sides of his face. "I think you'd better consult the doctor about these headaches. I could have him come by in the morning."

"That won't be necessary," Ewan said. He looked down at the blanket and sighed.

"No? But, Ewan—why not?"

"No doctor will do me any good. You must believe me, Maud. I'm too tired to explain, so you must believe me."

Maud watched as Ewan folded his newspaper, lowered himself to the bed, and pulled the covers up with visible effort. He closed his eyes.

Maud's heart started to race. Her dream from the night before returned to her with a sick sense of foreboding. She felt that same way now. What was she meant to do inside that fearsome house? How would she ever find her way out?

"All right, then," she said finally. "You rest now. But tomorrow—tomorrow I must know what this is. I must know what I can do to help."

THE FOLLOWING MORNING, as Ewan walked out the door to chauffeur yet another visiting minister to Uxbridge, he told Maud he would stop by the doctor on his way home.

"Doc called it a nervous breakdown, not an illness or anything of that sort," Ewan announced when he arrived back at the manse. He said it loudly, not quite looking at Maud or at Stuart, who had hurried into the entryway to greet him. With slow steps, Ewan walked toward the dining room. "I'm going to work on my sermon."

Maud felt a pull in her legs to follow him but stopped herself. She worried that if she tried to move, she might topple over. She needed to sit. She needed Frede.

A nervous breakdown? Other people had nervous breakdowns. People who were young and risking it big in cities, people's long-lost sisters spoken of in hushed tones. Not fathers with mouths to feed. And certainly not small-town ministers!

Ewan always had been the steady one of their pair. The one who stayed loving and dependable while her moods vacillated like the weather.

Maud told Stuart in the most normal voice she could manage to run along and play outside with Chester.

Not a second later, she heard Lily's voice calling, "Mrs. Macdonald?"

How had she forgotten about Lily? Only for a moment, but still. And Lily had ears like an elephant. Why had Ewan spoken so loudly? Lily was known for her penchant for gossip. She could have this news about the minister's breakdown spread around town in no time. Their lives would never be the same again.

After a few quick steps to the kitchen, Maud let out her breath at the sight of Lily unpacking eggs and milk. She had been at the store; she had just gotten in.

"Ah, you have the shopping finished," Maud said.

"I'm behind," Lily said, "what with all these big eaters, one after another."

"Our guests, Lily. Today is the last of them."

"Well, I'd appreciate your help with supper."

"Of course; I said I would help. Tell me what's on the menu, and we'll divide it up."

They made quick work of the meal. As she chopped and stirred, Maud kept her eyes on Lily for any sign of suspicion and her ears on the dining room for any odd noise. She felt tired, but this was no time for relenting.

THE LAST OF the visiting ministers had the good sense to go to bed early. Maud told Lily the dishes could wait.

Maud reached the bedroom only minutes after Ewan, who was changing behind the closet door.

"Dear," she said, her eyes on the ceiling, "I'm at my wit's end. I've wanted to give you time and space. But I cannot wait any longer. You must tell me more about what's happened at the doctor."

Ewan took his time emerging from the closet. When he finally spoke, he sounded so sad that she momentarily regretted asking. "Doc diagnosed a nervous breakdown, like I said," Ewan said. "He said I should go away for a bit, breathe some different air."

"Well." Maud took a breath. "You hadn't told me the part about the fresh air. It's a good plan; it will just be a matter of a few arrangements. Did he give you any recommendations on the type of place? We'll have to find ministers to supply for us, but there are plenty available these days. I can make some inquiries tomorrow, and we can start working on travel arrangements—"

"I only wish it could be that easy."

"Ewan—" Maud's voice caught in her throat.

"I'm sorry, Maud," he said.

"Ewan, help me understand." Maud took a few long breaths, trying to still the shake in her hands. She started over. "When you said the other night that no doctor would do you any good, I didn't understand what you meant. It sounded like it might be something more than headaches."

"It's simply a fact," Ewan said with a resignation that made her concern grow deeper. "Something I know to be true."

"A fact?"

"The fact is that I'm lost."

"You're lost." She couldn't be sure she'd heard him correctly.

"Eternally, I mean. I mean there's no hope for me in the next life."

"Oh, Ewan." Maud nearly laughed. "Is that all?" She felt her abdomen release in relief. Ewan—literal to a fault—couldn't harbor such a belief for long.

"I mean it, Maud."

"You can't possibly believe such a thing."

She was about to say more when a memory edged back into her consciousness. A conversation they'd had years ago, on their honeymoon in Scotland. Ewan had told her about a preacher from his youth with eyes that bore into each soul of his congregation. "Fixed on the idea of predestination." Ewan's words had been light enough, but it was not like Ewan to bring up the past. It had stuck with him, what that preacher said.

Maud's voice grew softer. "We've talked about this, how neither of us believes in that blasphemous idea that the old preachers preached, of people predestined to a hell of fire and brimstone. 'With God, all things are possible.' And 'it is with your mouth that you profess your faith and are saved.'"

"I've tried my hardest to believe otherwise," Ewan said now. "Tried to come as close to God as I could, being a minister. I've wrestled, but it's no use. It's all I can think about these days." He lumbered into bed, dragging the sheet halfway across him.

"Wrestled—what do you mean exactly?"

"Well, there was a while I thought I was mistaken, or I never would have—" He looked at her. "Maud, I never would have had children if I hadn't convinced myself otherwise. I never would have involved you in this."

Involved her in this? In a single breath, he seemed to be calling into question their entire relationship. Their decision to have children.

Maud's stomach churned; she thought she might be sick. "When did you first have these thoughts?"

"As far back as my childhood, I suspected the truth. And—" He stopped.

"And?"

"That winter I went to study in Scotland, after I proposed to you. You know I came back early, without a degree. But I never told you the whole of it. I was a failure, Maud. I arrived full of my success in Cavendish, full of your belief in me, but then I met my classmates, and they all knew so much. I couldn't bring myself to attend my lectures. It was then that I felt sure—God had turned against me. You must have known something was the matter."

"I remember those strange postcards . . ." She wasn't sure what she knew anymore, then or now.

"I tried telling myself it was the place; I needed to get out of that place. When I came back, I was still a minister, and you were still around, and mother was still giving me her encouragement, and I made myself believe again in my own future." He shook his head.

"Ewan." It was all Maud could manage. Looking away for a moment, she got a glimpse of Ewan's toes sticking out from the bottom of the sheet. Bigger versions of Chester's toes.

She started walking the length of the room. Eventually, she stopped at her dresser drawer and opened it, searching under her clothes. An idea had occurred to her, and now it was all she could think about.

"Ewan, you've hardly been getting any sleep. Did I ever tell you I had a prescription for sleeping medication back on the Island when I had those restless winters? I've saved it. It might help." She paused and took the pills from her dresser. "I'm not sure what to make of all this. But let's take a night to digest."

Ewan didn't respond right away. But when she handed him the pills, he took them compliantly. "Thanks, dear," he whispered before closing his eyes.

Once she brought herself to settle down beside Ewan, Maud told herself it would all be all right. She'd been through bouts of melancholy herself and come back around. Why shouldn't she permit Ewan the same? He should be able to have a few days of headaches without her losing her bearings. The sleep medication could be just the thing for him, making those pesky fantasies about doom and destiny recede like a bad dream.

But try as she might, she could not convince herself that Ewan's confession had been a passing episode. No—what Ewan had said tonight felt like a bucket of black paint that had the potential to coat their entire lives. Was this a premonition, or her imagination getting the better of her?

Regardless, now her imagination was off to the races. She pictured Ewan locked away in this very bedroom for the remainder of their lives, the awful bandanna attached to his forehead like a flag signaling defeat to anyone she dared let enter their home. He would grow fat and morose on meals delivered by Lily. So many explanations would be due—to his congregations, to her women's circles, to her volunteer organizations, to her publishers, to their relations back on the Island. None could be told the truth. She would have to do some of her best work, contriving explanations bland enough not to elicit questions but elaborate enough to be believed. Worst of all, she pictured the boys begging to know what was the matter with their father, stashed away behind lock and key. Pulling on her shirtsleeve and asking her questions she couldn't bear to answer.

None of this could happen. She wouldn't let it. She was a resourceful woman—she simply needed a plan.

24.

"S tella." Maud opened her arms again. "You can't know how good it is to see you. Six years—can you believe it?"

Maud was speaking to Stella but watching Ewan. He'd managed a polite greeting before returning to the bench at the train station where he and Maud had been waiting for Stella, his winter cap pulled down low over his forehead—never mind that it was the middle of summer—and sitting hunched so that his belly rounded out over his pants, showing his recent weight gain. He had a newspaper open on his lap—but the way he was looking at it! Maud rotated her body so Ewan would be fully out of Stella's sight.

Frede was the only one of the Campbell sisters who had taken a liking to Ewan, with Stella liking him the least of any. What must Stella be thinking now?

"I can't hardly! Wonderful to see you!" Stella said over Maud's shoulder, swaying side to side a few times in their hug. "Even after the most tragic of times, with Frede," she added only a little more quietly as she pulled away. "Now, is there anyplace to get a decent hot meal around here? When does Ewan's train depart?"

"His doesn't leave for a few hours," Maud said, "but our connection leaves for Uxbridge in not too long. There's decent food on the train—much better than at the roadhouse next to the station, and we don't have time to go out in Toronto. What do you say to a meal on the rails? When I bring you back in a few weeks to catch the night train we can be sure to leave plenty of time for a steak supper."

"Well, all right," responded Stella, doing nothing to hide her disappointment. "Although you should know I've had my fill of train food the past few days. When do we head to the gate?"

"Might as well be now," said Maud, lifting the heaviest of Stella's luggage. "It's just down those stairs and to the left. Ewan will be just fine here, won't you, Ewan?" she called.

Ewan looked up from under the brim of his cap to give Maud a nod.

Stella took her other two bags and walked a few steps toward Ewan. "Have a fine trip, then, Ewan! I'll take good care of your girl, so don't you go worrying. We'd probably bore you stiff with talk of the old times, anyway. Nice that you're off to be with your own folks, I say."

It looked like Ewan might have said something in response, but Maud couldn't be sure. Stella had already started lumbering toward the staircase.

Maud had just reached Ewan's side when Stella's voice barreled up from the steps. "Come on, now, Maud—you're the one with the directions!"

"Coming!" Maud called in the direction of Stella, then turned back to Ewan. "Give my love to Flora. I do believe this trip will help, Ewan. Please, you must try to believe it. Allow your mind a chance to change."

Maud kissed Ewan's still lips, then waited a few seconds before starting to walk away.

"Try to have a good time," Ewan said after she'd taken a few steps. "Like we used to with Frede." His voice was chalky, but sincere.

Maud stopped walking and looked back at him. "I'll try if you do," she said. "Please make the best of this trip. Doctor's orders." She managed a lift of her cheekbones that was almost a smile.

"I NEVER KNEW Ewan had family in Massachusetts," Stella said as she settled against the crushed red velvet booth in the train's dining car. After brushing a few crumbs off the seat, Stella kicked her feet up to rest on the opposing booth, moving the tablecloth a little to cover her legs. She sighed.

Maud scooted a few inches away from Stella's legs and their characteristic bounce.

"Ewan's half sister, Flora, lives in East Braintree," Maud said, signaling for the waiter. "Along with her husband. Nice folks. Ewan hasn't seen her in quite some time." Maud was sure she'd mentioned Flora in her letters.

"That's right." Stella leaned in and pinched Maud's forearm, with no indication that she actually remembered. "Say, remember that grand time we had in Boston back before the war, when the fancy publisher invited you for a visit and you agreed to let your old cousin Stell tag along? 'Course you never would have done it if you hadn't gotten so guilty about all that money you spent on Frede's degree." She chuckled. "Guilt or no guilt, that publisher just about spoiled us silly— I'll never forget watching a taxicab pull up for us. And that meal you had after the Harvard-Yale game; I was almost green with envy to hear about it."

Maud smiled. Different as Stella was from Frede, they still shared a history. "You're right—I lived so much in those few weeks. I would never trade them."

"And to think, your soon-to-be husband had family right there. Of course, you were still putting him off back then. How long after that was it that you finally decided to marry him?"

"It wasn't as simple as that, Stella." Maud gave a pointed look, the kind that Stella often made necessary.

"Now, I didn't mean anything," Stella said, adjusting a hair clip that had started to slide out of place. "Touchy today," she added in a loud whisper, her head tilted like she was talking to someone beside her.

Maud turned her attention to the tea that had just arrived. When she finished stirring in milk, she picked up her purse and weeded through it, pulling out a novel. She smiled at Stella as though the silence had come on naturally and opened her book.

The minute the food came and Maud put her book down to eat, Stella spoke again. "So I trek all this way by train for my first visit in years, and Ewan heads off for his own summer holiday, does he? Not that I'm taking it personally," she said. "Seems he could use it," she added under her breath.

So Stella had noticed the change in Ewan. Of course she had.

"A holiday on doctor's orders," Maud said. "Ewan's been suffering from some terrible headaches that have been keeping him up at night. He's not quite himself. It's lack of sleep that's most to blame, I think. So we're following orders—a few weeks off from work and a trip away to new surroundings, staying with Flora. It should be just the thing. He'll see a specialist in Boston, too, and hopefully get some medications."

Maud was watching Stella closely, searching for signs of skepticism. But by the time Maud finished speaking, Stella was looking down at her own knees, bending and flexing them with a wince and a grunt.

"I could use a specialist myself," Stella said, "what with these knees I have. I tell you, they never stop acting up nowadays. Not to mention my head, especially in the heat. If Ewan gets any good headache medication, you'd better let me know. I sure hope it won't be too hot at your house in

Leaskdale. I've gotten used to the cool Los Angeles summer nights, come to depend on them. And I don't know but ever since I crossed the border into Canada, I've felt the specific gravity rising and rising. It has had such an impact on my nerves."

Maud covered her mouth with bent fingers, stifling a laugh.

Then, instinctively, she felt her body turn heavy. There would be no next letter to Frede to share the joke.

CHESTER HAD BEEN too young during Stella's last visit to remember her, and Stuart hadn't been born. But Stella's laugh was just like Aunty Fred's to them. All the Campbell girls had that laugh, with its hearty, broken-up notes that got wheezy as they went on. The combined effect of Stella's laugh and presents from California won the boys over immediately.

"Aunty Stell," Chester said the next night at supper, "tell us another of your stories."

The meal was Stella at her best—mashed potatoes with the flavor Maud never could get out of them, roasted turnips, pot roast, and three kinds of cake.

"Oh now, boys, you know your mother's the real storyteller." Stella paused, her half smile growing full. "But I suppose I'm not so bad either. Has she ever told you the one about my brother and the barn?"

"No," Chester said, leaning forward in his chair.

"Well." Stella's voice was full enough for an auditorium. "Let's be glad for that, because it gives your Aunty Stell something to tell."

Stella got them going until they were all laughing together, the boys' high voices complementing Stella's and Maud's like parts to a song. The laughter built on itself as Maud told a story, then Stella again.

It was almost enough to make Maud feel like her old self,

sliding in and out of stories with Frede and Stella years ago in this same dining room soon after she and Ewan had moved into the Leaskdale manse. Also, she remembered, hoping for children. And now she had them, two of them, and their smiles were unencumbered, and they had all their dreams still inside of them.

"You boys go on up and ready yourselves for bed," Maud said when Stuart's eyes started to close. It was far past their usual bedtime. "I'll come check on you in a few minutes."

"I'm exhausted too," Stella said with a yawn. "Your mother kept me up too late last night, rehashing old losses and solving the family's problems. I'll be right up after you." She rose and ruffled both boys' hair. "You boys," she said. "You remind me of my brother."

To Maud, after the boys had gone upstairs, Stella spoke more softly. "I still can't quite believe he's gone. That any of them are. Being in California made it hard to realize fully. It will be hard on me to see Park Corner next week." Stella cleared her throat. "You'd better be thankful, me going all by my lonesome to sort things out."

"I cannot leave the boys right now, not while Ewan's away. But I'm happy to help in any way I can." Maud's voice cracked, and Stella's expression softened.

"I miss her too," Stella said.

The tears that came next were full, clean ones. Maud found her head on Stella's shoulder, taken over by a hug full of warmth she hadn't expected. She'd forgotten how well the Campbells could hug.

Maud decided that she'd made the right decision, spending the money to bring Stella out. Stella might be a sad ember of Frede's former glow radiating through the house, but Maud clung to that ember. She didn't dare confide her full worries about Ewan or her full heartsickness over Frede, but she and

Stella could share some good laughs and dote on the boys. Maud wanted the boys to have all the family relations they could—especially now, with their most cherished relative gone.

Maud felt a clutch in her chest, remembering how hard it had been to explain Frede's loss to Chester and Stuart on that awful snowy day she'd returned to the manse. How Chester hadn't been able to look at her. How Stuart's lower lip had quivered. She could tell the change in Ewan was affecting the boys now too.

It had been wonderful to laugh around the table again.

ONCE THE BOYS and Stella were settled for the night, Maud went to her bedroom, guilty for the relief she felt at being alone. She was tired but couldn't think of sleep yet— not when she had this time to herself and an uplift in her spirits from the evening with Stella.

After Ewan left, she'd brought a set of folders up to the bedroom to sort through for writing material. She pulled out a folder labeled "War News" and started making a pile to discard. She hadn't made it very far when a headline grabbed her attention. It brought her right back to those heart-thumping days when she'd scoured the newspaper as soon as it arrived, marking any progress it reported on her map of Europe. She remembered the way she had waited for Ewan to bring home the paper, pacing the floors in the bedroom until she heard the creak of the front door opening, then studying Ewan's footsteps in hopes of deciphering that day's news before he got to her.

It wasn't all that different now, but instead of war news, it was word from Ewan that she was waiting for. She shook her head. "No news is good news," her grandmother would say.

For the first time since losing Frede, Maud pulled out the spadework for her new novel. She'd promised herself she wouldn't dip into her savings if she could help it. That money was for the boys' educations (and her own peace of mind). She couldn't put off writing any longer.

She'd already decided that it would be another novel in the Anne series—the last, she hoped. Her publishers were demanding it. But there was not much more to be said about Anne and Gilbert. Their middle-aged happiness had started to bore her silly, if she was being honest. So this novel would focus on someone new: Anne and Gilbert's youngest daughter, Rilla, nearly fifteen at the start of the war.

Maud read over her notes for the first few chapters.

Gertrude Oliver. A good name. She would have boarded with Anne and Gilbert's family the past year and shared a room with Rilla. Old enough to have some wisdom but young enough for the reader to allow her to talk about dreams.

Rilla would be busy getting ready for a party and worried over the sensation she hoped to create with her hair and dress. She would tell Gertrude Oliver about her dream of showing up to the party in her bedclothes.

"Speaking of dreams," Gertrude Oliver would say.

Gertrude would tell Rilla about her own dream of gray waves breaking over faraway fields. How she was sure they would come nowhere nearby. But then the waves would break at Gertrude Oliver's feet, and they would wash away everything—the whole town. When she tried to draw back, the edge of her dress would be wet with blood.

And how would a girl like Rilla respond to a speech like this? Maud smiled. Rilla would only be miserable over the possibility that Gertrude's dream predicted bad weather for her party.

"Incorrigible fifteen!" Gertrude Oliver would respond. "I don't think there is any danger that it foretells anything so awful as that." Maud closed her notebook. Good to end the scene with a little humor.

Maud was struck by memories of how she used to laugh to herself, writing Anne's lines. She couldn't remember the last time she had laughed out loud at her own writing. But this was not a place to dwell. What did it matter if it had become rote to spin turns of phrase her readers would appreciate? The point was that her readers would appreciate them. Nor could she be expected to have the same amount of affection for poor Rilla that she'd had for Anne. Anne was an original. A dear friend—at least, she used to be.

FOR THE REST of Stella's visit, Maud slept better than she had since before Frede died. She kept working on *Rilla* at night. After a few days, letters from Ewan started to arrive; each said he was a little better. He was enjoying visiting with Flora, and his headaches were starting to subside, just as the Leaskdale doctor had hoped.

Maud made sure they left early enough for Stella's departing train to make it to the steak supper she'd promised. The restaurant was the kind Maud liked, with white tablecloths and more glasses than they could ever need on the table.

Supper started out well enough, but the last of Maud's patience was used up during the meal. Not only did Stella never say thank you, for meal or trip, but she picked a choice moment, with Maud's fork raised midair on its way to her mouth, to announce precisely how many mosquito bites had been inflicted on her during her stay at Leaskdale—some of which, she was sure, had come while she was sleeping. Topping it off was the request Stella shouted from the train steps as she boarded, loud enough for people two hundred yards away to hear: "You must be sure to tell me if Ewan has any success with the medications for his head!"

A half-hearted wave was the best Maud could manage in farewell.

25.

The grandfather clock in the Leaskdale parlor struck a quarter past the hour again, sounding its four descending notes. The same no matter the day, no matter the hour. Reassuring to Maud now in its constancy.

Ewan was out, having left for a night to attend the Toronto Exhibition with an old friend. Maud and Ewan had gone to the Exhibition together in the past, but this year Maud declined, explaining that she hated the idea of leaving the boys just then. Or perhaps it was the idea of supervising Ewan.

"You go, though," she'd said. "Doctor's orders were to get out and about whenever you can."

True, this was one of the top recommendations given by the specialist Ewan had seen during his time in Boston. Not that the so-called specialist had earned much of Maud's confidence with his unsatisfying attempts at diagnosis.

"I am inclined to think that his thoughts of eternal doom are simple melancholia. On the other hand, they might be an indication of something deeper, like manic-depressive insanity," the specialist relayed to Maud over the phone, using the same tone he might use to deliver a report on the weather. "He does say he's been having these thoughts for quite some time. Aside from getting plenty of water, which should help with the headaches, and encouraging him to get out and about, the most important things are not to argue with Reverend Macdonald on the subject of his phobia, and not to frighten him with either of these potential diagnoses. But do take close care of him. Keep your eye out for any signs of things worsening. And most important of all, make sure he takes the barbiturate and bromide medications I've prescribed, at the times of day they are indicated."

Maud must become Ewan's mother, in other words. A mother to her own husband.

She had succeeded in becoming one for the near month since Ewan had returned to the manse, making things as easy on him as she could. But now, with Ewan away for the night, Maud itched for a distraction.

"A horrible idea," Maud said out loud to the thought that came next. The boys were in bed, and she was sitting at the parlor table in her robe and slippers. "It won't make anything better."

But she went upstairs anyway and pulled out a stack of books from the lockbox—her journal from her Cavendish school days and the blank books for recopying.

Since Frede had died, Maud hadn't recopied any more entries. She had started reading back over her oldest surviving journal a few times and couldn't quite believe it was herself, this girl who named people Snip and Snap and worried over recitals and arithmetic. Each time she had picked up the first formal volume for recopying, she'd put it aside again. But tonight, it might be just the diversion she needed.

Maud turned back to the first page of her original journal and read her own words under her breath. "I am going to begin a new kind of diary." She had been a few months shy of fifteen. "I have kept one of a kind for years—ever since I was a tot of nine. But I burned it to-day. It was so silly I was ashamed of it. And it was also very dull."

Well, she was honest if nothing else.

The thought of her childhood journal lost to the fire still

hurt. She remembered how long it had taken to burn in the kitchen stove, second after second for her to imagine how much might be salvaged if she pulled it out now, or now.

Maud ran her finger along the bound edges of the ten blank books, identical in size and color. She spread the first volume open in front of her and turned forward several pages to where she had left off recopying. Immediately, her mind returned to that dreadful night when she'd gotten the telegram about Frede, copying an entry that called herself "Pollie," of all things. She almost closed the book again. Then one line caught her eye; she blinked a few times and read it over: "Snip calls law a dirty trade." She thought of Nate, living out west with his wife and children and practicing law—so happily, by his telling. What would he say if she were to show this entry to him now?

The question piqued her interest. Once she started recopying, she did not stop for hours. The effect was so much greater than she had anticipated. Self-contained dramas and long walks all over Cavendish. It was hers, this time; she had lived it once, and now she could live it over again.

She should be able to manage fifteen minutes of recopying every day. Fifteen minutes entirely away from whatever worry the day brought, from dosing out pills to Ewan to soothing the boys' fears. She could relive parts of her past that were not clouded by the present. Recopying might do her some real good.

26.

The irregularity of Ewan's inhales caught Maud's ear from where he lay close beside her. Some had a whistle at the end. Some had a chortle in the middle that she recognized from the few times she'd heard her grandmother snore. Maud counted the length between the breaths, wondering if Ewan was altogether healthy. Could he have something the matter with his throat? But this counting exercise only caused her to become more fully awake. Which was not her intent, since the sky was still black, and she could feel the tired ache behind her eyes and a yawn in her throat. She tried instead to match her own breathing to Ewan's. But this only got her thinking about the difference between his loud breaths and her quiet ones. Would Ewan always snore? And if so, would lying awake like this be a daily occurrence when she and Ewan were married?

She had almost slowed her heartrate down sufficiently to return to sleep when another, long chortle issued from Ewan's mouth.

Enough.

Gingerly, she released Ewan's hand from where she was holding it up against her chest. How natural it was for a hand to hold and to be held. How naked her hand felt now without his around it.

Ewan's fingers softened in a way that assured her he was in a deep sleep. She moved out from under his arm and felt the sudden separation between their bodies as a dull ache through all her limbs. But here was another snore that sent her heart beating fast, and she knew there was no hope of returning to sleep.

She dressed in a hurry and went outside to meet the sky of early morning, now more gray than black. She started out on a well-known path. Maud didn't think much beyond the sound of her own footsteps until the deep gray relented into a clear, light blue. Then, with less ache behind her eyes and more energy in her gait, she could start to sort out what she felt about Ewan, parsing what had occurred the night before.

Yes. The word flew at her like a bird at a window, landing with a thud. Ewan had asked her to marry him now. She had said yes.

What did marrying now mean? In a week? After a few months? Ewan's eyes had been urgent. Serious.

Oh, does it really need to be sorted out now? What an exquisite night it was. Might you just dwell in the afterglow of it all, for a few more hours at least?

It had been an exquisite night. Maud felt longing brew again in her stomach. Excitement and fear are close cousins, she knew.

I am quite convinced now that Ewan really is the hero of our imaginings, with poetry and melancholic eyes. A bit shorter and rounder in the face, less profound in his speech, but does any of that matter so much?

It did not matter. Not to Maud, and not to Anne either.

Maud had begun to sketch out the start of Anne's turn in her feelings for Gilbert in the sequel. Anne's realization that romance can emerge from a friendship, like a rose emerging from an ordinary green nub. A friendship was not Maud and Ewan's beginning, but their romance had been just as much a slow bloom—one now at the height of summer.

Still, Maud's early morning unease would not relent, and Anne's interjections were aggravating it further.

Anne was precisely the problem, Maud realized as she passed an old home that she had always loved for its tall rafters and the stained-glass window at its front. Anne wouldn't exit Maud's mind. Anne's next chapters compelled her.

Maud had no idea if her first book would sell. It could be a dismal failure. But success mattered far less than continuing did. If she didn't get a foothold, if she didn't take the momentum that came with the first publication and use it for the next book, she feared she might give up writing altogether.

With this thought, Maud felt the wash of excitement she'd been bathing in since Ewan's arrival the night before drain from her body.

Writing was what she cared about most. It was the one thing she could not bear to lose.

What she wanted revealed itself in the rhythmic landings of her footsteps on the path of fallen leaves. She wanted to wait a few more years before marrying, before having children. She wanted to write first, and do these things second. The reverse order, she feared, would sweep her up in mothering and the ministry, squandering any chance of becoming who she might become.

But how could she ever put this to Ewan?

You must simply tell him.

Tell Ewan that her writing surpassed him in importance? Mention it casually over breakfast?

I told Mrs. Rachel Lynde the precise truth about her, didn't I? That she was fat, clumsy, and devoid of imagination? Nothing you say to Ewan could be any worse than that. And somehow, I think she respected me more for it, in the end.

Some tactics work better in fiction than in real life.

What makes you think Ewan won't understand?

This, she realized, was the mouse buried in the pudding, the truth she most wanted to hide—both from Ewan and from herself. As much as she knew he cared for her, Ewan might never fully support her writing, or understand it either.

She needed to grow more solid in her career before marrying him. She must wait until her writing became a mature tree, self-sustaining and immovable.

You might at least give him the chance of knowing your full self, with all your ambitions, and coming to accept them. Tell him you are worried that he can't understand, but you need him to try. He has ambitions too, don't forget. He has that speech coming up.

True enough. But there was no question it would hurt Ewan deeply to tell him not only the importance of her dreams, but also her lack of faith in his understanding them. What if they couldn't recover? What if he left the house today and never returned? She thought of the weight of his arm, wrapped around her at night. The warm press of his body against hers.

Maybe he will leave, and maybe he won't. But the most important thing is that you will have opened the book of your heart and allowed him to read it. That idea has its own romance, doesn't it? He could turn into a full confidant.

A full confidant. Some part of her had always wanted this in a husband, even if she had not believed it possible.

An ideal that may have less to do with being understood than with being revealed.

Perhaps so. Maud turned around now, steeled and ready to return home.

27.

*T*he worst of 1919 remained in her original journal notes from that year.

How few days in a life end up truly mattering? If only there was some telling in advance what days those might be. A power reserved for the Lord—and the novelist.

On a single day, she had written the first lines of Anne, and one of the men who would most influence her life had entered it.

On another day, that same man would say the worst words imaginable to her in the bedroom they shared, and a second man would enter. The pages in her hands described that day, in the plainest of terms.

Her hands shook as she reread. One last time before ensuring the safe disposal of these pages into the flames.

28.

Maud's jaw was set tight. She couldn't believe the words that had just come from Ewan's lips. A mouth she had kissed more times than she could count turned ugly and terrifying by the carelessness with which he had just spoken about Chester and Stuart.

"Family used to be everything to you!" Maud screamed.

"I've already failed my family," Ewan answered bleakly from where he lay flat on his back in the center of the bed.

Maud took a breath, steadied herself. When she continued speaking, her voice was quieter, but she hated its desperation. "It cannot continue this way. We have two children. We are responsible for them, Ewan. They need us—both of us."

Maud had come into the bedroom to dress for the Mission Band quilt-making event later that day and found Ewan in bed, with the awful red bandanna returned to his head. It was past noon, and he was half-undressed.

"Yes," Ewan said now, "and I wish from the bottom of my heart we never had them."

He had turned to his side so he faced fully away from Maud.

Maud watched Ewan's back for several minutes, frozen.

This was a nightmare come to life. How could this be

the man she married? The man who wanted children even more than she did, who adored and supported them every day since they were born. Had it all been an act?

No. It couldn't have been. Ewan was no actor. That had been plain from the day they met, with his sheepish eyes and stilted speech.

It didn't matter. Whether an act or not, the Ewan of their past was gone. In a single sentence, he had trampled the part of himself that she loved most. The part she had come to depend on.

But just who was the Ewan of their future—this man who had just wished their children out of their lives without so much as a sigh of regret? This was not a man Maud knew at all.

A fierce sort of protectiveness started up inside her. A Mother Hen with her chicks. She cringed at her old, happy metaphor entering back into her consciousness at such a serious moment. But a Mother Hen she had become, providing for and protecting her boys with all the warmth and skill she had in her.

What Mother Hen needed to protect her chicks from their own father? To make sure they never felt the depths of his indifference, to make sure they knew, always, how much they mattered?

Maud waited until she realized that Ewan had no plans to move or speak again. Then she checked the bedroom door to make sure it was locked. She folded herself into the small sofa they kept in their bedroom with her knees to her chest and sobbed. The noise she made felt disconnected from her body; after a while, the sounds slowed and subsided.

They'd had such a good few weeks after Ewan had returned from the Toronto Exhibition. But the last few days had been terrible. Ewan kept asking for more medication, a few more doses; his head just wasn't right. For the past twenty-four hours, he had hardly seemed to move a muscle. His moaning lethargy had worn Maud's self-control down to a nub.

Lean on each other, Frede had instructed on her deathbed. But how was Maud meant to lean on a man who relied on an increasing number of pills to get himself through the day?

She imagined rising up and hitting Ewan as hard as she could in the face with one of the couch cushions.

She shook her head, and the tears started again. She told herself this was Ewan's delusion talking—his idea that he and the boys were fated to hell. He wasn't wishing away the boys, he was wishing away their eternal damnation.

Even if true, it didn't lessen how much his words hurt. It also did nothing to change the need to protect her boys from becoming casualties of their father's illness. But how was she meant to do this alone? Without Frede, without a single friend in whom Maud would dare confide something so awful?

Maud pulled a tasseled sofa pillow up toward her ear, hoping to mute the sound of Ewan's breathing, and curled up even tighter.

Ewan's voice seemed to come from directly above her head when he finally spoke again.

"Well," he said, "now I am late to meet Smith."

For the next few moments, with her head still under the pillow, Maud's mind rolled over that word, "smith." Black-smith, silversmith. The Smiths were a family from the Zephyr congregation. But Ewan wouldn't be preaching at Zephyr today.

Then it dawned on her. Captain Edwin Smith was coming to supply for Ewan tomorrow, one in a long chain of supply ministers they'd had the past few months while Ewan was ill. The captain was one of Ewan's old friends from seminary. He planned to stay at the manse with them until Wednesday. And that meant Ewan's state could not stay hidden. Maud's stomach turned over at the thought. She rolled onto her back and thought she might be sick. So far it was only the specialist in Boston who knew the whole of it; she'd been so careful. But with Ewan leaving the house in his current state, there was only so much she could say to explain. Most of the time, when the delusion reappeared, Ewan was more or less subdued. But given what had just occurred, today he might say anything.

Maud buried her head again under the tasseled pillow. She lay half-asleep until the sound of the front door closing behind Ewan made her legs jerk.

Up, she instructed herself.

Then she was at her dresser, inspecting her face in the mirror. The half sleep had taken away some of the redness from her tears, but she could make out most of a floral pattern from the pillow embroidery on one cheek. She applied powder quickly, then hurried to her closet to replace her wrinkled dress. She was late already for the Mission Band charity meeting, and no one in that group was the charitable sort.

"Boys," she called out as normally as she could manage, opening the bedroom door, "are you ready? We've promised to go help make that quilt for the hospital."

THE AFTERNOON LIGHT on the walk home from the Mission Band meeting was nice enough to be startling. Maud stayed a ways behind the boys as they passed the neighbors' wide front lawns. She watched them run to find and inspect sticks, raking them through the fallen leaves and competing over them while the sun painted streaks of their hair orange down from the crowns of their heads.

Even now the outdoors could take her full attention. But instead of filling her up as it usually did, this walk outside emptied her. She felt flimsy inside all this light, as if the slightest touch would ripple her body like a pebble in still water. She wrapped her arms around her torso, holding it in place.

As soon as she was back home and had the boys safely occupied making supper with Lily, she went to her desk and took out the journal notes she had started to keep, a cruder journaling practice she'd begun now that she had her formal volumes for rewriting. She found herself spelling out each of Ewan's terrible words from earlier that day, wringing herself out in the old way. At some point, she heard the front door open, followed by the muffled sound of voices.

Never mind. She had to keep writing.

When she finished, she felt easier in her movements. She assuaged her guilt with the thought that these notes never needed to end up in the formal volume. The Reader never had to know.

Nearing the bedroom door, she grew conscious for the first time of laughter, distinctly male and bellowing up from the first floor.

CAPTAIN EDWIN SMITH sat smiling in Ewan's armchair, his arms spread wide against the chair's arms and his head resting against its back. His eyes were mostly closed, which made Maud think of a jungle cat, feigning rest, fooling most.

When he opened his eyes enough to notice Maud and Lily bringing in tea, Edwin's hands pushed against the arms of the chair, and all at once he was on his feet. The deliberateness of Edwin's gestures—the confident masculinity of them—was such a contrast to Ewan's recent meekness that it startled her.

"The famous authoress," Edwin said to Maud with a bow of his head.

"Good to see you, Captain. It's been quite some time," Maud said.

"The pleasure is mine," Edwin said.

"The captain and I have been talking over his wartime experiences," Ewan said. "You won't mind repeating some for Maud's benefit, Captain? She took a real interest in the war. Maud, did you know Edwin was involved with those submarine chasers in the Channel?"

It was the greatest number of sentences Maud could remember Ewan stringing together in days. Enthusiastic ones, at that.

"I've read some of it in the news, but I'd love to hear it from the source," Maud said. She situated herself on the sofa next to Ewan, and immediately his hand rested against hers. When she looked at him, he smiled. After all that had happened not hours before, Ewan seemed back to his old self. Maud felt the energy of the change reverberate between her ears. She was determined to make it last. "What can you tell us?" she asked Edwin eagerly.

Edwin paused. "Well." He looked at her as if taking measure of her interest. "I was stationed for four years in the English Channel. Captain of a fleet of submarines. Really, it was a patrolman's role, scouting out German subs. Not unlike your local cop." Edwin smiled, looking around to ensure the attention of his audience, which no longer included Lily.

"You undersell it, I'm guessing," Maud said. She met Edwin's eyes when they traveled back to her.

"I'll say—quite a step up from old Pine Hill seminary," Ewan said before Edwin had a chance to respond.

"How naive we were back at Pine Hill," Edwin said. "Thinking we had such a solid grip on the world." He looked at Ewan. "I thought so, anyway. I'm sure you were more reasonable."

"Oh no, I wasn't," Ewan said with a sheepish smile.

"Remind me—how many classes apart were you at Pine Hill?" Maud asked.

Daffy took a flying leap then and landed straight on Maud's lap, which gave them all a good laugh. Daffy took his time settling into slumber, and Edwin poured himself more tea.

"Ewan was a good six years my junior," Edwin said after he finished pouring, remembering Maud's question. He smiled and added, "I'm the old man around here."

"Hardly!" Ewan said. "I got a late start. We're not too far apart in age, if I recall."

So Edwin was nearing fifty, as she'd thought. Still, referring to himself as an old man was laughable. In part it was the lack of gray hair, and the same unlined, good skin she remembered from twenty years earlier when Edwin presided over Ewan's induction at the Cavendish parish. "That man is too good-looking to be a minister!" her friend had said of Edwin that day.

It was even truer now. She'd seen Edwin's picture a number of times in the paper over the years—in reports of his speeches and essays about Canada, as well as his wartime heroics—but she hadn't seen him again in person since he had inducted Ewan as a minister. Recent pictures didn't do him justice.

"None of us should be calling ourselves old, Captain," Maud said. "Middle-aged at worst. And with interesting stories to tell. How many ordained clergymen do you suppose have commanded one of his majesty's ships of war?"

Edwin cleared his throat. "Just one, that I know of."

"Quite something," Maud said. "I read that you were personally thanked and decorated by the king?"

Edwin nodded. "I was drenched from being caught in the rain just before. Standing there ready to shake the king's hand, I think I was more nervous than any day at war." He chuckled.

"Really?" Maud said, putting down her tea. "In all that time as an officer, did you never feel you were under any sure danger?"

"A number of times," Edwin said. "But I think you may be underestimating the danger of inadvertently offending the king."

This line drew a laugh from Maud and Ewan both.

"Yet you're here; you survived," Maud said.

"I'm a lucky man," Edwin said.

"So it would seem," Maud said, holding the teacup close to her mouth before taking a sip.

Edwin looked at her. "Some men say they were spared for a reason. But I can't believe that there was any rhyme or reason to it." He shook his head. "Not after what I saw. It does make me want to live as well as I can from here on out. Try not to squander anything good."

Maud nodded, looking down. "The bind of the survivor. The problem is knowing what to do with the time we have been given that others have not. I sometimes think—if only someone could come down from on high and tell us our ideal path, how much simpler life would be."

"Simpler, but not nearly so interesting," Edwin said.

"What's this I hear about you selling insurance now?" Ewan asked. His tone was chipper.

Edwin took Ewan's change of tone and subject in stride. "Imperial Life Insurance Company. I'm an agent for them. It's good money, and I like the change. I've always had a hard time sticking with any one thing for too long. 'Forever a dreamer,' my wife sometimes says. But I do miss parts of the ministry.

Any chance to serve as a visiting minister like this one, I'll take." He looked at Maud. "Thank you again for inviting me. I really am thrilled to have a few Island folk not too far away. I'll always prefer islanders to mainlanders, no matter how long I live here."

"I feel the same way," Maud said, smiling.

She kept smiling until she heard Ewan clear his throat. His eyes had lost some of their humor from earlier. Ewan never liked when Maud talked longingly about the Island.

"Well, we are happy to have you nearby as well," Maud said, now eager to exit the conversation if it meant that Ewan's spirits stayed up. "If you'll excuse me, I'll let you two keep catching up and go check on our supper."

I really am thrilled. She rolled Edwin's words around in her mind as she walked to the kitchen. They sounded oddly familiar.

Then she remembered—Edwin had said the same phrase nearly twenty years earlier on that hot July day, preaching for Ewan's induction in the Cavendish Presbyterian Church. "I really am thrilled for the town of Cavendish to have the likes of my friend Reverend Ewan Macdonald as a minister." He smiled down at the Cavendish congregation when he said it.

Maud had made a point of approaching Edwin that day on the church lawn. He'd started to make a name for himself giving lectures throughout the Island about Canada's natural beauty, and she was eager to meet him in person.

"I hope you don't mind my asking," she'd said after they exchanged pleasantries, "but what part of Canada made the biggest impression on you?"

"I'll let you in on a secret," Edwin had said. "Not the theme of my lecture—but this Island beats all."

Someone had called for him soon after that; he needed to catch his ride. But Edwin had taken Maud's eyes briefly as he went, and she remembered feeling his smile clean through her clothes.

MAUD WOKE UP to the sound of Ewan humming a tune from the night before. He had started up the Victrola after supper with Edwin, and they'd all danced, the boys included. What sweet relief it had been to Maud, seeing the boys happy and laughing with their father. She had allowed herself to bask in the moment, stuffing Ewan's terrible words from earlier that day into a back drawer of her mind and turning the lock. If nothing else, life with her grandmother had taught her about locked drawers.

Now it was a new day, and here was Ewan, out of bed at a reasonable hour and dressing himself.

"Good morning." Maud used the lightest tone she could.

"Mornin', monkey," Ewan called back from his closet. "We'd better get going if we mean to watch the captain preach. It's sure to be entertaining." He came out of the closet fully dressed. "Can you believe he did all he says in the navy?"

"Hardly," Maud said. "Of course he always did have a hobby for boating, studying navigation and all. He even got that motorized yacht, well before anyone had heard of such a thing."

"Quite the leap from a boating hobby to joining up with the British admiralty," Ewan said.

"What do you think his family thought of it—his wife especially? It must have been hard on them."

"Surely they were supportive."

"I'm not so sure," Maud said. "Putting himself in that kind of risk when he has children—and seven of them at that! Taking a leave from his congregation at Avondale Presbyterian too." She shook her head. "Now that he's come back safely, of course it's all right. And with stories to tell."

"I'm eager to hear more of them."

Maud was up and straightening Ewan's collar. She searched his eyes as she did, looking to glean more about this recent turn of events. She found her gaze settling on her own nightstand behind them, with Ewan's pill bottles sitting on top.

It had been nearly eighteen hours, she realized, and she hadn't dosed Ewan a single pill. After days of his requesting more pills than she could count. She frowned. A coincidence surely. This was doctor-prescribed medication, meant only to help.

"You go on downstairs. I'm sure the captain is already up," she said. "I'll dress and be there soon."

Still, she might as well check the bottles for any signs of Ewan's clumsy tampering. Make sure she could report the facts accurately to the specialist in Boston, should he ever ask.

A careful inspection showed the bottles just where she had set them, with no evidence of meddling. So Ewan was medication-free and humming. What was she to make of that?

MAUD SNAGGED A spare hour after services while Edwin was still out to write a chapter of *Rilla*. She tried for more, but she had a hard time keeping her eyes open. She rarely napped, but the past few months' cumulative lack of sleep seemed to be catching up with her. Something to do with the adrenaline lifting from her veins after Ewan's recent about-face, surely.

She'd just made her way from the table over to the bed when she heard two fast knocks on the bedroom door.

"Mother! Mother!" Chester called.

Maud squeezed her eyes shut before rising to open the door.

"Now, Chester," she said with a smile, "haven't we talked about how there's hardly ever any need to yell?"

"But I really needed to tell you something," Chester said.

"What is it?" Maud walked toward the bed, motioning when she got there for Chester to come sit beside her.

"Did you know the minister staying with us was a real ship captain, in charge of whole ships, and that's why he's called Captain?" Chester said. He sat beside his mother, looking down at his knees as he kicked his calves forward and back.

"I did know that," said Maud.

"Right, well, do you know how he got to become a captain?"

"I don't know exactly how," Maud said, looking down at Chester's mussed brown hair, the handsome bridge of his nose and wide eyes that she'd memorized the day he was born. "Do you?"

"Yes! He offered himself to the king."

Maud held back a smile. "It was something like that, yes. He offered his services—not directly to the king, although he did meet the king."

"Oh," Chester said, looking up at her. His legs had stopped moving. "And now he sells ensuring," he said.

"Insurance, actually, 'ance' instead of 'ing,'" explained Maud. "Have you heard of insurance before?"

"Maybe," said Chester, starting up his legs again with a smile on his face.

"I can explain to you what it means if you'd like."

"Okay."

"Well." Maud paused, assessing what level of detail would be interesting. "For life insurance, which is what Captain Smith sells, a whole group of people pay a small amount of money and pool it together in case a bad thing happens to one of them. Because we never know when bad things might happen, do we?"

"Like to Aunty Fred?" Chester said.

"Yes, darling. Just like that." Maud worked to keep the emotion out of her voice. "If something bad does happen to you, the insurance will help by giving you money."

Chester nodded, rotating his feet back and forth with his legs fully extended.

Maud put her hand on Chester's head, fixing his hair around the cowlick.

Maybe she should consider an insurance policy herself. Even if Ewan kept well, it wasn't Ewan who made the money they would need for the boys to attend good schools. She was thinking she might ask Edwin about a policy when Chester said, "Anyway, it's what I'd like to do. Be a captain of ships for the mother country."

Maud coughed. "Well," she said. "And you've gotten this idea from Captain Smith?"

"Not from him—because of him."

"It's good to be thinking about your profession now. It is important to love something and to keep at it, and I mean to support you in that." She swallowed and looked at Chester. The possibility that her boys would grow up someday and go to war had never occurred to her. It made her feel sick. "But it's also good to keep an open mind. Do you know what I mean by that?"

"All right, Mother," said Chester. "But it'd be good if you'd start calling me Captain."

Maud laughed. "I'll call you that if you are one someday, just like we don't call anyone a minister until they have special training like Father. Until then, you will be Chester—the name I gave you."

Chester looked up at her, his usual smile still on his face but anger in his eyes. Then, using one arm to push himself off the bed, he used the other to give Maud's shoulder a hard shove. As Chester ran out of the room, Maud fought back a yelp. She couldn't believe how strong he'd become. But exclaiming might turn this into an incident, and she couldn't add anything to her list of worries right now. He was just a boy. Boys did these things.

Chester left the bedroom door open wide behind him, and Maud could hear voices downstairs. Edwin was back, and the conversation had started up again. She willingly abandoned any thought of Chester's shove and started wondering what she had missed.

"It's a silent film—a modern marvel. All footage taken during the war," she heard Edwin say.

Maud walked into the hallway.

"We could see it sometime—the British government gave me my own copy after the war. I'd be happy to show you."

"Well," Ewan said.

The pause that followed made her quicken her steps. This was an important guest, a man as good as famous. Ewan could not be trusted to show sufficient enthusiasm. Rushing down the stairs, she told herself it was her good wifely duty to show Edwin the appreciation he deserved.

A FEW WEEKS later, Maud jotted down a few notes about Edwin's visit on scrap paper for later inclusion in her journal.

"He has an almost boyish face, surprising in light of his age and the good deal of change I'd expected in him after going to war. He served as an officer in the British navy, and he entertained us brilliantly with tales of wartime adventure. No longer preaching and not sure he'll ever go back to it fully. A shame, given his considerable talent."

"I met him once a number of years ago after he spoke at Ewan's induction in Cavendish—very handsome I thought then, and clever too."

"I've been particularly interested in him always, as a writer of articles and a fellow enthusiast of Canadian beauty, so this visit was of a good deal of concern to me. And it turned out to be a good deal of help to Ewan. He is interested that I am writing a war novel and wants to hear how I am planning to tell it."

"After Edwin, Stella came through for a few days on her way back to Los Angeles, and Ewan was as good a conversationalist as ever. The day after Stella arrived, he preached without difficulty."

Maud paused before adding a final dash. Incidentally, she noted, an insurance company recently found her heart, kidneys, lungs, and blood pressure all normal. She'd bargained quite the deal, and had taken out a twenty-thousand-dollar policy on her life.

She saw no reason to mention with whom this hard bargaining had taken place. Certainly no need to mention her several visits into town to meet with the salesman over lunch.

Nor did the Reader need to know that she no longer could depend on Ewan's career to provide for the family should something happen to her—that her reverend husband was intermittently taking a heaping dose of pills with his water that might just be harming him more than they helped. She had done her best to explain to the Reader her understanding of Ewan's malady, along with his visit to a specialist to cure it. That felt sufficient for now.

The point of the insurance—the only point that mattered—was that her boys would be provided for, no matter what.

29.

E ntering the old house, Maud breathed in the smell of toast and fresh butter. Ewan and Frede must be having breakfast. She felt a pang realizing they had started without her, but what did she expect after having been out walking for hours without a word to either of them?

"I'm back!" Maud called as she walked down the hallway toward the kitchen, resolved to share her mind with Ewan as soon and as earnestly as she could. "I woke up early and took myself for a walk."

She entered the kitchen to see Frede sitting at the table, her frizzy hair unpinned and her face still bearing a sleep crease down its side. One of their grandmother's prized china plates and a half-full teacup sat in front of Frede, who looked up at Maud from a textbook wedged between her torso and the table.

"It's only me. Ewan's gone out looking for you." Frede shook her head. "I told him he had nothing to worry about, that you like your walks. But he was determined, and I saw there was no use in arguing."

"Oh no! Do you know what direction he headed?"

"I don't," Frede said, closing her book. "But I told him

on his way out that he should turn around in a half hour if he didn't find you. That you'd be coming back, and he may not catch you. He agreed. So he should be back in"—Frede looked up at the small kitchen clock—"no more than twenty minutes."

Maud sighed and nodded. "I suppose I may as well wait here for him, then."

"Now don't go frowning away. He didn't seem upset. More excited to see you as soon as possible than worried over you, I think." Frede studied Maud's face. "It must have been a good night."

Maud sat down beside Frede and picked up a piece of crust from Frede's plate. "It was," she said, putting the crust in her mouth and looking out the kitchen window.

"So distracted by the memory that you have resorted to eating leftover crust!" Frede said. "Of all Grandmother's lessons, her idea that presentation is half the taste is a good one. I'll make you a new slice."

Maud smiled. "You are wonderful."

"I'm sorry we didn't wait for you to eat, but we both woke up with holes in our stomachs. I for one was craving more of that cake, but the bread sufficed."

"Did you have a good chat? Did he say anything of interest?" Maud felt like a schoolgirl suddenly, asking her friend for gossip.

"Well," Frede said as she placed a slice of bread in the newfangled electric toaster Maud had purchased last year with some of her story money. Frede then busied herself retrieving a plate and a mug, which made Maud anxious. It was not like Frede to hesitate.

"You of all people wouldn't dare hold out on me," Maud said.

Frede turned, and Maud saw the serious look on her face.

"I don't know that it's my place to say. Really, I don't know if you'll mind in the slightest, and I'm sure he'll tell you himself soon enough."

"Frede," Maud said.

Frede came to sit down.

"We got to talking about when we'd be leaving today, and Ewan mentioned that he needs to leave by noon to stop over at Reverend Edwin Smith's. The minister who delivered Ewan's induction, do you remember?"

Maud remembered. She nodded, eager for Frede to get to the point.

"Well, I asked what he planned to meet Reverend Smith for, and that's when he got to explaining about the speech." Frede looked over at the toaster, which had just chimed its completion.

"The speech?" Maud couldn't place the meaning of this.

"The one Ewan was planning to deliver to the General Assembly."

"Of course. I couldn't get him to say much about it last night—" Maud stopped, registering Frede's words fully. "What do you mean, he 'was planning to deliver'?"

Frede swallowed. "Apparently, he's stopping by Reverend Smith's hotel to turn it down."

"To turn it down," Maud repeated. She looked down at Frede's plate and took another piece of crust. "What does Reverend Smith have to do with any of this?"

"He was the one to offer the speech to Ewan, apparently. He's been so busy that he couldn't do it himself." Frede got up and started to ready the toast. "I'm sorry to be saying any of this," she continued, looking at Maud behind her. "This is between you and Ewan." She spread the butter and returned to the table, delivering the toast to Maud. "Only he said it to me reluctantly, a little like it was a secret, and Lord knows I don't want to lug any secret information around. My loyalty is with you, always. And I wasn't sure what your reaction would be, but I can see on your face plain as day that you are disappointed." Frede's knees were bouncing now.

"Did he say why?" Maud asked.

"He didn't," Frede said. "Just that he would be meeting with Reverend Smith to turn it down today."

Maud reached for the toast and devoured it in uncharacteristically large bites. Then she stood up and brushed off her skirt.

"You," she said, looking Frede in the eye, "are a dear friend. And I detest secrets. Other people may not want to know things of this nature, but I always do. Please know that."

Frede nodded. "I do."

Maud's eyes grew serious. "Do you mind giving me and Ewan a few minutes alone when he arrives back?"

Frede nodded again. "You won't punish him for this, will you? He looked so sorrowful talking about the speech. And so dearly happy when the subject turned to finding you on your walk."

Maud shook her head, her face softening. "I won't punish him," she said. "I'll simply try to understand. I have some things to share with him too."

"One other thing," Frede said, eyeing Maud carefully. "I saw him put a draft of his speech notes in the rubbish bin."

"You don't say," Maud said, her eyes traveling immediately to the bin.

Just then, they heard the creaky turn of the front door handle.

"I'll be upstairs, buried in this treasure trove," Frede said in a loud whisper, nodding down at her textbook. Frede headed up the back staircase as quietly as she was capable.

30.

*H*er fantasy life in the first nine months of 1920 had been the most active of her entire life. Whole new futures imagined, and much of it captured here, in her journal notes.

Her senses were dulled now, but it was still a delicious time.

Looking down at herself again from on high, she saw a small figure before a dwindling fire, an ordinary-looking set of papers in her hands. Who would think some old pages could turn that figure's heart from aching to pounding in a span of a few minutes?

These notes were always intended to be kept private. They had to be. The Reader would see this as a betrayal or worse—a flight of fancy. Proof that reality was so far from what she imagined it to be that she could not be trusted even to tell her own story.

Oh, but one last indulgence. One more time to relive, for her and her alone. The fire would still be there when she was through, ready to leap back to life.

31.

Leaskdale, Ontario
January 1920

Gibbon's *The Decline and Fall of the Roman Empire* had a nice weight to it. The jacket was torn in a few places, and she knew parts of it by heart, but it had never lost its hold on her.

Reading Gibbon again now was research—reminding herself of the historical tolls of war for *Rilla*. She finished underlining a passage.

"Lily!" Maud called, walking toward the library door with the book still in her hands.

"Yes?" Lily said back from the kitchen.

"How's supper coming? The captain will be arriving any minute now, and I want to make sure it's ready." Maud felt her heart pick up at the word "captain."

"Ready soon enough, not to worry," Lily said, without any of the urgency Maud had hoped for. Edwin's visits had become something of a habit that fall and winter, but he was still a guest.

LATER THAT EVENING as they sat in the parlor, Maud's eyes traveled toward Ewan every few minutes. He had been in a dosing pattern for a while now, nodding his head in a slow rhythm most of the time and every once in a while jerking it up and mumbling incoherently in his sleep.

"He's been tiring early with the headaches," Maud had explained to Edwin, even though in truth it was Ewan's barbiturate and bromide medication that made him so groggy. Not that grogginess stopped him from asking for higher and higher doses. The specialist in Boston did not seem concerned. "Bodies do habituate. Is he sleeping better?" the specialist wanted to know. "Any more delusion talk?" With her answers of yes and no, he seemed to be satisfied, and he increased the prescribed dosages.

At least there had been no more terrible remarks about the children over the past several months, no more wishing them away. She thanked the Lord for that much. And if increased grogginess meant another few months of needing ministers to supply for Ewan, well, there were certain advantages to that too.

"Just supposing you happened to be living in the same time and place, both members of the literary elite—do you imagine yourself a friend of Gibbon's?" Edwin asked now, his eyebrows raised.

"It matters quite a bit what time of his life you mean," Maud said. "Surely not in his early days—converting to Catholicism, can you imagine?"

"During the writing of his masterwork, then, surely. Reading him a third time suggests quite the spiritual kinship." Edwin tilted his head. "A passion of sorts."

"Certainly nothing like that—have you seen his portrait?" Maud asked.

"I am not sure that I have," Edwin said.

"Well, if you had, you would understand," Maud said, laughing and pouring tea.

"In all seriousness, what is the appeal of undertaking it now again—all six volumes of it?"

"Well, he has a fine style, and wonderful dedication to the

primary source. But most of all, it is the scope of the work that I like—and the big swallow of perspective that scope brings with it." Maud paused. "Do you ever feel a need to be taken out of yourself and put your troubles in perspective? Viewing my life and circumstances through the wide lens of human history can calm my nerves like nothing else." Noting Edwin's lack of reaction, she raised her eyebrows. "But perhaps you are beyond such things as troubles."

"How little you must think of me to believe I have come through this life unaware of my own troubles," Edwin said. "Which I have, as you know. Or should know by now."

Maud spoke slowly. "You don't mention any."

"We don't mention any," Edwin said, matching her tone.

Maud felt a jolt of energy through each of her limbs; she turned her attention to the teapot, pouring more and wiping a few drops.

"That's true," she said.

"You'll forgive me for taking certain things as implied," Edwin said.

"I find it refreshing, actually," she said. "People these days can be so literal."

Edwin nodded. "I do understand what you mean about a wider perspective," he said.

"It's important," Maud said. "But at the same time that reading Gibbon calms my nerves about my own troubles, it also starts me worrying about all of human trouble. The sheer terror of war. When I'm through with each volume of Gibbon I read a novel—the most frivolous I can get my hands on—to turn my pulse back normal. He's almost as awful for my heart as astronomy, which I had to give up reading a number of years back."

"Astronomy—really?"

"Yes. I used to love it."

"Do you miss it now?"

"Sometimes. But I'm sure astronomy's continued on very well without me to worry over it. Ever proving humankind smaller than we thought we were the year before."

Edwin nodded into his cup. "We are but a speck of dust."

"Yes," Maud said. "One among the 'baffled millions who have gone before.'"

"I've always admired Lord Byron."

"So have I."

"Historians like Gibbon and astronomers have a certain advantage, I will say," Edwin continued, sitting back in his chair. "But we cannot live our entire lives up in the sky or back in the past, can we, now?"

"Quite right." Maud's heart was beating quickly now, begging the conversation along. Just another moment of this, please. And then another after that.

She couldn't recall ever having felt quite this way with a man. Not this combination of intellectual stimulation and attraction—yes, attraction; she might as well allow herself the word. She'd had banter with Nate about writing, and about their eventual scholarly professions. But that was child's play. Nothing like this talk—adult, smart, with just the right amount of innuendo. Her conversations with Ewan were nothing like this, even at their best. As angry as she had been with Ewan for months now for his carelessness in the face of his malady, her anger softened for the moment into a sympathetic sadness. This kind of talk simply wasn't in Ewan.

Edwin cleared his throat and continued. "Have you found dear Gibbon to be quite the tyrant against Christianity that he is supposed to be?"

"I find him honest, which is the important thing," Maud said. She looked Ewan's way for the first time in a while and made sure his chin was still on his chest, his eyes still closed. "I am convinced now, more firmly than ever, that God and the church are not always one," she added.

"You mean since the war?"

"I mean a number of things."

Edwin was leaning forward now. "Such as?"

"Such as." She stopped. "Such as I cannot tell you how long I've felt that I'd be better off Sunday mornings going out in nature and spending some time with my own soul instead of sitting upright on a hard bench with nothing above me but plain brown rafters. There!" She laughed, then gave another sideways glance at Ewan. "I've said it. To a minister, no less. It almost makes me believe in the good of Catholic confession." They both laughed.

When their laughter died down, she added, "Though I've never been able to think of you as much of a minister, even when you are preaching for Ewan. 'Captain' is more fitting."

"I've felt the same. It may be half the reason I enlisted."

Edwin stretched his arms even wider on the chair, moving his knees closer to Maud's on the couch so they were just touching. He didn't look down to notice, but it had to be intentional. She smiled to realize it.

"I was a far better student at the Royal Naval College than I ever was in seminary. Take from that what you will," Edwin said.

"In all seriousness, though, why did you go to war? Was there any of God in it?"

"Why do you ask?"

Maud paused. "Mostly I picture the mothers' and sisters' faces," she said. "The ones Ewan preached to, telling them their sons and brothers were doing God's will. The way they nodded at his words and regretted their own gender, that they couldn't do more. The way many of them stopped nodding eventually, and then stopped coming to church at all." Her eyes traveled again to Edwin's knees. "The only answer, as I can see it, is that God is good but not omnipotent. And certainly not an ultimate arbiter of good and evil."

Edwin looked down at the floor and said, "I didn't feel God in the war. Guiding my actions, or on one side or the other." He looked up. "Right as I believe we were."

Maud nodded.

"I did feel God sometimes in my pain," he said. "In my fear."

Maud looked at him. "Well—that's what we hope for, isn't it. That's something." She shifted so more of their legs touched.

After a while Edwin said, "So how will you do it in your novel? Portray the war, I mean?"

Maud smiled. "It won't be a war story of the sort you are thinking, I'm afraid. Of the sort you lived. That's for you to write someday."

"I just might," Edwin said, looking away.

"So you do want to write?"

"I do. I always have. I just can't see trusting myself to stay with a book all the way to the finish. I don't know how you do it." Edwin's gaze was fixed out the window. The uncharacteristic fear in his voice made Maud hesitant to respond. "But enough about that," he said, turning back to her. "You were telling me about the war as you are planning to write it."

"Right." Maud cleared her throat. "I write what I know, and that's the view from the other front, at home. I'm focusing on Rilla, the youngest daughter of Anne and Gilbert—but you probably don't know who they are."

"I know Anne and Gilbert well." Edwin grinned.

Did you hear that! He knows us!

Maud nearly jumped from her seat, stopped only by years

of well-honed propriety tempering her movements. Anne's voice—at this of all moments.

Regaining herself, Maud channeled her excitement into a close-lipped smile. "Well," she said, looking Edwin in the eye. "Isn't that something."

Quite a bit more than something, you silly goose! I cannot recall the last time I've had such fun. Let's keep this one around, shall we? He has shown himself to be a man of exquisite taste.

Edwin cleared his throat. "How does religion fare in this tale of the home front?" he asked.

"It comes out well—of course—but not unscathed. It's not all worked out yet in my mind. The impact was anything but simple."

"And Anne?"

"She comes out well. But not unscathed." Maud smiled.

"Yes," Edwin said. "Nothing was left unscathed."

"Yourself included?"

Creases Maud hadn't noticed before on Edwin's forehead softened. "I'm selling insurance now, aren't I?"

They both laughed until they heard Ewan stir.

At the first sign of Ewan awakening, Edwin yawned, stretching his arms out behind him and then pulling them back quickly like he was noticing them for the first time. The movement shifted his knees away from Maud's.

"Thank you," Edwin said. "This tea—and the company—was just what I needed on a cold winter night." He stood.

Lily came into the room just as Maud had started to move the pot and saucers closer together. As Lily cleared, Maud went over to Ewan and rubbed his elbow, rousing him.

MAUD'S THOUGHTS RACED as she settled into bed that night. After losing Frede, she thought she might never enjoy a conversation so much again. Guilt and excitement coursed through her in equal measure as she replayed the evening in her mind, trying to recall each turn of phrase and gesture.

Once she had it all burned to memory, she attempted to match Ewan's even breathing, willing sleep to wash over her nerves. But sleep proved elusive.

She told herself she'd done nothing wrong—it was only a conversation—but something was nagging her. Glancing over at Ewan, it struck her in a single word. *Ugly.* Ewan's face always had been one of his fine points, something she could depend on being drawn to. But at this moment, she found it downright repulsive. She turned away, hoping to banish the realization as quickly as it had come. A passing feeling, surely. Or could it be punishment—the Lord's consequence for allowing herself to be attracted to another man?

She knew better than that. She'd been attracted to more than one man before. She knew attraction could not be willed nor coerced, either out of being or back into it.

Maud felt a weight like her grandmother's hand on her shoulder. She knew like second nature what her grandmother would say. This was all temporary. Ewan would recover, he would take back those awful words he'd said about the children at the height of his illness, he would become a dependable man again, and surely her attraction would return. The thing to do in the meantime was to avoid extended conversing with Edwin. Attraction was one thing, courting disaster quite another.

Avoid a kindred spirit? You will do no such thing! The older one gets the harder real joy is to come by, and I will not have the terrifying notions of an old lady echoing from the grave and stamping out our joy.

Anne's words came to Maud like honey stirred into bitter tea. Drifting into sleep, Maud knew she would do anything for that voice, to keep it with her awhile longer.

32.

Maud pulled out her trowel mid-dig. She'd been making her way down the sunny side of the house, planting lavender and willing the spring thaw they'd been having to last. Lily hadn't told Maud she was expecting a visitor, but now Maud was certain she could make out two distinct peals of laughter coming from the kitchen. Lily must think Maud was out visiting the parishioners, or she'd keep her volume lower.

Then Maud heard Lily say the words "Captain Smith," drawn out and with intention.

Maud dug the trowel into the ground and stood up. A few throaty giggles followed. Maud walked toward the kitchen window, keeping close to the side of the house.

"And he's just moved his entire family only forty-five kilometers from Leaskdale," she heard Lily say. "Mrs. M. will be grateful to have her dear friend living that much closer, I tell you what," Lily added, followed by more of the ridiculous laughter.

Maud had started walking quickly and was inside the kitchen before Lily's friend had a chance to respond.

"Good day," Maud said to the friend with a smile. Looking Lily square in the eye, she added, "Lily, I was hoping I might trouble you for a moment with tonight's supper menu?"

A slight waver at the beginning of Lily's recitation of the planned menu was the only sign of self-consciousness she showed. When Lily finished, Maud excused herself with two nods, explaining that she was going to finish her planting along the side of the house.

"Don't have too much fun now, you two."

AS SHE WORKED in her garden that night, Maud watched the dusk come on particularly gray. The air was dense with humidity. Lily should have called for supper already.

Then she heard Ewan's voice say, "Evenin', Captain," his accent turned a thicker Gaelic than she had heard in a while.

A car door shut loudly, and then Edwin laughed. She felt that laugh from the base of her stomach all the way through her toes. She had missed him.

"I thought I might have the fun of a surprise visit," Edwin said to Ewan.

Maud entered through the kitchen and scampered up the back stairs in a way she hadn't since she was a teenager. After closing the bedroom door, she barely paused for a breath before making her way to her closet to change.

It had been a few weeks since Edwin's last visit, and she had begun to wonder when he would reach out next.

A surprise was just like him. Equal parts infuriating and gratifying. She hated Edwin for not allowing her the fun of anticipation. On the other hand, now she got to feel everything in a single, wild dose.

"I'VE DECIDED TO kill off poor Walter," Maud told Edwin later that night, looking up at him while taking half a cookie expertly between two fingers. Cigar smoke still clung to the air from earlier; Edwin and Ewan had smoked while Maud and Lily cleaned up from supper.

"Remind me," Edwin said, leaning forward in his chair. "Walter is Rilla's favorite brother—the poet?"

Edwin took a sip of the wine Maud had taken to pouring during his visits. A rarity in their house.

"That's the one." Maud smiled.

"Killed on the front? Before he has any chance at literary success? No—that can't be right."

"But it is."

"Do I see a smile on your face to boot? I never would have imagined Lucy Maud Montgomery had it in her to be maniacal."

"Not maniacal," Maud said. "I smiled predicting your reaction. And I predicted right."

She took a sip of wine, then went back for another.

"So I'm turning into an open book. I better work on that." Edwin cleared his throat. "But really, I don't see how killing off Walter could be necessary. What about the other brother? He was eager to go to war, wasn't he? Not as interesting of a fellow? The reader wouldn't take that so hard."

They sat in their usual positions, with Edwin in Ewan's chair and Maud on the end of the couch nearest him. Ewan had gone to bed after cigars. Maud kept a check on her knees, though, and her posture. Lily might be anywhere.

"Why should I spare the reader what wasn't spared any of us?"

"That's hard of you."

Noting the tenderness in Edwin's expression, Maud's tone changed. "Grief creates a need in us, I suppose. I may have written Walter out of that need. A need for I don't know what exactly." She took a long draw out of her wineglass. "I gave him some literary success, anyway—a poem published to great acclaim, written in the trenches."

"And Rilla, and Anne? Losing their brother and son?" Edwin asked.

"They will keep moving—which is the harder thing to do." Maud's voice caught, then grew softer. "We always have a choice about whether to keep on or let grief take us under."

"I suppose that's true."

A few visits ago, after more than one glass of wine, Maud had told Edwin about Frede. He'd already sensed the hollow in her heart. She hadn't had to say much. She could still feel the strength of his hand wrapped around hers after she spoke about the loss, not too hard or too soft. How solid he felt to her then—and now. How safe. Someone she could lean against without any thought of him falling over.

"When our women fail in courage, shall our men be fearless still?" Maud said now.

"Who said that?" Edwin asked, his eyes brightening.

"I did." She paused. "I thought it during the war, and I've put it in the book. A line for Anne."

"A nice one," Edwin said.

A bit too grave and wizened for my liking. But nothing has been quite to my liking since I entered middle age. I cannot wait until I am old and gray and free again to say just what is on my mind and spend my days chasing whims! I don't believe I even thought about whims when I was young, they were so baked into my existence.

"Don't go feeling so awful over Walter. I've thrown my readers a bone of sorts—a character for Rilla to love. Not nearly so interesting as her brother Walter, but he should appease them."

Edwin adjusted in his seat, moving closer. "Won't this lover have gone off to war too?"

"He will, but he'll survive. I'm not sure quite what will come of his returning, though."

"Planning to write an out-and-out sex scene like the kind appearing in many books these days?"

When he saw that he had caught her off guard, Edwin leaned his head back and laughed. He lowered his chin, and the corners of his eyes stayed wrinkled in a way that surprised her.

She added her own laugh to the end of Edwin's. Then she said, "You have just hit on a topic that you might not hear the end of from me."

"Excellent," Edwin said, clasping his hands behind his head. "Count me interested."

"We can be thankful that Ewan has gone off to bed. He hates to hear me out on these things," Maud continued. "But I've never been one to shy away from the subject of sex—with an appropriate audience. Not our parishioners, of course."

Maud studied Edwin for his reaction. He reached for his wine. "Happily, I'm not one of them," Edwin said after a long swallow.

"Yes."

"So you better have out with it."

"I'll try to put it briefly—"

"I wish you wouldn't." Edwin laughed.

She smiled. "Many so-called modern novels seem to be only about airing out filth—the more grotesque, the more people like it. It's not the inclusion of sex itself that I object to. It's the bias against beauty and toward the lack of it. As if it's harder work to tell an ugly story about an ugly place and make it believable. I've found the opposite." She looked up at Edwin. "I do wish that my publishers would allow me more room. 'The readership,' they say, 'you must mind the readership.' 'The readership' won't allow more than a chaste kiss, apparently—preferably out of doors."

Edwin laughed. "Your publishers sound like they could benefit from having their minds expanded."

"My intent has always been to write a different kind of

novel someday, one that may not sell quite so well. The story of a single life, in all its difficulty and splendor. One showing the basic sameness in all of us—and the whys of the differences. One that makes people stop and think—yes, this is life as it really is."

"I wish you would."

Maud looked at Edwin. "I'd like to show sex as it really is too—not making it gratuitous or romanticizing it either."

"Sex as it really is . . ." Edwin looked right at her and smiled. "I'd love to experience it. Your telling, I mean."

Maud cleared her throat. "If only it were really possible."

"Why isn't it?"

"'Possible' isn't the word. It's impractical."

"In what way?"

"The disruption to my family—"

"Disruption?"

"They count on my income, on my reputation being what it is. I must think of my children first."

"I understand. But it's important, don't you think, the word 'possible'? Some days possible is what I get out of bed for," he said.

Then Maud's shoulders jumped. A dish clattering—Lily? Would it have sounded so close if it had been in the kitchen? She turned her head toward the parlor door, but she didn't hear anything more.

"And what about love?" Edwin said, unperturbed. "With Rilla and her beau—do you believe them to be in honest love as you are writing them?"

"I'm trying to work that out," Maud said.

"How so?"

"Rilla is the first of my characters whose ambition centers around a husband. Not my ideal character, but it's true of many women."

"True of most women, I'd say," Edwin said.

Not true of me. And I'm most thankful for my ambition. Without it, I would not be nearly so interesting to myself, let alone to anyone else. Although now, having achieved most everything I dreamed, I worry I am not nearly so interesting as I once was. Funny, isn't it, how our dreams matter far less once we achieve them?

"I've always thought there are different kinds of love—passion and friendship and worship. Telling the truth about love is made difficult by the fact that I've never had them all at once with the same person."

"No?" Edwin was looking her straight in the eye, his wineglass near his lips.

She studied him. "I should like to be able to tell the whole of love honestly someday."

It occurred to her that the wine might be going to her head. Then—was that another noise from the kitchen? Lily should have been well done with dishes by now.

"I'd like that too," Edwin said.

Maud tried to remember what she'd said a moment before.

"I'll be interested in hearing what you decide to do with *Rilla*," Edwin continued. "But mostly, I'll be waiting for that next book. The one about a single life as it really is." Edwin smiled.

"I wouldn't go holding your breath," Maud said. "It may not come anytime soon."

"As long as it comes while I'm alive. I'm a patient man." With that, Edwin flattened his palms against the chair and readied himself to stand.

MAUD WAS MANAGING fairly well with *Rilla*, especially now that she had Edwin to talk it over with.

She was nearing the end of the war.

Not long before the armistice, the papers had reported that the British line was broken and German shells were falling on Paris. "And so Canada will change hands like the stowed-away set of dishes that comes with the dowry," Maud had whispered to Ewan at the time. Only later had they learned that the British line had broken only in one place, and the shells were falling from far away. Far less dire news than they'd thought.

Maud opened her *Rilla* manuscript and started a new chapter.

"Oh God," Gertrude Oliver would say, hearing that the British line was broken.

"Is God dead?" the little boy Jims would ask in reply.

And Rilla would doubt God, right up until the news that the British and French had checked the German offensive. Only then could she rest assured. "Evil cannot win," she would say.

But what exactly would have been the meaning of a different outcome? Could faith depend on it?

"Historians and astronomers have a certain advantage," Edwin had said. "But we cannot live our entire lives up in the sky or back in the past, can we, now?"

Maud opened her spade notebook and jotted down a few lines for Gilbert. "Perhaps students of the canals of Mars would not be so keenly sensitive to the significance of a few yards of trenches lost or won on the western front," Gilbert would say.

So the book would have a little of Edwin in it. Maud smiled. She wondered if he would recognize himself.

33.

"Mrs. Macdonald!"

Had Lily's voice always been so shrill? Maud held her pen still for a moment and then continued. She had momentum on her final edits to *Rilla* that she did not want to lose. Lily never could be trusted to moderate her tone appropriately based on urgency.

When Lily's call stopped Maud's hand from moving for the third time, she sat her pen down and unlocked the library door.

"Yes, Lily?" Maud said into the hallway.

Lily came out of the kitchen then, one of her hands deep in a bowl of bread dough. "I've just had a visit from Mrs. Leask," she said, still working the dough with her hand. "Apparently she's seen your cat over there in her yard, dying. I thought you'd want to know."

"What? You don't mean Daffy?"

"That's what she said," Lily said on her way back to the kitchen. "I've got to get this bread in the oven."

Maud was changing her shoes to go out the door when she heard the pops and creaks of the boys' feet stampeding down the stairs. They could hear so well. She must remember that.

The boys crowded around Maud, not saying anything.

"We should go right away, boys," Maud said. Then she saw Stuart's lower lip quiver. "Or maybe you'd better wait here.

I'll come back with Daffy." She enveloped Stuart in a hug, reaching out a hand to squeeze Chester's shoulder.

She could get there more quickly herself. And who knew what she'd find when she arrived.

THE STILLNESS OF the soft gray form registered first; Maud slowed her run as soon as she saw it. No animal with any wild in him is ever that still in an exposed area, not with footsteps approaching. But the shape looked too small to be Daffy.

Then she saw the subtle stripes down his sides, the angle of his nose. She started running again and calling his name. He had curled himself up into the tightest ball he could, his nose and ears pointing down into the ground, his eyes shut. Closing in to protect himself against whatever pain he could, not realizing it might be coming from inside.

She'd first understood death in its plain form watching her childhood kitten die of poison. He'd been the first in her string of gray cats. "One day," her grandmother had said, seeing Maud's tears at losing the kitten, "you might experience real grief." She never did seem to remember that the death of Maud's mother had been Maud's loss too.

Maud had experienced grief now in many forms, and still she could picture the confused face of that kitten; still she could feel the particular combination of nausea mixed with despair that she had felt that day, watching an animal suffer that doesn't have any understanding of what is happening. She felt it again now.

With cupped hands, Maud picked Daffy up off the gravel. As soon as she lifted, she nearly let go. He'd made a noise that startled her. Now he was shifting slightly, reacting to the lack of assurance given by her hands. She had added to his discomfort.

She wrapped him up in both arms, begging forgiveness with her gentleness. Slivers of green showed through between his eyelids.

Daffy had been sleeping on her bed when she read the letter accepting *Anne* for publication. There when she received her first bound copy and leapt around the room. He'd been several days on the train alone, shipped from Park Corner to Leaskdale after she and Ewan returned from their honeymoon. She'd barely slept those few nights, wondering if he'd been sent with enough food. But he'd made it, and he'd been there to cry outside the room during the births of all three boys—Chester and Stuart, and her middle son, Hugh, Maud's father's namesake. Hugh lived only a few minutes, but Daffy had met him. In his fourteen years, Daffy had seen as many sides of Maud as anyone. He had become almost human to her, more of a personality than most people she knew.

MAUD TRIED TO keep calm in spite of her tears as they sat around the glass table where Daffy lay, dying on the porch while the long summer twilight came on around them. Maud had covered with a blanket the bloody section of Daffy's fur, which she'd discovered after she found the red smear on her dress. An errant shot by a groundhog hunter, probably.

She explained to the boys as gently as she could. "A mistake; sometimes people make mistakes."

"Do you remember that time I saw the dead groundhog, Mother?" Chester asked, looking out at the front yard. "It was all bloodied up, laying on the side of the yard. I tried to move it, but I didn't have anything to move it with, and—"

"Not now, Chester," Maud said, putting her hand on his head.

"But Mother!"

"We need to keep calm for Daffy now. He needs us to be as calm and loving as possible."

Chester sighed and got up from his chair. A few seconds later, he started to ask questions. He was curious about the burial and where Papa would dig the hole.

Maud couldn't bring herself to respond. Instead, she did her best to keep her focus on Daffy.

When Stuart started to sniffle, Maud put her arm around him, drawing him close. "I know, darling," Maud said in Stuart's ear.

Hearing this, and seeming to notice his brother's tears for the first time, Chester came around the table and gave Stuart a hard shove.

"Crybaby!" Chester exclaimed with a laugh. "I'm telling Papa!"

Maud looked up long enough to see Chester run off the porch.

She wondered about Chester sometimes, about his sharp-elbowed way of dealing with the world. He often responded to situations with emotions that didn't quite fit. But he was also a boy. She didn't know what to expect from boys his age, and Ewan wasn't any real help in that area—especially not these days.

Maud would talk it through with Chester later, letting him know it wasn't okay to push his little brother. But right now, she couldn't bear to leave Daffy.

Stuart, who had kept perfectly quiet despite his brother's exclamation, drew even closer to Maud's side, wiping his eyes.

"Will he be okay, Mummy?" Stuart asked suddenly, after Maud had given him a squeeze.

Maud let out a sob. "Oh, darling, I don't believe he will."

"Not Daffy," Stuart said, looking down at his toes. "I mean Papa."

Maud knelt down to Stuart's level, taking her hand off Daffy. "I didn't know you worried about Papa." She paused to collect herself, noticing Stuart's seriousness. His gaze was still cast down to the floor. Maud saw a glimpse of Stuart as an adult, her measured but deeply empathetic son, so concerned with the wellness of others. She saw his younger self too, the inquisitive way he used to look up at her as she nursed him. Even as a baby, Stuart had begged for more understanding of this world they were living in.

Tell him the simple unvarnished truth. That's all I ever wanted when I was his age.

"Papa has been sick for a little while now. I am not sure how long he will be feeling this way." She stopped to see how her words were registering. Stuart was looking at her now instead of the floor, paying close attention.

"What kind of sick?" Stuart asked.

"It's what's called a mental sickness, so it affects the way he thinks. That's why it's hard to know when he will get better—harder than if he had a cold or flu like you've had before. But a doctor is helping him. He's taking medications to help too. Those medications make him extra sleepy, which you've probably noticed."

Stuart looked down again. Maud felt her heart sink, seeing the dejection on Stuart's face. She hated that she couldn't better answer his questions—that she was still asking the same questions herself.

It had been over a year since she had felt half normal with Ewan. Since they'd even kissed.

"You can come to me with any questions you have about Papa, sweetheart, all right? We can keep talking about this."

Stuart nodded.

"But it's not your job to figure out what's wrong and take care of Papa. That's my job and the doctor's job. Your only job is to keep being my Stuart, my very dear boy."

Daffy let out a soft meow that drew their attention back to the glass table. They stood there together silently, Maud's hand on Stuart's head.

Daffy's last breath was obvious, much longer than usual. Maud put a few fingers on Daffy's forehead with the lightest touch she could manage, and watched as Stuart did the same.

Feeling Daffy's last breath shake through her fingertips, then counting long enough to realize it was his last, Maud thought of her three caretakers after Chester's birth: Frede, the nurse, and Daffy. None was alive today. The thought nearly brought her to her knees.

LATER THAT NIGHT, lying awake in bed, Maud returned to stillness. The sobs had shaken themselves out of her system, and she came back to the words she'd often repeated on the days since Frede's death and Ewan's illness: Her boys needed her. Both of them in different ways, maybe now more than ever. And somehow, in some ways, life remained interesting.

The thought of Edwin flickered through her mind. She pictured his strong arms wrapping her up in a hug, holding her on his chest while she cried. She felt a pang of guilt, but she reminded herself that they hadn't done anything wrong. They hadn't betrayed anyone.

He's a gift to your imagination is all! A possibility your mind can occupy itself with when the nights get especially long.

And the return of Anne's words, well, that was a saving grace.

34.

Maud copied another sentence. She'd kept to fifteen minutes a day of recopying her old journals, an undertaking she found increasingly rewarding the further along she got. She was particularly pleased with the opportunities it afforded for curating. She'd maintained a good clip in her edits so far, finding it easy to tell what parts of her past would reflect well, but tonight's entry stopped her.

Ewan had proposed in the fall of 1906, and this was the entry describing it. Even knowing what was coming, her pulse quickened. She felt sure her naïveté would reveal itself from the very first line.

She'd started the entry teasingly. Knowing what she was about to spring on the unsuspecting Reader. Oh yes, even then she'd written her journals with a future audience in mind. Not so consciously as on recopying. But the Reader was there always, a critical eye peering over her shoulder for as long as she could remember.

Ewan Macdonald—she'd written out his name with a particular flourish—had come to say goodbye before leaving for Scotland to study, and she had his little diamond solitaire on her left hand.

She continued reading, cringing at her own unsuspecting delight, until a sentence stopped her. "The life of a country minister's wife has always appeared to me as a synonym for respectable slavery."

In some ways it was a comfort. She was never fully naive.
And yet.

As she read on, the tone of the entry changed back to
frivolity. Could it have been she who wrote this all out?
Sounding downright giddy just after saying something important and wise?

She would delete some of this enthusiasm on recopying.
A happy benefit of the project. No harm in sprinkling in a bit
more wisdom and premonition either. She hadn't been without premonition back in that day—the sentence about being
a country minister's wife proved that much.

"I would be content with a workaday, bread-and-butter
happiness," she informed the Reader now in the recopied
volume. "But suppose a marriage with Mr. Macdonald would
not give me even this. I would make him unhappy, too, in
that case."

"Or, worse still," she wrote, holding her breath as she
did, "suppose that, having married him, I met a man whom I
could love as it is in me to love." Her pen stopped. Had she
said too much? "The type is uncommon and the chances are
a hundred to one against his ever coming into my life. Yet, if
the thing should happen, the result, I am absolutely certain,
would be tragedy of one kind or another to me, and it might
be to others."

A tragedy to herself, and it might be to others. Yes. She
closed her eyes and let the ache make its way through her.
Several minutes passed before she started up again.

"I think I have done the wisest thing in assenting," she
concluded. "But the future alone can prove that. One takes
a risk in any marriage—the very 'for better or worse' of the
ceremony shows that."

How she longed now for more of her easy schoolgirl entries to recopy. But she'd been surprised to learn throughout

this project what insights the past could hold for the present. Maybe she'd find some clues about Ewan in the entries that would follow—about what could help him. Or her. Or them both.

FOR THE NEXT few weeks, Maud worked longer than her typical morning stretches on *Rilla*, with her editing bleeding into the evenings when the boys were asleep, and into the mornings before breakfast. Before long, she'd finished all the necessary tying up.

"To the memory of Frederica Campbell MacFarlane," Maud wrote on the final page. "Who went away from me when the dawn broke on January 25th, 1919—a true friend, a rare personality, a loyal and courageous soul."

Maud couldn't bear to look at that page too long, so she took out her journal from its lockbox.

"August 24, 1920. To-day I wrote the last chapter of *Rilla of Ingleside*," she wrote. "I am done with *Anne* forever—I swear it as a dark and deadly vow."

She paused for a moment, waiting to see if she would hear Anne's voice expressing her dismay. But no voice came.

It was better this way. She told herself Anne would prefer not to be written about again anyway, at least not until she was an old woman. This didn't mean the end of Anne in Maud's mind; only Anne on the page.

Shaking her head, Maud started a new paragraph. "And I want—oh, I want to write—something entirely different from anything I have written yet."

"*Juvenile literature*," a recent reviewer had written. "*Wonderful stories for girls.*"

Tears welled unwelcomely at the corners of her eyes.

"I am becoming classed as a 'writer for young people' and that only. I want to write a book dealing with grown-up creatures—a psychological study of one human being's life. I have the plot of it already matured in my mind." She sighed. "If I had only time to go to work on it—time and leisure. But I haven't as yet. The boys are too young—there are too many insistent duties calling me—I can't give up my profitable 'series' until I have enough money salted down to give the boys a fair start in life—for my 'real' novel will not likely be a 'best seller.'"

She thought about describing more fully the book she had in mind, using the journal as a sort of commitment device. But she stopped herself. What if she never managed to write this book? What would the Reader of her journals think of her then?

She was relieved to hear Lily call for supper.

"WE'VE GOT TO leave in just over an hour." Ewan's voice traveled faintly through the locked parlor door. With *Rilla* in her publisher's hands, Maud and Ewan were finally set to make the trip to visit Edwin's family they'd been talking about all summer.

"All right, dear, I'm packed. Just finishing up," Maud called back.

Since finishing *Rilla*, Maud had redoubled her journal recopying efforts. She was almost through the journal entry about the letter from the publisher accepting *Anne*. She was surprised to remember that she'd been reading the Charlotte-town *Patriot* when her grandmother brought in the mail, and that day's issue had included an article touting the Reverend Edwin Smith as one of the continent's finest speakers. The irony.

"Maud," Ewan called, knocking now at the parlor door. "Half-hour warning. We don't want to keep the Smiths waiting."

Ewan's voice was noticeably different from the one she'd

heard in the old Cavendish kitchen the day she wrote *Anne's* first lines—flatter, and without any of its old earnestness.

"I'll be ready!" Maud said.

For nearly a year now, it had been in the back of Maud's mind to look through her old scrapbooks for the newspaper photo of Edwin she thought she'd pasted in one of them. Her journal entry made her even more keen on finding it. She started to sift through her scrapbooks.

It wasn't long before she saw it: a photo from an article in the *Patriot* dated January 25, 1908. She studied the page. Not all too different from the face she'd seen a month ago, announcing himself in her entryway.

Above Edwin's photo she'd glued a maple leaf—fitting for the man the article called the "Great Ambassador of Canada." And above that a poem by Clinton Scollard that she barely remembered until she started to read it.

"Winter in Lovers' Lane," it was titled. "Lovers' Lane" was her own name for one of her most beloved Cavendish haunts, and also Anne's name for a place in Avonlea. And here it was in someone else's poem. She'd cut the poem out of the magazine where she found it.

Now she tapped her fingers on the table as she read out loud. At the last two stanzas, she stopped tapping.

> *Those tremulous trystings, are they done.—*
> *The meeting joy, the parting pain?*
> *Will hearts no more be wooed and won*
> *In memory haunted lovers' lane?*
>
> *Ah, wait till April's bugle call*
> *Reigns, rich with rapture, up the glen.*
> *Till may once more her flower thrall*
> *Weave amorously—and then—and then!*

Maud shut the scrapbook. The anticipation that had been building in her stomach flooded her body, not letting up as she walked away from the table. She felt wild in her heart. Seeing Edwin's picture right underneath this poem? In a scrapbook she'd made years ago? She didn't believe in the deterministic fate of Ewan's delusion, but she couldn't ignore the fact of this coincidence.

She unlocked the parlor door. "Ewan! I'm ready now. Boys, are you here to see us off?"

Stuart stood waiting, and Maud wrapped her arms around him, glad for the distraction.

"Now remember, we'll only be gone a night," she said over Stuart's shoulder, gesturing with her eyes for Ewan to start moving their bags out to the car.

She stood and put her hand on Chester's head after he emerged from the kitchen. "I'll be back before you know it, and you'll be on your best manners for Lily, won't you?"

The sound of her own voice bothered her. Could the boys sense the strangeness in it? She moved toward the door, calling out instructions to Lily as she did.

OVERSTUFFED. THAT WAS what Maud kept thinking as she took in Edwin's furniture. Worse, everything matched, in a floral pattern better suited for curtains.

"Grace," Edwin was saying to his wife, "you of course are familiar with the reverend's wife, Mrs. Macdonald—the one who turned our little Island into quite the tourist spot. The descriptions of the Island in her novels are superb, and her fans are flocking there because of it."

Maud tried for a good-natured laugh. She looked at Grace. "Your husband isn't taking nearly enough credit for the on-slaught of tourists. Leaving for us to fill in the fact that he laid the foundation for tourism on the Island well before me with those speeches to packed halls." Hearing no response, Maud turned to Ewan, who was rubbing his left temple. "I've—Ewan and I have—been so eager to meet you."

"Pleased to have you," Grace said. She took her time lowering herself onto one of the plump sofas and gestured for everyone else to sit as well. "You have shown my husband excellent hospitality. Opportunities to preach too. His old congregations sure do miss him—always begging for him back."

"I have not been blessed with either of our guests' gifts of steadfastness in career," Edwin said, lighting a cigar after taking his seat. "Visiting preaching is just the thing for me." He glanced at Ewan. "Care for a smoke, Ewan?"

"Oh," Ewan said, looking up from his lap and around the room like he was seeing it for the first time. "Not now, thank you," he added when he saw Edwin holding out the cigar.

As Ewan's palm traveled to his forehead, Maud cleared her throat. How long had his silence lasted?

"Where are the children today?" Maud asked.

"Off with some friends who live down the street," Grace said, folding her hands in her lap.

"I hope we will meet them tonight," Maud said.

"You'll meet them at supper. They've all just started their fall terms, so they will have plenty to say." Grace looked at Ewan. "I do hope you like pot roast. My husband was no help at all in letting me know if there are any foods you don't care for."

"Pot roast will be wonderful," Maud answered, adjusting herself on the sofa. "You have a lovely home here. Perhaps you could tell me its history. I'm always interested in the stories that accompany old homes."

"We didn't learn much about any story, I'm afraid." Grace's

expression had barely changed since they'd come in the room. "Can I offer you some tea, Mrs. Macdonald?" she asked. "Reverend Macdonald?"

"Please, call us Maud and Ewan," Maud said. "I'd love some. I'm sure Ewan—"

"Actually," Ewan said, his voice drowning out Maud's, "I think I'll take a nap before supper. I'm afraid I have a headache starting up."

Ewan had slumped down unattractively into the sofa without Maud noticing. Maud leaned forward, hoping to block as much of him as she could from Grace's sight.

"I'm sorry to hear that," Grace said, unaffected. "I'll show you to the spare room."

After Grace stood up, Maud looked directly at Edwin for the first time since they'd entered the parlor. He sat far back in his chair, smoking, and quieter than she'd ever seen him. His silence was making her nervous.

"You know," Maud said, "I could use a short nap myself."

In a moment she had Ewan off the couch, placing upward pressure on his elbow as they followed Grace out of the room.

"NICE OF YOU to come up with me, dear," Ewan said with what sounded like genuine gratitude.

They settled down together on the guest bed, and Ewan was asleep within minutes. When Maud heard the familiar gurgle of his snore start deep in his throat, she reached into her purse and pulled out the small yellow notepad where she'd been keeping her journal notes.

"Mrs. Smith is a nice but uninteresting sort," she wrote.

She set her pen down, then picked it up again. At the end of a caret, she added the words "likeable, however."

Maud glanced down at Ewan. She couldn't possibly sleep

herself—she'd barely slept in the last few nights—but she could try to make her heart stop beating so ridiculously.

EDWIN BARELY SPOKE during supper. There were seven children at the table to do the talking for him, but there was also the intent way he studied the potato pieces on his dinner plate. And the fact that he never, not once, looked in Maud's direction.

Maud asked to use the washroom twice. Each time, she apprehended herself in the mirror, shaking her head at the wrinkles that showed up all over her face in the soft light.

Back at the table, she couldn't help but keep looking toward Edwin at intervals so short they embarrassed her. Her legs crossed tighter, and she felt a bead of sweat trickle down from the back of her knee to her ankle. Not all that different from the way she usually felt around Edwin—the same restlessness that made the minutes expand and the hours contract—but now with an added dose of nausea that made it difficult to eat.

And yet, she'd managed the right number of questions, the right timing for laughs. There wasn't a thing for which Grace could fault her.

"UP TO YOUR rooms, now—it's gotten late," Grace said to the children as soon as they stood up from the table. Maud excused herself again for the washroom.

When she came out, she found Edwin leaning against the doorframe to the parlor. She started to speak but stopped. His eyes were focused out the window on two yellow specks among the shrubbery. A raccoon's eyes, she thought at first, but changed her mind. The specks were too unwavering to be any sort of animal. Still, she felt the itchy sensation of being observed.

"Where's Ewan?" she asked.

"He followed behind Grace," Edwin said, still looking out the window. "Seemed pretty tired; his eyes were glazed over like they get. I assume he's gone to bed."

"I see," Maud said, drawing close to Edwin's side. "He's continued to struggle with his health."

"A shame."

"It is." Maud moved so the side of her hand rested against Edwin's, fidgeting at first like it might have been an accident. "How are you?"

"Fine enough." He rubbed his eyes, which was not like him. Then he returned his hand next to hers.

"You don't seem fine," said Maud.

"This day has felt strange," Edwin said, not looking at her. "Having you here."

"Strange in what way?"

Edwin turned his face toward her, but his eyes stayed away. "You must see it, the way it is around here."

"I'm not sure I know what you mean," Maud said.

"I didn't want you to see it. All this ordinariness. It is not what I intended, you know. When I was young. I hoped for so much out of life."

"We both did. I still do."

"I know you do." His voice was soft when he said it. Her arms ached to pull him in, to hold him, to have him take her away somewhere. Anywhere.

"I cannot help but hope," she said.

"But don't you feel it sometimes? The need to face the truth of what things are?"

Maud's breath caught in the back of her throat. There wasn't enough air. She nodded because she couldn't speak.

Edwin put the back of his hand to his face and wiped away tears that Maud only just noticed.

"Nothing to be done, is there?" he asked.

"About what?" Maud stepped even closer.

"About old choices," Edwin said, leaning now so the side of his body was against hers. He took her hand fully in his.

Her desperation to have him—more of him, all of him—was overwhelming. They could make a life together.

You could write together!

She could inspire him to focus the way he'd always wanted. They could move back to the Island and give joint speeches to packed crowds. No more dabbling in insurance sales, visiting minister posts, and other hardly fulfilling pursuits. And the children—well, the children could all play together. It would be good for Chester and Stuart to have older influences.

Oh, how this vision fills my heart with gladness of the solemnest and sincerest sort.

They could be social in a way that being a practicing minister's wife never permitted. They could host visits and dance late into the night. She would never have to fear that Edwin might make an awkward comment or an ill-timed exit. They would be each other's closest friends.

She started to say something but stopped herself.

"We could try," she said finally, gripping his hand. She gritted her teeth at the sound of her voice, which had come out high in the way of a schoolgirl.

Suddenly no part of Edwin was by her side. "Maud," he said, and turned to face her. "We both know that's not possible." He looked at the ground.

Maud shut her eyes, and when she opened them, Edwin was already at the top of the stairs. She heard a bedroom door close.

Only after that could she hear the impossibly gentle tones of a child's story carry down the stairs. She wondered if Grace had been reading all along. She wondered how much Grace had overheard.

35.

Maud stared at the ledger sheet she kept of her earnings. Nearly one hundred thousand dollars she'd earned by her pen—a lifetime's worth for an affluent family.

"Reward once tasted soon loses its flavor." One of her grandmother's truisms. And hadn't that first five-dollar check for a short story carried with it more joy than the thousands she'd earned from recent novels? She'd tucked the check under her pillow for a full week before she could bring herself to cash it.

Whatever the consistency of heaven might be, it couldn't be reward alone. Maud wondered what Edwin would have to say about that.

She shook her head at herself; the familiar pain in her chest returned.

It had been five and a half months, a full turn from fall to winter, and not a word from him. Worse, not a word from Anne. She hadn't been able to bring herself to write during those months, or recopy any journal entries either. It wasn't just pain that was stopping her this time, the way it had after losing Frede.

"I feel hopeless," Ewan had told her on one of his worst days, moving his head back and forth against the pillow.

Hopeless. Yes, it was something like that.

"ENOUGH IS ENOUGH," Maud said, walking the perimeter of the braided rug in the parlor a few days later.

With past loans included, Maud had given Stella nearly ten thousand dollars. *The Bank of Maud, Dedicated Lender For Life—No Interest!* Frede might have joked.

Now Stella was asking for a few thousand more.

Maud picked up the letter. "You simply *must* lend us," it said.

Maud pulled out a clean sheet of paper and started her reply, but her pen stopped after the first line. An image came to her of Stella's hair, wild and curly around her face— the same hair as Frede's.

"Stella," Maud whispered in the educational tone she sometimes used with her boys, "is not Frede. Stella is living on a cattle ranch in Los Angeles. With a husband to support her." It was confirmed now. Despite occasional glimmers of hope, Stella would never be a kindred spirit.

Maud continued writing her denial of Stella's request, pausing only over the salutation. "Sincerely," she wrote finally. Stella would note the change and add it to her case against Maud. But the point was to have the letter over with and in the mail before she succumbed and wrote another check.

Once she finished, Maud crunched Stella's letter into a ball, rolling it against the oak desk in the library until it was as small as she could make it. She threw it in the silver bin a few yards away. It dropped right in, without hitting the rim.

"A regular ball player," she said.

But it hadn't been satisfying in the way she had intended it to be.

The sudden feeling of a warm hand on her shoulder made Maud's toes raise off the ground a few inches. One of the boys, it must be.

But she was standing, too tall for either of the boys to reach, and the hand too big.

She turned her head, verifying. Ewan rounded both of her

shoulders with his arm in what used to be a regular gesture of his.

When she finally spoke, her voice came out in a hoarse whisper. "Ewan."

"It's Valentine's Day," Ewan said, his voice deeper than usual.

"Is it?" Maud asked, leaning back and surrendering to his embrace.

"It's been a rough time—for both of us. For a while now. But I've come to tell you that you are truly the dearest—" His voice caught. "The dearest little wife in the world."

Maud started to turn. As she did, she thought she felt Ewan's arm pull, drawing her closer and resisting her effort to turn to face him. She pulled his arm across her collarbone instead, weaving her fingers through his.

"Happy Valentine's Day, Ewan," she said.

A knock on the library door sent Ewan in backward motion; Maud barely kept hold of his hand.

"Never mind whatever that is," Maud said. She gripped Ewan's hand tighter, but he was distracted, looking at the door like it might open any second.

"Come in," Maud said finally.

Lily stopped abruptly when she saw them. "Didn't realize I was interrupting."

Maud took a small step away from Ewan. "What is it, Lily?"

"Only—supper tonight. Mr. Macdonald made some specific requests—"

"Requests?" Maud looked at Ewan.

"Duck," he said slowly. "I know you like duck, so I asked for it." Ewan extracted his hand from Maud's. "Shouldn't have interfered. I'll leave you and Lily to talk it over."

"Ewan, thank you," Maud called after him.

Stepping back behind the desk, Maud watched the door until it closed behind Ewan. Then she looked at Lily.

"Well?" she said.

"I need to know supper timing," said Lily. "'The clock ticks swiftly only for those who fail to attend to it.'"

"What's that?"

"You said that once, some time ago." Lily paused. Her mouth turned up at the corners.

"I did?"

Maud could tell Lily was playing another one of her games. Delighting in something she wasn't saying. In the past when this happened, Maud had always managed to stay on her toes. But not today.

"It was the last time Captain Smith visited. I'm sure you remember," Lily said. When Maud said nothing, Lily added, "Captain Smith's turkey did battle with our oven. Simply refused to be cooked. That's when you said that line about the clocks ticking. Anyhow, it was a while back, like I said." She waited. "Any plans for the captain to visit again soon?"

"I don't believe we'll be needing him to supply as a minister anymore, so my guess is no. But Ewan would be the one to know," Maud said.

"Oh," Lily said. She sounded surprised, and a little sad.

"Timing, you asked about timing," Maud said now, her voice toneless. "Anytime for supper is fine."

"The boys, I noticed, are out—"

"They are just down the street. They should be back with plenty of time before supper."

"Well—" Lily stopped. She seemed to be searching hard for something else to say. "I think that's everything. Thank

you, Mrs. Macdonald," she said finally. Her tone was the closest to apologetic Maud had ever heard it.

LATER THAT DAY, waiting for the duck to cook, Maud
found herself up in her bedroom, opening the lockbox where
she kept her journals.

Saying the words out loud to Lily had taken away any last
vestige of hope: They would not be seeing Edwin again.

Once she had the lockbox open, it took only a few minutes to find the page she was after in her most recent set of
journal notes. Her entry describing Edwin's first visit, now
more than a year and a half ago.

"A rather universal genius," she had written. Other flattering things too.

She wrote a caret after that line. She thought for a few
minutes before adding, "I rather think he lacks steadiness of
purpose." Then, "Surpassed in his professional career by men
who were far his inferiors in mental capacity."

She skimmed the next several entries detailing Edwin's
stays at the manse. Many edits would be necessary, but this
was a start.

Then, thinking that she'd heard a noise, Maud stuffed the
journal notes back into the lockbox and hid the key away.

THAT NIGHT, MAUD lay in bed and stared at Ewan
for a long while. He had the red bandanna tied over his
eyes. She thought for the first time about putting it over
her own eyes and tying it tight. The thought was strangely
appealing.

Instead, she pulled closer to Ewan and laid her head on
his chest. She felt his arm encircle her. In the way his fingers rested against her arm, Maud remembered with surprise
the tenderness of Ewan. She remembered the shy young

man who couldn't get his hands out of his pockets, and later couldn't get his hands off her. Whose dimpled smile had made her smile right along with him.

All that goodness was buried somewhere deep inside the heap where they both lay together now, each lost in their own pain.

"Dearest little wife in the world." It wouldn't be so hard to live the rest of her days by that description. It could be a relief, actually. She could stop trying to force her way through molasses that seemed to harden more and more every day. To let go of wanting for good. To be the dear little wife Ewan always hoped she would be.

Lean on each other, Frede said.

She let herself believe that Frede would approve.

A FEW NIGHTS passed with Maud sleeping on Ewan's chest and dressing haphazardly in the morning. Not writing, not reading, not journaling, not trying at a single thing. It was easy only because of the heavy weight of sadness and loss lodged in her chest that made trying seem impossible.

Lily managed the meals just fine without instruction. And the boys, occupied with schoolwork and friends, hardly seemed to notice a difference.

Then, as Maud was falling asleep one evening, the wind picked up. She woke in the middle of the night to the sound of a branch breaking off a nearby tree. She stirred, hot and uncomfortable.

She had been dreaming of fires again. Fire had always had a hold on her, ever since she was a little girl poking her first journal into the stove.

But her real fascination began the night of the Cavendish brush fire.

She soon found her fingers running across her recopied

journal volumes from her Cavendish years. She pulled one out and starting paging through.

November 13, 1907. Here it was.

She started reading.

Anne had been accepted but not yet published. She was wearing Ewan's diamond solitaire on her finger. And the evening had been mild enough, despite it being November, for Maud's usual walk. She'd started out at the final fade of twilight, keeping to the road between the school and graveyard instead of any of the narrower paths. The air had smelled like pure winter, with the pines pushing their scent out ahead of the decaying leaves.

She'd heard it before she saw it, a sound like the rush of water, far more of a rush than the brook a few yards away had ever produced. Pulling everywhere on her body, urging it closer.

Past the valley where the brook ran nearly dry and halfway up the hill, a brush fire burned, bright orange in the center and red along the edges.

She was out of breath by the time she reached it.

The fire grabbed at the air with a forceful sort of need; its roar exposed the spaced-out pops and cackles of chimney fires for the imitators they were.

Maud's eyes spit tears and her skin sweated and she moved closer. She watched the fire take an aged, misshapen tree by its upper branches. Her thumbs twitched at the destruction until she noticed that the tree appeared willing, bending itself toward the flames.

The fire was not a destroyer, she realized then. It was a container that anything—a tree, a house—could pour itself into, coming out no different than the earth underneath it. The ground afterward a pile of dark crumbs. Dark, of course, but no darker than anything else at night.

She laughed in the face of the relief that flooded through her. All the pressures she ever felt—gone. All the wrongs and rights—gone. It was a wonderful idea. Absolutely wonderful.

She knew she'd need to describe this fire in her journal, but she hadn't been able to think of any words fresh enough. All the words seemed like old towels, sullied by their history of use.

Then she moved closer and didn't think anymore about words. The sky was slashed with orange and red, and the stars seemed close at hand.

Looking down again, she saw that the flames were nearer than she thought. Her heart delivered a throttling so hard she felt it in her temples. The fire could have caught up to her in a matter of seconds if the wind shifted. She began a slow retreat, checking back over her shoulder every few steps.

Later that night, she'd pulled out her journal.

As she did her best to put words to the indescribable, Maud could still feel that perfect mix of comfort and awe, that tremendous heat that stirred peace through her body with its utterly indifferent, crackling spoon. The fire hadn't cared a lick more about her than anything else on earth. Fire brought things down to their essence.

Now, she thought for the first time of what had grown out of those dark crumbs left by the Cavendish brush fire. A new field, green as ever not even a year later. New trees too.

There it was—the kernel she'd taken away from that night, a kernel she'd kept buried inside her.

The fire didn't just destroy. The fire remade. Transformed. Cut a path for new growth.

All she had to be was willing.

THE NEXT MORNING, the wind stopped, and Maud felt the heat of the sun on her skin for the first time in a while.

Soothed by stillness and sun, Maud thought first of her journal recopying project. The fire remade, and so could she. Shaping her own narrative now seemed like the most important of any writing project she had undertaken. She would apply the same discipline she did to the rest of her writing. She would spend hours recopying every day, rather than fifteen-minute spurts. She would catch herself up to the present, and in the process, she would give her life the sense of order that it had been lacking now for years. Things she did not understand fully—Ewan's malady, Edwin's disappearance from her life—could be minimalized. Or reimagined.

Her heart pounding with an energy she had not felt in weeks, she pulled out her journals and her pen.

SHE DID HER hours of recopying at night, after the boys were in bed. They were hers during the day, and Maud intended to be their mother as fully as possible. She listened closely to Stuart, who remained concerned about Papa getting better. And she kept her eye on Chester, trying to soothe his upset before it escalated. As often as she could, she tried to see both boys through Frede's eyes, devoid of worry and comparison.

Maud held Ewan's hand in bed at night too, and she kissed his cheek before closing her eyes. Her anger and angst had diffused, replaced by something new: sadness lined with understanding. She could see herself now in the red spiderwebs surrounding Ewan's black irises. She could see herself in his trembling hands, shaking his pills out of their bottles. Saw every day in him the other side of a decision she had barely found the strength to make.

On the day she finished recopying the final journal entry from her Cavendish years, she found herself in bed with several of her grandmother's handkerchiefs by her side, using up one after the other as the tears came. She let them run.

"March 13, 1921. Today I finished copying my Cavendish diary," she wrote in her journal notes.

Perfect happiness. The phrase was circling her mind like a noose. It was what she had thought she most wanted, in all her Cavendish years. What Anne had wanted and received. But why was happiness the ultimate victory? Why the only aim? Hadn't Anne also become relegated to the background of her own story?

"Perfect happiness, I have never had—never will have," Maud wrote.

And yet life remained interesting.

She looked back at her page of journal notes.

"Yet there have been, after all," she added, "many wonderful and exquisite hours in my life."

36.

E wan rested at the kitchen table while Maud washed the breakfast dishes. He had just finished saying how sorry he was not to have caught her on her walk. He had hurried in his search for her, and he was only now recovering his breath. He was also eager for a morning kiss, which she had happily given him.

"Frede tells me you are off to see Reverend Smith this afternoon," Maud said carefully.

"That's right," Ewan said. "He's a good friend."

"You were in the seminary together, is that right?" Maud asked, indulging the diversion while she gathered her own thoughts.

"We were," Ewan said.

"He's making quite a name for himself these days." Maud thought of an article she'd been reading in the Charlottetown *Patriot* the day she learned that *Anne* had been accepted for publication. It touted Reverend Smith as one of the continent's finest speakers. In every province, and American cities too, he'd had audiences on their feet with applause, showing images of the Island's natural beauty. She'd had a daydream that morning of herself in the shoes of Reverend Smith, speaking to audiences across the United States and Canada.

The acceptance letter had dropped out of her grandmother's hand not minutes after the daydream ended.

"He sure is," Ewan said. Maud turned away from the dishes to look at Ewan. The newspaper he had picked up on his walk covered most of his face.

"Frede said you meant to talk to Reverend Smith about the General Assembly speech you planned to give." She paused. "The speech on the best means of improving the Canadian ministry."

Ewan cleared his throat. He did not lower the paper. "Edwin offered me the speech in his place. He's too busy this week to give it."

"Ewan, is it true that you are turning the speech down?" She walked closer so she could see his face.

Ewan glanced up at Maud quickly and then back down. "Yes, I mean to."

"But why?"

Ewan put his paper down, finally, and shifted in his seat. Then he rose up and took both of her hands in his. "You are more important than any old speech."

Maud felt her resolve to understand weaken in the face of the sentiment. But her thumbs were twitching against Ewan's.

"So you came here for my birthday instead of preparing? On top of finding another minister to preach for you today?"

He nodded. "Of course I did."

"Oh, Ewan, you shouldn't have." Maud's head shook. "Not for my sake. As much as I've loved having you here. This speech is a once-in-a-lifetime opportunity." She squeezed his hands then, an idea occurring to her. "What do you say to staying here this afternoon and working through the speech instead of turning it down? I could help you write it." She was desperate to retrieve his notes from the rubbish bin, to see what they might say. But she didn't dare let on that she knew about those.

Ewan backed away from Maud then, sinking down into his chair. "I don't think so," he said.

"But why not, Ewan? We could have such fun." She went to a kitchen drawer and pulled out a pad and pen. "I love to sketch out ideas. I've spent a long time practicing, you know? You just say them out loud, and I'll write them down here. I think we'll make a splendid team."

What an idea this was. She and Ewan could be collaborators. Colleagues. A happy old couple they might make one day, holding hands on a front porch swing while they talked through his sermons together.

"I don't think so," Ewan said again. He stood suddenly and straightened his spine. "I appreciate the offer and all. But I don't want to give the speech is the truth. I simply don't want to. And you wanting it for me isn't going to change my mind." He said this with a grave resolve she had never heard before in his voice.

"All right," she said, tilting her head to the side as if it might help her see him more clearly. "I thought you wanted to give the speech," Maud said slowly. "I was mistaken. I see that now."

"Thank you for understanding," Ewan said, and she could see his face soften in relief as he sank back down into his chair with his newspaper.

Maud thought suddenly of the postcards Ewan had sent from Scotland, back before he dropped out of his graduate seminary studies. The sad, black-and-white sketch of a penguin with droopy eyes on the front of one of them. Never more than a few, sorry sentences on the backs, and the last one entirely blank. She remembered how little she had understood Ewan's reasoning for dropping out of school. Much like now.

Ewan's eyes looked a little like that penguin's, glancing up at her from her grandmother's kitchen table. Where was the man from last night, with his sure-footed command of himself?

A pattern began to press its way up into her consciousness. Ewan's expression became like the sad penguin whenever the conversation turned to his career or hers. Ewan was ruled by a fear of failing. She saw this now, plain as day. So he never fully gave himself a chance. Her writing couldn't be easy for him; of course it couldn't. Seeing her cast her line again and again, and finally get a large bite.

Maud studied Ewan as he studied his newspaper, trying to grasp at the roots of her feelings toward him now. Had they changed?

She didn't think so. She had seen something like this in him all along. She also knew that he was devoted. Devoted to her. Devoted to family. She and Ewan could create the sort of home she'd never had, comprised of adults who loved the children they raised without an ounce of resentment. Without Ewan, there was no hope of this. Not at her age.

Equally plain now in Maud's mind was the fact that Ewan would never understand writing as her priority. Not only would he not understand, she realized with a sinking feeling—he would never accept it. She, to him, was paramount. And the well of self-doubt inside him would never accept being anything less to her.

"Ewan," Maud said quietly, sitting in the chair closest to him and pulling it even closer. "I need to tell you something."

He looked up at her with worried eyebrows that softened her heart.

"I cannot leave grandmother, Ewan," she said. "I must remain with her in this old place until she passes." She swallowed. "I know you have been waiting. And I know what I said last night. But I don't suppose it will be too long yet." Her thumb twitched against her forefinger under the table, waiting for his response.

Ewan sighed. "I half suspected as much," he said, his face surprisingly calm. He reached under the table for her hand and stroked her thumb. "I love how you care for your family, Maud. It's one of my favorite things about you. I would do the same for my mother if she was ever in need."

Maud felt her stomach turn queasy. A bad batch of butter? But Frede and Ewan had eaten the same toast and butter as her.

This was a good thing, she told herself. Ewan understood what she had said. He wasn't angry. And he didn't seem nearly so sad as when she had asked him about the speech.

Still unsure of her feelings, she willed Anne's voice into her mind. But no voice came. The Fox and the Old Hen were uncharacteristically silent.

Well, she had achieved the result she wanted. She had bought herself time to keep writing. Hadn't Anne decided to stay with Marilla at Green Gables after Matthew died? So why then did she feel like a knot had tightened between herself and Ewan when she had meant for her words to loosen its grip?

"It will be all the more wonderful when we can be together," Ewan said, pulling her in for a kiss. "Just like last night," he whispered. "And in the meantime, we will belong to each other. We will always belong to each other."

Belong. The word rang in her mind like a bad chord on the old church harp she used to play. But here she was, nodding and issuing a half smile of consent.

This is what she would owe Ewan for waiting.

THE TEMPTATION WAS irresistible. The minute Ewan left the kitchen to wash up before leaving, Maud was at the rubbish bin, digging beneath toast crusts and setting aside tea bags until she had Ewan's speech notes in hand.

Watching the door, Maud read quickly.

Her stomach sank.

It wasn't that his ideas were terrible. They were simply—ordinary. Similar to the notes he would make for a regular Sunday sermon. First, a standard Biblical passage. Then, a few fairly traditional ideas on its meaning, followed by several sentences of trite wisdom about ministry on the Island.

It was clear now that Ewan would not have risen to the occasion. Out of lack of capability? Or lack of effort?

No matter.

Glancing down again, she turned the paper over. The back was blank. No points of redemption to be found.

She shook her head at herself. She was being harsh. But the disappointment she felt ran so deep, it nearly cut off her airway. Disappointment in Ewan? No, that was not it. She didn't fault Ewan.

The disappointment resided within herself. It existed in the space between reality and what she imagined reality to be, where most of life's pain—and most of life's pleasure—existed.

Ewan was a decent orator, but he would never be a great one. Even if he overcame his insecurity one day, Ewan would never hold an audience captive. They would never sit together at night by the fire, editing each other's work, reading their words out loud with laughter and wine.

The paper in her hands had turned, with each passing realization, into a tighter and tighter ball. Suddenly, she hated that ball with a vengeance. A record for all posterity.

No, what would posterity care?

A record for the judgmental soul that lived inside her. The Reader with his watchful eye.

She closed her eyes, crunched the ball even tighter, and then—

Burn. The word came to her like a high note sung by the church choir, lifting her spirits instantly. She turned to the old stove in the corner, where the coals still gleamed red.

She eyed the kitchen door again, feeling a moment of guilt. But this paper was already rubbish to Ewan.

In went the ball in one delicious swoop.

It took its time burning, which bothered her. Too compact. Or maybe moisture from her hand was to blame.

When at last it lit, she felt the satisfaction she had been longing for. What a thing, fire. Every bit as beautiful, and as destructive, as its innocent cousin water. Yet no one would call fire innocent. Why was this? And what did it say about her that she was so drawn to one above the other?

Not simply drawn, though. That wasn't all of it.

She didn't just want to be close to the flames.

She envied them.

III.

Embers

Those who can soar to the highest heights can also plunge to the deepest depths, and . . . the natures which enjoy most keenly are those which suffer most sharply.

—LUCY MAUD MONTGOMERY,
Anne of the Island, 1914

37.

A final hurrah. Not nearly so big as the last fire. It did not need to be.

Still, the flames did their job, rising high over the dirt patch in the corner of the yard. Greedy for more, but they had already taken all there was to burn, and they had almost taken her nightgown too.

If she hadn't thrown the folder of journal notes into the flames, she might never have let it go. A mess. A travesty. There was no recovering it now.

On last reading, the words had all looked like sticks and stones to her. Disconnected nonsense. What was the expression? Sticks and stones break bones. But not words.

Well, that was a bunch of hogwash. Words broke plenty. As every broken soul in the world could attest.

Oh, but every healed one could attest to the opposite.

A voice from the past. Not welcome here. A daughter? The next best thing, for a time.

Her notes for the final volume were almost gone now, reduced to a glowing rectangle of embers. The eleventh volume. It might have been the most honest of them all.

A laugh, hollow and low. She spun around. No one in sight, nothing moving aside from the fire, and the shaking of her own belly.

38.

Despite her lack of experience with the route, Anita maneuvered the sharp left turn with ease like the good Island girl she was. Maud let out a sigh of relief. Seeing Anita's eyes travel toward the passenger seat, Maud righted herself and loosened the grip of her hand on the side of the seat cushion.

"Thank goodness for you," Maud said. "I cannot tell you how nervous it has made me, the way Chester drives. I knew it wouldn't matter that you'd never driven anywhere except the Island. An Island girl's skills can compete with the best of them. A Webb girl especially."

Maud's hands returned to the knitting she had brought along. Out of the corner of her eye, Maud caught Anita smiling.

"What's this event we're going to exactly?" Anita asked.

"An address to the local women's guild," Maud said, successfully containing a cough. "Run-of-the-mill, I'm afraid. I hope you won't be bored."

"Surely not, Aunt Maud," said Anita. Maud liked that Anita had always called her "aunt," even though in reality their relation was more distant. Anita Maud Webb was the youngest daughter of Maud's third cousin Myrtle. Anita had been born just after Maud left the Island, and named in

Maud's honor. Of all the next generation of family members back on the Island, Anita was the one Maud had come to like the most. Just a few weeks ago, Anita had arrived in Toronto to become Maud's new maid.

"You'll speak about your novels?" Anita asked.

"The novels, yes. A little on my background, on the state of Canadian literature, and the Island of course. People always like to hear about the Island. I have a set of remarks pre-prepared and memorized for these sorts of events—right turn here, dear, this is where we park! I should have mentioned it earlier."

"Not a problem." Anita managed to slow the car just enough to keep the turn into the parking lot smooth.

Maud felt her jaw relax even further. "Now be sure to tell me if you have any suggestions for improvement, either in the speech or in my delivery."

"I'm sure I won't. I am so looking forward to hearing it."

Anita turned off the car engine and took her purse. Quick on her feet, she was at Maud's side of the car in an instant, extending her hand.

"So it's official—I look even older than I think I do!" Maud said, laughing as she put away her knitting.

Then she took Anita's still-outreached hand and said, "Good girl—always help an old lady out no matter what she might have to say in protest."

"I DON'T KNOW that I've ever been so interested in someone speaking in front of a room!" Anita said after starting up the car. Anita's eyes were directed toward the passenger side of the car instead of the road, which earned her a wary look from Maud. But Anita didn't seem to notice. "The rest of the audience too—you had us all right from the first. Are all your speeches so clever?"

"Well, they don't differ too much, if that answers your question. Although the Spanish Inquisition at the end was not exactly customary. They could have warned me about that—"

Maud winced as Anita braked hard.

"No more taking your eyes off the road now, Anita! Surely this afternoon couldn't have distracted you quite so much."

"I'm sorry, Aunt Maud," said Anita. After a few seconds, Anita picked right back up again with the same tone, her eyes now on the road. "We all knew you were a famous author, but no one in the family ever told me you could speak so well. And the honors they mentioned in your introduction! What was the acronym that young man used? O.R.B.?"

"O.B.E. Order of the British Empire, it means." Seeing Anita look toward her, Maud continued. "The king's idea, all coming out of the Great War and his desire to honor certain noncombatants, including people in the arts. Nice of the British government to reach some modicum of its attention clear across the ocean to a Canadian province." Maud picked up her knitting.

"But when did this happen? I don't remember word spreading on the Island."

"Nineteen thirty-five," Maud said, her hands at work on her knitting. "It was about a year after I learned before I got back to the Island. By then it was old news, and no one likes old news. I did show Aunt Emily the insignia when I visited. All she managed to say was that it was quite pretty." Maud laughed.

"Aunt Maud! You should have told us all."

"Oh hush."

"And the Canadian Authors Association that put on the event? So official sounding. You must be one of their most important members."

"If only you knew," Maud said under her breath. She watched Anita's eyebrows cinch together.

"What's that?" Anita asked.

"Only that looks can be deceiving. It's an old adage but a true one, as I expect you'll discover for yourself during your time here." Maud delivered the last of her words with finality. She busied herself fixing a mistake in her knitting.

THE NEXT NIGHT, as they cleared the table from supper, Maud looped her arm through Anita's elbow. "I have an idea," she said.

Anita pulled away a little to face Maud. "An idea?"

"The movies. Let's escape for a few hours, what do you say? My old friend from Leaskdale goes all the time, apparently—on a whim, she said once. Doesn't that sound wonderful? To act on something as perfectly insignificant-sounding as a whim." Maud coughed. "We have just enough time to make the evening show."

"Now?" Anita had new energy in her voice. She pushed the kitchen door open and set a stack of plates on the counter. "What about the dishes?"

"I'm through worrying about dishes. What fun is getting older if you can't give up some of the old worries for all the new ones you have to contend with—a lesson my poor grandmother never did learn, by the way. The dishes will be here when we get back. The hours at the movies we may never get again." Maud coughed hard then, shaking her head at herself. "Now, that's a morbid thought. You just ignore anything morbid that I say, dear, that's some sound advice."

Anita laughed. "All right, Aunt Maud. Are you sure you feel well enough?" She put her hand on Maud's shoulder, her touch so gentle that Maud flinched.

"Not entirely well, but we can't let a thing like that stop us. I'd never go anywhere these days."

Anita followed Maud to the front entryway and took her purse from its hook. "Should we ask Uncle Ewan?"

Maud breathed hard out of her nose, then laughed.

"I'd love to hear what he would say to that," she said, mostly to herself. Turning to Anita, she added, "Movies are not an interest of Ewan's."

"He seems to keep to himself, I've noticed," Anita said. "Though it's farm men I'm used to, I suppose. There's so much for them to do around the property. I need to stop expecting it all to be the same in the city."

"Oh, don't go taking Ewan as representative of city men. He does things his own way. He's always been one to give me my space around the house—in all my pursuits, really." Even now that his malady had forced his retirement from the ministry and he had less to occupy him, Ewan had continued to carve a path through his days that seemed conspicuously designed to avoid her.

"That's a good thing, I suppose. Surely he must love your books, though."

"I do not believe he has read a word of one," Maud said. As she pulled on a light sweater, she caught Anita's expression. A flicker of old yearning came back to her, for a husband who would take a real interest in her work. She had fooled herself once into believing that Ewan could be that husband. "Books are nearly all the same to Ewan. Not of interest. It's his nature, which is very different than mine—nothing he ever could help. You'll see soon enough."

"All books." Anita let the question lie flat at the end.

Maud opened the front door and looked straight out into

the dark. The wind caught several strands of her hair and lifted them up and away from her face.

"Maybe mine especially," Maud said.

"GOING ON MY third week of illness," Maud wrote in her journal notes. "Dr. Lane has diagnosed bronchial-pneumonia."

Maud's eyes watered as she coughed into the stained blue handkerchief that had become her grandmother's when her mother died.

"In a small fit of energy that lasted half an hour," she wrote, "I booked a train ticket to Prince Edward Island to leave next month. It will no longer be the height of summer, but it shouldn't be too cold yet. It has been years since I've been, and I don't know that I'll ever go again. Some part of me senses that I will not. Only Providence knows these things, of course; my will is powerless in her wake."

Just then Maud heard the front door slam into its frame. As soon as she could secure her notes under the mattress and settle her legs and arms back into their normal positions, Chester was in the master bedroom, not bothering to knock.

"Hello, Mother," Chester said. He walked to her bedside and kissed her forehead. She moved over to make room for him to sit beside her.

"Chester. A surprise, as usual, to see you." Maud attempted a smile.

She watched Chester study the room. Collecting data. His eyes made their way to the balled-up handkerchiefs beside her legs, then to the newest prescriptions from Dr. Lane on the bedside table.

While his eyes were in route, Chester said, "You can probably guess what I've come about."

Maud coughed quietly into a new handkerchief, neatening the pile of used ones. "I'm not up for a guessing game right now, Chester," she said, her tone weaker than she intended. She coughed again. "I've been ill."

"I can see that," said Chester. He scooted closer to Maud on the bed but looked past her in the direction of the dresser. "I've come because I haven't received my copy of the revised will. It's on its way, I hope?"

Maud sat up straighter. "What revised will, Chester?"

Chester rose from the bed. His hands had turned into fists.

"The revised will that you promised—"

"Promised?"

"When I reconciled with Luella and was 'situated in a home' with her and the children. I have reconciled, and you saw me situated with your own two eyes. You have managed to pull me through law school by the grip of your teeth, and I am gainfully employed as an attorney. What I mean—" He stopped. "I mean exactly what we discussed and agreed to, you and I."

"Chester," Maud whispered. She started over again, trying for a sturdier tone. "Chester, all of this is very new, your—situation. I have been ill. Your father has been ill. And legal changes do not happen overnight. You must understand why we are moving slowly. You must understand, given the history, our cause for—trepidation."

"What I understand," Chester said, his voice suddenly thunderous, "is that you—and leave Father out of this, we all know he doesn't control a damn thing around here—are revoking your promise. After I have done every single thing that you wanted."

He began pacing the length of the bedroom. After a few round trips, he stopped near the middle of the bed, looking at

Maud for the first time and just soon enough to see her slink down a few inches in the covers. She saw a flicker of a smile as his face registered her movement.

He lowered his volume. "I always thought my mother, the famous Lucy Maud Montgomery, was a woman of her word."

A few tears slid down Maud's face. Eventually, she said, "This is something I need time to consider—when I am well."

Chester sighed and walked over to the bed. Slowly, he settled himself beside her, resting his forehead close to hers.

When he eventually spoke, his voice was different. "Dear Mother." He paused. "You show such preference for Stuart. You always have. You can't know how badly that makes me feel. And I cannot see why. It's not as if he is so much better at being what you want than I am." Chester moved away slightly and turned to face her.

She felt the hurt she so often felt with Chester, made worse by the kernel of truth in his words. Stuart always had been more comprehensible to her. But had she shown so obvious a preference? She loved Chester so. Looking at him straight on, she could still see his face as a baby, round and chubby cheeked. Her firstborn. He woke up each day with eyes and mouth wide open, keen to see and taste the world.

As a young boy, Chester had perpetually disheveled hair. "Outside, mother, outside," he would say with the same wide, unchanging smile. Chester never could get enough of the outdoors. He was always bringing sticks and other discoveries inside, tucking them under his pillow at night. Maud would find his sheets covered with dirty remnants and tell herself that he was a nature lover after her own heart.

As a teenager, Chester's face changed. He no longer wore a smile like a favorite hat. Maud could see him think before each smile and frown, contemplating when to flip the switch. He was smart. He did well on every test he chose to show up for, without a moment of study that she had ever observed. Stuart was smart too, but in a different way. Stuart loved to study. He came to her, shared what he was learning, and even asked for her help from time to time. With Stuart, she always knew her value.

She could not remember when she had first started to worry about Chester, for Chester, whenever she was with Chester. She could not recall when the now-familiar pang had started to sound its same sorry note in her chest. Each time Chester's responses were outside of bounds. Each time he betrayed the rules of right and wrong—rules so deeply ingrained in Maud that she had never understood them to be optional.

Still, she loved him so. Still, she hungered for him to be settled. Content. Right in his heart and sound in his mind. And he knew it. Oh yes, he knew it.

Chester gave an exaggerated sigh, then continued, "I didn't want to bring this up if I could avoid it, but I feel I owe it to you to tell you. You think Stuart's finished with Joy Laird, but I have it on good information that he is not."

The slump left Maud's back. "What do you mean?"

"I mean," Chester said, smiling a little, "that he's sent her his medical school pin. Just recently too. And I can't imagine that gift didn't come with some letters and visits alongside it. So you see, Mother"—he stood—"your golden boy isn't so golden as you think. Still running around with a girl with a drunk for a father. Certainly there's no justification for treating me so shabbily by comparison!"

He paused and studied Maud's face. Apparently seeing what he wanted, he kissed her cheek.

"I've got to be going—familial responsibilities, you know," he said.

Just before pulling the bedroom door closed behind him,

Chester looked back and said, "I'll keep an eye out for a copy of the new will in the mail."

When Maud heard the bedroom door latch click into place, she sank down further in the bed and rolled over on her side. Coughing loudly, she reached for the bedside table, pouring from a near-empty bottle of cough syrup without sitting up. She lay still for a while, until her legs felt restless.

She needed to turn over, that was all. After she did, she scooted further toward Ewan's side of the bed. She closed her eyes. Then she sighed and scooted even further, reaching her hand into Ewan's bedside drawer and pulling out a bottle of pills. Ewan's lifeblood for the past few decades. She took three. It couldn't hurt, and it might just help.

THE NEXT DAY, Maud returned to her journal notes.

"I've had some unwelcome news concerning an old worry," she wrote. "One that haunted me for years and that I thought had lifted from my shoulders for good. Not that it should surprise me now."

She put her pen down and thought about how to put this; as with anything difficult to touch, it was all in the handling.

She shook her head. These were only notes. She was well into the tenth of the set of formal volumes purchased back in Leaskdale, and the decision of what to include in that volume would come later, when she had better information.

She licked her finger and touched it to the corner of the notepad so that only the top page lifted.

On the next page she wrote, "To put it plainly, which is all I can muster these days, it seems that Stuart has given the daughter of a bootlegger his medical school pin. I let myself believe we were out of the woods when he started up with the girl next door. She was the sort he could have a good life with. Stable, and from a proper family.

"But Joy Laird. He's always had a soft spot for her. He tells me she has a good heart and her family is better than I suppose, but I can't help but imagine the way the neighbors would talk about a marriage like that. After all my difficulty with Chester, it is the last thing I can handle right now.

"Joy Laird is the only thing that ever has come between me and Stuart, and I let myself believe she never would again."

She paused. "Of course one must always consider the source of such information. And I do not have a reliable one. Time always does tell, whether we want it to or not."

Chester's words came back to her then. "A woman of her word," he'd said. "My mother," he'd said, drawing out the first word. She felt like he had spoken inside her own chest, somewhere between her ribs. He knew exactly what he was doing, which didn't stop it from working.

The next thing Maud knew she was standing by her bookshelf, rummaging through a set of files. Her expert fingers found her old will quickly. Sitting at her desk with the will in front of her, her eyes grew heavy. Sighing, she forced her eyes open and took her new black felt tip marker to the first few lines, drawing it thick across the page so the old words became only curls and sticks.

THE NEXT MORNING, Maud came down to breakfast late.

Ewan never read the front page of the newspaper anymore; his fingers seemed to know how to find the comics without looking. But sitting across from him at the dining room table gave Maud easy viewing of the day's top stories; she could tell in a few seconds whether it was worth checking Ewan's pet spots for the discarded newspaper later that day. He never could tell her where he'd put something down.

Maud took a sip of coffee and lifted her eyes from her spadework. It was her first attempt at writing in several months, and it was slow moving. She found herself hungry for a distraction.

"September 10, 1939. Canada declares war on Germany." The headline took Maud's eyes with it; down as Ewan let the newspaper sag with his chuckles and up again as his expression dulled and he pulled the page straight.

"It's official, then," she said.

Ewan said nothing.

"It's official," she said more loudly.

Ewan's eyes finally moved in her direction. The newspaper remained spread out in front of him, covering his mouth and half of his nose. "Canada declares war" was written over the place where Ewan's mouth would have been. But she could still see his eyes perfectly—eyes that had aged more than any other part of him, becoming cloudier with each passing year.

"The same as last time," Maud added when Ewan still said nothing. "They will say it might be quick, but it will not be quick. It will be drawn out. It will last a lifetime and take many lifetimes away from us." Her left forefinger and middle finger twitched against each other during the long pauses between her sentences. "You know what this means."

She raised her voice. "You know what this means, Ewan."

After a few seconds, he lifted his eyes again in her direction, and she continued. "All those boys. And their mothers. I can see their faces in my mind, the worst terror followed by the worst sadness, and now—Stuart." Her fingers stopped twitching. "They will need doctors. Stuart may have to go."

"Stuart may go. Right away?" Ewan spoke finally, softly. He lowered the paper.

"Not right away, dear, no."

"Oh," Ewan said.

"But eventually. And Stuart is not built for war. He is too good and bright and cheerful. I'm not built for war either. You saw what it did to me last time. Now I feel it in my bones, as an inevitability, this war will take . . . I'm not . . ."

Maud watched as Ewan slid down further in his chair. His head sat too far over his neck. She knew better than to upset him like this. She'd let blind terror do the talking.

She walked over and put her hand on Ewan's shoulder.

"Go back to your comics, dear," she said. "Never mind all this."

When she got to her bedroom, Maud took out the revised draft will. Her pulse quickened as she read through it again.

"To be divided equally," it said about all her personal effects and literary income. Between both boys. But she'd kept Stuart as literary executor. Only he would have the right to decide when to publish her journals.

To revert to whom if this sickness finally took her, or if Stuart went to war? She felt the thought skitter across her mind and shook it away like a spider on a towel, firmly and without looking too closely.

She'd be off to the Island before long. She could put these thoughts aside for a while.

39.

M aud planned her visit to the Island carefully. She decided to stay in one place instead of moving around from one night to the next as she had during past visits. There would be no appeasing everyone, no polite hellos to every relative and neighbor who wanted to claim an association with her. She was simply too tired, and that was not the point of this trip. She even contemplated a hotel in Charlottetown, but she knew her relatives would have balked at that.

In the end, she chose Myrtle Webb's farm in Cavendish, largely because she thought they could talk mostly about Anita and avoid less pleasant subjects, and also because the farm had good associations, being the green-gabled inspiration for Anne's first home. Myrtle had inherited the house from her great-uncle and his sister, who lived on in part through Matthew and Marilla.

"A godsend, your girl has been," Maud said to Myrtle at supper on her first night in town. "What a job you did raising her. I cannot thank you enough for letting her come out to us." Maud had offered to bring Anita along for the trip, but Anita had insisted on staying in Toronto to feed Ewan and keep the house in order.

"It was all her idea," Myrtle said. "She's always been crazy about you. I swear a piece of that independent spirit of yours leapt right into hers the day we made her your namesake. She's always seemed cooped up in this small town. I hope she might meet someone out west. A nice young man she can settle down with."

Maud tensed. "I've been talking to her about going back to school," Maud said. "She's a driven one, you know. With many talents. I can see her doing well in a number of different professions."

Myrtle looked up quickly.

Catching Myrtle's expression, Maud added, "Of course, there are plenty of eligible bachelors in Toronto as well."

After that, the conversation continued smoothly enough through the rest of supper, and Maud excused herself immediately afterward for bed.

But the next morning the talk grew more stilted, with Myrtle looking worn around the eyes in the brighter light of daytime, and Maud lacking her old knack for filling a silence.

"Green Gables Golf Course, they are calling it," Myrtle was saying now, seemingly out of nowhere. Myrtle's words were nonchalant enough, but the spaces between them caught Maud's attention. "I'm assuming you've heard?"

The porch where they sat drinking tea was all white wicker, with green-and-white-striped cushions and a low wicker table with glass nested in the top. It reminded Maud of other teas in this same spot. A porch always full of the happy percussion of crystal pitchers knocking against porcelain cups and spoons stirring in sugar.

The white paint was wearing away now, in too many places to count.

"That's the first I've heard about any name," Maud said. "What parts of the forest are they taking for the golf course?"

"I'm not entirely sure," Myrtle said.

Maud frowned.

"But it's not worth your furrowed brow," Myrtle said, shaking her head. "It won't be so bad."

"Won't it?"

"They're also planning to turn a good amount of the shoreline and forest into a national park, which will be nice."

"I suppose." Maud looked down.

"And the government will preserve our farm, just as it is now, for the tourists to visit."

"Your farm!"

"Didn't I tell you?" Myrtle asked. "I am forgetful these days. Only a smidgen of my old mind left. They are doing right by us, don't you worry. We'll be able to keep the house in our family and make a good amount of the proceeds off the tours and such."

"Oh, Myrtle," Maud said.

"Not too different than the tourism we've had for the last twenty-odd years, only now it will be better regulated."

Myrtle took in Maud's expression and reached out, putting her hand firmly on Maud's shoulder. Myrtle waited for a while to speak again. Then she said, "You know, these people who come to visit, it's because you've touched something inside them. More than that, you've gotten at the heart of this old Island. You made something permanent out of a place and time that otherwise would have been forgotten as soon as an old rag. How many other authors can say that?" Myrtle took a sip of tea, then nodded. "You put us on the map. And now our coastline is never going to be piled up with houses like so many of them are. It's your doing."

Myrtle put her tea down and squeezed Maud's shoulder, then reached for her handkerchief to wipe a few tears.

Sometimes these days, Maud did not notice that she was crying herself until she spotted a dark circle on her dress or a pillow. But when she lifted a finger to the undersides of her eyes, they were dry.

"I'm glad if something good for this Island comes of my work. I worry so," Maud said.

"Now, now," Myrtle said. After a long drink of tea, Myrtle sat back and changed her tone. "Say, I heard from a boy down the road that the former prime minister said he'd read all your books he could get his hands on two or three times. Had you heard that?"

"Something like it," Maud said.

Maud used to love anecdotes like these. Now she heard Myrtle's voice like it was spoken through water. It had been a little better when Myrtle was leaning forward, looking Maud in the eye. Now that Myrtle had pulled away, it was harder.

Maud excused herself not long after. She told Myrtle she was in need of a walk.

STRAIGHT ROWS OF trees ran along the edges of Gartmore farm, forming a natural fence. Maud's palm pressed against a large oak; she braced herself against it and allowed herself a brief look at the garden. Immediately, she drew a deep breath.

Nearly sixteen years earlier, Stuart and Chester had run ahead of Maud to the spot in this same garden where May Gartmore had pointed from her kitchen window. A basket of red peonies sat against that window and put most of the ground out of Maud's sight. But then a flash of gray had emerged in a playful leap.

Maud went out to join the boys. The sun hung thick in the air like a mist that day, clinging to the boys' hair and upper shoulders.

Good Luck—Lucky, as they ended up calling him—was

the biggest of the kittens and the boldest, approaching Maud with his tail raised and his round eyes set on hers. The other kittens tried not to notice the new inspectors and huddled close together in their play. But not Lucky. He'd seemed wise to her even then, looking at her like a grandfather might apprehend a new granddaughter.

Stuart noticed the letter first—a shape on Lucky's side like a clover leaf with a black M inside it.

"M for Mummy," Stuart had said.

"Or M for Maud," she'd said.

"Or Macdonald," Chester had said.

"Or Montgomery. I think he's for us. Don't you, boys?" Maud asked.

She never thought she could love a cat again the way she had loved old Daffy. But anytime she came home for the next thirteen-and-a-half years, Lucky was the happiest of anyone to see her. During the days, he followed her everywhere she went in the house. When she wrote, he lay on her papers; when she cried, he put his paw on her face. And when she got into bed, he waited until she nodded and then came to lie by her side. She'd never had any comfort like him. The gods had a lot of score to even after a gift like that.

Maud walked to the edge of the Gartmore garden and pulled up a straggly orange mum—the last of the season from the looks of it, and growing not more than a few feet from where Lucky and the boys had stood that day when the air had been thick with humid sun.

Now the air was crisp and invisible; no animal was in sight. As quickly as Maud had come, she walked away, leaning her back against the same oak as before but facing the other way, studying the tree branches above her in the way she used to. When she held the orange mum to her nose, her fingers brushed against her face and twitched with surprise. Still no tears.

THE NEXT DAY, Maud woke and went immediately to the Cavendish shore.

The underside of the rock she'd gone in search of was smaller and less cavernous than Maud had remembered. Far smaller than it seemed in the photo tucked inside her pocket—the photo of herself at Cavendish beach thirty-six years ago, looking out to sea.

Occasionally these days when she saw her whole body in a mirror, or dimly reflected in a pane of glass, this photo was the image of herself out of which her mind startled, and she would turn away and then glance back, confirming.

In the photo, Maud's hair almost disappeared into the shadow beneath the overhang of rock. Her bathing costume— if you could call it that, sewn from some old scraps and minimal enough to be scandalous at the time—glowed bright white against her thin, pale limbs. She held her arms with confidence; the bend of her leg was sharp and refined enough to earn some attention. But she thought she'd come out looking rather frail on the whole, set up against the mass of orange sandstone, which showed up in the photo only slightly darker than the looming blue-gray sea behind it.

She remembered just how important those few simple moments when the photo was taken had felt back then, sitting on a rock and looking out at the ocean. Remembered thinking back on them just before she began writing *Anne*.

Maud found herself now standing by the same rock, waiting for a mother to pass with her son, a small boy running a few steps ahead with cherub cheeks and blond curls so tightly wound they were resilient against the breeze.

Assured that there was no one left in her periphery, Maud

tucked the photo back in her pocket and moved to wrap her palm around one of the shelves of sandstone jutting out in the place where the photo had been taken, feeling its graininess under her hand. She'd forgotten this texture, raw and scraped. She'd forgotten how the sand coated everything too, spread in a thin layer across the eroding discs of sandstone that gradually descended to the sea. She bent down and swiped a finger through the sand.

How long ago were these particles part of the sandstone? Years? Minutes? *We all wear away*, she thought. Particles separating and dispersing and consolidating, if they ever do again, into something else entirely. The incredible part is what holds any of us together in the meantime.

Her eyes closed; she heard the distraught-sounding bellow of a seagull. Walking to where the water slid thin and clear over a flat layer of rock at high tide, Maud let her open palms lead her down, her knees following and bending until her hands connected with the surface of the water. Its surface tension clung to her hands like pudding as she slowly lifted and lowered. The shock of the cold drilled down her spine, and with it, finally, came the old feeling.

She had never felt cold the way she'd always felt touching this water, delicious in its contrast with the air. The air had nothing like the water's bite. And with that bite, something in her skin's natural defenses stripped away; the water burned the life back into her. Then the spice of the water was on her cheeks and lips; she had lifted her hands to her face.

The experience reached a place inside her that nothing else had in years. Her fear—all her worry about Chester and Stuart and their futures and her reputation—turned momentarily small and manageable.

She had forgotten this relief. This perspective. Nature never had its same claim on her anywhere except the Island.

She loved her yard in Toronto well enough, and she still took walks from time to time. But nature on the Island was Technicolor, Toronto black and white.

Days spent exploring her old Island haunts came back to her now. She saw her small body packed to the brim with feeling as she walked, reaching out to touch treasured trees and friendly flowers. She must have been a silly sight to those watchful middle-aged townsfolk. A lonely skipper, strange in her contentment.

Only she hadn't been alone. Always, there had been a character. Always a voice in her mind. And best of all had been Anne.

How she missed her. Anne girl. Maud hadn't allowed herself to realize how much. Anne's turns of phrase, her peculiar ways, felt so distant to Maud now. Her own creation turned terribly, painfully foreign.

Maud wiped her hands against her skirt and reached into her pocket for the other photo she'd brought with her. Nearly eight years after the Cavendish beach photo and two weeks before her marriage to Ewan, Maud had finally walked out to New London point. Here was the proof of it, sitting flat in her hands.

A dark figurine against a backdrop of near-white sea and sky, Maud stood at the end of the point in a stately black dress that came up high on her neck and a large black hat, her face barely visible between them.

A point of departure, she remembered thinking then. Frede had just written that she had assembled all the ingredients for Maud's wedding supper. Stella had ordered the garland for the mantel. So Maud would marry. She would leave the Island. Standing at the tip of New London point had been a lifelong dream, and the reality was gratifying in the way she had dreamed it, and when she rode away in a carriage she did so sadly and wished for the dream again.

Maud took the Cavendish beach photo out of her pocket again and held the two side by side, examining her younger self dressed in white in the first photo, in black in the second.

Then she turned and began walking away from the water, past the rocks and toward the sand dunes with their scattered knots of vegetation. She passed the same dune now that she had used for cover when she changed clothes the day the first photo was taken.

She shook her head.

The dune seemed a little shorter, less shapely at the top, but that was only natural with age.

RETURNING TO THE Webbs' house that evening after treating herself to hours more of walking alone, Maud kept her steps light. She shut the front door so carefully she was sure no one could have heard.

Finally reaching the bedroom where she was staying, Maud breathed out audibly. On the desk were her journal notes.

She felt like writing now, and her hand felt steady, which was remarkable compared to what it had been. She took out the picture of herself on the rock at Cavendish beach and propped it up against a cut-glass vase on the desk.

She thought again of that day taking the photograph, of the way she had seen the rocks and the sea like they were delivered up only for her. The gift—just that momentary gift—of seeing something more than ordinary on a day not unlike many other days. On a shore unlike any other shore.

40.

T he new dress from the Easter catalogue laid out on Maud's bed less than a day ago with a flush of something like excitement looked colorless now. Gray against the white bedspread, the bed frame also gray, the carpet a gray rope spiral coiled like a snake and ready to spring.

Maud picked at a string hanging a centimeter down from the hem of the skirt. Pulling on it cinched a few inches of material together at the hemline. She let go, not bothering to pull the material straight, and turned away.

She found herself a few minutes later sitting in the chair at the table in her bedroom.

"Dissolved," she wrote in her journal notes, her lower jaw moving back and forth against the upper. She must write this horrific news out. All of it.

"That's the word Chester used, with no more care or concern than he might say the word 'Hello.' (Or 'Mother,' for that matter.) So there you have it: the legal partnership that I put $2,000 into, as gone as salt stirred into water. 'Dissolved.' Some of it no question paid out to Chester, although where it has ventured from there I refuse to speculate. Not into clothes and food for his children, that's for certain.

"I know how the record will read—Chester's law partner

did not mince words, after all. 'Unkempt and lazy,' that's how he described Chester. 'Taking a risk.' 'It won't be my fault if he fails, you must understand that before we begin here.' 'He's bright as they come, but that can only get him so far.'

"Then there was something else the partner said, right at the beginning of my meeting with him. 'You, like all mothers, surely think your son is perfect.' What did my face look like then, I wonder? I would hate to see a photograph of it.

"Tomorrow is Stuart's graduation from medical school, and I am to attend. People will be wearing suits and dresses and taking photos by the spring gardens. Just now, I can hardly see going in anything but my bedclothes. Dressing up to see my son graduate his way into a war tanker hardly seems proper.

"'Tomorrow is a new day with no mistakes in it yet'—I wrote that once."

MAUD'S LEGS JUMPED at the sound of the front door opening. She nudged her way out from under the covers where she had spent most of her days since Stuart's graduation, pushing herself into a seated position against the headboard and listening. If the news was all right, Ewan's steps up the stairs would be faster.

No, Maud's steps would have been faster. She could not remember the last time Ewan had sped up his steps for anything. How many times had she assumed with him, interpreted his movements the way she would have interpreted her own?

Then again, Ewan had gone off his pills for two straight days before this little trip to talk with Chester. For the last twenty-four hours, his speech and eyes had been clearer than they had been in a long while.

For years now, it had been impossible to separate Ewan's

illness from the barbiturate and bromide medications he took to manage it. Maud didn't like to think about this too closely, especially with how much she'd recently come to depend on Ewan's medications herself. The delightful anticipation she felt after she swallowed a few, knowing that in a half hour, her mind would no longer be the same uninhabitable place. Instead, her mind would be cloaked in a heavy winter comforter. Heavier it would get, then heavier still, until nothing mattered, nothing was the matter, and blessed sleep took hold.

Maud felt her hand reach for one of Ewan's pill bottles now, but she stopped herself. Such indignities were best kept private—even from Ewan, who was unlikely to notice.

As the bedroom door handle turned, Maud's eyes closed. When she opened them, Ewan was sitting on the end of the bed, scratching the back of his head.

"Please tell me you have good news," Maud said, her voice full. It surprised her, this voice.

Ewan grunted. "Wish I could," he said.

"So Luella is determined to leave Chester, then? Obstinate girl. I suppose I'll have to make a visit myself. Give her a few days, then go to her and say it straight. All of us need a little straight talk from time to time, but especially a girl without a mother. I promised her mother when she was on her deathbed that I would take care of her girl, and it's what I mean to do. Clearly, you and her father weren't up to the task." Words were getting away from her now, but she couldn't contain them. She was seething.

Ewan waited a few breaths before speaking. "I haven't said why."

"The question was never supposed to be why. There was never meant to be any question, for that matter. There was only meant to be a message. A one-word message, at that.

'No.' That could have been the end of it, delivered with proper authority—"

Ewan muttered a few words under his breath, ebbing the current of Maud's speech.

"What is it? If you spoke this softly and unconvincingly to Chester and Luella, it's no wonder—"

"She's ill."

"Ill? Is she in need of a doctor?"

"She's seen one, she said, that's how she knows."

"We can surely arrange for medical care if money is the issue."

"Don't suppose she'd take our help. Not now."

"But why, Ewan? If the girl is sick, well, that's an issue we can solve. Why are you slumped there looking so grim?"

"It's a certain kind of sickness."

"Please, Ewan, don't be cryptic."

Ewan turned toward Maud. "I can't," he said. His eyes were pleading and watery. He turned back around. "It's venereal. It's from Chester."

Maud hardly paused for a breath. "That's impossible. The girl's a liar." Her son, a carrier of venereal disease?

"She's not lying. I looked at Chester when she said it. Luella's father is going tomorrow to move her out. The children too."

"She told you this, in the room with Chester and her father?"

"Yes."

Maud picked a piece of lint off her sweater and held it between her fingers, rubbing it absently. She should be thinking of Chester, or better yet of poor Luella. But rage had narrowed her focus. All she could think of now was the Reader. That high-minded presider over her journals and novels who had evolved over the course of her lifetime into an ever older and more skeptical man. He looked at her now through lenses half down his nose, a single eyebrow raised. How would she ever explain this to him?

Ewan said, "It was cold today, even though it's summer. Cold in the house, and there was no fire going. Luella says there is never enough money for coal. She burns boards from an old barn nearby. Says Chester never is home in the evenings. Says she does not know where he is." His words were monotone, the same dull note played again and again.

"Damn it all," Maud said, because she couldn't contain herself any longer. This was her fault. It had to be. She had been too busy with her writing and other obligations. How else could things have reached this point?

Maud rose from the bed, pulled the bedspread up over the pillow on her side, and then tugged at the corner until the wrinkles were gone. She walked quickly past Ewan and out the bedroom door, slamming it behind her.

LATE THAT EVENING, Maud set her pen down, closing her eyes. When she opened them, she drew a line across the page, continuing on below it.

"I reread part of my journal from 1922 today—opened it to a random page. In the entry I turned to I'd gotten it in mind to write to my great-granddaughter. I had just finished recopying my last old entry into the bound volumes, and I suppose I was feeling sentimental."

Rediscovering the hope she'd felt writing a note to the granddaughter of one of her boys tapped the well, and Maud's tears began to flow. The yearning she had when she wrote these words. The difference between this moment and that one. She could no longer concern herself with the Reader; she needed to write this out.

"I wrote those lines full in my heart with the thought of

my boys in the next room, young and merry-eyed. Now one of those boys—changed at once and before I had time to notice into a grown man—will surely go off to war in a conflict no less deadly than the last, leaving my only hope for sympathetic descendants in the son whose actions make me sick at heart. Proof, if ever, that I only bring bad things to people I love. So predestiny it is, in the end. It cannot be otherwise, in light of all that I have put into trying to influence. In light of all that my efforts have been powerless to prevent."

ANITA'S BREATH RELEASED like a slow leak from the other side of the bedroom door, then inhaled with a sharpness that made Maud's head jerk.

How long would she stand there? How long had she been close by? All the time that Chester had been in the room?

Anita would have heard the crack of the dresser breaking against Chester's fist even if she'd been downstairs, most likely. Then she would have come up and heard the worst of it—the surrender, the "okay" coming quick and high out from Maud's throat like the squeak of a cornered mouse. Anita might have heard the amount of money Chester demanded.

Now here Anita was, standing put. Worried. Worse, one of the only people left who would bother about worrying. Anita would need to come in eventually to give Maud her painkillers and take down dictation for the day. There was no use in pretending she wasn't there.

"Come in, Anita," Maud said with as much authority as she had left in her.

A hesitation—deciding whether to pretend she had not been just outside the door, no doubt—and then Anita was in the room, opening the drapes and hurrying to Maud's side, a hot water bottle, no longer even warm, in hand. Anita settled the bottle behind Maud's back and adjusted the pillow under the now dingy white cast on Maud's arm from when she'd fallen on the stairs a few months back. It was upset over Chester that had been the cause of the fall, making her forget to watch her step.

Anita studied Maud's face—looking for traces of pain, most likely.

"It surely will be a relief to have your cast removed," Anita said, the back of her palm on Maud's forehead. Maud hadn't noticed the half-full glass of water Anita had brought with her and set on the bedside table until Anita handed it to Maud along with two chalky painkillers, a little wet on the bottom and cut into thirds to make them go down easier.

Maud nodded and began taking the pills.

"I know you're concerned about having full range of motion," Anita said, "but we'll get you back in no time. It's a matter of strengthening and stretching. I've been reading about it."

"Have you," Maud said.

"I'm quite the expert now. First, though, there's the matter of your eating."

"My eating," Maud said when she saw that Anita was waiting for a response.

"Rather, the lack thereof. You've never been a shrinking violet, but you're quickly becoming one as far as your physical self is concerned." Anita spread a sheet out in front of her to fold, covering her face. "Down next to nothing, and sending back plates of food." As she made a third fold in the sheet her eyes met Maud's. "I can only imagine what your grandmother would have to say about that, from what I know about her."

"Grandmother never would have condoned you wasting good food on me, knowing I have no appetite these days. Better to give it to any still-growing relatives we have, she would have said. Did say, in fact. Cheese and preserves was all that woman ate for the last several months, and little of it at that."

"She was very old, and you are not," Anita said. "And I don't want to hear any different. Speaking of, what do you say we try for another one of our movie dates? Now, don't say no right away. I don't mean we have to up and go immediately. I'm just planting the seed; you can tell me when it's been planted long enough to grow."

"I'm sorry, dear, but I cannot see doing that anytime soon." Maud let out a breath that felt like it had been folded up inside her for a long while.

"Like I said, doesn't have to be now," Anita said. "At least let me bring you your manuscript. Maybe you have a few ideas I can jot down for you. You haven't written in months. Even Chester said something about it. Stuart is beside himself."

"Not now, Anita," Maud said. "If the boys are concerned, they can come tell me. While we're on the subject, please go ahead and cancel all my speaking engagements completely. No use continuing to put everyone off."

"But—Aunt Maud—"

"It's important to face these things head-on. When is my next doctor's appointment?"

"Dr. Lane needed to push it back a day, but he'll be here for a visit on Thursday, day after next. If there's anything you need in the meantime, I'll do whatever I can." Anita straightened the pillow behind Maud's back and pulled the lukewarm water bottle away. She felt Maud's forehead again and then pulled the quilt off her lap. "Should have known you'd be too warm with this quilt in late summer. Can I get you some iced tea? One of your books?"

"My books?"

"I mean any book that you might want to read."

Maud thought for a minute. "Do be a dear and pull out

one of my old journal volumes from the lockbox in my closet. Any one will do—surprise me."

"Your—your journals?"

"You know where I keep the key."

"I don't!"

"I'm not accusing you of anything except being observant, dear." Maud paused. "Have you ever thought of writing in a journal yourself? Journal writing, I fear, is dying out with the age. A shame. My journals have been to me—" Maud's voice caught on the saliva in her throat, now chalky with the pills. "What friend does any of us have for our whole lives, any time we might want them? Need them?"

"I've never thought of journaling that way."

"Well, maybe you are lucky and will have a few real-life friends like this," Maud said. She thought of Frede, and her voice broke. "I had one early in my life. I've had many friends since, but never one quite like her. Anyway, what friend persists in telling our story long after we are gone, for as long as anyone else might like to listen?"

"You know," Anita said, "I never tire of listening to you myself. What if we plan an hour a day where we talk together, and you tell me stories? Not reading your journals, of course, just telling me anything you'd like to remember. I'll tell you anything you'd like to know about my life too."

Tears welled in Maud's eyes. The words of a kindred spirit, if she could still bring herself to believe in such things.

She felt a dull throb, realizing how Anne would lament this sentiment. To no longer believe in a kindred spirit would have struck Anne as a tragedy beyond all comprehension. But Anne's voice had left her long ago.

"That would be just lovely, dear," Maud said to Anita.

Anita opened the lockbox and picked out a journal volume.

By the time she turned around, Maud's eyes were closed. No use in Anita seeing tears in her eyes and thinking her an old sentimental fool.

Anita smoothed back the hair from Maud's forehead, tucking a few falling strands behind her ears. She pressed the journal into the down comforter near Maud's outstretched hand and left the room as silently as her flat feet and sturdy gait could manage.

AT A PACE of a few pages a day, Maud had just made it to the end of the journal volume Anita picked out for her when the final few fall leaves, with brown tips curling in on their red fronts, spun off the oak tree closest to her window, moving impossibly slowly and then landing out of sight.

In the first half hour of each day, when she felt most alert, Maud alternated between rereading (and, on some occasions, razoring out undesirable pages from) the journal volume picked by Anita and jotting down a few contemporaneous notes for possible inclusion in her newest volume. Maud was exercising considerable economy in her journal notes now. It was easier than she would have expected. Short phrases fit the mood of her days. And an hour each day swapping stories with Anita made her feel less need for long entries.

Now she wondered when Anita might be coming with her toast and a new question or two about happier times. Maud wasn't hungry, but she'd been saving up all week the news that she finally meant to agree about going to the movies. Anticipating the way Anita would smile had given Maud's mind a place to settle into sleep the night before. These days, she clutched at anything that could settle her heart temporarily.

> *"The heart asks pleasure first/ And then, excuse from*
>   *pain; / And then, those little anodynes/ That deaden*
>   *suffering; /,"*

she wrote now in her journal notes.

Emily Dickinson. She'd quoted these lines in her journal before. She half smiled at herself for remembering.

But now here Anita was, and she wasn't carrying toast. She had a piece of paper in her hand. "My brother," she said.

"Your brother what, dear?"

"Keith, he . . ."

"What is it, Anita?"

"Keith's wife, I mean. She died during childbirth. Maud, I must go, as soon as I can. My mother, she cannot care for two baby girls alone." Maud had never seen Anita like this, shallow breaths taking her voice an octave higher and faster than she'd ever spoken before.

"Anita—slow down, child. We can handle this one step at a time, you and I."

"Aunt Maud, I must make arrangements now. I must let them know that I will come immediately."

Her steps started going in the wrong direction, away from the bed, and then she was gone.

After Maud had stayed in one position for so long her legs started to twitch, she turned to Ewan's bedside table. She took a bottle, spilled some pills out into her hand, round and white. She moved them around on the table for a while. Closing her eyes, she took them all.

So it was. Anita would be gone too.

41.

The first time the doorbell ever rang in the Toronto house was the day Mary Powell came for an interview.

Stuart later told Maud he had admired Mary Powell's voice from the start; she spoke in distinct syllables. It was true, her words did pierce through the air—air that had only grown thicker in the months since Anita left, with dust showing up like smoke in the light that streamed through the window past the bare winter trees. Mary Powell couldn't keep anything clean.

Now, remarkably, the doorbell rang regularly. Maybe Mary Powell had given an instruction to visitors. Or maybe something about the formal way she answered the door demanded it of them. With Anita, visitors had given only a knock, or sometimes not even that, since Anita seemed to have eyes and ears quick enough to know who was coming and when. A visitor would have barely crossed the front hedges and Anita would have the door open wide, hollering her hello.

Each time Maud heard the shrill reverberation of the doorbell, her body jerked.

After a while had passed since the latest ring, Maud found herself falling into a light sleep. Then, suddenly, another noise.

The doorbell again? Maud's hand covered her mouth to stifle the sounds of her tears. Too soft, Maud hoped, for Mary

Powell to have heard anything, and yet not a minute later here she was.

"Another call from next door," Mary Powell said as she lined up a glass of water, a cup of tea, and three pills appropriately sized for horses in a straight line on the side table. Maud noticed the point of Mary Powell's chin set against her too-small skull. Her perfectly regular way of breathing.

"I let her know that you are not well." Mary Powell took Maud's wrist and felt her pulse, then touched the top of Maud's forehead with the back of her hand, her eyes set all the while on the clock at the top of the dresser.

Maud moved to sit up in bed. Slowly, with her mouth feeling full of cotton, Maud spoke, "I'll be needing you to transcribe another letter. This one to a correspondent I've had for a time. Literary correspondent, you know. He'll have been wondering about me."

Mary Powell nodded. "I'll be back at half-past four to take dictation."

There was no sign in Mary Powell's body of having recognized a noise outside the door, but when she opened it and saw Stuart on the other side, she said hello as if she had expected him.

"Hello, Mummy," Stuart said, staying near the door. "I'm sorry to interrupt. I didn't hear voices or I would have waited."

Maud's lower back slackened. "No matter, Stuart. We were barely talking."

"How has today been? I apologize I'm later than usual. It was a busier day at the hospital. Have you slept? Have you taken your pain medicine?"

"Yes, today's been just the same as every day. You should go get some rest, darling. Were you up all night?" Maud yawned.

Stuart gave a reluctant nod, then walked over to Maud's bedside table, inspecting. He picked up the three pills sitting there and broke them each in half. He handed them to her and watched to be sure she took them. Then he studied his mother until his gaze seemed to lose its focus. So tired he always was these days—long shifts with little sleep. She worried for him. He felt her forehead and started to say something.

But now they could hear Chester's voice coming up the stairs.

"I won't have it, Mother," Chester said, his voice dropping when he saw Stuart.

Chester looked Stuart up and down slowly until Stuart sighed and turned to leave. Stuart put his hand on Maud's knee as he walked out, leaning for a moment like he might keep it there.

But Maud's eyes were on Chester.

Once Stuart had passed Chester's side he said, almost to himself, "She's tired, Chester. Leave her be."

"Looks like you're the one who could use some sleep, brother," Chester said.

When Chester heard the door close, he waited a few seconds and then continued as if he had never stopped. His voice crescendoed quickly to an impressive volume, one that Maud did not think he had quite reached before.

The will. He was upset again over the will. But she had revised it. She thought about this for a moment. Yes, she was sure of it, back before Mary Powell, before she fell and broke her arm.

Something was bothering her about her eyes now. She blinked them open—they must have closed without her realizing. She turned her concentration to keeping them open. She never should have taken three of Ewan's pills, knowing Stuart hadn't come yet and was sure to notice and make her take her own. That was a mistake.

And then—

"There is also the matter of the journals. It's simply not right, Mother!" Chester had taken her ankles now, one hand on each over the covers. He gripped and shook, lifted and threw them down.

"The journals," Maud said, suddenly clear in her speech. "What do you mean, Chester?"

"You know precisely what I mean! Giving all control to Stuart! As if I was nothing—just—nothing!"

When he went to grip her ankles again, he found empty caverns in the sheets.

Maud was sitting up straighter, her knees folded back and to the side. No longer looking at him.

Chester pounded the spots where her feet had been with two flat palms; then, shaking his head, he gave one long yell straight in her direction. It seemed to hollow out the room, that yell, and in the emptiness that followed it they both noticed for the first time the humming. Subtle and unperturbed, something like a nursery rhyme. The notes scaling up and back down methodically in the way children like.

Maud took her time looking over. When she did, she could see the naked backside of Ewan, two folds on the sides of his torso and dark, sparse hair from his pant-line down, matted to the side in places. His robe lay around his ankles as he picked up a bottle from the dresser, studying it and rubbing it along his armpit with the cap still on, all the while humming.

"You'd better leave, Chester." Maud's voice could have filled an auditorium.

Chester started toward the door. He kept his eyes on his father as he walked out.

When the door opened, Maud called for Mary Powell.

"Would you please take Ewan, Mary?" Maud asked when Mary Powell came in. She watched as Mary Powell pulled up and tied Ewan's robe and ushered him out, still showing no sign of any particular interest.

WHEN MAUD WAS alone and had the relief of closing her eyes, she didn't find sleep. Instead, the memory of Chester's birth played itself out as vividly as it ever had. She saw a spider crawl slowly across the ceiling, scampering and slowing in rhythm to her screams. She saw her own naked fear mirrored in the bloodshot eyes of the tired nurse, and later in the eyes of the cat Daffy. Then, like an aftershock, she felt the part she was most ashamed to remember: the source of her fear, which was for her own life, no room in that moment for anything else.

It wasn't until later that Chester appeared and changed everything. A bag of stones comprised of equal parts love and responsibility came down on her, laying her out flat.

She'd written something about this once, back nearly thirty years ago when Chester was born. A few years ago, she would have been able to remember each of her own words immediately and in the right order.

To find and reread that journal entry became a singular focus like she had not had in months. She pushed hard against the bed with her good arm to lift herself and made her way over to the shelf in the closet that housed the lockbox with her journals.

"Nineteen twelve," she whispered, pulling out the volume. It wasn't more than a few minutes before she found it.

"What a terrible thing it is to be a mother," she'd written. "Almost as terrible as it is beautiful! Oh, mothers of Caesar and Judas and Jesus, what did you dream of when you held your babies against your beating heart. Of nothing but sweetness and goodness and holiness perhaps. Yet one of the children was a Caesar—and one was a Judas—and one a Messiah!"

"Yes," she sighed, leaning her head back and closing her eyes against the words.

"And what did the mothers have to do with it?" she whispered, sitting up a little straighter now and rubbing her forearms. "How much control did they have? Some, surely. But all of it?"

She shook her head and tried to believe her own words, but they were muted in her mind, like they belonged to someone else. Then, her voice suddenly at top volume, she continued, "Why should their lives be at stake?"

With a ferociousness she did not know she had, she took the journal containing the 1912 entry with the best grip she could manage and swung it across the room toward the bare wall. Half expecting the book to swing itself back at her, Maud rose from the bed and approached slowly. She bent down and picked up the volume. A small white mark on the bottom of the spine seemed to be all the damage. She inspected the pages to be sure. She laughed a little in spite of herself.

She'd always thought the anger inside her, if unleashed in any real way, might just leave her dead on the floor. Instead, it had barely left a mark.

She went to her writing table and took out a set of scrap paper she had collected in a folder. The folder would house the notes for what would become her eleventh journal volume now that she had nearly reached the end of the tenth.

The fact that her life would comprise eleven journal volumes upset her more than she cared to admit. Ten was a superior number.

But here she was, with ten volumes almost complete, and life still plodding along.

"Feb. 3, 1941." She began to write on the top of the next

page of notes, in large and messy font. Her right wrist ached through the center tendons after the effort of her throw.

No matter. These words were hers and hers alone. They did not belong to the ten-volume set. They did not belong to the Reader.

She could rip these words into shreds, now or tomorrow. She could burn them to a crisp. Hers, for any time she was still living. Hers like nothing else she had known.

42.

It was hot again in a way that made the less sturdy leaves on the trees droop during the day and regain their rigidity only at night. Maud's palm sweat around her pen; she kept having to release it to run her grandmother's handkerchief between her fingers, then behind her ears.

She'd made it about halfway through the list of objects, well over one hundred of them, that she was leaving Chester. Personal, sentimental objects. Not the journals, but enough to make him forget about those, she hoped.

Maud's handwriting grew slack as she neared the end of the list. Her eyelids started to droop.

No. She had not stopped taking Ewan's pills for the first time in weeks just to fall asleep at her table with a task half-finished. She had to get through to the signature, to make sure the new will was delivered to Mary Powell for mailing while she was still right enough in the senses. She couldn't bear it much longer, feeling as exposed as the trees in the dead of winter without the blurring effects of the pills.

She had not known she was going to make the new will conditional until she saw the words spew out on the page.

"The foregoing is conditional," she wrote—and it had to be—on Chester living with Luella and the children at the time of Maud's death. If he was not living with Luella, the items must go to Luella and be held in trust for her grandchildren. What influence did she have besides that? What hope? And she could never let go of hope for him. She could never stop being Chester's mother.

Two round drops fell in the ink and stood at a standstill until she swept them across the page. Sweat or tears, she could not be sure.

Her journal notes for the eleventh volume had become the light spot in the middle of her days. She pulled out the folder of notes and opened it wide, so that it hid any view of the revised will underneath.

She'd started writing without censorship. Without any semblance of coherence. Coherence was what she'd done all her life. The relief of writing without it was sometimes enough to get out of bed for.

"June 24, 1941—revised will today," she wrote hastily. "—scant earnings all year—$6,996 in the ledger in 1940, a good amount—this year's more than half through and I've scarcely crossed $500—nothing new can be made now— I've decided to cobble together something from parts of old writings—squeeze out what money I can from my dwindling fan base—dwindling, yes—a few of the old stories strung together and a few attempts to link them—need to support my grandchildren, to do what I can—

"—or perhaps I should recall some of those old loans to PEI folk, or to Stella—wouldn't that be a riot, seeing what excuses would come out of the woodwork."

She paused and started a new line. "Cobbling it is."

THE NEXT ENTRY came on a relatively good day—which meant more pills and no visit from Chester—and Maud's cursive turned rounder.

"Sept. 4, 1941. 'The Blythes Are Quoted,' I'll call it—I swore I'd never go back to those characters, Anne and Gilbert and the rest—that they were all dried up. But who am

I to say? If it were up to me, their lives would have ended
long ago. No, that's the mistake, believing that an author has
any control. It's the Reader—always the Reader. No different
than real life, with the children. The husband. The gods.

"When Chester was nine, I heard him from the Leaskdale
kitchen pitching a fit in the yard, talking loudly to himself.
'Causing a ruckus'—as grandmother would say. I looked out
the window and smiled to myself as I saw him jumping up
and down—remembered my own stomping episodes at that
age. Stowed away in my room of course—Grandmother never
would have tolerated anything more public. I thought—
Chester's legs look just like mine—his arms and shoulders
solid and stout like Ewan's. I remember thinking, *What a
miracle*.

"I sent the maid out that day to call Chester in for dinner.
I'll never forget the look on her face—'Mrs. Macdonald,' she
said. 'You mustn't go outside. Chester's collected mice, and
no better way to say it, he's had off with their heads. By his
own boots. We really must clean them, the soles of them. I'll
work at it. Never mind. He's just a boy. He's a boy.'

"There was no letting anyone but me face that scene. I
did it myself, with a shovel and a sponge. A pale gray bucket.
A burial for the mice. Didn't look Chester in the eye again
until he was sitting at the table for supper, his fingers perfectly folded—his eyes closed like he was praying—flesh of
my flesh—and then he opened them. I couldn't very well say
anything after that.

"Ewan looked nearly the same as Chester the morning
after—his incident. Here I am again, using dull words. Dull
words when it's only me that this account is for, and Lord
knows I could use some excitement.

"Near shooting, that's better. Ewan brought the gun into
the dining room just like that—like he might walk in with

a plate of ham—only Ewan never would—a deck of cards, then, or a match to light the candles with—and then he flailed it around, aiming it at no one and everyone—the other people at the table!—mumbling nonsense and then saying suddenly, 'Watch your heads!'

"'Watch your back!' Chester said, just before flinging a book at me last week. My own book at that—one of the original copies of *Anne*. It did not hit, so he must not have been trying his hardest. 'Indecency!' he said. 'I can only guess what you've said in your journals about me that has led you to leave them to Stuart—lies and blasphemy, but who will know that? What is my account compared to the all great and renowned Lucy Maud Montgomery?'

"Slimy is how my name sounded at the end—positively slimy—the name of his own mother. Flesh of my flesh.

"—His father's though too."

After Maud had stared at her journal notes for a number of minutes, the page started to take on new life. It danced a little, puppeted, or rather Ewan and Chester puppeted out from it; she could dance them around, play their parts. Then she imagined them as puppets flattened to the page, where they became more manageable.

She shook her head. She'd make sure the lockbox was secure.

The eleventh volume must never be shown to anyone; it was settled now.

43.

When Maud first heard rustling near the trees along the side fence in the backyard, she thought the neighbor's dog must have come to supervise. But when she turned, she couldn't see anything. She sighed and took a half step back from the fire, which she immediately regretted. The warmth was comforting on a cold December evening.

Maud had a knack for knowing when she was being watched, and she knew someone was nearby now. It didn't bother her, though, not like it would have once. It was Ewan, probably, paying no real attention.

Letters fell from her fingers one at a time. She watched gladly as the flames licked their edges before devouring them. A few of the letters were so old the paper was yellowed, and others she had received not a few months ago.

Maud teetered on her feet as she moved to pick the next set of papers from a large box she had dragged into the yard.

She was so frail these days, that was the problem. Especially a problem in important moments like these.

She really must eat a little more so she had enough strength when she needed it. She didn't have to want to eat to be capable of it. Yes, it was time for a return to discipline.

She registered the sound of a throat clearing as something animal at first, then realized that the noise had come from too far off the ground to be a squirrel or a chipmunk.

Next came a soft voice. "It's me, Mrs. Macdonald."

Luella.

"I thought I'd come by," Luella said. She clung to her jacket, not coming too close. "To let you know that we're all right. We're doing a little better now that I've gotten a job."

"You and Chester?" Maud asked.

"Me and the children," Luella said.

"Oh, of course," Maud said, looking toward Luella for the first time. Maud's knees were shaking; she could see her skirt quiver as she let the shaking resolve itself.

"Your grandchildren." Luella hugged herself tighter, pulling on her scarf.

"Grandchildren, yes. My grandchildren. How I have worried over—" Maud's voice cracked. She straightened and turned back toward the flames. "I should tell you that I've given Chester plenty of money over the years. I'm sorry now that I didn't give it straight to you. Don't let up, Luella. Threaten him legally to get all the support you can. Lord knows he's not a motivated enough lawyer to put up a good fight." Maud patted her hands against her skirt.

"You've given him money?" Luella paused, taking this in. "I never knew, Mrs. Macdonald."

Still facing the flames, Maud shook her head in anger at Chester's audacity. Then her eyes lost focus. She began to shift from one foot to another. She picked up a book and let it fall, knowing the fire would grow with it.

"You know," Maud said, "I read my first book on my own when I was five years old. Or about that. Flat devoured it. I couldn't stop asking for more. Always I was fascinated by how it was done. Whole worlds opened up for people that they couldn't otherwise experience. Whole lives. To destroy a book, well—I never could have imagined it then. And now look at me." Maud gave a soft laugh. "Well, they're mine. My notes in the margins. The world won't mind one less copy."

"I'd better be going, Mrs. Macdonald," came the confused voice from behind her.

"All right, dear," Maud said. Then she turned in the direction of Luella's footsteps. "I'm glad to hear that you are taking care of yourself and the children. You are a good, brave girl." She swallowed. "Far better off without my son."

Maud turned back, and chose the next set of papers for the fire. Her exchange with Luella had given her a strange new energy. She had said her piece. Luella had her judgments, no doubt, but for the first time Maud could remember, she could not bring herself to worry over them.

She had much more to go, and now she relished the thought. Sick with delight, she decided to revisit each paper or book before it fell. To feel each piece of her private life before it burned—lost, forever, to history.

THE WEEK AFTER the bonfire, Maud sorted the letters she was preparing to write on her desk in the bedroom. She'd addressed them and written salutations at the top.

She'd been off the pills for a few days, so it was a good time; the only time maybe.

After finishing off letters to two long-time correspondents, Maud turned to the two final sheets of paper on her desk. To a young aspiring writer in Chicago, Maud wrote that she was very ill. "Broken, really, and I do not know that I shall ever recover. So I'll tell you what I've been meaning to tell you for some time now. I'm going to tell it straight. The only way to find out if you are any good is to write and submit your writing. Submit it to magazines, and if you are rejected, submit it again. Only you can know when it has been enough, when you're through trying. For me, I'm not sure I ever would have been through, no matter how many times I was denied. As it is, I cannot count the number of rejections before my career finally took hold.

"Then again, even I have my limits.

"I've thoroughly enjoyed our correspondence. You can't know what a breath of fresh air it has been. But fresh air cannot seem to reach me in the place I reside now. So farewell, good friend. And for heaven's sake, keep at it!"

As she wrote, Maud found her eyes drawn toward the top of the door to the bedroom closet. After she finished the first letter, she went to the closet door, looking at it like she might look at the door to a house where she did not belong.

She spotted the box immediately when she entered the closet. Its awkward dimensions took up most of the top shelf. It was a good thing this house had high ceilings—higher than any of the other houses she had lived in. It was a beautiful home, really. Working bathrooms, rich wood floors and paneling, and a large yard backing up onto a stream. The house she'd always dreamed of back in the day when she'd had the kind of hope that dreams require.

After taking the box down, Maud closed the closet door and returned to the fresh sheet of paper she had laid out for another letter.

"Dec. 18, 1941," she wrote at the top. "Captain," she wrote, adding a large dash after his name.

Just the word triggered a wash of pain.

"How many years has it been? More than twenty now.

"That's something sentimental folks would write at the start of a letter, and I assure you I've only become less sentimental with age. But still, it's what came from my pen, and I don't have the patience to start over.

"I think sometimes about you and that brood of children. I hope they are well. I hope you are well. I've kept an eye out for your name in the papers and haven't seen it. That may be considered rude to write—in the second paragraph of a letter twenty years in coming especially—but occasional rudeness is another quality I've grown into with age.

"I like to believe you've settled into a quiet sort of life. Gardening and watching after grandchildren.

"If you've been looking for my name in the papers, you may have seen it, although almost certainly not in an esteemed light as of late. My writing has gone out of favor, it seems. Doesn't it all, though, sooner or later? There are times I can almost see the joke—of public opinion—yes, PUBLIC OPINION, that falsest, cruelest of Gods—and of the fickle fancies of readership. But now I sound defensive and not a little bitter.

"What I mean is there are times I can almost bring myself to step back and see the comedy of it all. See the ways in which it's all an unpredictable sort of dance—the writing, the audience, the congregation, the husband—the children. See how all I can really control is me and what I choose to look at. I learned this, once, but not fully enough. Sometimes another way of being in this world seems out there just beyond the tips of my fingers.

"But then, I get a wrenching feeling in the pit of my stomach. Like the realization on waking up from a good dream that reality is something else entirely. My reality—not something I can look at from a distance and choose, but something woven into the very fibers of my being. So I cannot bring myself to laugh.

"I used to wonder why you stopped coming for visits—why you stopped even writing.

"But then, of course you did. We both knew why.

"I am sorry—have been sorry, all these years—for the gossip that may have crawled its way through your community after it pervaded mine. It was my maid Lily who was responsible. She always suspected something between us. If only she knew the extent to which we held back so she would not be right.

"I'm sending this letter along with a package, which requires explanation. It is old, as you'll see when you open it, and not the most functional. But it is the typewriter on which I typed up *Anne*—the original one. It's a keepsake of mine, and I don't see anyone in my family caring to have it. You, at least, are something of a writer. Or, you were once.

"Maybe this will inspire you to write that tale of your wartime experiences you were keen on years ago. You are a man of more than one extraordinary talent, and ambition squandered is poison to the soul. Unless, that is, other poisons have begun to stand in ambition's way—in which case you have both my deepest understanding and regret.

"In the end, I can say this: I never respected a man like I did you. Never felt as at home with one either.

"Thank you for the hours we spent together. Thank you for what time we had."

"L.M.," she signed at the end, with the carelessness of an afterthought—both familiar and incomplete.

44.

Maud shuffled into the kitchen, retrieving a box of graham crackers from a cabinet. She put one in her own mouth and sat another on Ewan's newspaper. She watched his chin dip and catch as though he was falling asleep, but then she saw that his eyes were open and unusually focused. She followed them until she spotted the object of his attention—a fly lifting and lowering from a bit of food on the floor.

"Something to eat, dear," she heard herself say, watching him. When Ewan did not respond, she raised her voice. "To eat."

Still watching him, she took a large bite of her own cracker and chewed slowly. She watched Ewan notice his cracker and lift it to his mouth, a line of drool following on its way back down.

She went to the sink and spit out the remains of her own cracker, throwing the rest away and rinsing her mouth. The effort made her dizzy, so that when she turned to leave the kitchen, she was forced to slow her steps. As she did, she noticed the latest order of pills sitting on the counter in its paper bag from the pharmacy. She removed half its contents, two brown containers with her name on their labels. It hadn't been hard to persuade Dr. Lane of her need for them.

"'Those little anodynes,'" she said as she pocketed the bottles, "'that deaden suffering.'"

"What, monkey?" Ewan asked. It was a phrase from another time in their life, one so removed from the present that it made her wonder where she was.

"Part of a poem," she said, watching to see how his face registered the words. She almost let herself believe she saw his head nod in recognition until the noise of the fly made itself known again, and she realized that Ewan's head was only tracing the fly's path across the room.

"Never mind, dear," she said.

She returned to the bedroom with her mind tossing about restlessly, eager for the small but reassuring thrill that came at the end of remembering a poem in its entirety. She'd once been able to recite this Dickinson—most Dickinson—cold.

She began walking the length of the room.

"The heart wants—no, the heart asks—pleasure first, and then, excuse from pain, and then, those little anodynes that deaden suffering; and then, to go to sleep; and then—"

She stopped, willing herself to remember.

"And then, if it should be the will of its Inquisitor, the liberty to die."

Of course that was it.

One of her old journal entries had been itching at the back of her mind, and this recitation made her think of it again. She remembered the bones of it without the details.

It took a while to page through past volumes before finding it. But here it was, two months shy of twenty years earlier, from May 10, 1922.

"Personally, I have never felt the horror in regard to suicide that some feel. . . . it is a cowardly thing to do if the doing of it leaves our burden upon others—ay, and a wicked thing. But if it does *not* I cannot see that it is wicked." So she'd written it right out. Plainer even than she'd remembered.

But then she'd written, "I don't think *I* would ever be *really* tempted to commit suicide as long as I could get enough to eat and wear by any means short of begging. Life, with all its problems, has always been an extremely interesting thing to me."

She never would have imagined—even with all the imagination she could summon back then—life losing interest in the way it had. Or maybe the interesting parts were still there, but they'd become untouchable pockets of pain she kept tucked away. Ewan. The boys. Her work, at least the way people viewed it now. Her journals.

But not all her journals. Not her scribbling book, as she'd come to think of her notes for the eleventh volume. A folder with content mostly full of wobbly and ugly lettering, the occasional black line drawn so deeply that it bled several pages through. The closest she'd ever come to drawing out a feeling.

She pulled the folder out and shook her head in embarrassment just to see these pages. *Nonsense*, her grandmother would have said. Proof that Maud had gone off her rocker.

On the other hand: No one would see these pages, so what did it matter how they looked? They were hers and hers alone.

She felt a strange giddiness rise up inside. She could write precisely what she wanted, each day, in these notes. When had she ever done that? Even in her fiction. Always sequels, always more of what the Reader demanded. Always with an audience as a shadowy presence in the foreground.

She drew a large "X" on the next, full page of notes. Why not? On the next she drew one large circle with three circles inside and then scribbled all over the small circles. Her laugh was furious and a little malicious and it welled up from something that felt like an underlayer—a dark, large pool that had previously sat unnoticed just under the surface of her skin.

Maybe she hadn't needed to write all those sequels.

The sound of Ewan's footsteps coming up the stairs started

a churn in her stomach. Her eyes darted back and forth like a child caught at forbidden play.

She shouldn't laugh so loudly again.

When she heard Ewan enter the other room—he generally slept in Chester's old bedroom these days—she pulled out the tenth volume. The last of what she had come to think of as the formal journals.

She thought she'd better provide some explanation, now that the eleventh volume would never see the light of day. The Reader might be wondering just what had happened since 1939. The Reader might appreciate a summation of sorts. Not any real detail, but the facts of the matter. She wrote a single line for 1941 and then turned to a fresh page.

"March 23, 1942. Since then," she wrote, "my life has been hell, hell, hell. My mind is gone—everything in the world I lived for has gone—the world has gone mad. I shall be driven to end my life. Oh God, forgive me. Nobody dreams what my awful position is."

EACH OF THE days in early April seemed to drag on long and narrow as spears. But a new chapter of the Canadian Authors Association was being organized in Prince Edward Island, and certain tasks needed accomplishing.

When the phone rang, Maud knew it had to be either Stuart checking in or Eric Gaskell from the Authors Association calling about contacts on the Island.

"Hello," she spoke into the receiver. It was Eric, nearly out of breath and jumping into questions straight away.

It was not a sense of duty that compelled her to answer Eric's calls. Not after the way the Association had treated her of late. It was the Island, mostly. Her oldest flame. Something solid enough to grip at a time when everything else she had once cared about felt slippery in her hands.

As she spoke, her pinky finger jutted back and forth against the handset, and her other hand involuntarily shook for several seconds at a time against the counter in front of her. But Eric couldn't see that.

"Other than that, it sounds like you are all set to leave," she said. "Is there anything else I can do for you, Eric?"

She'd come to believe over the past few weeks that the dependable contraction of her jaw was all that held her exterior world intact and apart from her inner one. She clenched it harder now.

"Not at all. You've done plenty." Eric paused. His voice turned less certain. "The Association will be forever in your debt, I hope you know. Your influence and impression on readers will be my welcoming wagon to the Island, even without you being there."

"Yes, well," Maud said too loudly. "Give those I have mentioned my best, and other Islanders too. Especially those who say something real of my work."

"Of course."

She fingered the letter sitting at the top of the Authors Association file she'd placed by the phone for reference during her calls with Eric. The letter naming her an honorary member of the Association in recognition of her contribution to Canadian literature.

An honorary member. The recognition that should have come after her death; a subtle pronouncement of her irrelevance following the not-so-subtle election of the new executive. Also known as the execution of the sentimentalists. A literary movement that felt strangely personal.

Paving the way for modernism—for the dark, hard themes that had come into favor—naturally came with a changing of the guard. But it was her, more than anyone else, that they seemed to care about ousting.

"Well now—" Eric said after Maud had paused for too long.

"I do wish," she said, "people wouldn't think of me only as a writer for children."

"Oh," he said. "But that is a wonderful thing to be."

It was something Anne would have said. How Maud resented Anne's naïveté now. How she longed for it.

"Well." Maud's voice caught on the word and then changed, assuming the grandmotherly tone that now felt like a comfortable old jacket. "Breathe in a bit of the Island air for me, will you? Good day, Eric, and best of luck."

Her jaw slackened with the touch of the headset to the receiver.

"I'D BETTER BE going. I'll be seeing you next week, Maud. The same time, I assume."

Maud's neighbor uncrossed her ankles and rose onto her feet, her oversized legs straining with the effort.

"I doubt very much that I'll be here, dear." Maud spoke the words in the same tone with which she might have said that she would see this same neighbor after dinner the following Sunday.

She heard some noise coming from Ewan's corner of the room and looked over to find him swatting at what might have been an insect. Mostly the pests were in his imagination these days, now that Anita had come back and the house had returned to order. But swatting at insects had become a habitual movement of Ewan's.

Maud had given up trying to keep Ewan in the other room when company came.

"Well, we'll be in touch," the neighbor said. Already near the door, she did not look at Maud as she spoke. "If not next week, then the week after."

Hearing the door close, Maud nodded. It could be that simple.

Then she heard the familiar rustling in the kitchen. A few shaky breaths later, and here was Anita, a tray of food in hand. She placed one plate on the table in front of Maud and one in front of Ewan.

"At least a few bites today," Anita said, kissing Maud's cheek.

Maud shifted uncomfortably in her seat. She'd thought Anita was still at the store.

"I was about to go for a nap."

"A few bites first," Anita said.

Ewan had started taking slow mouthfuls, using his entire fist to hold his fork.

"You'd better go get yourself some food, my dear," Maud said.

"You don't worry about me." Anita took a blanket and laid it over Maud's lap.

And then—

"Where are you thinking of going off to next Sunday?" Anita asked, looking down at the blanket as she smoothed it.

So she had been listening with those careful ears of hers. She'd sure done some work at quieting her feet since her return.

To be fair, it also could have been the low-level buzz in Maud's head these days that prevented her from hearing Anita's footsteps. A by-product of the pills.

"What do you mean?" Maud asked, summoning a distracted cough.

"I mean what you said just now to the neighbor."

Maud gave a low laugh. "Oh, I wouldn't dare walk out that front door without your steady hand beside me. Don't you worry about that, dear. I've never once doubted the reliability of your attention."

"You never should," Anita said.

"You are a blessing in this life, Anita—never forget that, will you?" She coughed again. "I could really use some hot tea for this cough. Would you mind terribly?"

She looked up and saw Anita trying to meet her eyes; Anita's mouth was firm.

Maud knew her eyes were watery now, but there was the cough to blame for that. She told herself to hold Anita's gaze, but the effort was too much. She moved her twitching forefinger and thumb down to the plate instead, taking a cracker. She lifted it to her mouth, bit a piece, and chewed until she heard Anita say, "Of course, Aunt Maud."

As soon as Anita left, Maud put down the rest of the cracker and closed her eyes. She must find a way to keep Anita at bay.

STOWED AWAY INSIDE her bedroom, Maud sat with her folder of notes for the eleventh volume.

"April 22, 1942," she wrote on a new page. And then at the top, the page number: "176." Quite the number of pages her scribbling book had amassed.

She was starting to feel the reality of her decision in her body as she had not before. And now she found herself writing that feeling out.

This was a letter, she realized by the end. She had written a letter.

"What an end," she concluded, and the noise in her head quieted. She could feel her nerves like tiny fissures all over her body. "To a life in which I tried always to do my best in spite of many mistakes."

A letter did not belong in the folder with her journal notes.

A piece of the eleventh volume for the Reader, then. A page of it preserved. But nothing more.

45.

Watchful not to catch the hem of her night-gown in the flames, Maud stood before the small fire she'd set in the same large patch of dirt where she had presided over the bonfire a few months earlier.

Anita would have sniffed out the fire in a minute. Maud had to scheme, making a phone call to ask one of Anita's friends to take her out for a new movie. Anita surely needed some fresh air, Maud had instructed, with her and Ewan both so ill lately.

Fixated by the flames as ever, Maud thought of herself at age fourteen holding that old pink journal up next to the stove coals, then pulling it back, and then finally poking it in. Desperate to rid herself of any record of her younger voice. The idea that she'd been embarrassed by any of this now seemed like impossible naïveté. The series of incidents and foibles in those years were what fed her novels.

What would she have thought at fourteen if she could see herself now?

What an education she could give her younger self about appreciation. About the number of choices available to her in those days before life narrowed and narrowed, until it finally settled into the present—the endless straight.

Now she could hardly see a single choice left available to her. Her eyes went to the folder of journal notes she held in her hands.

Well, here was one choice.

What would it mean to put these pages back in her lock-box for someone to discover eventually? Better yet, what would it mean to line this folder up on the bedroom shelf for publication as she planned to with the other ten volumes?

What would it mean to come out and say just what she thought to everyone in her life? To tell the truth to poor Ewan, and to file for divorce? To tell Chester no, and to mean it? To write precisely what she wanted to write and nothing else for the rest of her days?

The thought made her laugh, so much that her eyes ran with tears and her nightgown shook down over the fire until it was about to catch. Seeing the flames lick her nightgown, Maud felt like a bird was batting its wings inside her chest. She backed away, just as she had from the brush fire so long ago, during her Cavendish days.

She shook her head at the cold, familiar salve of adrenaline running through her veins. For all that she'd told herself about no longer being afraid of death, here she was, jumping back from the flames. Part of her still yearning to save her own life.

She tossed her notes for the eleventh volume into the fire like something vile, then stood for a while, watching.

When the fire finally died down, her eyes took a long time to acclimate to the dark; they canvassed the trees for the path to the back door.

BACK IN HER bedroom, Maud pulled out her manuscript. Her mind strangely clear, she finished copying the final missing piece of *The Blythes Are Quoted* from a story she had written once. A recycling effort, truly. But now it was finished. Anita had prepared a box to mail the manuscript the next day.

As Maud picked up the manuscript to fit inside the box,

she had a sudden glimpse of herself running out into the yard and burning it. Trading the manuscript for the folder of journal notes even, and sending those to the publisher instead. She laughed to herself, but the laughter sounded foreign.

This was childlike thinking. The folder was gone. The publishers were expecting this manuscript; she'd told Stuart the income would be coming and that she meant for it to go straight to Luella and the grandchildren.

She put the manuscript in the box and sealed it.

MAUD SAT BESIDE the bookshelf in her bedroom where she had placed a complete collection of her novels and the ten formal volumes of her journals, removed from the lockbox with edits complete. She ran a finger across each of their spines, catching a little in the places where one spine met the next until it settled on one. *The Story Girl*.

She thumbed through the pages until she found one she had dog-eared.

"Truly," she read out loud, "we had had a delectable summer; and, having had it, it was ours forever. 'The gods themselves cannot recall their gifts.' They may rob us our future and embitter our present, but our past they may not touch. With all its laughter and delight and glamour it is our eternal possession."

A sigh of approval. A sigh Anne would give, but that couldn't be.

Anne didn't belong in this moment.

Maud set the book down and closed her eyes.

"You're the best woman I'll ever know," Ewan had told her once, his voice sluggish with exhaustion and contentment. It was just before they fell asleep in the same bed for the first time, on the night of her thirty-third birthday. *The weekend of nothing ordinary*, Frede had called it. An entire weekend with

Frede—the sheer luck of it! They'd had a scrumptious cake to celebrate. The taste and smell of that cake came back to her with the vividness of a recurring dream. Dark chocolate. The cake and the day had become one and the same in her memory, crafted to her liking and perfectly sweet.

"That's a lofty conclusion," Maud had replied to Ewan then, her eyes already closed. His arm was laced under her neck. "I'll settle for being the most interesting."

The day had been full of laughter, so many different parts all long and drawn out, and the joy had loosened up her speech.

"I have no doubt you'll be both," Ewan had murmured, pulling her closer.

Had she succeeded in the latter, if nothing else? Would Ewan have said so, back when he still had most of his mind intact?

The usual number of pills already in Maud's system made her vision hazy around the edges. Still, she'd been sure to be coherent enough. She took one more.

She could make that the last one and no one would ever know a thing.

The rest of the pills in the bottle went down easily, like warm milk; welcomed as they were, the sensation still surprised her.

Alone. This was how it ended. For everyone, too, it ended this way. For her sons. For her parents. One body; no one else's. She had always known it. And yet.

She laughed. Impossible. Lying down on the bed, she ran her finger along her collarbone, back and forth, sweeping across it. Her own. She took a deep breath and felt her breath enter and fill up her stomach, her ribs, her back. Full, so full. Each time a choice; each time a relief. Always in the background, always.

How could this have been available, always? How many breaths had she taken? How many breaths had she noticed?

"I did feel God sometimes in my pain; in my fear," Edwin had said once. She wondered if it had been a feeling like this.

She let the breaths rise and fall until some noise—she couldn't place what—came from somewhere in the house, and her heart started up, the rapid, fluttery beat to which she'd become so accustomed.

She stood and made her way to the dresser. The mirror. She blinked, apprehending what others must be thinking every time they looked at her. Old. Old, wrinkled face, wasted and pale. Mother, weakest of mothers. Passé impersonator of a writer. Spent, wife—a minister's wife. Dearest little wife in the world.

Kneeling now, her head in her hands. Now crawling, grabbing for the sheets, knowing she needed to make her way back to them.

On the floor and gripping for the sheets, staring at her hands, could this be how it ended?

With her last energy, she made it up to the bed and under the sheets. She situated herself on her back, placed her hands at her sides.

Presentable now, Maud. Peaceful, even. Look halfway decent. She tried to smile a little.

Then the breath; there it was again, coming in, releasing. She had almost forgotten the comfort she'd realized not a few minutes before.

It was her own. Just hers. What she needed, so simple, and her body already knew.

Another noise from downstairs. Her head thrashed from side to side. The mirror again.

Inside. Only. Only inside. That's all that matters now.

Slow, heartbeat. Slow. You've worked so hard. Taken such care.

46.

Cavendish, Prince Edward Island
April 1942

A crowd gathered outside the church on the day of the burial, blocking cars from passing on the street.

At the end of the service, the reverend read Psalm 23. "The Lord is my shepherd; I shall not want," the reverend said.

"Who is dead?" Ewan asked from the front-row pew, in the direction of no one in particular.

The reverend was saying, "He maketh me to lie down in green pastures; he leadeth me beside the still waters."

Then the reverend looked at Stuart. Stuart adjusted in his seat and lowered his chin in his father's direction, whispering.

"Who is she?" his father said again, just as loudly. "Too bad!"

"This is a sad day," the reverend concluded, "but we must also feel a lift in our hearts to know that Mrs. Macdonald will be buried in the Cavendish cemetery, where visitors surely will come in future years and feel their pulses quicken at the thought of their proximity to the dust of one who painted life so joyously, so full of hope, and of sweetness and light."

"Who died?" Ewan asked again as they walked down the church steps, and again as they rounded the corner to join the crowd of mourners.

Chester walked ahead and away from the crowd, but Stuart stayed with his father.

Each time Ewan asked who was dead, Stuart answered. Each time afterward, Stuart found the farthest point that he could see and focused his gaze there.

But with their turn into the graveyard, his father's composure shifted. Stuart felt himself relax even before he looked over to notice any change in his father. When he did look, his father was reaching out with his hand and taking Stuart's wrist—to steady himself, maybe—but then Stuart felt a squeeze. A squeeze and release. Maybe the most surprising gesture he had ever experienced.

Stuart studied the continuing movement of his father's hand, watching it reach out to graze a pine bush, now the new leaf of a low tree.

The procession turned inside the perimeter of the graveyard, where the trees and shrubs formed a natural fence, past tall stones and short ones, past his grandparents' and great-grandparents' graves, until they reached the large gravesite his mother had chosen for herself and his father.

"I thought you'd want to be in the graveyard you helped restore, among the trees you helped plant," Stuart had overheard his mother say more than twenty years earlier, pushing the grave site order form across the table in his father's direction. "I've chosen a headstone inscription as well," she'd said.

One by one, onlookers took their places by the hole in the ground, their eyes fixed on the elaborate box that would fill it and the headstone that would preside over it.

"Lucy Maud Montgomery Macdonald," the headstone read. "Wife of Ewan Macdonald."

Normally cold winds blew from the north in April, but on that day a warm wind from the south came instead, on its way to soften the ice in the Gulf of St. Lawrence. Shoulders relaxed from underneath dark overcoats, and cheeks wet with tears tilted up until they found sun. Among them, a man who an hour ago had been hunched over halfway to the ground now stood as tall as he had in years. He studied the headstone with tears in his eyes and a branch with a single stray, new leaf gripped in his hand. A few songbirds sang in the distance.

47.

Frede's luggage sat half-open by the front door. Maud set the casserole dish inside it, scrubbed clean and bearing the silky sweet scent of their grandmother's signature soap, made with lye extracted from sugar maple ashes. Frede would appreciate the scent—one of their mutual favorites. Maud laid the dish carefully among Frede's rumpled nightgown, pens, and thick textbooks, their edges scalloped by water spillage.

Maud started to laugh out loud at a bag that could only be Frede's, but an ache in Maud's chest stopped her laugh halfway to her lips. Ewan would be leaving soon, and Frede would follow soon after that. Ewan was upstairs finishing his packing. He had already returned the two armchairs from the entryway to their habitual places in the parlor, and the entryway now seemed to gape its disapproval.

Perhaps it is sacrilegious to say so, but a queer feeling comes over me many Sunday afternoons, at week's end. Especially when it is a week I have anticipated with the whole of my being. It's as if I have swallowed a rock that has made my body heavier than it was only hours earlier—but when I look in the mirror, I can hardly notice the difference.

Maud shared Anne's sentiment, but it did seem sacrilegious to indulge in it. Particularly so on a Sunday when no one in the household had been to church.

How different life would be if one looked in the mirror the way one felt inside. Oh, how I would delight in having every sun-drenched meadow and shadowed forest of feeling shine through, plain for everyone to see. Maybe others would understand me better then too. Maybe they would believe once and for all how high I can soar and how low I can sink on the wings of my imagination alone.

An appealing idea at first, but terrifying on further reflection. A world without a hiding place.

"There you are," Ewan said now as he ambled into the hallway from the kitchen with his suitcase in hand, the floorboards creaking under his heavy footsteps. "I found her, Frede!" he called out.

"Well done," Frede said, following behind Ewan. "Not the happiest-looking of birthday gals, I must say." Frede plucked Maud under the chin as she passed, a few stray garments laid over her arm.

"I am a drag with endings," Maud said.

"You are." Frede tilted her head in Ewan's direction, and his head bowed in agreement. "Too sentimental for your own good. But we'll have all the time in the world together soon enough, once you two are married and have a house of your own to invite me to," Frede said as she stuffed the loose garments into her luggage and attempted unsuccessfully to fasten the closure.

Frede's words only made the ache in Maud's chest deepen. *All the time in the world.* A fiction made possible by Frede's youth.

If they did have all the time in the world, would the day before have glowed nearly so bright?

Maud caught a glimpse of Ewan, who was placing his luggage next to Frede's. Maud hadn't missed Frede's suggestion that she and Ewan would be married and settled before they knew it.

"You have a perpetual invite to any home we have," Maud said.

"That's right," Ewan said. "You most certainly do. We'll leave a place at the table for you." He thought for a moment, then flashed a dimpled smile. "Aunt Frede's seat," he added. He looked to Maud for recognition of the child his comment implied. This sort of subtlety wasn't typical for Ewan. She smiled and nodded her understanding.

Then Ewan looked at his watch. "I'm very sorry, ladies, but I must get to Reverend Smith's hotel in the next two hours if I mean to catch him."

Frede nodded. "I imagine Father will be dropping off Grandmother in not too long, and then I'll be off too. I doubt the old lady could tolerate staying much past breakfast." Frede looked toward the door as if she half expected it to swing open of its own volition.

Maud laughed and ran her hand along the back of her neck. "That's a safe bet."

"This does seem to be a rather sad final note." Frede thought for a moment, and then all at once her shoulders drew together behind her back. She clapped her hands. "What do you say to a toast before Ewan is off?" Frede asked.

Maud pursed her lips to the side, then relaxed them into a smile. "That sounds like a perfectly unordinary plan. I think we have just enough strawberry lemonade left from yesterday for three glasses."

"It's settled, then," Frede said. She took Maud by the arm and led her in the direction of the kitchen.

WHEN THEY RETURNED, Ewan was standing by the door, his hands at loose ends by his sides.

"Will you join us, Ewan? Do you have time?" Maud asked.

"Of course he will," Frede answered, putting a glass in front of Ewan and turning him around by the elbow. With his hands now occupied, Ewan seemed to relax.

"I'll do my best," he said.

"Good then, I'll start," Frede said. "I have two toasts. First, to Maud, for the book that will soon be published—famously, I'm positive. To our dear girl's persistence and her bravery."

Maud shook her head and gave a close-lipped smile as she joined her glass with Frede's. It took a clearing of the throat from Frede to break Ewan away from his own thoughts. He held out his glass to meet theirs.

"And next," Frede said, "to Ewan, for his good taste in both poetry and partners. May you both always know the fortune of finding each other."

This time all three glasses met at once.

Maud looked in her friend's eyes and thought for the first time that she might be seeing loneliness there. A desire for partnership. She'd have to see to that going forward—she should not let Frede get away too long with pretending not to care about marriage. Maud knew that tack too well.

"And I will toast to both of you," Maud said, looking from one of her guests to the other. "I will always remember our time together this weekend. To the holy goodness of comradeship—and the holy goodness of that cake!"

Their glasses met in laughter, which softened into silence after they swallowed. Eventually, both women turned toward Ewan.

"There's a reason I make notes for my sermons," Ewan said eventually, smiling and running a hand through his hair.

His eyes studied the ground until Maud looked down far enough to catch them.

Seeing the sheepishness in his gaze, Maud thought of Ewan's dreary speech notes, now reduced to ashes in the stove. Could he have spotted them missing from the rubbish bin? Could he have apprehended what she had done and grown even more self-conscious? No. It was not like Ewan to go looking, or to put two and two together if he had. She raised her chin, and Ewan lifted his with her.

Then, all at once, Ewan assumed his full stature. His mouth grew solemn. Now turned preacher, he looked down at her instead of up, and Maud remembered the night before, her arms underneath his shirt, the musculature of his torso so different from her own. Of all the women who had seen him preach, she alone knew him in this way.

"A toast to Maud," Ewan said. A faintly dimpled smile, and then he assumed a deeper tone. "'Thy word is a lamp unto my feet, and a light unto my path.' That is Psalm 119, and it is what you are to me. At times, I've thought that I was destined for darkness. But in your radiance, my path is light. As long as you are on my side, I know I cannot falter." He said the final words slowly, his eyes as kind as they were the day they met, but more saturated now with feeling. Maud's stomach clenched at the same time that her face grew soft at the sentiment.

"Thank you, Ewan," Maud said, raising her glass. After taking a long, final draw from her lemonade glass, Maud stepped close enough for a kiss. As their lips met, she noted with satisfaction the familiarity of the stubble across the surface of Ewan's chin, the varied texture of his lower lip. She had kissed his lips long enough to learn them.

"Thank you for the poem, for the flowers, and above all for

the gift of this weekend," Maud added. She lifted Ewan's hat from the entry table, placed it on his head so it sat just right, and then brushed her hands together and opened the door. "Frede and I will see you out."

"UNCLE'S BUGGY JUST crested out of sight," Maud announced with a sigh, peering out from the parlor window with her nose not much further from the glass than her grandmother's had been the previous morning, waiting for the buggy to pull up.

Goodbyes with Frede had been full of jolly humor and holiday plans. Her grandmother had come back later than expected, and Maud's feelings had waited to sour until now, after Frede's wild hair was no longer visible.

"Maud, dear, with that tone of voice, you would think it was a hearse you were staring after rather than a buggy," her grandmother said to Maud's back.

Maud's head dropped back. "When have I ever been so dramatic?" she asked in the direction of the window. Then she turned, smiling at herself, and took her grandmother's hand. The responsive tightening of fingers brought a flood of warmth through Maud's veins. The affection between them might have been the slowest-growing of mosses, but it was perceptible now in everyday moments.

"You'll be happy to know that Frede and I put together a supper for us," Maud said as she led her grandmother in the direction of the kitchen.

"A supper finished off with cake, I hope."

Maud grimaced. "I'm afraid Frede and I finished the last slices earlier today, after Ewan left. I'm as sorry as you, because having that cake to look forward to was twice the fun of eating it."

Her grandmother's abdomen shook with silent laughter. "What a dour sentiment that is." She looked at Maud. "I'll survive, I assure you, my dear. Any food will do."

"Fine," Maud said. "Let's have supper, and you can tell me all about your tribulations with the dreaded great-grandchildren."

"I do wish we could talk about something more stimulating," her grandmother said with an exaggerated sigh.

Maud laughed. "It can't have been so terrible."

Her grandmother released Maud's hand and went straight for the kitchen sink to wash up, not even bothering to go to her bedroom to do so. Travel had clearly loosened her up in the joints.

"Upon my arrival," her grandmother said as she lathered the soap, "one child had locked the other in the barn and hidden the key." She scoffed, then looked toward the ceiling. "I think that about sums it up."

Maud pulled her chair up to the kitchen table and began removing the cloth coverings from the food she and Frede had set out. "That sums up nothing," she said as she readied the table. "I will be woefully disappointed unless I hear the full story, top to bottom."

"I couldn't be bothered to ascertain the full story, I'm afraid." Her grandmother's back was still turned toward Maud as she lathered up for a second time, with no apparent regard for the waste of soap. Maud liked her grandmother this way.

"I do know that the boy child lied to his parents over it, and the girl child has never been trained in the proper etiquette for tears," her grandmother said.

"Oh, Grandmother, you couldn't even bother learning their names?"

"I did learn them," her grandmother sighed. "I just didn't see a need to retain them." Turning on her heels after several rounds of hand scrubbing, her grandmother made no effort to hide her surprise at apprehending the table setting. "You've set the kitchen table, I see."

"Yes," Maud said. She sat tall and met her grandmother's gaze straight on. "I have."

"A clever trick, knowing I would be too tired to argue over the propriety of a dining room for dining," her grandmother said, sitting down so firmly that the old wooden chair creaked a loud greeting. "You always have loved this table best."

"Look at how the west window frames the sunset, grandmother. You always say sunsets on this Island beat all."

Slowly, her grandmother turned her head toward the window. Maud saw a hint of a smile cross over her grandmother's face, the private kind of smile that she had only ever seen before when her grandmother didn't think anyone was looking. The pink light of sunset smoothed her grandmother's face and turned her, momentarily, years younger.

"It's good to be home," her grandmother said as she lifted her fork.

THEY BOTH ATE together in a contented silence, until her grandmother's last forkful was complete. Her next words issued with the same precision used with each prick of her needlework. "So what have you decided, Maud, dear?"

"Decided about what?"

"About Frede coming to live with me."

"Oh, that."

"What else could I have meant, chi—dear?"

Maud cleared her throat, steadying herself. "I mean to stay here—"

Her grandmother's brow furrowed. "So you didn't ask Frede?"

"Frede offered to move in of her own accord."

With eyes wide, her grandmother paused and took her time folding her napkin on the table. "Did she. Well, it's settled, then."

"It is settled, but not in the way you are implying. I mean to stay here with you and to keep on with my writing."

Her grandmother wiped the side of her hand across her forehead, then inspected her palm as if she might find something disagreeable on it. "Do not tell me you have put that poor gentleman off completely."

"I have done no such thing," Maud said. "You will be happy to know that I have solidified my commitment to him further."

"I do not know what 'solidified' means, dear, if you will not be marrying him now."

"It means exactly as it sounds."

Her grandmother's lips were kind but firm. "I will tell you how it sounds. It sounds as though you've decided to have that cake of yours and eat it too."

"Ewan is happy to wait, grandmother."

"Happy to wait for you to write?"

"Happy to wait for me to care for you."

Her grandmother scoffed.

"What is it?"

Her grandmother shook her head and poked at her empty plate with her fork. "Men sense more than they say." She paused. "Now, don't go thinking that I am not mighty appreciative. I do not want you thinking that. But I care for you, Maud. For you more than my own tired self, I suppose." Her grandmother's eyes widened at these words. She thought for a moment and then nodded. "My thoughts are for your future happiness."

Maud studied her grandmother for a good long while before she spoke. "Future happiness seems no more predictable than the hare who stalks our vegetable garden," she said finally, and hearing her own words, she noted with satisfaction that she heard nothing in them of the child she used to be.

Rising from the table, Maud kissed her grandmother's cheek, feeling the soft pliability of its creases. "Now you get yourself off to bed, and I'll clean up from supper. You must be exhausted."

Her grandmother looked up, and a hint of her sunset expression returned, pink-hued and content. Only this time the smile was directed at Maud. "You are a dear. My knees in particular thank you. Your uncle drove that buggy as if being chased by a vagrant."

SETTLED IN HER bedroom that night, Maud sketched out a new scene for the sequel to *Anne* based on the bones of the story her grandmother had told from her time away, of one great-grandchild locking the other in the barn and lying about it. The sequel needed the flavor of a young one getting into scrapes and learning for the first time that telling falsehoods was wrong. Anne the school ma'am would impress that lesson upon him.

With her sketch of the scene complete and the last of the light drained from the night sky, Maud took to her journal.

It sounds as though you've decided to have that cake of yours and eat it too.

Her grandmother's words cartwheeled through her mind, stopping her pen without more than a sentence written. They had met their mark, those words. They might even be true.

"I know as well as any," she wrote, "how a single choice can make a story, just as easily as a single choice can break it. In this way, the storytellers among us have something on the rest of humanity. A storyteller knows that every choice is chasing a tale."

Maud lifted her pen. She looked out the window into the night and thought a moment. "Of course, some choices are more complicated than others. In these past few days, I have made a choice that foretells an unpredictable intersection of ambition and marriage (the latter at a time still yet to be determined). But I think I have made the right one. Regardless, it is a choice with writing as its centerpiece, as a result of which I feel sure of at least one thing: this old journal will be more interesting for it."

She licked the tip of her finger and used it to turn the page. She had not specified the nature of the choice. Should she now? Or had she already said too much?

She would read this over and decide tomorrow. Thankfully, if she regretted an entry later, there were means of mending. A page or two could be removed, if need be.

Or perhaps someday, at a calmer time in life, she could sit herself down and recopy all her old journals, one by one. A delightful idea. Careful handwriting filling a neat stack of volumes. Recopied, and revisited.

The idea of a set of recopied volumes put her body at ease. She could afford not to be so future-minded. She could afford a mistake.

With this, she let her mind return to the present. Here, in her bedroom. Here, with the empty page before her, with her sentiments doused in Frede's humor and Ewan's care.

Anne would never spend her energy on morbid thoughts of what might come after. For Anne, a single day—a single hour—could hold as much grandeur and fascination as a lifetime. It was simply a matter of the dose of attention devoted.

Maud turned her attention to the hours just lived. She resurrected the long walk she had taken through leaves fallen at their most colorful peak, her dear woods uncharacteristically quiet. She rediscovered the splintering diamonds she'd found at the beach, the cake she'd brought home with a scent like another voice in the room. She put a few of Anne's lines in her journal as they'd occurred to her that day, inserting their bold advice and unmeasured delight.

Her Island. Her creation. Her heart humming with anticipation at what life had in store.

Author's Note

Anne of Green Gables was a fixture in my adolescent imagination. I treasured the books, and I watched the Canadian Broadcasting Corporation's series each time I visited my grandparents at their beloved old home in small-town Iowa.

Years later, I read a few details of Lucy Maud Montgomery's life and got chills. I told my husband I had to know more about her. The more I researched, the more compelled I felt to tell Maud's story.

Maud wrote twenty novels, and she also wrote and then rewrote personal journals intended for publication. While reading her journals from beginning to end, I was struck by the contrast between Maud's life and her art. Maud's fiction paints the world in soft and forgiving hues, with perpetual happy endings, but she experienced so much sorrow. Her life ended in suicide—a fact kept private for generations until her granddaughter publicly disclosed it in 2008. Yet, like her best-known heroines, Maud also lived vibrantly and boldly.

I found myself asking: Who was this consummate editor who crafted and then recrafted her life story? What drove her tragic end?

Maud's life is beautifully documented not only in her journals but in the biography *Lucy Maud Montgomery: The Gift of Wings* by Mary Henley Rubio, a lifelong scholar of Maud's work. But there are questions and emotional realities of Maud's life that remain a mystery. That is the space where fiction can enter.

In *After Anne*, I strove to create a novel that stayed true to the well-documented record of events and people in Maud's life, while also imagining what Maud might have withheld from her story as she told it in her journals.

Maud recopied her journals into formal volumes beginning in 1919, sometimes removing recopied pages with a razor and rewriting them. She later took notes on scrap paper that she fleshed out in the formal volumes, making edits along the way. We will never know what she excised from her first drafts or why. Maud also burned boxes of letters, books, and papers near the end of her life—a final editing device.

Learning that Maud's journals had gaps, and understanding that she likely edited out the events hardest to comprehend or to share, my imagination took hold.

I grew fascinated by the page number "176" on the paper found on Maud's bedside table at the end of her life. That paper was long assumed to be a suicide note, but it actually appears to be the final page of a collection of journal notes reflecting the last three years of Maud's life. The first 175 pages have never been found. Many things could have happened to those pages, but it seems most likely to me that Maud purposefully removed them from her life record. She included two short entries summarizing the whole of 1941 and 1942 in her tenth journal volume, indicating that she intended those to be her final entries, and not anything else from the 175 pages of journal notes. Given her relationship with fire—burning her first journal, watching the Cavendish brush fire in awe, and burning papers again at the end of her life—her final set of journal notes voicing significant inner pain would have been a prime candidate for burning. Regardless, the disappearance of these pages leaves a striking gap in Maud's account of her final years.

Maud's journals also leave lingering questions about the

emotional intricacies of her decision to marry the Reverend Ewan Macdonald and about his mental-health condition. Maud razored out and replaced the pages telling the story of her courtship with Ewan in her formal journal volume—a sign of editing even after recopying. And although Maud paints a generally dire portrait of Ewan's mental health beginning in mid-1919, it remains difficult to understand the full nature of his condition. Ewan, a kind but insecure man, almost certainly felt threatened by Maud's success, and his heavy use of prescribed barbiturates and bromides—the addictive depressants that killed Marilyn Monroe—likely contributed to his continuing decline.

The nature of Maud's relationship with Captain Edwin Smith is another mystery. Maud hints at intimate conversations between them once Edwin began to visit and preach in Ewan's stead in the fall of 1919, including their discussion of sex "as it really is." At some point, Maud gave Edwin the typewriter on which she typed *Anne of Green Gables*. Yet her mentions of him in her journals stop abruptly. What we do know suggests to me that Maud's true feelings for Edwin might have been too difficult to share with readers given her deep sense of propriety.

The Birthday Weekend is my invention and a later addition to the novel. Maud does not mention her thirty-third birthday in 1907 in her journals, although this would have been one of the most forward-looking times in her life. *Anne of Green Gables* was soon to be published, and Maud was engaged to Ewan and regularly buoyed by visits from her best friend and cousin Frede Campbell. Curious why such a birthday would remain undescribed, I envisioned a formative weekend that Maud might have chosen to excise from her journals because of all that she had not understood at the time, but also one that she might remember in her final moments, in the way the best memories can return to us in the bleakest hours.

Many sources were invaluable to me in my research, including: *The Selected Journals of L.M. Montgomery, Volumes I–V*; *The Complete Journals of L.M. Montgomery, The PEI Years, 1889–1900*; and *The Complete Journals of L.M. Montgomery, The PEI Years, 1901–1911*, edited by Mary Henley Rubio and Elizabeth Hillman Waterston; *L.M. Montgomery's Complete Journals: The Ontario Years, 1911–1917*; *L.M. Montgomery's Complete Journals, The Ontario Years: 1918–1921*; *L.M. Montgomery's Complete Journals: The Ontario Years, 1922–1925*; *L.M. Montgomery's Complete Journals: The Ontario Years, 1926–1929*; and *L.M. Montgomery's Complete Journals: The Ontario Years, 1930–1933*, edited by Jen Rubio; Maud's fiction, especially *Anne of Green Gables, Anne of Avonlea, The Story Girl, Anne of the Island, Anne's House of Dreams, Rainbow Valley, Rilla of Ingleside, Anne of Windy Poplars, Anne of Ingleside, Chronicles of Avonlea, Further Chronicles of Avonlea*, and *The Blythes Are Quoted*; *Lucy Maud Montgomery: The Gift of Wings*, by Mary Henley Rubio; and *The L.M. Montgomery Reader, Volume One: A Life in Print*; *The L.M. Montgomery Reader, Volume Two: A Critical Heritage*; and *The L.M. Montgomery Reader, Volume Three: A Legacy in Review*, edited by Benjamin Lefebvre.

A visit I took to Prince Edward Island with my husband and parents while researching the book filled me with a sense of place. Walking the shoreline and woods preserved because of Maud's impact, and visiting her gravesite in the Cavendish cemetery that Ewan helped beautify, I understood Maud's devotion to the Island.

Maud's story has woven its way through my life in the years I have spent in its company. Each time I thought I was finished writing this book, another layer would appear. Maud's grit, the striking range of her imagination, her ability to remake herself in the face of deep loss, and all she could not bring herself to reveal, have spoken to me in moments big and small.

We are all one personal tragedy away from being a different version of ourselves—a weathered version, perhaps, but also a deeper version. Maud suffered two such tragedies in 1919, with the death of Frede and the onset of Ewan's mental illness. She suffered another late in life as her son Chester's nature revealed itself. She persisted in living as interesting a life as she could, until she could not.

I wrote this book with reverence for Maud and for her work—above all for her tremendous journals, which are the "psychological study of one human being's life" that she always hoped to write.

Acknowledgments

I owe this book's publication to two women who shared my vision that Maud's story must be told. First, thanks to my agent, Abby Saul. Abby is the kind of agent who answers every email thoughtfully and promptly and who cares enough to send baby gifts. She is also an editorial mastermind. She believed in this book early in its evolution, and she provided invaluable notes and guidance.

Second, I am endlessly grateful to Tessa Woodward, exceptional editor and fellow Anne aficionado, whose pivotal insights helped me see the story within Maud's story and bring it to life.

Thanks also to the rest of the wonderful team at William Morrow who helped in the making of this book: Madelyn Blaney, Kelly Dasta, Hannah Dirgins, Jennifer Hart, Kelly Rudolph, Liate Stehlik, and the whole sales team.

Special thanks go to early readers whose insights and encouragement proved invaluable: Dawn Amos, Emily Green, Alex Davies, Lisa D'Annunzio, Ashley Berry, Megan Rietema, Paul Rietema, Bob Wright, Diane Green-Kelly, and Geoff Kelly.

Finally, thanks to my family. My parents, Jeanne and Steven Steiner, have always championed my dreams. They read draft after draft and never stopped clapping their hands. My grandmother Dorothy Ann Logan Schenk sparked my love of Anne; she shared Anne's gumption and Maud's Scottish humor. My brother Ben Steiner left this world too soon.

It was in his honor that I stopped talking about writing and started writing. My daughter Noa came into the world alongside this book. My tremendous love for her inspired me to rewrite the motherhood scenes. And my husband, David, read the book first and more times than anyone, always with a keen eye for story and character, always with insight and encouragement. You believed in this story before anyone else, and you kept believing when I did not. You are not only my partner in living, but my partner in writing, and I cannot thank you enough.